EVER SO GENTLY

"Why must you continue to challenge me?" Cole asked. He shifted his weight to lift his hand, tucking a stray lock of hair gently behind her ear.

"I . . . I just . . . I don't want to be here." She could barely get the breath out of her lungs. His angelic face lowered to mere inches above hers. If she lifted her chin, her lips would touch his. Did she dare?

"I don't want you to be here, either. But you are. We could try to enjoy it, Bailey."

His voice was seductive, low . . . like a caress.

BOOK YOUR PLACE ON OUR WEBSITE AND MAKE THE READING CONNECTION!

We've created a customized website just for our very special readers, where you can get the inside scoop on everything that's going on with Zebra, Pinnacle and Kensington books.

When you come online, you'll have the exciting opportunity to:

- View covers of upcoming books
- Read sample chapters
- Learn about our future publishing schedule (listed by publication month *and author*)
- Find out when your favorite authors will be visiting a city near you
- Search for and order backlist books from our online catalog
- Check out author bios and background information
- Send e-mail to your favorite authors
- Meet the Kensington staff online
- Join us in weekly chats with authors, readers and other guests
- Get writing guidelines
- AND MUCH MORE!

**Visit our website at
http://www.kensingtonbooks.com**

ROGUE

KAYLA GRAY

ZEBRA BOOKS
Kensington Publishing Corp.
www.kensingtonbooks.com

ZEBRA BOOKS are published by

Kensington Publishing Corp.
850 Third Avenue
New York, NY 10022

All Kensington titles, imprints, and distributed lines are available at special quantity discounts for bulk purchases for sales
promotion, premiums, fund-raising, educational, or institu-
tional use.

Special book excerpts or customized printings can also be created to fit specific needs. For details, write or phone the office
of the Kensington Special Sales Manager: Attn. Special Sales
Department. Kensington Publishing Corp., 850 Third Avenue,
New York, NY 10022. Phone: 1-800-221-2647.

Zebra and the Z logo Reg. U.S. Pat. & TM Off.

ISBN-13: 978-1-4201-0190-4
ISBN-10: 1-4201-0190-0

First Printing: January 2008
10 9 8 7 6 5 4 3 2 1

Printed in the United States of America

For my mom and dad.
Thank you for inspiring me to learn
and encouraging me to dream.
In a perfect world, every child would have parents like you.

Special Thanks:
To Tina St. John (a/k/a Lara Adrian) for critiques that make
me think beyond what I believed myself capable of;
for generously sharing your limitless expertise on the business;
and best of all, for the priceless gift of your friendship.
You are amazing in every way.

To Gaelen Foley, for great advice, loving support,
patient critiques, and much laughter.
You are a wonderful talent and an even better friend.

To Hilary Sares, for making another writer's dream come true.
As many times as you must hear that, the call was a treasured
moment; and I will carry that day in my heart forever.
Thank you for your patience and for sharing your wisdom.

And to my love, Brian. You're the other half of my heart.
Thank you for believing. I love you. We're on the same team!

Prologue

London, 1713

Cold spikes of rain drizzled from a murky black winter sky. Colby Matthew Leighton barely felt the sting against his cheeks, or the trickle of droplets that fell from his clenched jaw. He felt numb, like the walking dead, and a bit of icy water wasn't nearly enough to retrieve his spirit from the black depths where it now resided. He was fixed on a single purpose—vengeance—a purpose that had brought him across the ocean from his family's Virginia plantation to this affluent address in the West End of London.

Cole stood under the protective canopy of an oak tree and pulled a crumpled letter from his pocket. The frigid January wind caught the paper, but Cole's gloved fingers gripped the missive, refusing to yield it to the winter elements. A nearby street lamp shed a dim orange light upon the letter, the words set down in elegant script. Words he'd read at least a hundred times: *love . . . sweetheart . . . missing you . . . all my heart.*

Disgust coiled in his gut at the familiar handwriting. It was his mother's, words written not to his father but to his mother's lover.

Cole's eyes fixed on the first line of the letter, one meager clue that had aided him in getting this far.

My dearest love, M—

This letter, along with the small amount of information he was able to gather from his mother before she died, had led him to London. But it was more a stroke of luck that had brought him here, to 28 Leicester Square. Built out of the ashes of a great fire in 1633, the long rows of extravagant homes had been modeled after those in Pall Mall.

Cole tucked the parchment back in his pocket and walked across the cobbled street toward the gray stone residence of Lord William Montrose. Twinkling chandeliers spilled slivers of light from each of the lower windows, cracked slightly to allow for a bit of circulation in the crowded house. The aroma of roasted meat and sounds of a merry gathering escaped into the street.

Cole's purpose was anything but festive.

He reached for the doorknob and hesitated, noting the ornate brass door knocker made in the likeness of a dragon's head. "How fitting," he muttered to himself, scoffing at the careless vanity of the man he was here to kill.

He should have finished the bastard off two nights ago. But patience would serve him well this night. He wanted the earl exposed in front of as many of the peerage as possible, and as he shoved the door open and stepped inside, he was pleased to see that the party was indeed well attended.

A startled manservant rushed forward to hold the door and offered to take his coat. Cole brushed past the man, ignoring him. He stalked across the marble foyer, his determined footsteps echoing above the din of voices.

He followed the lively sounds and soon found the ballroom, sparkling with hundreds of golden candles reflecting in ornate mirrors lining the side wall. He paused in the wide threshold, surveying the crowded room. Rivulets of water flowed down his hair and black cloak, pooling around the clumps of mud that clung to the soles of his boots.

He felt wide-eyed stares and heard hushed whispers from the women standing by the refreshment table. Scathing glares followed him as he rudely cut through the crowd, dripping rainwater on any who did not clear an easy path. One burly fellow huffed his displeasure and stepped up, dabbing at his wet shoulder with a handkerchief. Cole spun to face the man, issuing a silent challenge with an unflinching stare. He felt a heavy pulse in his clenched jaw, his eyes daring the tipsy noble to make a move. The man muttered and shuffled away as fast as his unsteady legs could manage.

Cole continued across the room, shoving through the bodies, his black attire a stark contrast against the sea of colorful gowns and powdered wigs. Like a starving hawk, Cole's focus was trained on snaring his prey. As he broke free of the crush of taffeta and velvet, he spotted Lord Montrose lifting a glass in toast to a small group of guests.

In two long strides, Cole was on him. He lifted the man by his embroidered velvet frock coat and pinned him against the wall. A woman in the group screamed. A startled violinist hit a screeching discord, causing the room to fall eerily quiet.

"William Montrose." Cole spat the name as if it was poison on his tongue, his threatening tone filling the uneasy silence of the ballroom.

The man's bulging eyes darted about. He stammered and shook his head in terror.

"Don't bother to lie. I followed you to the dockyards two nights past. What business does a man of your station have on the East Side at two in the morning, Montrose?" At the earl's hesitation, Cole tightened his grip on the man's collar, lifting his considerable weight clear off the floor. "I'll allow you one more breath, and if you use it to tell me what I want to know, I may be generous and allow you another."

An overpowdered matron gasped in outrage. "What is this? My husband would never go to those docks—especially in the middle of the night, like some kind of . . . criminal. How dare you? Who are you, sir?"

"Lady Montrose, I presume." Cole eyed the woman with a slight tilt of his head before returning his attention to her quivering husband. "You may consider it fortunate to have a wife with such courage, Montrose, but I will have no qualms about shutting her up if you don't."

Montrose's blanched expression registered the seriousness of the threat. "Victoria, stand clear. I am fine."

"I will do no such thing. You are not—"

"Do it, woman! Henry, get her out of here, will you?" Montrose bellowed to one of the gentlemen guests he had been toasting. The man shut his gaping mouth and ushered Victoria and her two female companions to a safer distance.

"Please, sir, what is this about?" Montrose asked, visibly attempting to remain calm.

"You." Cole released him long enough for the portly man to slide down the wall to his feet, but whipped out a dagger before the man could speak.

"Do I know you, sir?" he squeaked out.

"You know of my family." Cole's voice was deadly calm.

Montrose looked as though he'd been struck hard in the gut.

"Are you . . . him?" he asked, his voice lowering to a conspiratorial whisper.

Cole stared at the man, wondering at his odd question. Was there someone other than himself who hunted the wealthy earl?

"Are you . . . my son?"

Cole's eyes narrowed. Was the man stalling or did he seriously believe he could feign ignorance? Whatever game he was about, it mattered naught. Nothing would save the bastard tonight. Cole dragged the blade upward, nicking the fine silk of the man's purple waistcoat and popping off two silver buttons. Montrose sucked in his breath, his face draining of color as his costly buttons rolled across the floor.

"Please . . . don't . . . kill me. We can work this out," the portly man squawked. "I've wanted to reply to your letters, but you've never told me how I can reach you."

"What the hell are you going on about, Montrose?" Cole bit out. "Don't think you can sway me with your nonsensical tripe."

"You haven't been sending me the letters?"

"What letters?" Cole glanced around, suspicious that Montrose was trying to distract him with this balderdash, but no one was trying to come to the man's aid.

"The threats against my life," Montrose said, his words coming out in an excited rush.

"It doesn't surprise me that there are others who want you dead, Montrose. Pirates aren't looked upon too highly, if you hadn't noticed."

Montrose gasped. "Pirates! Good Lord, man, what are you accusing me of?"

"I'm accusing you of being a scurvy deceiver and a murdering pirate," Cole roared. "Do you deny it?"

"God, yes! Of course I deny it. That is preposterous! Oh, thank goodness, if that's what you're here about, then you haven't been sending those letters after all."

Cole eased the pressure of the dagger and moved one step back from Montrose, who looked considerably relieved.

"You have nothing to relax about, Montrose. Unless you welcome the idea of dying this night."

"You must be insane, man. I am an earl, for God's sake!"

The man's brave attempt to sound haughty only served to inflame Cole's bloodlust. In one quick movement, Cole shoved Montrose against the wall. He drove the long knife blade through the collar of the man's velvet coat, effectively pinning him to the hand-painted wallpaper. Cole heard Victoria shriek behind him. Montrose cringed at his wife's distress.

"I should finish you right here in front of your wife and the rest of the gentry. But perhaps I'll tell them your secret first.

Once they know what you've been doing, I doubt even your dear Victoria will shed a tear over your cold body."

Montrose moaned pitifully. "Please, oh please, what is it that you want?"

"Justice," Cole said, impatient with the man and his houseful of edgy, gaping guests. "But for now, I'll settle for a private place to discuss my considerable annoyance with you."

"Yes, yes, of course. We can go to my study."

Cole eased up on his knife, releasing Montrose. The old man wiped the sweat from his forehead, white powder creating a smeared mess across his bloodless face.

"Don't give anyone the slightest reason to follow us, or I'll disregard my good manners."

Montrose nodded and swallowed hard. In true English upper-class form, he collected himself and pasted a smile on his face as he turned to address his guests. He waved a hand, motioning for the musicians to play.

"Ladies! Gentlemen! Please, please, go back and enjoy yourselves. Dance, drink, eat! This has been an unfortunate misunderstanding, that's all," he finished, attempting to regain his composure. Montrose's wife rushed up to him, her face flushed with worry and anger. "Take care of our guests, Victoria. I'll return shortly," he said, cutting off her protest as Cole nudged him away from the many curious stares that continued to rest on them.

Lord Montrose closed the door of his study and went directly to a fully stocked lowboy. He poured himself a liberal draft of scotch with a shaky hand. He downed the liquor in one swallow and splashed more into his glass. Clearly unsettled, he carried the bottle with him to his chair and sat.

Cole realized with dark satisfaction that he likely resembled a minion from hell, his uncovered hair plastered to his face and neck, his eyes rimmed with dark circles from lack of sleep. He felt none of the heat emanating from the roaring fire. His wet clothes soaked the fine leather of the chair, but he didn't care.

"Speak," he growled at Montrose, still suspicious, still prepared to deal death to the little man.

"I pray, sir, what more can I tell you?"

"You claim you are not the pirate I seek. Prove it. Convince me you are not the Dragon. Unless you've no wish to live out the night."

"But . . . but, how can I prove it? What would you have me do? Whatever it is, I will do it," he insisted. "Can you at least tell me why you think I am him?"

A lingering silence filled the room. A log slipped in the fireplace, popping loudly and shooting sparks onto the brick hearth. Montrose jumped, spilling his scotch on the Persian rug. He refilled his glass and drank deeply.

When he finally broke the silence, Cole's voice held no inflection, no indication of the extent of the wrath that filled him in saying her name aloud. "Catherine Leighton."

He watched as Montrose's face wrinkled in genuine confusion.

"What? Who is Catherine Leighton? Does she have something to do with the letters? Does she know my son?"

Cole felt like every nerve in his body had been twisted into knots. It was becoming painfully clear that this was not the man he sought. He couldn't fathom how, but he had made a mistake somewhere along the way. Every carefully gathered clue had led him here and he had anticipated the sweet taste of vengeance he would have had this very night. Now that taste had turned sour as he faced yet another failure in his quest to avenge his family's honor. Still, he couldn't shake his gut feeling that he had been led here for a reason.

"Tell me about these bloody letters you keep going on about," Cole demanded in vexation.

Montrose took a moment to calm his breathing and gather his thoughts. His eyes showed fear and genuine confusion. "I am being blackmailed. And threatened. The person sending the missives says he is my son."

"A bastard son," Cole guessed. "And your dearest wife knows nothing about him."

Montrose nodded his head, then lowered it in shame. "I didn't want to hurt her. I love my wife."

Cole shrugged. "Love is for fools." He narrowed his eyes at the curious inquiry in Montrose's gaze. "The letters. What do they say?"

"The writer identifies himself as my forsaken heir. He swears he will destroy me, then claim all that is rightfully his. He promises that I will see his face clearly before I pay for my sins against him with my life." Montrose plucked the wig off his head and rubbed the sweat from his graying temple. "But what I don't understand is how you fit into this, Mr., uh . . . sir." His voice trailed off uncomfortably.

"Suffice it to say that I received information that led me from Virginia to London and then to you. It would seem that your bastard is warming up to the surname of Montrose in advance of your demise."

"He is using my name?"

"Apparently. Though not so openly that I have been able to track him easily. I believe this man is also the pirate known as the Dragon. By any chance do you own ships that have been attacked?"

"Yes, as a matter of fact. I've had three plundered off the coast of the Colonies in the last year alone. The brigands killed every man on those ships. Do you think it was him?"

"Likely." Cole nodded, crossing his long legs in front of him at the ankle. "The Dragon does not leave survivors. If he was recognized, his plan to take over your name and your fortune would not be possible." Cole felt his pulse quicken as he became more and more convinced that the man he was seeking was Montrose's bastard son. "I've heard enough, Montrose. Where do I find this son of yours?"

The question was not a request, it was a command that left no room for denial. He watched Montrose squirm under his expectation, his mouth bobbing open and closed several times before any sound emerged.

"I . . . I don't know. The truth is, I've never laid eyes on him," he said, his words rushing out of him in explanation. "I sent his mother away when she told me she carried my child. I recently discovered that she died four years ago. There is no record of her son. It's as if he disappeared completely. The only contact I have had is through the letters. I was ordered to meet some-one at the docks that night you saw me. I assumed it was him. I was hoping to put an end to this madness, to pay him what-ever I could to be rid of him. But he didn't show himself."

Cole shrugged. "The docks seemed unusually overrun by lowlife that night. He could have decided there were too many witnesses around. He has yet to take any risks that leave him in the open. But it doesn't matter. Eventually, I will find him."

"You sound as if you would search to the ends of the earth."

"Or beyond." Cole's smile was knowingly icy. "He has been lucky to elude me for this long. His luck will not last forever."

Montrose visibly shuddered. He stood and returned his empty glass to the lowboy. "I have no love for my bastard son and, truth be told, it would be a relief to not live under his threats. But I have to say, now I can't help but pity the scoundrel." He shook his head and braced his hands on the rolled edge of the bar. "I can only imagine what you will do to him if you find him."

"Not 'if.' When," Cole growled through clenched teeth, as Montrose turned back to face him.

The old man looked grim. "There is not an ounce of pity in you, is there?"

Cole was not offended by the question—it was the plain truth. "Your son is as good as dead. His only salvation will be if I die before I find him."

Montrose nodded slowly. "I swear I have no other knowledge of the man. Now, I beg you, leave my wife and me in peace."

Cole remained measuringly watchful, motionless, except for his slight wave of dismissal. "Go back to your party. I will see myself out momentarily."

He nodded impatiently for Montrose to leave and the man did so without hesitation, arranging his wig back in place as he scurried across the room and shut the door behind him.

Cole sagged back against the puckered leather of the chair and stared into the dancing flames in the fireplace. He tried to convince himself that coming here had not been a waste of time. He was narrowing down the identity of the man he hunted, though the bastard was out there, like a ghost drifting in the air, taunting him at every turn before disappearing into the mist.

The hopes he'd had for acquiring his vengeance here tonight were gone. Burnt to ashes, like the logs being swallowed up by crimson flames that popped and cracked in the heavy silence of the study.

Chapter One

Beaufort, North Carolina, 1717

Bright orange claws of flame shot skyward, spiraling among swirls of black smoke, smothering the brightness of the full May moon. Bailey Spencer crouched in the shadows next to the outhouse, just inside the edge of the woods.

Pirates!

Dear Lord, three—no, four of them!

She watched in horror as the fire they'd set ate greedily at the thatched roof of her small home. Bailey could only hope that the thick smoke and ash would bring help from the folk who lived in the heart of the sleepy port town.

But not soon enough for her dear father and brother.

Fear choked her at the thought. She had no way of knowing if they'd gotten out safely, but she couldn't take the chance. Pulling her dark cloak closed over her white nightdress, Bailey darted along the tree line toward the house. An agonizing cry rose above the hissing roar of the growing blaze. Her heart skipped a beat as one of the attacking pirates emerged from her home. His body was engulfed in a hellish death grip of flame.

Bailey bit into her fist to keep from screaming at the gruesome sight. Two of the three remaining pirates ran to aid their burning mate.

Now was her chance.

She left the woods and ran through the open brush to the rear of the burning structure. Her eyes teared and smoke burned her lungs as she struggled to see in the window.

"Adam! Father!" *Please, God, don't let them be dead.*

Scorching heat forced her back and she stumbled to her knees. At that moment, the left side of the roof caved in, shooting sparks high into the air. There was no hope of getting inside the house. Choking back a sob, Bailey prayed that her father and brother had somehow escaped the inferno.

Perhaps they'd run into the woods, or slipped away down Adam's secret path leading to the beach. Yes, they must be waiting for her at the beach. She had to hurry, before her father came back—

"Well, well. Hello there, sweetness."

Brutal fingers twisted in her hair, jerking her to her feet. Panic welled in her throat, her scream becoming strangled as she choked on bits of thick ash.

Bailey was yanked around to face a black-masked pirate. She kicked him with her slippered feet, but he only laughed. He dragged her by her hair as she pulled and scratched at his hands and arms.

"I admire your spirit, sweetness, but it won't do you any good. You are going to die tonight."

"No! Bastard!" she croaked. "Let me go!"

She felt the raging heat of the fire weaken as he dragged her away from her home, in the opposite direction of the beach path. He threw her to the ground, kicking her onto her back. Pain exploded through her rib cage. She moaned and tried to escape, but he dropped to his knees over her before she could roll away.

"Leave us alone!" she gasped. "Please! Take what you want and leave us alone!"

"Oh, I intend to take what I want. And I thank you in advance. Shame I have to kill such a lovely chit. I think I could enjoy you for a long time."

Bailey tried to spit in his face, but her mouth was filled with ash. She landed a solid punch to the pirate's chin. Her fingers caught in a chain hanging around his neck. The heavy links broke as she yanked free and the pirate snatched the gold from her fingers with a curse. Then he laughed and backhanded her hard across the face. "Here, sweetness, let me show you what it feels like to belong to me," he said. "Just for a moment or two." The pirate's cruel fingers dug savagely into her skin as he forced her fingers apart. Fighting to stay conscious, Bailey didn't resist when he shoved the gold ring that had hung from the chain on her first finger. She knew if she passed out, she would never wake up again.

She needed a weapon. She looked around, trying to find a branch or rock.

"No. Look only at me. Do it!"

Her chin was yanked with cruel fingers, forcing her gaze to lock with piercing eyes beneath his black mask. The pirate took out a dagger and dragged it against her throat. She felt a sharp sting and then a warm wetness dripping down the side of her neck.

"That's a warning, sweetness." The pirate's white teeth showed stark in the firelight as he spoke low against her face, his hot breath laced with the smell of liquor. "Fight me some more. I like it," he urged.

His lust-filled voice sounded crude, though aristocratic as well. He braced his hands on the ground above her shoulders, his gold-flecked eyes piercing into her like blades. One of the other pirates looting her family's belongings passed too close, dragging a sack of goods. Distracted, her attacker turned to curse at the interruption.

The blessed moment of inattention spurred Bailey to action. She kneed the pirate hard in the groin. He fell forward with a moan and she rolled out from under him. She saw the orange glint of the jeweled hilt of his dagger in the firelight. He had dropped it! She grabbed the weapon and scrambled to her feet. His left hand snaked out to grab for her ankle. She dodged him, then delivered a solid kick between her attacker's legs.

Moved by sheer terror, Bailey gathered her nightdress together and ran. Sparing a last glance around for her father and brother, she then fled as fast as her legs would carry her. Her bare feet sank in the cool, damp grass as a light mist began to fall. She ran into the cover of woods, losing her slippers and tearing her nightdress on spindly branches. Old pinecones and low brush poked into the soles of her feet as she ran, though she dared not slow her pace.

How had this horror happened? There had been no warning sounded from the watchpost at the beach. She always heard the bells ringing, even when her father didn't. Had the watchmen fallen asleep? Maybe they weren't even there. Beaufort hadn't seen a pirate attack in nearly a year and that had been well off the coast. The residents had become increasingly relaxed in their efforts to remain prepared. Now, they were all paying for the mistake.

Rain began to fall more steadily now, pattering against the canopy of leaves. Bailey ignored the waves of nausea that assaulted her and struggled to get her bearings. James's house was just a mile from hers, and as children they'd worn a path between them. The Fultons were like kin—they would know what to do.

Bailey broke through the trees and stumbled forward. Her feet began to sink in the earth as the forest floor gave way to mud. Shards of moonlight shone through a break in the mass of clouds. She had reached the old road. It was rarely used by anyone other than the few families who lived near Crystal Cove, since it was too narrow for anything more than a single horse and rider.

But that can't be! Bailey wrung a knot in a torn edge of her nightdress. As she went on, the road gave way to tall marshy grass. *That means I'm on the wrong side of the creek.*

The old, broken-down quay had been abandoned long ago. Even her father and the other fishermen had taken their small boats to the newer, larger wharf closer to town. Bailey stopped for a moment to get her bearings, the low song of frogs a familiar, oddly comforting sound.

Quickly deciding which way to go, she tried to move, but the sandy water bound her by the ankles. She lost her balance and stumbled, watching helplessly as the dagger sank into the marsh beneath the thick reeds. Bailey struggled to rise, and then began the arduous task of pulling her feet out of the deep muck. Each step was more difficult than the last but, finally, she was out of the grassy wetland.

That old dock should be around here somewhere.

Then she saw it. A heavy cloud released the moonlight for a moment as it swirled past, briefly illuminating the rickety dock. A lone ship lay in the water, creaking a gentle, though mournful song, her tall double masts rising into the night sky.

Sweet Mary, no!

The pirates' ship! There was no jolly roger flying, but Bailey knew that meant little in a midnight land raid. The fearsome symbol was usually raised on the open sea, to take ships off guard and intimidate them into surrender.

God help her, she had stumbled right into them. She swung around in alarm, expecting her attacker to be right behind her. She strained her eyes, but with another storm cloud shrouding the moon, Bailey could see little beyond her outstretched arms. The only sounds came from the wind in the leaves, the gentle lapping of water against the dock, the low groaning of the wood on the rocking ship.

And her own frightened, ragged breathing.

She stood frozen with uncertainty, panic rising up, ready to swallow her like Jonah. Her frightened mind conjured visions of the masked pirate just beyond her, in the darkness. Waiting for her to move the slightest bit before he would take her down. She started to cry, tears of frustration at herself—at her weakness. At her fear. And at her utter failure to help her family.

No!

She would not accept that she had failed them. Not yet. She blinked back her tears. As long as she had breath left, there was hope. She had to make it to the woods and somehow find her way back to the fork in the path that would lead her to James's house.

She swung around, too fast, for the movement sent a stabbing pain into her injured ribs. She felt faint, then her knees gave out beneath her. Breaking her fall with her hands, she cried out as tiny rocks jabbed painfully into her palms. She knelt still, trying to clear her head. The sound of a man's voice rang out over the singing frogs and clanking rigging of the ominous ship. She held her breath, her eyes focusing on the dark tree line a stone's throw away. Could she make it?

Another voice sounded, louder than the first and angry, his foul curses carrying on the wind. With her head pounding, she couldn't make out which direction the voices were coming from—the ship or the woods. Desperate to hide herself from a further assault, Bailey summoned all of her remaining strength and rose. She stumbled, and as blackness enfolded her, she realized the worst. She had lost her fight.

The pirate had won.

Chapter Two

Was she dead? Bailey felt as if she was floating, an oddly pleasant sensation that competed with the severe pounding in her head. She opened her eyes, blinking several times to clear her blurry vision. She was lying in a bed, but it wasn't her own. As she glanced around the dimly lit room at her unfamiliar surroundings, recollection came swift and ruthless.

The fire.

The pirate ship.

The voices.

God's mercy! She was on board the pirates' ship.

She sat up, nearly passing out with the quick movement. A red blanket that she had been covered with slipped to her lap and she sucked in her breath.

She was naked! She frantically searched her mind for any trace memory of what had occurred after she had heard the voices. Nothing came to her. She spied her nightdress in a rumpled ball on a chair against the far wall. She tumbled out of bed in her haste, snatching up her wet linen gown. She stared at the ugly stains of mud and blood, a testament to the violent night she had endured. Her hands trembled as she slipped the garment over her head, easing it down her bruised body. The nightdress had been a favorite—altered from one of Mama's

own. Bailey blinked hard and swallowed the emotion hardening in her throat. Now was not the time for tears.

Moving on shaky legs, she made her way to the porthole.
It was a double window, large enough for her to fit through,
if she could just get the latch to open. She pulled with all her
strength, but the brass hinge wouldn't budge. Next, she went
to the door, knowing with dreadful certainty that the lock
would be secure. She just prayed no one was keeping watch
on the other side. The lock held as she jiggled the knob, but
at least there didn't seem to be anyone out there.

There was only one option left: she would have to fight her
way out.

She began looking around for a weapon. The large room
had an elegant, yet masculine feel and seemed infinitely in
opposition to the slovenly clutter Bailey would have expected
to find in a pirate captain's cabin. She assumed the ship must
be the prize of a past attack and the unfortunate captain and
his crew were probably buried deep at sea now.

Papers, charts and instruments were scattered about the top of
the mahogany desk, along with a worn-looking map. She looked
at the lettering across the top of the map—*Bahamas*—and her
heart began to race. She flipped the papers around the desk, shuffled through drawers, and checked the small shelf under the bowl
on the washstand—no blade or weapon of any kind.

Spinning about, she scanned the room, her eyes landing on
a large sea chest at the foot of the bunk. She hurried to the
chest, ignoring the lovely ivory work and wide brass name-
plate bearing the initials CML. Whoever CML was, she
prayed he had a weapon in this trunk.

Clothes, a patchwork quilt, books and three bottles of some
kind of liquor were the only contents. With a groan of distress, Bailey dropped the heavy lid and backed away from the
trunk. Her eyes burned with the threat of tears, but she refused to give in to them. She turned and caught sight of herself in the mirror above the washstand. Her face was a mass

of bruises, purple and black, her lip swollen on one side, the gash at her neck red and caked with dried blood. Her shoulders bore small, round finger-mark bruises and her body ached deeply from the beating she had sustained at the hands of the murderous brigand.

No more, she thought. He had done his worst. He had killed her family.

"And he may kill me as well, but he will have no more of me," she whispered to herself. She worked to free the mirror from the pins that held it in place on both sides of the washstand.

Soon she heard voices above, some shouting orders to get under way, others in answer, and some she couldn't make out at all. Her nerves seemed to stretch to their limit as she waited, breathless for what seemed an eternity. All too soon, the sound of boot steps on the wood planks of the deck echoed down to her. Determined in gait, bold and purposeful, they fell with a cocksure stride. No doubt, those footsteps belonged to the pirates' leader.

Her attacker was back. With a last frantic pull, the mirror came loose. She plucked a crisp white square of cotton from a brass rod on the washstand and wrapped it around the mirror, then dashed the glass to the floor. She retrieved the largest, sharpest piece and wrapped another of the fine towels around one end like a makeshift handle. She dragged a chair to the corner behind the door, figuring she would have only a second or two before the pirate realized she was hiding.

Minutes dragged by, yet she remained poised on the chair clutching the mirror shard with white knuckles, waiting . . . waiting. Dawn was just breaking and she could see through the foggy, rain-streaked porthole that they had left the cove. The ship rocked and dipped against a building storm as they moved out to deeper water.

There would be no turning back now. Whatever happened to her, she was stuck on this pirate ship with very little possibility of escape. Her only consolation was in her determination that the pirate would not escape, either. She would see to it.

But that did not keep her heart from leaping into her throat when finally, the heavy footsteps got increasingly louder against the wood planks as the pirate neared. She eased herself up to crouch on the chair. She raised the jagged blade in her trembling hand as the door opened, blocking her from her enemy's view for a few precious seconds.

She held her breath and watched through the narrow crack between the door and jamb as the pirate ducked his tall form under the door frame. He hooked his booted toe around the bottom of the oak panel and pushed it closed. As he started to shrug out of his wet oilskin coat, she saw her chance.

Bailey hurled herself from the chair with a strength born of desperation, her torn hemline wrapping around her legs as she flew through the air. The ship responded to the wind's raging whims by shifting violently, throwing Bailey off balance just as she pushed up from the chair. The weapon she had hoped to slash the pirate's throat with missed that vital mark, instead cutting a long gash down her enemy's rain-soaked arm as he turned. Her powerful forward momentum caused her to fall painfully on the oak decking and tumble into the table, but she held fast to the bloodied shard of mirror for all her life.

"What the—?" he bellowed.

A mug he had held landed with a loud crack, spilling steaming black liquid across the floor. He spared no time to check his wound, but threw himself at her with a curse, slipping in the spilled coffee and landing with a loud *crack* on his forearms.

With the power of fear rushing through her veins, Bailey jumped to her feet. Ignoring the pain, she reached the door with lightning speed. Her sweaty hand slipped off the handle once, then again, and she glanced back to see his look of fury as he growled and tossed a chair across the cabin, out of his path. She screamed and whirled around to stab at his dark, angry face, but he leapt back and she heard the loud *whoosh* of the sharp weapon mere inches from his jaw.

"Give me that damn—"

He was interrupted as the ship lurched again and he bumped against another overturned chair behind him. He fell backward over the obstacle, giving Bailey the time she needed to fling the door open and run. She fled down the passageway, half-blinded by tears, half by fear.

Lord, what had made her think she could kill this pirate devil? She tripped up the ladder steps on her torn hem and slid back down, crying out as she bumped her shins. Daring to turn around, she could see he had regained his feet and was closing the space between them. Bailey yanked the linen up to her thighs, vaulted up the steps and raced onto the rain-slicked deck.

"Stop, you little hellion!"

He was catching up with her. She darted past a hulking bearded man, oblivious to his stunned expression as she flew across the deck. But the rain had made the deck too slippery. Bailey lost her footing, fell to her knees and slid several feet before grabbing at a line and pulling herself up.

She was at the railing in seconds, her lungs burning for air. Tears stung her eyes as her courage was swallowed up in the mix of rain and sea spray. She prayed for the strength to climb up and jump out of this hell. She was a strong swimmer. She would stand a chance in the ocean but, God help her, she would not survive another beating at the hands of this black-guard.

Throwing one bare leg over the railing, she heaved herself upward. A steel grip fastened around her middle. She was yanked off the polished wood with so much force that she fell into the beast and they both landed on the deck, face-up, Bailey on top of her enemy's hard, wet body.

"Let me go! Let me go!"

She struggled like a wild animal, then rolled over his injured arm. He cursed roundly while grabbing her by the back of her nightdress. She felt the wet material give as she struggled to get away. Just as his other hand reached up for her arm, the old linen began to split, slipping off her shoulder as she gained her footing and ran. Rain stung her face and blurred the figures of several sailors who had gathered on the deck to gape.

"Gadso! We've a real live sea nymph onboard, boys!" yelled one.

"A demoness!" cried another. "She's gonna take us to the bottom of the sea!"

Out of the corner of her eye as she darted past, Bailey saw the young sailor cross himself.

"Get the hell back!" the pirate ordered in a low growl.

It was him! He was gaining on her. Bailey scrambled past the sailors to the railing and started to climb but the pirate was on her in a flash, slamming into her back, knocking her sideways to the ground and then pinning her beneath him.

"Be still, wench!"

"Murderer! Get off me, pirate bastard!" she cried, beating her fists against him.

The pirate captured her wrists, holding them in a hard grasp. She thrashed upward, trying to throw his weight from her and felt her head hit the boards of the deck. The hard impact blasted the back of her skull, filling her vision with a wave of darkness. She fought the pull of unconsciousness, struggling against the hopeless feeling that she was about to die.

She felt his weight lift as he straddled her, pinning her arms above her head. Determined to stay conscious, she opened her eyes to stare into the unmasked face of the devil. Water streamed in rivers from thick spikes of dark hair that were plastered to his tanned face. His thick, muscled forearms rendered her upper body immobile, but what really kept her still was the deep fury reflected in his cold gray eyes.

"Who the hell are you?" He ground out the words through gritted teeth, his unmasked face inches from hers.

Gray eyes! "You are not . . . him!" She shouted the fact with more than a hint of accusation in her tone while her mind grappled with the sudden unexpected realization. *Dear God, this was not the same pirate!*

A spark lit in the depths of the man's gaze but no warmth followed. If anything, the dangerous narrowing of those piercing orbs gave evidence of an even colder, more brittle anger than moments before.

"Who! Who am I not?" His angry command would have been drowned out by the pounding rain and billowing sails if he had not shouted the words so close to her face. His deadly expression told her it would be a mistake to lie to him.

"The . . . the pirate on shore. The one who tried to kill me."

Though not much more than a whisper, she knew he had heard by the way he inclined his head and eyed her with—what, suspicion? Interest? She did not understand the strange way he was looking at her as if she had sprouted a third eye.

Without a word, he released her arms and leaned back on his knees, his icy glare sliding from her face down her body and back, making her acutely aware of how the damp, torn linen clung to her body. She threw her arms across her breasts and felt a hot flush descend upon her cheeks as she began to struggle underneath his weight.

"I advise you to cease your fighting," he warned, leaning so close she could feel the warmth of his breath tickle her ear. He raised up again and called out to one of his men.

"Bastard! Let go of me!" Bailey tried to keep the trembling from her voice.

The man did not answer but glared down at her as he shoved wet ebony locks back from his face. He turned his attention to the bearded man who approached them, the man's considerable height emphasized by Bailey's supine position on the deck. As he towered above them, she averted her eyes to inspect the giant's boots, fear spreading through her chilled limbs. She held her breath. The giant removed his heavy coat, handing it to the gray-eyed man that he acknowledged simply as *Captain*.

Taking the garment, the captain dismissed the giant, then turned his dark head to bellow out orders across the deck. The men who had gathered to gawk now scattered like rats. Drawing a ragged breath, Bailey's attention returned to the man who straddled her, his muscular thighs pressed firmly against her cold skin.

"Murderer! You took everything! Why did you bring me here? What do you want now?" Her voice rose with each question, hysteria threatening to break to the surface through her fear.

"You are in no position to ask questions," he said matter-of-factly as he began to rise, scooping her up roughly as he stood. "But you had better be prepared to answer all of mine. And, wench, you'd best hope that I am not displeased by what you have to say," he added with menace. His brow lowered with his frown as he captured her chin, lifting it to meet his cold stare.

She stood before him stonily, trying hard to be brave as he reached around her, trapping her within the coat, her arms straight down by her sides. He then picked her up as if she were nothing more than an empty sack and dropped her over his shoulder before moving with long strides in the direction of his quarters.

Chapter Three

Cole was not accustomed to being taken by surprise. In truth, he hadn't let his guard down once in the last five years. Not since he felt the lethal bite of betrayal that had made him swear two things: he would never trust a woman again, and he would never stop until he avenged his father's murderer.

So, it was his own fault that he found himself standing here, in his ransacked cabin, a long gash stinging his arm and the cause of it struggling wildly over his other shoulder. He had known the girl was here—Owens and Dewey had told him how they found her in the wet reeds, so near to death she wasn't expected to live.

Near death, like hell! The wench had nearly sliced his neck open. Damn. If he hadn't been in such a hurry to question her, he would never have been so careless.

He shifted the girl's slight weight off his shoulder and dumped her on his bunk in a rumpled ball of arms, legs, and his first mate's soaked overcoat. He crossed to his desk and pulled out a bottle of brandy, pouring himself a shot while watching her from the corner of his eye. She righted herself, pulling the coat around her and holding it in place with her arms crossed tightly in front of her.

"Stay away from me!" she cried.

Cole frowned at her. "Believe me, wench, ravishing you is the very last thing I am interested in. What I want from you are answers."

She sat unmoving, quietly watching him, wide-eyed as a mouse about to be swallowed whole by the kitchen tabby. He reached in the drawer for a second glass, poured a healthy amount of the amber liquid and moved toward the bunk. His boots crunched in the broken mirror on the floor, the violent pop of glass startling the girl. She shrank into a dark corner at the head of his bunk and eyed him warily.

"Here, drink this. It will give you a measure of courage."

The slight shake of her head was barely perceptible from where she huddled in the shadows.

"I insist. It's plain to see I won't get any answers from you if you're cowering in my bunk all day." He knew the lull of the brandy would loosen her tongue and make her less inclined to lie.

She reached out a trembling hand and snatched the glass from him, as if touching him might burn her to ash.

"What happened to the hellcat? Not so full of bloodlust anymore? Or is it just that your courage has abandoned you, now that you are unarmed?"

She downed the amber liquid in one swallow and choked out a cough. "I thought you were . . ."

"*The pirate*," he finished when her trembling voice failed her. "Yes, I heard that. Tell me what you know about him."

She clutched the crystal in shaky hands. "I don't know anything about the vile beast. He's one of *your* men, why are you asking me about him?"

"Careful, wench. The brandy is making you overly bold. Or are you ready to be disposed of so soon?"

The threat was successful. Color drained from the girl's face, except for the dark bruises that now stood out even more against her ghostly pallor. She held out her glass obediently when he brought the bottle over to splash more in the large bowl of the snifter.

"I don't explain myself to anyone. However, since you are at a grave disadvantage, I'll forgive the transgression this once. The pirate who attacked you was not my man. The Dragon and his men are responsible for what happened to you last night."

The girl gasped, pressing a slender hand against her breastbone. She took a gulp of the brandy and fell into a fit of coughing. She covered her mouth and winced at the contact with her split lip.

"You've heard of him, then."

She nodded, coughing. "Everyone in my village knows of him. He is the devil," she spat. "But, then . . . who are you?"

"I won't be answering the questions here, wench."

"Would you stop calling me that?" she snapped, her voice slurring the tiniest bit.

Cole sighed, debating the wisdom in giving the girl liquor. She was injured and weak and apparently had never imbibed before.

"Give me your name, then."

She opened her mouth, but hesitated to speak, her eyes filled with mistrust and fear.

"So, it is to be 'wench' after all."

"Bailey Spencer."

"Aye," Cole nodded and spoke, more to himself than her. He removed his soaked shirt, squeezing the rainwater out in the washstand bowl. "Johnathan Spencer's daughter," he said over his shoulder.

"How do you know—?"

He turned back to her and saw her flinch, a look of alarm on her face. She was staring at the thick line of blood running down his arm.

"Feeling remorseful, Bailey?" He drawled out her name with a slow emphasis that made her cheeks flush. "Or are you just now realizing what a serious mistake you made in missing your mark? You did mean to cut my throat open, didn't you? I suppose I should be grateful for your lack of skill."

"The . . . the ship hit a wave. I fell. I . . . I didn't intend to kill you. I just wanted to get away."

"Don't lie," he growled. "If there's one thing I won't tolerate, it's a woman who lies. You'll do well to remember that. As for this," he said, glancing down and swiping the blood away with the crumpled shirt, "if this is the worst damage you can inflict, you'd best be thankful that I'm not the Dragon. That maggot would have skinned you alive for this scratch. I, on the other hand, believe you may be useful. If so, then that is where your worth begins and ends with me. Otherwise, you are useless baggage. So, the sooner you cooperate, the sooner you can be on your way. Make this as easy or difficult as you wish, it matters naught to me. I *will* get what I want from you, either way."

He thought he saw a light of anger come to life in her wounded eyes. He supposed he couldn't blame her. He would have thrashed anyone who insulted his worth in such a manner.

He steeled himself against the inkling to soften. Her father had been responsible for the attack. He had brought the Dragon's fatal wrath down upon his family. Bailey might know more about the pirate than she realized or admitted. It was imperative that he find out with all haste. Her tragedy was not his doing and he could not let it be his concern. He had spent years searching for an end to his own family's tragedy. So far it had all been in vain. But now . . . This girl was very possibly the luckiest break he had gotten in a long while.

"Damn," he muttered in irritation, watching the blood continue to trail down his arm. He didn't want to waste time getting stitched just now; he was impatient for answers. "About last night—the pirate who attacked you—did you see his face? What did he look like?"

"I . . . I'm not sure. It was dark. I can't remember," she answered vaguely. From the mistrust in her eyes, Cole could see that she still wondered if he had played a part in the attack.

Rain beat heavier against the porthole now, the ship dipping and swaying against storm-tossed waves slapping against the hull. The girl's teeth were chattering against the chill in the cabin, her small form drooping against the wall in the wet coat she still wore.

Cole sighed, running a hand through his damp hair, realizing he wasn't going to get any answers if the girl died on him. He didn't know the extent of her injuries, but from what little skin was visible, he could see she suffered an ugly gash on her neck. He retrieved the patchwork quilt from his sea chest and handed it to her, taking the empty snifter from her chilled fingers.

"Here. Take off your clothes before you soak my bed down to the mattress. You can wrap up in this. Don't move from that spot—I won't be forgiving if we have a repeat of the last time I walked in here. Understand?"

Satisfied with her shadow of a nod, he turned and left the cabin.

Chilled to the bone, Bailey wasted no time shedding the enormous wet coat and wrapping up in the dry quilt. But the man was mad if he believed she'd part with her shift. The ruined garment was her only bit of modesty against a blackguard who had heaven knows what in mind for her. She was feeling unstrung in the presence of this dark-haired, gray-eyed man who spoke to her with what seemed to be barely held restraint.

That information is where your worth begins and ends with me . . .

His voice had been filled with such a deadly calm, but his threat was clear. The cold certainty in his eyes and the hard line of his mouth showed her plainly that he was a dangerous man who would not be denied. Though he seemed capable of as much cruelty and mayhem as the black-masked pirate, he seemed willing to bide his time with her.

Even though she had tried to kill him.

With that dismal reminder, waves of nausea assaulted her. She shivered, despite the warmth of the cotton quilt. Did he really just want information? God's mercy, what was to become of her if she couldn't tell him what he wanted to know? Try as she might, she could remember only bits and pieces of the previous night. Had her father and brother gone to the beach? Were they safe? She shook her head in misery. Her father would have no idea what had happened to her. But he would move the heavens to find her, of that she was certain.

The throbbing in her head became unbearable and the knot of fear in her stomach increased her nausea. She was not accustomed to being afraid. Her father had always said she had her mother's strong will, but she couldn't seem to draw upon it now. She had to keep her wits about her and toughen up. If her father was alive, God willing, he would come for her. No matter what this vile lout threatened her with, she had to be strong and survive if she wanted to get out of this nightmare.

"No more stuttering little girl, quaking every time he raises his devil's eyebrow at you," she whispered to herself. "As long as he wants answers, you will be safe. You will be brave without giving him any reason to hurt you. And soon, you will be going home," she promised herself, with a glance heavenward for extra assurance.

"Who are you talking to, Bailey?"

"Don't you knock?" she snapped in surprise. Her eyes fell on the clean, white bandage encircling his upper arm.

"Not on my own door. Now, answer my question."

"I was talking to myself, if you must know." She lifted her chin and tried to keep her voice level.

"Perfect. Just my luck to get burdened with a daft woman." His voice was heavy with sarcasm.

"You would not be burdened with me, *sir,* if you had not

taken me aboard this ship and sailed away from my home." The effects of the brandy must be to blame for her unwise inclination to sass him.

"I see you're feeling better." He smirked, rolling his sleeve down over the bandage." You were taken aboard my ship as an act of mercy by two soft-hearted dunderheads on my crew who are now doing extra watch. I wanted only to question you. I would have been perfectly content to have returned you to the marsh in which you were found, but a storm was approaching and we had to sail immediately to get in front of it. If you had had the courtesy to wake up sooner, you would not be here right now."

Bailey gasped, shocked to her core. The man was the most callous brute she had ever encountered. "Very well. Ask me your questions so we may then happily part company."

The big knave laughed harshly, his eyes darkening, giving him the ominous appearance of a pirate. She had to remind herself that despite his good looks, he had not denied being one of them, and she must not lessen her guard.

"So, the hellcat has returned. Do I need to search you for a weapon, or are you hoping to cleave me in two with that sharp tongue of yours?"

"No!" she cried, pulling the quilt tighter around her. "Stay there. I will do my best to answer your questions."

She chided herself silently for continuing to allow him to menace her. He had said he wanted information and he seemed eager to be rid of her. Surely he would let her go once she told him what he wanted to know. She prayed her memory would return soon.

He grinned wickedly, a crooked turn of full lips that revealed a line of white teeth. In a flash of memory, she recalled the appearance of the pirates from last night. They had been unkempt and ragged, to say the least. The man standing before her now, though frightening enough, held himself like a gentleman. He had a strong jaw, straight nose and shiny, dark hair.

She could easily picture him riding through the pristine streets of Williamsburg in a fine carriage, pulled by proud, black horses. In fact, he would be downright handsome, if he didn't have a continuous scowl on his features. Sweet Mary! What was she thinking? The vile beast was a pirate!

"Dash it all! What's wrong with you? You aren't going to dissolve in feminine hysteria, are you? I told you, Bailey, I'm not interested. I avoid blushing virgins at all costs."

She gasped in embarrassment. It was a relief, of course. But still, his tone was insulting, his words crude, and she felt her cheeks fill with heat. "Good! Enduring one filthy pirate's claws on me was more than I could stand. I'm certain I don't need to be assaulted by any of the rest of you."

At her insult, his dark brow raised a notch. He tilted his head at her and dragged a chair back from the table in the center of the room. He appeared calm, terribly so, even as his eyes filled and then danced with unbridled silver menace. He had the ability to make her feel breathless with merely a glance. He sat and began drumming his long fingers with deliberate slowness on the mahogany, appearing to study the highly polished finish with great interest.

"Now that you have that out of the way, I am going to have to insist that you refrain from any more dramatic outbursts. I don't have the time to waste and you are beginning to drain my patience."

"You are the one who insisted I drink the brandy," she replied tartly.

"I promise you will not like me if you continue to push," he said in a low, warning tone.

"I doubt there is anything you could do to make my opinion of you any worse." The contempt she had wished to convey had become diffused, even to her own ears. Damn the man, despite the scruff of beard on his chin, his dimpled cheek made him appear nearly angelic.

"You are no match for me, Bailey. You had better accept my word on that, rather than find out for yourself."

"Since when is the word of a pirate worth anything?" she challenged. She didn't know if it was actually the brandy or her own stubborn personality that made her continue on so unwisely. But startled by her growing appreciation of his pleasant appearance, she decided the only way to survive this man was to hide her conflicting fear and fascination.

He shrugged, his features remaining hard.

"If I tell you what you want to know, then you will let me go immediately." She meant it to sound like a demand, rather than a request. She just hoped he missed the slight tremor in her voice.

He looked around him and gestured with both arms lifted. "Where do you suggest I let you go? Off the bow or the stern?"

His humorless laugh rankled her. She should have realized he would not care for her plight at all. "See here, pirate, if you think to ransom me, you must know that my father is not a wealthy man. You will get nothing from him."

"I am well aware of that, Bailey."

Her name slipped off his tongue like warm honey, but it was his tone that confused her the most. It had seemed to carry the slightest edge of compassion. The cabin seemed to be closing in on her, the pirate's overbearing presence suffocating her. And to make matters worse, the pain that seared her body like hot spikes seemed to be stealing her sanity and tossing it to the winds. She was pushing him too far, but she had to know how he knew her father.

"What do you know of my father? He is a good man. He would never consort with the likes of you." A sickening realization struck her in that instant. "Sweet Mary, were you there?"

She tried in desperation to remember if she'd seen him last night, but her memories remained elusive. She glared at him from the safety of the shadows in the bunk, damning him for what she was afraid he might admit to next. Her body tensed. Pain streaked through her bruised muscles.

"You have to start accepting your circumstances, Bailey. You have no other choice. No one is looking for you. No one is coming."

"I don't believe you!" she shouted. "My father will never stop looking for me. You are despicable to say such things." A wave of dizziness passed over her. The cabin seemed to spin.

"Your father is dead. Your brother, too."

She barely heard his soft words as the blood rushed in her ears. She gasped back a sob and sprang to the edge of the bunk. "How do you know that? How do you know? What did you do?" she cried, condemning him with her eyes.

His own eyes went flat, like bits of gray stone, increasing the dread that filled her.

"Why won't you say anything?" she demanded, all caution forgotten in her desperation for the truth. "Say something, blackguard! Did you kill them?"

He wrenched her to her feet, holding her arms in an iron grip as she clutched the quilt to her breast. "I am warning you—" he growled before thrusting her roughly away from him.

"Warning me? Murderer!" she accused. "Damn your pirate's soul to hell!" she cried and leapt up from where she had landed on the bunk. She rushed him, throwing punches at his face and chest. He reacted instantly, capturing her fists in one large hand. He caught the quilt as it slipped from her shoulder and wrapped her tightly in the folds of cotton.

Drained of strength, she sagged against his unyielding form, sobbing and accusing him over and over. He had succeeded in crushing the small glimmer of hope that had kept her going. The deep ache in her heart bespoke the truth and would not be ignored anymore. She knew his words were true. It was useless to wish for the impossible.

Her father and Adam were dead.

With that hope gone, her world seemed to crumble to dust

at her feet. The walls began to spin in earnest, making it impossible to focus on any one object. She tried to push away from the pirate, but his hold on her was unyielding. She felt the tickle of fresh blood as it wet a path down from the cut on her neck. She looked up into her captor's hard face. His grim expression blurred as the room grew dimmer and dimmer. She had to get away. She fought against the heaviness of her lids but failed, and as she closed her eyes, a dizzy weightlessness came over her.

Chapter Four

Cole sighed and rolled up the set of island maps he had been studying. It was useless trying to form a strategy when all he could think about was the girl in his bunk. He had been scornful earlier when she'd demanded to be released, but in a way, he was thankful for the convenient excuse that kept her here. Despite every soul-deep inclination to relieve himself of the burden of this woman, there was a deeply shrouded part of him that felt an intense need to protect her. The pain in her eyes when he'd so coldly announced that her family was dead had struck an emotional nerve in him that he had purposely buried long ago. Apparently not deep enough, he thought peevishly.

A single rap sounded on the door, bringing him back to the present. He called out permission to enter as he tucked the maps on a specially designed shelf above his desk. Thin strips of hemp and hooks kept rolled documents from flying off the shelf in bad weather.

Though Marcel was officially the ship's cook, he had the heart of an inventor, even if some of his creations had been less than successful. Cole had liked this particular idea so much that he allowed shelves just like this one to be built elsewhere on the ship.

"Mon Dieu! The mess! What happened in here? Ahh, *la petite femme! Elle est mortes, sacrebleu."*

"Marcel, you are rambling in French again."

"Pardon, *Capitaine.* She is so still, I fear she is dead."

"If weeping is any indication, then she was alive five minutes before you arrived," Cole replied. He turned halfway in his chair, just as Marcel straightened and with a sigh of relief, confirmed that the girl yet lived. "She is in restless slumber. Her body will need better sleep to recover from such wounds."

"Can you do anything?"

"Oui, but of course. I am the ship's doctor, *non?"* he chuckled.

"Aye, but you're rarely called on for anything more than cooking, old man," Cole responded with a grin.

"Ah, you won't admit it, but you believe in my odd ways of healing, or you would not have asked me to help the girl. You are a kind man, this I believe about you, *Capitaine,* even though you don't believe it of yourself."

"Enough, you old fishwife. Just get to work—I need her to tell me whatever she can remember about the Dragon."

"Sacrebleu, then it is true? She truly escaped that devil with her life? Remarkable."

"It would be remarkable, at that, if in fact, it was him."

"Was it not?"

"I'm not certain yet. There were no witnesses other than the girl. And if you don't start healing her, I may never get any answers."

"Oui, of course." Marcel moved then, his white hair bobbing as he set out bottles of his mysterious healing herbs and two jars of thick salves on a chair that he dragged next to the bunk.

Cole righted the table and other chairs, lit a lamp and brought it next to Marcel. He avoided looking at Bailey's tormented features but watched Marcel's weathered hands move over her body in the air just above the quilt. He paused often, holding very still, his thick brows wrinkling in concentration. Cole didn't pretend to understand the ancient healing art Marcel had learned during his years in Japan, but he'd experienced the old man's gift himself and would not question its odd power.

After a few minutes, Marcel leaned back and exhaled deeply, then began tearing off a clean strip from a small roll of cloth.

"Will she live?"

"*Oui*. Not a single bone is broken—there is no damage inside that will not heal. She is a strong one, this girl. *Oui*, she has much life in her," he concluded as he mixed a dab of salve and herbs in a small bowl.

"Good. What about that?" Cole asked, leaning in to take a closer look at the angry wound that ran a finger's length across the base of the girl's slender neck.

"This will keep infection away," Marcel responded, dabbing the smelly concoction generously on the cut. "It will leave a scar that no young lady should have to bear, pity shame. But such a scar won't make a difference on this one. *Elle est tres jolie, non?*"

Cole didn't respond. He told himself her appearance was inconsequential. Still, he was drawn to study the girl's face while Marcel wrapped the linen around her neck. Long brown lashes feathered against her cheeks, below her lids—closed against eyes he recalled were the same startling blue as the water surrounding his island home.

He straightened and turned away from the bunk, seeking to distance himself from his unwelcome musings. His boot slipped in a pile of crushed mirror as he made his way to his desk. His pride faltered at the reminder of how easily Bailey had taken him by surprise. To think this mere slip of battered girl could have killed him—on his own ship, in his own damn cabin—it was too much. He never for one instant considered the girl could be a threat to him.

He had almost been taken down for that one careless mistake. He would not allow himself a second.

Time seemed to drag by as Marcel worked, preparing his

salves and mumbling in broken French. The girl was restless in unconsciousness, her low mournful moans filling the room and grating against Cole's nerves.

"*Merde!* This is the Devil's work, I tell you. No one but a devil could do such a thing to an innocent *damoiselle*," the Frenchman muttered in disgust.

Cole let the goose quill drop from his fingers. He shut his eyes and rubbed his forehead above the bridge of his nose. A dark splotch of ink stained the parchment, bleeding into the unfinished entry.

It hardly mattered. He had only been able to write three lines in the ship's log since sitting down. The agonized sounds coming from behind him were distracting enough without the old cook having to cluck like a mother hen over the girl.

Dash it all! He had succeeded in constructing a solid barrier around his heart. But he found himself relating to the hell she had endured. Despite his urgent business with her, he was beginning to wonder if Bailey Spencer was more of a burden than he wished to take on. He would be glad to have her questioned and out of his life.

Another moan drifted to his ears.

And the sooner, the better.

He replaced the quill in the pen stand and retrieved a small jar of sand from a drawer. He sprinkled a bit on the round pool of ink and watched it soak up the stain. "Are you almost done performing your voodoo?" he asked, turning in his chair to observe the old cook.

"*Non, Capitaine,* she has many injuries. I wish to be gentle with her, the girl looks so delicate."

Cole doubted there was anything delicate about her. "Don't be fooled by appearances, Marcel. She fought off the Dragon, for Christ's sake. A delicate girl would not be alive to keep me from my work."

Marcel chuckled. "Very true, *Capitaine*. I admire her. For such a small girl, her spirit is strong."

"Fine. Then I suppose she won't die while you see to dinner. I won't have my crew starving because you wish to coddle the girl."

Marcel opened his mouth to speak, then shut it again. His face held an expression of surprise. Cole held up his hand and sighed heavily. Whatever strain he was feeling, it was unlike him to take it out on a loyal member of his crew.

"You have done much for her. Let her be for a while. You can come back and finish later."

Marcel grinned and nodded felicitously. He lined up his balms on the table and chattered out loud about which vegetables might still be fresh enough to add to the stew.

Moments later, Cole heard the click of the latch as the door closed, leaving him alone in the cabin with Bailey. He returned his attention to the ship's log, entering more about their time in Beaufort. The quill scratched across the parchment, each word illustrating the bloody violence that Cole had witnessed when he discovered the bodies of the man and young boy who had been Bailey's family. The more he wrote, the more her moans seemed to haunt the stillness of the cabin.

And the more she suffered, the more Cole's past seemed to come alive. Memories he had long kept buried now surfaced to torture him as the image of his dying mother formed clearly in his mind. She had cried with much the same agony as Bailey did now, yet Cole had felt little sympathy. He had been too angry. She had brought on her own misery, by her selfish, dishonorable actions. She had cast that dishonor up on her sons, who were left with the aftermath of her betrayal for the rest of their lives.

Cole had not thought of that day—the day he stood by her bedside as she begged for forgiveness—in months. His only focus had been on the practical, methodical steps he was taking to hunt down the bastard who had started it all.

But listening to Bailey's pain echoing like the beckoning

of an old ghost had brought it all back. With a relentless vengeance.

And despite how hard he tried, he couldn't keep himself from turning in his chair to look at her again. She lay in his large bunk, tossing restlessly. She landed on her back and as her head rolled toward him, her brows pulled together in a grimace of pain. Her left arm dropped out from under the quilt to hang off the edge of the bunk. Dark, ugly rings encircled her wrist and several fingers bore small cuts, as if she'd been defending herself against the blade of a knife. Angry scratches left red streaks up her arm. She whimpered and tossed her head toward the wall.

Blast it! It was plain enough that he wasn't going to get any work done.

Cole glanced at the bowls lined up on the table. Perhaps if he finished putting the ointments on her, the girl would quiet down and sleep. He pushed back from his desk and moved reluctantly to the table, studying her dispassionately as he neared.

He sank down in the chair next to the bunk and studied the ointments. He chose the most pungent-smelling one and set the bowl on his knee, dipping a finger into the sticky concoction. He reconsidered for a moment, perturbed at himself for doubting his ability to remain aloof. Determined to do just that, he reached out and lifted her limp arm, dabbing the ointment on her bruised wrist. He smoothed the balm on her fingers, so small entwined with his own, large, awkward ones. Next, he made his way up the cuts on her arm. Her skin was soft and warm under his calloused fingers.

He muttered a curse and leaned heavily against the back of the chair. He stared at her in indecision, his emotions at war with his logic—or was it bitterness? His logic told him that she may have answers he desperately wanted. But the bitterness warned him she was poison. He had learned logic from years of school abroad. The bitterness had come to him in the flash of deplorable sins committed by a mother he had once cherished.

Aye, Bailey Spencer was problematic enough in her mere presence, without his having to take on this undesirable task. He would leave the rest to Marcel. He flipped back the quilt to place her arm by her side and saw the ugly line of injuries down her body and legs. How had he not seen these when she had fought him on deck? Had he caused any of them? He swore again. No, he had nothing to feel guilty about. He had merely restrained her, hadn't he?

Bailey stirred, turning on her side. The backs of her calves bore scrapes as if she'd been dragged across the ground. Cole sighed. He might as well finish what he'd started. The sooner she healed, the sooner he would get his information and the sooner she would be a distant memory.

He spread the ointment on her left side and then tilted her toward him and stood to coat her right side with the medicine. He lowered her back to the mattress and she rolled to face the wall, shivering. Cole began to cover her and noticed the gashes on the bottoms of her feet. An irrational anger filled him on her behalf as he imagined the blind panic that must have numbed her to the pain as she ran for her life, barefoot, over sharp twigs and rocks. He gently coated her feet with the balm and then pulled the quilt up to her shoulders.

Cole returned to his desk and braced his hands on the carved edge, staring at the map hanging on the wall. It was useless. Even unconscious, the girl refused to give Cole a moment of peace. She invaded his thoughts as she invaded his very cabin. He couldn't help but respect the magnitude of strength the girl possessed. After all she had been through, and despite believing he was no better than the pirate who attacked her, Bailey had still stood up to him. She had shown real courage in fighting him on deck and in facing his resulting anger. Grown men had cowered before him for less reason more times than he could count.

He turned as her soft murmurs reached through his thoughts. She spoke in broken whispers, pleading for the lives of her father and little brother. Her brow wrinkled in her deep sleep as she cursed the pirate's soul and vowed to see him hang. She began to struggle under the quilt, her cries of distress drawing Cole to her side. She freed her arms and flailed them about, as if battling an unseen attacker. Cole caught her arms and eased her fists open, massaging each palm as he tried to calm her.

"You're safe, Bailey. It's over. The pirate is gone. He can't hurt you anymore."

"No . . . no . . . must get off . . . the ship."

"You're safe on my ship, Bailey. I promise you," Cole said soothingly.

She quieted and fell into a peaceful slumber. A niggling of compassion shook his soul from its well-practiced indifference as he rose and stared down at her. She lay helpless and defenseless, at the discretion of a man she believed was her enemy.

And when she healed and he was done with her, she would return to Beaufort, to . . . nothing.

Christ, what the hell was wrong with him? Had he misjudged his own fortitude in closing off his emotions? Beautiful, seductive women from every port he visited had given him pleasure and received pleasure in return. It had never been difficult to walk away.

Only now, he could not walk away. The vast ocean imprisoned them together as securely as chains. And even if they weren't at sea, he couldn't be free of her just yet. This woman might have something he truly desired. Information. He couldn't walk away until she had remembered everything.

But the bitterness of failure taunted him. His failure to stop his father's murder. His failure to catch the Dragon.

His failure to keep his heart closed to the troublesome girl in his bed.

No, he had not failed in that, yet. His heart was still closed. But he realized he would have to guard it more carefully from now on. Staring down at her angelic face, Cole suddenly felt an intense need for the brisk ocean spray against his face.

Chapter Five

Bailey stood at the porthole, watching the rain streak in vertical patterns down the glass. There was nothing but ocean as far as her eye could see, endless leagues of water, taking her . . . where? How was she going to get off this ship? Who was this grim, gray-eyed man who was taking her Lord knows where? He hadn't answered her when she asked him who he was.

He doesn't want to admit he's a thieving, murdering pirate, that's why he won't answer you.

She squeezed her eyes closed against the unbearable question she could not keep from thinking.

What was to become of her now?

She inhaled deeply, grimacing at the pungent odor that rose from her skin. Someone had cleaned up the glass, straightened the cabin, tended her wounds, bandaged her neck and dressed her—in a manner of speaking. Was it the pirate himself? Was it his shirt she wore now? It was large, like the man himself, the open neck plunging indecently low, the hem reaching just above her knees; still, she was grateful to have something more than her damp, torn nightdress to cover her. She couldn't picture the churlish man caring for anyone in such a manner, and the mere possibility that it had been his hands rubbing salve on her body brought heat to her cheeks.

She laughed bitterly and glanced heavenward at her embarrassed reaction. The humiliation she suffered last night was enough to make the most tarnished barmaid blush. Her innocent ideals were gone—stolen by a masked monster with cruel gold eyes that had shone with the thrill of his brutality. He had not succeeded in raping her body, but despite that blessing, she still suffered from a feeling of violation. It would have been more of a blessing if she hadn't begun to recall the raid, but the nightmare that had awakened her a few hours ago had now developed into fragments of memory that she couldn't escape.

Though she could remember only bits and pieces of the attack, she did remember the fire—the sight of her home burning to a mere pile of flaming rubble.

Before that, she remembered waking up, taking her rough wool cape from a peg by the door and slipping out to make her way to the outhouse, a short walk to the edge of the woods. Had she made it there? She struggled to remember, pressing her fists to her temples in frustration as she concentrated.

The sound of the door closing startled her out of her thoughts. She spun around to face the scowl of the implacable man whose presence seemed to fill every corner of the cabin. The expression on his face was unreadable, and she found it suddenly difficult to breathe.

"Are you feeling better?" He seemed to growl the question while casting her a black look.

"Are you a pirate?" The question hung in the air, her heart beating fast in anticipation of his answer.

"I see you are still intent on asking the questions."

"If you intend to kill me, I would simply rather know now."

A single dark brow lifted slightly, along with one corner

of his firm mouth. Was he mocking her fear? Though it would be foolish to show it, she felt her ire rising.

"Are you afraid that if you tell me your intentions, I will try to kill you again? Perhaps you fear I will be successful the next time."

He held up a hand to stop her, an unmistakable, cocky grin of pleasure curving his full lips.

"You win, Bailey. I will give you an answer. But then I expect some answers of my own."

He crossed the room in two long strides, then sat in a chair at the highly polished mahogany table. "I am not a pirate. Now, sit."

She released the breath she had been holding and moved to sit across from him. She held the neckline of the shirt closed with one hand, feeling next to naked under the man's direct study.

"Now then, let's start with something easy . . . How did you end up in the marsh?"

"I . . . I was running . . . There was a fire . . . My home was burning . . ." Her voice trailed off. "I was trying to get to my neighbor's farm, but the smoke was so thick. I was so afraid. I must have gotten turned around somehow."

"And ended up in the marshes."

"Yes. I remember, I heard voices. I thought it was . . . the pirates . . . coming after me."

He shook his head. "It was my men, Dewey and Owens. They found you, unconscious, next to the road."

"I see. May I ask you one more question?"

That infuriating brow rose, as a seeming look of amusement touched his otherwise stern features. "I doubt I could stop you, Bailey."

She hesitated, flustered by his continued familiar use of her name. "Who are you?"

"Colby Leighton. Captain of the *Barracuda*."

She let out the breath she'd been holding but eyed him

cautiously. The three ship captains she knew were honorable, respectable men. "Why did your men bring me aboard? How did you know my father? When are you going to let me go? Captain Leighton, you must let me go." She hadn't meant to, but the words spilled out of her in her eagerness.

"That isn't going to be possible."

Her mind refused to accept that response. "People will be looking for me. I assume you don't want anyone pursuing you."

To her utter disbelief, he simply shook his head. Unable to keep still, she stood and began pacing behind her chair. "I must see to my father and brother," she said, her voice more insistent.

"No."

"No?" She sent him a look meant to shame him to his toes, to no avail. "I have to bury them." She punctuated each word with a mixture of venom and tightly held emotion. "You cannot deny me that."

"I'm afraid I can. And I do." He reached out and plucked an orange from a porcelain bowl in the center of the table and toyed with it absently. "Bailey, you were the only survivor. As far as I know, you are the first person the Dragon has attacked and ever left alive."

"And you wish to keep me for your own selfish reasons. Well, you cannot hold me! You have no right. If you do not agree to let me go then I will find a way to escape you. I promise you that, Captain!" she railed at him.

The infuriating man began peeling the orange, completely unaffected by her challenge.

"Escape me? I hadn't thought of it that way, but if that's how you prefer it . . ."

She glared at him, wishing he would choke on the piece of fruit he had popped into his mouth. "Prefer it? You claim not to be a pirate, yet your actions and words say otherwise. If you are an honorable man, then you must let me go. You know it's wrong to hold me." She gripped the back of the chair, wishing it was the captain's neck. "Where is this ship going? I demand you take me to the nearest port. Immediately!"

Cole watched her pace the confines of the room, her tension palpable, nearing desperation. She went to the porthole and looked hard in both directions, searching for land, he supposed. He imagined she would like to rip open the latch and squeeze herself through the window if it meant she had half a chance to prove to him that she could escape him. Such a strong will, he thought. Such courage, though much too impetuous to be of good use. She was just like Duchess, he thought, smiling at the memory . . .

It had been a humid summer night, too humid to sleep. A thunderstorm hung in the air, threatening its fury at any moment. Cole had no fondness for thunderstorms, so he lay awake waiting for it to be over with. A strange and pitiful sound outside drew him to the window and he quickly found the source of the noise. A tiny kitten huddled in a crook of the huge oak that stood close to the house. The tree had been a source of fear for Cole when he was younger, its thick branches scraping eerily against the window glass during stormy weather.

But that had been long ago, and now he was a brave ten-year-old who intended to save the kitten. He climbed out of his window, scampering from branch to branch, until he sat squarely in the center *Y* of the tree, inches from the frightened kitten. But when he reached out to take hold of her, the kitten clawed at the trunk, scraping bits of bark as she clung with all her might to the tree. Cole spoke calmly to her, trying to coax her to trust him, but she puffed out her fur and arched her back in response. After some time, he gave up and settled himself next to the kitten, refusing to leave her alone as the thunderstorm approached and unleashed its fury on the world around them. They remained relatively dry under the thick canopy of leaves and though Cole had meant to go inside once the worst was over, he woke to find dawn tinting the morning sky.

The kitten lay asleep, curled in a contented ball of damp fur on his chest.

From that day on, Duchess had been his constant companion. She was fearless and smart and curious to a fault, getting herself in one fix after another. Until the night, two years later, when she became curious about a coyote that had been prowling around the plantation. Cole had found her on the lower roof of the chicken house, where she often went to lounge in the sun. From the looks of her, she had fought hard, probably never considering that the coyote would have been too much for her. Cole had been heartbroken that he couldn't protect Duchess, but he had long ago accepted her wild spirit, knowing she might not be with him long . . .

Bailey reminded him so much of that scared but courageous little kitten as she tried to no avail to pull the cabin door open. She spun to face him, her red-gold hair falling across her face and neck. Damn, if Duchess hadn't had the same red-gold coloring. Bailey brushed the waves out of her eyes, then planted her hands on her hips, looking at him as if he was supposed to say something.

"If you think to distract me from my purpose by staring at me as if you have no sense, you are wasting your time," she complained, resuming her pacing. "I already know you have no sense. But surely there is someone onboard this vessel who does not agree with their captain's propensity to kidnap women."

Glaring down at him with spit and fire in her blue-green eyes, she brushed past his chair and stalked back toward the door. As her slender fingers closed around the cool brass, he seized her wrist and turned her to face him, pressing her back against the door.

He stood so close he could feel the warmth from her body,

smelled the briny ocean and herbed ointment that clung to her skin. He bent his head close to her face and watched with some satisfaction as she swallowed hard, the fire in her eyes dulled to apprehension.

"You won't find anyone on the *Barracuda* who will aid you. Not a single one of my men would stand against me for anything you might offer in return for their assistance."

Bailey gasped at the rude comment, but he laughed and allowed his gaze to skim down her body. He felt her flinch and knew she would have slapped him if her wrists weren't still pinned to the door next to her shoulders.

"You are the rudest man I have ever had the misfortune to come across."

"I only speak the truth. If that insults you, I'm afraid that is your problem."

"You don't know the first truth about me. My morals are not those of a barmaid, as you seem to believe, and I did not ask to be on your ship or in your presence in any way." She struggled, trying to free her wrists from his unyielding hold. His eyes were the shade of a thunderhead, but the fullness of his ebony lashes seemed to soften the look of a storm brewing deep within them. There was hostility there, yes, but something more. No man had ever looked at her so completely, so intimately, as if he could see her very soul. The intensity of his attention brought all of her senses to awareness.

"You are not this cruel," she whispered.

Her wrists were free in a blink. She had caught him off guard and the storm in his eyes dissipated. He moved away to study a chart on his desk.

Resigned for the moment, she picked up the quilt and wrapped it around her, then went to curl up in the window seat.

"Captain, you must understand why I need to go back. I have to find out why this happened."

He pulled free of his pensive staring and turned to lean

back against the edge of the desk, crossing his arms over his chest. She tried to ignore the pure masculine dominance of his stance and the fact that his direct regard made it hard to catch her breath.

"Bailey, I am not trying to be a jackanape. And call me Cole, would you? You make my title sound like a curse," he grumbled. "It really is as simple as this: it is too dangerous. The Dragon won't forget about you until you're dead. Cad though I am, I am not depraved enough to return you to such a grim fate."

"That makes no sense. The Dragon took everything we had. Why would he want to kill me?"

His expression was deadly serious, she felt a sick dread fill her.

"He takes great care to assure there are never any witnesses left behind who could identify him. No one has ever survived one of his attacks—until now. Until you."

She shook her head, wishing she did not believe his words. "But . . . But I can't identify him. He wore a mask. I didn't see his face."

"He won't take that risk. The Dragon is more than a pirate. He moves among the most respected and wealthy families in the Colonies. He attends our balls and card games and strolls through our parks as if he was one of us. No one knows who he is—he could be my neighbor, or a Boston shipbuilder or even one of our highest political figures."

"That can't be possible! How, in Heaven's name could he get away with that?"

"He won't for much longer. I am going to find him."

"You look as if you wish him dead as much as I do."

"Wishing him dead does nothing. I will see him dead."

"Do you know who he is?"

"I am getting close."

"But why? Why my family? We were not wealthy, my father was a fisherman."

58 *Kayla Gray*

"Before yesterday, I wouldn't have been able to answer that question."

"And now you can? What do you have to do with what happened?" she asked, afraid of the answer he might give.

"I never knew your father personally. I followed the Dragon to Beaufort—and damn near caught the bastard," he growled. "After the fire, there was a meeting at the Morehead Tavern. Your father's friends were speaking freely. They had formed a group to stop the pirate raids along the coast. Your father was scheduled to travel to Virginia—"

"Yes, I know about that. He was supposed to leave in three days—no, that would be two days now, wouldn't it?" She concentrated to sort through the confusion of the last few days. "He said he was going to purchase some special sails for his boat."

"In reality, he was to meet with Governor Spottswood."

"Governor Spottswood? What business did he have with the governor of Virginia?"

"Some people believe that your Governor Eden is turning a blind eye to the pirate attacks. He's done little to try to stop them, and rumor has it that he is receiving payment in exchange for his lackluster attempts. Your father and the other men thought they'd have a better chance if they could enlist the aid of Governor Spottswood. The Dragon discovered the plot . . . And your father was killed for it. You and your brother were just in the way."

"Sweet Mary, why didn't he tell me?" So many thoughts swirled in her mind. The many nights of late when her father had claimed he was playing cards. The hushed conversations she had witnessed at the docks. Those men were his friends. She had grown up with their children.

Panic seized her. "What about the others? How could you leave when the other men's families are in danger? We must go back and warn them. Please!"

"They know. They were all at the tavern. They are prepared."

His voice was soft and low, breaking gently through the turmoil in her mind.

"The fire must have been a mistake—it called too much attention to the attack. I think the Dragon planned to slip quietly from home to home until all of the seven men and their families were killed. But the fire was seen in town and by the time we reached your home, the pirates had fled. Yours was the first that they hit, so they missed the opportunity to get to the others."

"But he will return, won't he?"

"Yes. But there's no way to know when. Despite his pomposity, he's not careless, and he won't risk being captured."

"That means the men will have time to prepare and the Dragon will no longer hold the advantage. They could catch him and put an end to this."

"No. I will be the one to end this."

It wasn't arrogance this time. This time it was simply the truth as he knew it. Bailey wondered if he was chasing his own death with such a promise. And if he cared.

"Why do you know so much about the Dragon? Who are you?"

"At the moment, I'm your only hope of staying alive," he replied bluntly.

Bailey's emotions were a whirlwind, the loss of her father and brother still a raw wound. The fact that Captain Leighton was holding the fragmented remains of her life made her terribly uneasy. He was a dauntless stranger with treacherous secrets. Secrets that somehow involved the pirate who had murdered her family—and who would hunt her as long as she remained alive. She couldn't help wondering what that meant to the captain. She was unwillingly indebted to him. If she remained with him, what was that debt going to cost her?

"I don't find much comfort in that claim, Captain. For all

I know, you are as much of a danger to me as the Dragon, and I don't plan to be with you long enough to find out."

The slightest grin curved along the sharp line of the captain's mouth, but a sharp knock at the door interrupted any reply he may have wished to make. He opened the door to a stout man, with white hair that flopped about his head. He entered the cabin carrying a silver tray laden with steaming food. A wiry young man followed on his heels with yet another tray.

It looked like a feast, and Bailey's stomach growled in appreciation. Food had been the last thing on her mind, but the wondrous smells of the stew and bread made her realize she was famished.

"Hmmm. Does that mean you plan to swim back to shore, Bailey? Perhaps you'd like to have something to eat before you go. You'll need a lot of strength to swim that far."

"*Mon Dieu,* what is this? Swim to shore? *Capitaine,* you cannot let her do this. You must tell her no. The poor girl, she must have injured her brain, she doesn't know what she's saying."

The white-haired man seemed frantic, his heavily accented words spilling out of him as he hastily put down the tray to plead with his captain. Bailey saw in him a fatherly protectiveness that drew her to him instantly.

"Sir, I assure you, it was not my idea or intention to swim to shore. I was trying to convince Captain Leighton of my desire to return to Beaufort, but he is not inclined to allow it. I must see to the burial of my father and brother," she said, shooting a meaningful glance the captain's way.

"*Non, mademoiselle,* you cannot go back there. It isn't safe. You mustn't ever go back there. The *capitaine,* he will take good care of—"

"That will be all, Marcel," the captain interrupted. "I'll serve." He took the bottle of wine from Marcel, who rubbed his thick beard between his fingers nervously.

"*Oui, Capitaine.*" He turned to leave, pushing the curious young man out ahead of him, but before he closed the door, he shook a crooked finger at her, and ordered in a warm tone, "No swimming, *d'accord?*"

Bailey nodded and attempted to smile. It caused her pain from the split in her lip but felt good all the same. Just this morning, she had sworn to herself that she'd never have anything to smile about again. But this strange little Frenchman's kindness had made her do the impossible.

Chapter Six

Cole stared at Bailey for a long moment, drawn by the smile that graced the girl's bruised face. It was as if she had bestowed a precious gift on the old cook, who beamed and winked a faded blue eye at her before shutting the door, leaving them alone. She turned and the smile vanished as completely as a doused candle when her eyes met his. Cole ignored the odd tightness in his chest and turned to pour the wine.

The little baggage could ply her charms on his entire crew for all he cared. Those blind fools might even fall under her spell. But he had learned well that a woman's smile was usually held up by a web of lies.

The girl winced as she sank into the chair and sampled the fragrant burgundy wine. She seemed determined to avoid looking at him and for a time, the room was filled with a heavy silence. Cole regarded her over his glass as she blew on a spoonful of hot stew. What was he going to do with her?

She didn't want to be on the *Barracuda* any more than he wanted her there. Bailey Spencer wanted to go home. Desperately. And she was desperate with the raw pain of loss. Cole knew all too well the destruction a desperate woman could wreak.

He wanted no part of it. Or her. But for the moment, he appeared to be stuck with her.

As usual, Marcel's stew was delicious, filled with thick chunks of fish and potatoes. Cole swallowed a tender bite of fish, then sliced the hot bread and passed a piece to Bailey. She thanked him, but with none of the warmth she had shown Marcel.

Clearly, she hadn't completely given up her idea of going home, and he also knew she was angry that he refused to comply. She wasn't trying to use her womanly charm or seduction to get her way, but he reasoned she was still too weak to put out the effort. He understood her anger and knew he would feel the same way, if he was in her place. But he would have enough sense to realize the danger in such foolish sentimentality. Why couldn't she?

She sat across from him, unaware that the mauve tips of her breasts showed through the linen of his shirt and equally unaware of his enjoyment of the provocative sight. Her fingers tore the warm bread as she glared at him with brilliant light sparkling in her blue-green eyes.

She had all the confidence of the most well-born ladies he had ever known, yet without the haughtiness. There was an uninhibited, wild look about her, as if she wasn't posed for effect. As if she didn't care what he thought of her hair or her dress or her family name. A pink flush spread across her cheeks at his persistent appraisal and he realized he was making her nervous.

He sipped his wine and noticed with some unease of his own how the thin linen caressed her nipples with her graceful movements. If it wasn't so ridiculous, Cole would have thought he was the slightest bit jealous of the damn garment. But that *was* ridiculous, of course. He needed to distract her from her anger and himself from her tempting curves.

"Do you have any family anywhere besides Beaufort?"

She sighed, pausing as she chewed a piece of bread. "No. There is no one else. My parents came here from England to own and work their own land. My mother caught the fever and died when I was twelve. Adam does not even remember her."

For a brief heartbeat, Cole wondered if her brother had not been lucky. He believed it was far harder to suffer the pain of betrayal than of loss.

"I mean . . . did not," she corrected herself softly. "Could I have some more wine, please?"

Silently, he filled her glass halfway. He felt uneasy at the obvious pain his question brought to her, but found himself at a loss of what to do about it.

She swallowed a bite of bread, then sighed. "I have to face the truth. I am on my own now."

"Some people prefer to live that way."

"That is fine and good for you—a man. This world belongs to men. I am a woman. Alone in that world, with no means of supporting myself. Now, you tell me how I should begin anew." Her fine brow arched up, a sad smile curving the bruised side of her mouth.

She was right, of course. He had spoken without a thought for her precarious circumstances. Being a man—and coming from a family with a considerable fortune—had given him many opportunities and privileges that most people would never know. Despite the fact that his family had been torn to hell, Cole could still go on living as well as he always had. He and his brother had inherited enough land and money to be secure for numerous lifetimes.

"You must have a skill. You are well spoken for a commoner."

She gave him a sour look and thanked him sarcastically. "My mother used to work as a seamstress for the wealthy ladies in town. After she died, Lady Hawthorne took pity on me, I suppose. She gave me a position helping with her children. Before long we became close friends and I was invited to attend many of her wonderful parties. I suppose I learned things simply being around her."

Cole had trouble picturing such a selfless relationship. He

leaned back and crossed his arms. "Well, then, looks like you'll be just fine. There are always families in need of a governess."

She nodded, then pushed the china plate back and rested her elbows on the table. "What is that?" she asked, changing the subject.

Cole got a glimpse of rounded breast before the lovely curves became obscured by her new position. She was pointing a slim finger, drawing Cole's attention to the leather pouch he had placed on the table when dinner had been brought. He had forgotten about it.

"This was found on you when you were brought aboard. I was hoping you could tell me about it."

She looked at him in question as he reached out and tipped the pouch to drop its contents onto the table. A ring? She picked it up, looking at the ring from every angle, confusion drawing her brows close together.

"I have never seen this before." Her brows knit in confusion. "You say I was wearing this?"

"Aye, you were."

He could see her struggling to remember as she leaned in closer to the candle's light, staring at the ring. Cole watched closely as her expressions evolved from wondering to understanding. To revulsion.

As if it had burned her, she dropped the ring and sat back in the chair. Cole picked it up and rolled it carelessly in his palm, examining the ornate *L* engraved into the heavy gold.

"I remember now. It's not mine," she concluded firmly.

"I know," he replied, drawing a questioning look from her. "This ring was my mother's. My father had it made for her as a wedding gift," he said with contempt.

"Your mother's!" she said, stunned.

"How is it that you came to be wearing it?" he pushed, impatient for her answer. No, he knew what she would say. But he was hoping to hear something other than the distasteful truth.

Her eyes brightened with emotion. She swallowed hard and

nodded. "That pirate. It was on a chain around his neck. I was trying to get away—I broke the chain when I hit him. He laughed and put the ring on my finger," she said, her voice threatening to break. The sickening memory threatened what little composure she held on to. "He said it made me his— that it bound me to him. Until he was through with me. He said he would take it back after he killed me," she finished, crossing her arms protectively in front of her.

Cole nodded curtly and snorted in disgust.

"How did the pirate get your mother's ring?" She looked at him almost beseechingly. It seemed she wanted answers almost as much as he did. She continued to try to put the pieces together. Cole wanted her to drop it, but he had started her down this road. Every sailor aboard knew bits and pieces about Cole's past, she was bound to hear something sooner or later.

"Did he steal it from her?" she gasped.

Her perception was beginning to get annoying.

"Oh, Lord, did he kill your family, too?"

He hesitated, deciding how much he wished her to know.

"Don't ask me any more questions," he ordered tersely.

"Of course not. I'm sorry, Cole."

He flinched at the sound of his name on her lips. It was the first time she had spoken it and his body reacted as if she had physically touched him. Intimately.

He was overly tired and off his guard. And apparently it had been too long since he'd had a woman. He would have to take care of that as soon as they reached their destination. Then he would be his old self and the mere sound of Bailey's voice would not affect him like a lover's caress.

"Here," he said sharply, rolling the ring across the table to her. "Take it."

She only shook her head, eyeing him as if he'd lost his wits.

"I have no use for it," he said with fierce conviction.

She looked unsure. "You might wish to change your mind."

He shook his head. After a minute, she hesitantly picked up

the ring. Another minute went by as she stared down at it, not moving. Not speaking. Finally, she slowly placed it on her middle finger and looked up to meet his gaze.

She appeared haunted. He could understand that. The ring held bad memories for him, too.

"This is very generous of you, Captain. This amount of gold could help me start anew. I imagine there wasn't much left after the fire."

He could tell she still didn't trust the gesture though she seemed to have come to the same conclusion he had. The ring would bring her enough money to survive until she found a position somewhere.

"I can tell you for certain, there is nothing left."

"No. I suppose there wouldn't be, would there?" she asked, staring down at her finger. "We didn't have any items of monetary value, anyway."

Cole fixed his gaze out the porthole, crushing a rising inclination to comfort her. Yes, she had been hurt. *He* had been hurt. Hell, the whole world was full of hurt. It was simply her time to learn that lesson and harden her heart.

That was the key to survival.

"Get some sleep," he grunted as he made his way to the foot of his bunk.

Letting her swim to shore was sounding more pleasing every minute. If they weren't so far out to sea by now, he might seriously consider it. He needed to be away from her to clear the aggravation from his head. He grabbed a clean shirt and breeches from his trunk, closed the lid and left the cabin to find a place to sleep.

Thin light filtered into the cabin as morning broke with more rain-filled clouds. Bailey stood in front of the mirror over the washstand and gingerly fingered her bruised eye. The sizeable, odd-shaped wedge had remained intact when she'd smashed it to the floor yesterday. Someone had rehung it and it tilted at a strange angle, a deadly sharp edge pointing toward the floor. She shuddered, remembering how close she had come to killing Cole. That he had not sought retribution for her attack on him surprised her. He did not seem to be a forgiving man.

She squinted and touched the deep blackish purple mark and noticed that the swelling was all but gone. She was amazed at how fast her wounds were healing and suspected that Marcel was a bit of a sorcerer. The Frenchman had come to the cabin just after dawn with more pungent ointment and a strong, fragrant tea. He changed the cloth strip around her neck and left her with the small jar and instructions on how to apply the medicine to her wounds.

A few minutes later he returned with breakfast and more of the hot tea. It tasted pleasant, and smelled like flowers. She pivoted to look out the window, sipping the tea and watching raindrops streak in random paths down the glass. At her request, Marcel had brought her a strip of leather that she had strung the ring on and tied it about her neck. She toyed with the gold band as she took another sip of tea, her thoughts turning back to Cole.

She remembered his face, the way his expression turned dark, almost savage, when he talked about the ring and his mother. He had attempted to hold himself in tight control, pretending the ring meant nothing to him even when she put it on her finger. But she had seen the pulse in his clenched jaw, the glint of violent hatred that burned in his smoke-gray eyes. It was a similar emotion to the one she had seen in the Dragon's cold eyes as he whispered his promise of death so close to her face. The two men were alike in that way—each a dangerous and unpredictable weapon. If Cole had his way, they were going to meet soon. And one of them was sure to die.

The ring was her security. The sole thing she possessed to bargain her way home, whether she bargained with Cole or with someone else. It didn't matter. As long as it got her away from both of them.

"I brought you some clothes."

She was so lost in her thoughts, she didn't hear Cole enter and close the door. She turned around, pulling the wide neck of his shirt closed in her fist.

"You startled me."

"This was the best I could do, under the circumstances. Tom Mills is a young man, not much bigger than you are. You'll need the rope to hold up the breeches," he said, gesturing to the short length of hemp on top of the pile.

"Oh, I couldn't ask him—"

"You didn't."

"And neither did you, I suspect." The poor sailor was commanded to give up his clothes, she was sure of it.

"I assumed you would prefer to don something more appropriate than one of my shirts. Besides, I don't need a mutiny on my hands."

"Thank you," she whispered, reaching out to accept the mussed wad of clothing. She wondered if she would ever get used to his bluntness.

He nodded. He was soaking wet, rain dripping from his coat, his hair, his nose.

"The sky is clear to the south, we should be out of the rain before long. It will be unbearable down here by noon, so you will find it necessary to come up on deck for the breeze."

Bailey nodded, watching the play of muscles in his back where the wet shirt clung as he shed his coat and hung it by the door. Deciding to ignore him, she set her teacup on the table to better inspect the clothes from Tom Mills. A rough, unbleached linen shirt, fawn-colored canvas breeches and a plain red kerchief. Simple but clean, and not the slightest trace of the captain's spicy scent on them. She wished he would leave so she could scrub her skin and put on the fresh-smelling items.

"You should consider going north once we sail back to the Colonies. Perhaps I could arrange to get you to Boston," Cole said, rubbing his hand across the dark stubble on his chin.

She took the quilt with her and sat cross-legged on the embroidered window seat, watching him as he went to answer a light knock at the door. After exchanging a few words with his seaman, he closed the door and dropped a pair of thick towels on the table.

"I will be going back to Beaufort," she pronounced.

He finished scrubbing his thick hair with one of the towels, then tossed it on the floor and ran his fingers back through the damp strands. He sighed heavily and scowled at her while peeling off his wet shirt.

"There's something I haven't told you," she continued. Bailey tried to keep her thoughts directed on what she was saying, but that was proving difficult. She became unwittingly preoccupied by the sight of the man's wide chest and how his muscles came to life as he dried his smooth chest with the towel.

When he was finished, he sat down and removed his boots and hose and dropped them in a pile on the floor. "Are you going to tell me, or are you going to gape at me all day?"

His arrogant tone was in clear evidence, accompanied by the single eyebrow that lifted slightly to mock her. Embarrassed, she leaned forward and retrieved her cup off the table. She took a calming breath and sipped the last of the cooled tea. "I do have something in Beaufort to return to. Well . . . some*one.*"

She put down the china cup and glanced up to find him watching her with interest. "His name is James. James Fulton. He is . . . He was supposed to be . . ." Why couldn't she just say the word? "We were supposed to become engaged."

"Were? What happened?"

His cynical tone irritated her. "Nothing happened. It just hasn't happened yet. I mean, he hasn't asked me to marry him . . . yet."

"But you know that he will. You are quite the confident one, hmm?"

"And you are insulting," she reprimanded him.

He shrugged his tanned shoulders, then propped his hands on his knees. The muscles bulged and curved along his arms, and to her dismay she found herself staring again.

"You don't understand." She lost the direction of her thought.

"I'm listening. With great interest," he added with a lop-sided grin.

"James and I have always been expected to marry. We grew up together—we've been neighbors and best of friends since we were children. He has always seen us being married some-day. Our families used to speak about our future together. It was just always assumed . . . that we would marry."

"So, that's why you are so anxious to return. Your true love awaits."

"Why did you say it like that?"

"Like what?"

"Like you don't believe in true love."

His eyes narrowed and darkened. "I don't."

"Well, I do," she said, meeting his challenging gaze. She would *not* give him the satisfaction of knowing she had never felt more than friendship for James.

He stood and began unfastening his breeches. "I'm sure James will be glad to hear it," he added with sarcasm.

Finished with the fastenings, he stripped off his wet pants, leaving him completely bared to Bailey's innocent eyes. He picked up the other towel and continued to dry himself, seem-ingly oblivious to her. She felt the heat of a blush as it crept into her cheeks, but she could not tear her eyes away from the magnificent sight of him. She had never seen a man like this—in all his glory—and despite her embarrassment, she was mesmerized.

For such a tall man, he moved with unusual grace, while at

the same time exuding power, even arrogance in the way he tossed his head and scrubbed the white cotton towel across his body. Her gaze shifted lower and the heat in her cheeks intensified as she wondered what mysteries that secret part of him held.

"You care to take a ride? I don't think James would approve."

Sardonic amusement was evident in his voice and he laughed outright at her startled gasp. She strangled out a refusal and leapt to her feet, turning her back to him, crossing her arms tightly in front of her body. She grumbled a few choice words under her breath and heard his deep laugh again, invoking her pride and courage to face him again.

She turned back, determined to not let him embarrass her anymore.

"I didn't think you were the kind of man to find humor in anything. I guess I was wrong, even if your sense of humor is not what is considered normal to most people."

He dropped the wet towel and placed his hands on his lean hips, cocking his head as he assessed her. The ship lifted on a swell, then dropped sharply, throwing her off balance, while the man before her remained firmly rooted where he stood. His bold assurance, along with the almost intimate way he watched her, made her feel uneasy in a way she never had before. Was it possible? Did she like this strange feeling? She caught herself on the window casing, and eased down on the cushioned seat, forcing herself to maintain eye contact with him.

"I don't care much about what people think of me," he said, his humor still intact. "However, I doubt that your true love would find humor in this situation. So, if you don't object, I'll just get dressed now."

When he winked at her, it was just too much. She felt a hot blush cover her face, and she spun to face the window. The rain was easing and the sun was attempting to break through the clouds. She heard him moving about the cabin, closing the trunk, shaking the wrinkles out of his clothes.

"You can turn around now. It's safe."

She didn't.

"Don't worry. James will never have to know your eyes have lost their innocence. As long as the rest of you is unspoiled, I promise you, he won't care. But Bailey, James or no James, you are not going back to Beaufort until I say you may."

"I don't need your protection, James is perfectly capable of taking care of me."

"I doubt that."

"You don't even know him!" she snapped.

"Don't worry, Bailey, James will wait for you. Or are you afraid he'll find another true love while you're away?"

She had had enough of his mocking her. "Don't you have duties to attend to, or does your cabin boy command this ship?"

He chuckled, pulling on his boots and standing to leave.

"Pity, I don't have a cabin boy. Guess I'll have to go command the *Barracuda* myself."

Once he was gone, Bailey let out a long breath, relieved to be alone. The man was impossible. Inappropriate. Crude. A rogue.

And disturbingly handsome.

Cole had barely reached the quarterdeck when his first mate approached him, carrying two steaming mugs filled with black coffee. He accepted the brew gratefully and glanced upward beyond the bow. Clouds were splitting apart to reveal blue sky dotted with random puffs of white.

"How does our reluctant passenger fare?" Cisco asked with a slight grin.

"She's fine," Cole answered tightly, raising a brass spyglass to his eye.

"She must be very frightened, eh? You didn't strangle her, or . . ."

"God's blood! Why are you so concerned about her? You know everything that takes place aboard this blasted ship, so you must know the wench tried to kill me," Cole railed. He punctuated the words with a stab of the scope in the general direction of his quarters.

"*Sí,*" Cisco nodded thoughtfully and stroked his wiry beard. "It is hard to believe that you have not bled out from that deathblow," he said, poking at Cole's shoulder. "She is obviously dangerous. We should put her in irons until we reach land. I'll have Dewey see to it right away, Captain," he said, his brown eyes twinkling.

"Blast you, old man! How am I supposed to maintain any dignity at all when you are always there to prick my pride?" Cole admonished half-heartedly.

"You could send me below and have the wench work her lethal magic on me," Cisco suggested with a lewd glint in his eye.

Cole snorted his disapproval. "You may call what she possesses magic, my friend. I see nothing extraordinary about her."

"Not even the fact that she survived the Dragon?"

"That is something."

"Did she see his face?"

"He wore the damn mask."

"One day he will make a mistake."

"That day may have just come, my friend."

Cisco shot him a wry look all too familiar to Cole. "Tell me the rest—I know there's more, I can see it fairly dancing in your eye."

"She has my mother's ring. It was on her finger when she was brought aboard. I was not even aware it was missing."

Cisco's dark eyes went wide. "You're certain it is your mother's?"

Cole unclenched his jaw and swallowed a mouthful of the

bitter coffee. "Positive. My father gave it to her before I was born. When I was a child she would often tell me the story of how he gave it to her. I never saw her without it on her finger."

Cisco let out a low whistle and shook his head. "How did the girl end up with it?"

Cole pivoted and tipped the pewter mug upside down over the railing. The last of the coffee and wet grounds disappeared into the frothy waves below. "A demented game the Dragon was playing with Bailey during the attack. He told her he would take it back after he killed her."

Cisco spat over the railing and cursed the pirate. "It's a true miracle the girl is alive. The Dragon will not take her escape lying down."

Cole shrugged, not sure if he should reveal more, even to his most trusted friend.

"You know that, though," Cisco added, accusation heavy in his voice.

Cole nodded, cutting his eyes sideways to glance at his first mate. He was certain his annoying friend could read his mind.

"¡Dios mío!"

Cole winced inwardly at Cisco's ardent disapproval.

"Tell me right now you are not thinking of using the girl in some way."

"I will do whatever it takes, old man. You damn well know that."

"Not even you could sacrifice an innocent girl."

"Don't think you know me so well, old man," Cole growled. His scowl would have intimidated any other man, but Cole knew Cisco would not back down. Cisco believed his purpose was to save Cole from himself.

"You intend to keep the girl until you decide," Cisco accused.

The sun burned with a bright intensity now, the azure canvas of sky broken only by gray and white gulls that glided and swooped about the sails of the ship. Their cries could be heard mingling with the steady flapping of the bleached canvas, but Cole was oblivious to them. He was trying his best to refrain from dropping his first mate to the deck with a blow to his substantial nose.

"What am I supposed to do with her? Toss her overboard? She wants to go back, for Christ's sake—she has no idea how foolish she is being."

"So you are going to keep her safe . . . how chivalrous of you." He chuckled.

"I don't have much choice. The Dragon will search until he finds her."

"Or until you offer her up to him?"

"If he's going to hunt her down anyway, then she's damn far better off with me. She doesn't stand a chance on her own."

"There is no one back in Beaufort?"

"She has no family left," he said, feeling a foreign stab of guilt for not mentioning James.

"But she wants to go back, Cole. She must have friends who will take care of her. They can keep her safer than you— none of them would consider using her as pirate bait."

"I haven't said anything about bait. That was your idea. And if you are so eager to protect Bailey, then I suggest you stop giving me suggestions."

Cisco grinned knowingly. "Well, then, how long do you suppose the girl will be in our company?"

"It's already been too damn long for my taste."

Cisco slapped a meaty hand against Cole's broad back and laughed heartily.

"Good God, man, you are going to knock me overboard. Can't you at least feign the proper amount of respect for your captain?" Cole complained to his incorrigible companion.

"You know damn well how much I respect you, Cole. As my captain and my reliable friend. We have seen each other through some foul times," he said, eliciting a nod of agreement from Cole. "But this is not so bad, if you ask me."

"I didn't," Cole grumbled.

"We haven't been this close to the Dragon's wake for two years. Revenge could be yours soon, now. And what the hell—if your beautiful bit of spitfire can play a part in getting you closer, then you should thank the fates for smiling down on your head."

"The fates are playing a cruel jest on me," Cole grumbled.

Cisco tossed the remains of his coffee over the railing and shook his head. "This girl—Bailey—she is not your mother, *mi amigo*."

"Do not speak of her," Cole warned.

"Why not? That is exactly what you are thinking about—that is all you think about. It consumes you."

"And you know why. I will regain the honor my mother took from our family."

"I know you will, Cole." Cisco heaved a sigh and leaned against the railing, crossing his thick, dark arms on the warm wood. "But not every woman has a web to spin."

"Name one who does not," Cole countered, raising the spyglass to his eye.

"My sweet, lusty Analee," Cisco answered, a bit of longing in the deep rumble of his voice.

"Humph. I'll wager she's the only one who does not." He copied Cisco's repose at the railing, elbow to elbow with his first mate, the only other person alive who knew the truth about his mother. Except for the Dragon.

"People change, Cole. Sometimes not for the better. Tragedies can turn people into something they otherwise would never be."

Cole cast a sidelong glance at the burly giant, whose expression held no apology or insinuation.

"I will stand by you, no matter what you choose to do. You can toss the thorny little rose overboard, you can deposit her in Charles Towne, or you can take her to New Providence and see if the little beauty can charm the serpent from his hole.

She is nothing to me, and even less to you. She should be grateful to you that she is alive."

Cole inclined his head in a slight nod. He squinted as he looked into the bright, endless sky, distracted by unwelcome thoughts of the girl in his cabin.

"You really think she is beautiful?" The curious thought slipped out before Cole could stop it. He wanted to bite off his tongue.

Cisco raised his unruly eyebrows as he moved away from the railing, gesturing to the bos'n, but he remained silent, to Cole's eternal relief. He was in no mood for Cisco's senseless opinion on the merits of love.

Cole cleared his throat sharply and turned toward his first mate, settling into his captain's role with an ease that came naturally with his love of sailing. "Now that the weather has cleared, trim the sails out—I want to reach Nassau with all haste."

"*Sí*, Captain. If the winds stay with us, we should reach port in two days."

"Good." He turned back and stared out over the rolling waves, mindless of the spray misting into his face. The past was bearing down on him, haunting him with increasing rancor and not just in the dark hours of night anymore. It seemed that the closer he got to the Dragon, the worse his memories became, until they very nearly seemed to breathe with a life of their own.

He fervently hoped the remembrances would diminish once he had regained his family's honor. No, not really the family honor, but his father's honor. His mother had proved in full measure that she had no honor. She proved how fickle a woman's heart is and how easily the fairer sex could be tempted to treachery.

Just then the wind caught a loose sail, which began to flap loudly, bringing Cole's attention around to the sailor who was scrambling up the mainmast. He was about to call out to the inexperienced pup, when the bos'n appeared beneath the young seaman and began to instruct him in securing the heavy canvas.

Cole sighed and rubbed his tired eyes. He couldn't remember when he'd gotten his last few hours of sleep. Having Bailey aboard had disrupted more than his schedule; she had disrupted his every waking thought. Since his mother's death, Cole had made it a point to limit his dealings with women, especially the eager young misses who chased plantation heirs like hounds on the trail of a red fox. Bailey was no barmaid, but she wasn't a pampered lady of society, either. She held herself proudly, was more educated than most women of her station, though she fought like no lady would dare. Her appearance was less than refined; with her face so smeared with dirt and bruises she could scarcely even pass for the fairer sex. How could the wispy little minx have survived the Dragon's attack when no one else was alive to make that claim?

There was something innocent yet intriguing about her and Cole found his curiosity uncharacteristically piqued. It shook him to his core.

Chapter Seven

Just after Cole had left his cabin, Marcel appeared with two sailors carrying a small copper tub. They made several trips, bringing warm water while Marcel crushed a mixture of herbs to ease her bruises while she soaked. When she thanked the cook for his thoughtfulness, he told her it had been the captain's idea. She suspected he was being kind. The captain had likely ordered her to bathe away the stench of sour marsh and stale smoke.

It didn't matter. She was grateful to feel clean for the first time in days. Now, she dabbed ointment on her throat, then wrapped a strip of linen over the cut and knotted it neatly behind her neck. The red kerchief wouldn't hide the bandage, but it would distract from it a little, so she tied it loosely over the white cloth. She rolled up her sleeves to her elbows and glanced at her reflection, smoothing her hands down the borrowed shirt. As strange as she looked in the sailor's breeches and shirt, it felt much better than being next to naked, as she had been before.

Shedding Cole's shirt had made her feel a little less vulnerable. She had found it difficult to sleep last night, as even her thoughts seemed to be under his control. It made no sense, she knew, but the garment seemed to hold a part of him and made her feel as if she had more of the man against her skin than just his clothing. Late into the night, she had dozed fitfully, anticipating his return, and with every creak of wood, she was startled awake, thinking he was there, standing above her. It felt so indecent, lying in his bed, breathing in the spicy, masculine scents enveloping her. She had finally drifted off to utterly shameful thoughts—imagining him lying next to her. Holding her.

Thank goodness she had come to her senses with the gray light of day. Captain Leighton was not the type of man that any woman in her right mind would want attention from. Her fanciful imaginings of the night before were just the result of being physically exhausted and emotionally raw from all she'd been through. She would see things more clearly once she was back in Beaufort. And since Cole wouldn't take her back, then she'd find someone who would. She reached up to touch the Dragon's ring that hung around her neck. It was the only valuable thing she had and she was counting on it to buy her passage home.

To James.

She thought of the sweet boy she knew wanted to marry her, but it did nothing to shake the strange hold the captain seemed to have over her. This morning he had had the same effect on her; she barely felt like herself when Cole was near. When he had so boldly stripped naked in front of her, standing as proud and hard as a Greek statue, her pulse had quickened, rushing hot blood throughout her body. Even her skin felt on fire. James had never invoked such a pure physical response from her, even though she cared about him deeply. She refused to believe that her reaction to the captain was anything more than shock at his conduct and lack of decorum.

Bailey sighed and picked up a silver comb from the shelf above the washstand and peered outside just as the sun made its final break from the dissolving clouds. She pulled the smooth teeth through her hair and then tied the damp waves at the nape of her neck with a narrow strip of brown leather. She straightened the cabin, made the bunk and restlessly circled the room. All too soon, the cabin became unbearably stuffy. The thought of going topside and facing all the men who had seen her humiliating display yesterday made her rethink the idea several times. But she longed to feel the sun on her face and breathe in fresh, salty air, so she swallowed what pride she had left and forced her shaky legs to move.

Reaching up for the last rung of the ladder leading up to the open deck, Bailey could feel the inviting sunshine warm her cheeks. She guessed it must be around noon, by the position of the bright yellow globe hanging overhead in the cloudless sapphire sky.

She heard Cole's voice booming over sounds of the rigging and sails, and her courage nearly failed her. *I will just make certain to stay on the opposite side of the ship,* she thought, trying to reassure herself.

"Can I help, miss?"

Bailey squinted, trying to make out the features of the sailor who was reaching down to offer assistance, but her eyes had yet to adjust to the daylight. She hesitated only briefly before extending her free hand to the young seaman. He lifted her up effortlessly and tipped his worn cap as he introduced himself.

"I'm Daniel Lewis, miss. At yer service. But everyone calls me Lew. You can too, if ya want."

Bailey exhaled deeply, unaware until now that she'd been holding in her breath, but a quick, nervous glance around told her the dark captain was nowhere in sight. She felt relieved, even while the raw edges of something akin to disappointment seemed to fold over her. Shaking those feelings aside, she turned her full attention to the young man before her, determined to forget about Cole Leighton.

"Thank you, Lew. I'm afraid I couldn't bear the heat down there a moment longer. I just need a few breaths of fresh air."

"Course not, miss. You shouldn't be holed up down there now, especially when there's such a good breeze on deck. An' the farther south we sail, the hotter it's gonna get. Most of us'll be sleepin' on deck from here out." He led her past some coiled ropes and around the rigging of the mainmast to an open space at the rail.

Bailey smiled in relief at how comfortable the young seaman made her feel. He didn't show the least inclination to discuss how she came aboard. Their conversation was easy and relaxed. He reminded her a little of how she imagined Adam would have been like at his age. She inhaled deeply to quiet the sadness that filled her when she thought of everything her little brother would never experience. As they talked, Bailey started to wonder if she could gain an ally in Daniel Lewis. Perhaps she could convince him to help her, once she figured out what to do.

"Is it true we are going to New Providence? I've never been away from Beaufort," she said.

"True as the sky is blue—it's in the Bahamas. It's like no place in the Colonies, or England or anywhere. You ain't never tasted fruit so good and the birds are just about every color you can think of."

"It sounds like a heavenly place. Maybe you could show me some of the island. When will we arrive?" she asked, affecting her most charming smile.

"Ah, well . . . We should be there in another day or two, but you ain't gonna want to go ashore. Oh, no," he added, his long tawny hair following as he shook his head back and forth.

"Of course I want to go ashore."

"Oh, no, miss. New Providence is taken by pirates. They

be a wild bunch, the whole lot. But don't you worry. We won't let nothin' happen to you, I swear on it myself. So, you can see why you'll be much safer onboard."

"But I'm afraid it's impossible for me to stay on the *Barracuda,* Lew. I'm not a passenger—you see, I'm here quite by accident, and Captain Leighton isn't prepared to sail back to Beaufort anytime soon. So, you see, I will need to make other arrangements once we reach the island."

Lew looked down at his bare feet and scratched his nose, screwing his face into an expression that showed serious doubt. "Ah, we all heard what happened. Marcel says the Dragon killed your family and you thought our ship was his an' that's why you were fighting with the captain on deck—oh, balls! We're not supposed to say nothin' about that. I'm sorry, miss. I swear I didn't see it happen, I was below decks yesterday morning."

Bailey swallowed her embarrassment before it could become a stain on her cheeks for Lew to see. She had prepared herself for the gossip that she figured by now had spread to everyone aboard. There was no going back to undo any of it, so she would pretend she didn't feel completely mortified about her nearly naked tussle with the captain, and with luck, the gossip would die down sooner than later.

"All I want is to get back to Beaufort, where I'll be safe, but I understand the *Barracuda* will not be going that way soon."

"No, I don't guess we'll be goin' back to the Colonies for a good while."

"That is exactly why I need to disembark in New Providence. Are you certain the only inhabitants are pirates?"

He shrugged. "It won't be no easy thing to find a respectable ship to take you home." He gave a worried shake of his tawny head. "Unless . . ."

"Unless what?"

"Unless one of them pirate hunters are in port. Governor

Spottsswood has been raisin' a ruckus about cleanin' out the Bahamas. He's got a few ships sent over from England to help. Maybe one o' them'll be in port. But I don't know, miss, there's an awful lotta them thieves, an' they ain't afraid of nothin'—not even the gibbet. Ain't natural, if you ask me."

She began to stroll, her hand trailing along the polished wood railing. She barely noticed as Lew fell into step beside her.

"That many?" she whispered as a cold fear threatened to sweep her courage aside. "Well, I'll just have to wait and see—and hope that one of the governor's ships will indeed be nearby." She glanced at Lew and tried to smile, feeling her courage slip. Could she go unnoticed among so many pirates? Would there be women there? Would they help her? Could she stow away on another ship? What if she ended up worse off than she was now? Sweet Mary, it seemed almost preferable to do as Lew said—stay safely aboard the *Barracuda* and out of sight until they were away from the pirate haven.

No, no. She had to find a way to get away from Captain Leighton. If he wanted to chase after the Dragon, then he could do it without dragging her along. And he could die without her bearing witness to it. She was on her own now—completely alone. She had only herself to rely on and so that's what she would do. She would find a way home or she would die trying. She stopped walking and tugged once on the frayed, cutoff sleeve of Lew's shirt. He paused and turned to her in question.

"I know what we can do."

"Aye, miss?"

She smiled sweetly, hoping it would aid her in getting her way, though she hated herself for stooping to the manipulative gesture. He grinned back at her, dimples poking tiny half-moons in his cheeks and revealing a black space where a tooth was missing.

"If you were to teach me to protect myself, then you wouldn't have to worry about my safety once we part."

His smile disappeared. "Oh, I don't know . . . I mean, if there's no ship to take you home then the Captain sure ain't gonna leave you there. You'll have to come with us. Why don't we just wait until—"

"Oh, Lew, you would be doing me such a good deed, don't you see? Even if there's no ship and I stay with the *Barracuda* for a bit longer, it would be good for me to know how to defend myself against louts of all sorts, don't you agree?"

"I suppose that makes sense," he said with a lingering edge of uncertainty.

"Oh, wonderful! When shall we start?" she asked, pinning him down with her most persuasive stare, the one her father used to lovingly chide her for using on him.

"Uh, well, how about tomorrow? At three bells. I'll come up here and look for you—how's that?"

"I'll be here. Thank you, Lew."

Lew nodded with a grin that seemed a bit shy, but his shoulders had lifted, and his gait displayed a masculine pride as he disappeared behind the mass of white canvas sails that arched with the force of a brisk wind. A wind that carried Bailey swiftly toward an island of pirates. She turned her face up to the sun, feeling the warmth of it melt the edge off her fears. Once she learned to protect herself, she would feel safe enough to venture about the pirate island, to find a buyer for the ring that hung like an anchor about her neck. She detested the black and gold band because of the memories attached to it, but it was the only thing she had to bargain with, so she would protect it as if it was the greatest of treasures.

She felt for the ring through the worn linen shirt, where it rested against her skin, safe from curious admirers. But she could not shake the feeling that someone was watching her, and when she turned from the railing, she found the cause of her suspicion. He stood alone on the quarterdeck, his broad chest bared to the sun, his black hair gleaming as shorter pieces whipped about his face. His eyes stayed on her, even as she glanced away and back, the butterfly wings starting their dance in her stomach.

Why did he affect her so? He was just a man, and though she couldn't deny he was wonderful to look at, he was decidedly not wonderful in any way that truly mattered. With that thought to bolster her, she lifted her chin and took herself to the opposite end of the ship.

Chapter Eight

The next day at the appointed time, Bailey strolled about the foredeck, the warm sunshine acting as a balm for the stiff muscles that still ached from the Dragon's beating. Somewhat earlier, she had gone below for a light meal and some more of Marcel's healing herb tea. Afterward, he had changed the bandage around her neck and marveled at how quickly the wound was healing.

Her senses stirred, and she looked to the helm, expecting to see Cole watching her from behind the large spoked wheel. To her surprise, it was not the captain who manned the helm but the bearded man called Cisco. Apparently her senses were as unnerved as the rest of her—it seemed she couldn't rely on them to warn her of Cole's presence after all. She reached the bow and gripped the railing, chiding herself for letting the captain occupy her mind so. She hoped she would have to endure him only a few more days, and silently vowed to keep away from him. If she didn't have to see him, perhaps she could purge the vision of his face from her mind. As if to seal that vow, she closed her eyes, letting the tangy salt spray mist into her face. Her troubled thoughts returned to the night of the attack. The black-masked image of the Dragon came to her, looming close, rimmed by a firelit sky. The frightening memory held her captive, the pirate's features blurred, save for the eery amber glow of his devil's eyes.

She was startled to feel a pair of arms come around her and suddenly she was being lifted and swung around, away from the railing. A scream tore from her throat, her heart leaping wildy in her chest as she struggled with all her might. Just as quickly as she was grabbed, Lew set her down gently, sputtering apologies while making certain she wasn't hurt.

"Balls! I'm sorry—I'm sorry! I just wanted to show you how a blackguard can sneak right up on you, that's all. Forgive me, miss."

Daniel Lewis fidgeted before her, his face a mask of contrition at the distress he had caused her. "I guess that wasn't a very good lesson to start with."

Bailey sucked in a deep breath and though she knew she was safe, the combination of the Dragon's image and being surprised in such a manner had her limbs shaking.

"It's all right, Lew. I'm perfectly fine," she said, her hand pressed flat against her pounding heart. "That was quite a lesson, and one I won't soon forget."

"Don't worry none. We'll start with somethin' eas—"

Bailey stumbled back as a seemingly unseen force lifted Lew and tossed him into the air away from her. He landed hard and with colorful protest, sliding a good distance before coming to rest unharmed on his backside.

Bailey spun on his assailant. "Are you mad? Have you taken leave of your senses? Answer me! What kind of man bullies the men under his charge in such a manner?" She punctuated her anger by smacking her palm against the offender's chest.

"The kind of man who would save an ungrateful wench from a sailor's unwanted attentions—or so I thought," Cole replied in a cool voice.

"Lew has done nothing more than what I asked him to do." She ignored the sardonic lift of a single brow and the crooked smirk that lit his face with mischief. "Captain Leighton, I assure you I am in no danger with Lew, so you need not trouble yourself further on my account."

"Have no fear, lady. I assure you, I will not make the same mistake of coming to your aid again. Best be careful not to fall overboard—the sharks in these waters are ravenous for soft-skinned females with sharp tongues . . . And he won't be of much help. Your suitor sinks in the water like a stone," he finished, gesturing to Lew, who remained silent a short distance away.

"Oh . . . you . . ." She backed away from him, coming up against the railing. "I cannot measure the extent of your incivility. Did your mother neglect to teach you how to speak pleasantly to people?"

"Don't speak of my mother to me," he growled, jabbing a finger in the air at her. "Ever! Do you understand?"

"Yes," she replied quickly, noting the grave tone of his voice—and something else. Was that pain she saw clouding his eyes to a dull gray?

"Come here, Lew."

Lew jumped up and approached his captain, showing not the least sign of trepidation, and stood directly in front of him.

"My actions were rash and apparently unnecessary. I apologize for being so rough on you. Are you hurt, boy?"

"No, sir, not a bit. I sure didn't mean to cause no trouble, Captain. I agreed to teach the lady how to defend herself, an' I was just showing her how a body can creep up on her."

"Defend herself?" His dark brows rose and he glanced with suspicion at Bailey, who was fervently wishing that Lew would stop talking. Lew wasn't so much a threat, but she felt certain that the overbearing captain would try to stop her if he knew her intentions. "Against who?"

"Well, sir, not against anyone in particular, I guess. But, you know, when we—"

"When we part, Captain, I will be alone in the world, as

you are aware. Lew thought it would be a good idea for me to learn how to handle any overeager passengers I may encounter on my voyage home. It was very chivalrous of him to offer his assistance. You should be proud of the fact that there is at least one gentleman on this ship."

Cole narrowed his eyes at her and she wasn't sure if it was because he didn't believe the weak story, or if he recognized the veiled insult she knew she should have resisted. He certainly knew how to draw out the devil in her, she mused.

By now several curious sailors had gathered about and Bailey was beginning to feel like a bird under a cat's paw.

"It looks like Captain Leighton doesn't approve, Lew, so I think we will have to leave off our lessons."

"No, no. By all means, go on ahead, Lew. I'll leave you to your—lessons. Just make certain you conduct yourself in a proper manner with our guest. And one provision: no weapons. Also, don't turn your back on her for too long." The last he said for her ears alone, as he leaned close to her and winked, a roguish grin turning the corners of his mouth and raising goose bumps on her skin.

"Your little sparrow looks serious about learning to battle her enemies. I wonder if she counts you among them, eh?"

"Can't you just say 'good afternoon' for once and keep your lackluster wit for the men on your watch?" Cole retorted. He accepted a dented pewter mug of steaming coffee from Cisco, then turned his eye to the small group of sailors near the bow. In the center of the cluster stood Bailey, mirroring Lew's movements, her small fists punching the air as she bobbed lightly from one bare foot to the other. Sunshine bathed her face, setting her wavy, shoulder-length hair alight with gold fire. She didn't seem to be distracted by those stray pieces that kept falling across her eyes, making her toss her head like a carefree child. She moved with grace, her ankles peeking out from the frayed breeches as she bounced on her toes. She reminded him of the wildly beautiful native girls he had once seen dancing in a wedding celebration in Jamaica, flowers encircling their heads and draped over their bare breasts. He took a large gulp of the bitter coffee, attempting to drown the unbidden image of Bailey dancing, adorned with nothing but a necklace of flowers.

"Christ!" Cole choked on the burning liquid. "Damn woman. Does she think the crew has nothing better to do than entertain her all day?"

"Seems there's not much to do at the moment, Captain. Wind's at our back, sails are trimmed, deck's shiny as a new coin . . . But I suppose I could break it up, if you—"

"No, don't bother. At least it will keep her out of my way," Cole muttered, fixing his eyes on the group once again.

Lew held up his hands, then made an unpracticed bow to Bailey as another sailor stepped forward. He stood close to her, demonstrating how a well-placed elbow in the ribs or heel to the shin could bring an opponent to his knees. He appeared to be encouraging her to try the moves on him, but she shook her head and started to move away. Cole crossed his arms and sighed as sounds of encouragement rose from his crew and the intended attacker held his arms up in invitation. Cole glanced sideways at Cisco, who seemed intent on enjoying the spectacle.

Bailey approached the sailor and turned her back to him, allowing him to advance on her. He took hold of her waist, pulling her against him with gentle force. The moment he placed his right arm around her neck, she reacted, elbowing him hard in the middle and sending her foot squarely into his shin. His yelp of surprise and pain caused raucous laughter and whistling to erupt in Bailey's favor, as she bent to apologize to her attacker. The sailor straightened, laughing as hard as the others and clapped his hands in approval. The others joined in, and Cole muttered an oath as he checked the compass for the tenth time.

Cisco laughed and slapped Cole on the shoulder. "The sparrow possesses the heart of a warrior. You seem displeased."

"I'm not pleased or displeased by her heart or anything else she possesses."

"You know, if you showed her a bit of your more charming traits, instead of scowling at her all the time, she might become a willing partner in your hunt for the Dragon. That is, unless your charms have rusted up like old iron."

"I do not need to charm the wench. If I decide she is of use to me, I will convince her in my own way."

"*Sí, sí.*" Cisco grinned. "Just like old iron. A warning then, *amigo*. If you don't wield your skills in practice, you may forget how to use them altogether. Women aren't to be treated roughly. Poetry and fine manners—that's what entices them. Ah, don't give me that look. Tell me you haven't thought just once about bedding the pretty little warrior and I'll know you lie."

Cole nodded. "You might have something there, old friend. A few compliments and a couple of glasses of brandy ought to bring her around. I'll have the innocent little bird snared and in my bed by dusk. After I seduce her, I'm sure she'll offer to sacrifice herself to the Dragon if that's what I wish. Perfect. Brilliant idea, old man, thanks," he finished, the sarcasm dripping like warm molasses.

Cisco rolled his eyes, a gesture that Cole knew only too well. He should actually go through with the unthinkable idea just to shock the wise-ass old man into silence for once. Did the crusty old Spaniard have to know him so well?

"You wield your wit as a weapon at times, Cole. Be careful it doesn't turn on you. We don't always seek the things we truly want—they find us on their own."

"Hell and fire, I believe you're turning into your grandmother right before my eyes."

Cisco laughed heartily. "*Sí!* Don't set aside my grandmother's words. She was a wise old witch who used her sight to help many people and she was never wrong, *amigo,*" he said, pulling absently on his thick beard. "You just wait and see, wait and see."

Cole grunted. "You didn't inherit her gift, you know. And even though you're beginning to act like an old woman—you aren't. And you don't have the sight. I suggest you reclaim your manhood while the crew still has a bit of respect left for you."

Cisco laughed and soon Cole heard his own deep laugh rumble up from some lost place inside. It was such a foreign thing for him to laugh. It felt surprisingly good, he thought as he followed Cisco's gaze back to Bailey and the zealous young men surrounding her like clouds dancing about the sun.

Young Miles Simpson stood bare-chested, not two feet from the girl, with what appeared to be a blunt piece of wood pointed at her middle. He jabbed the air, stopping short of her belly, then continued with several quick, stabbing motions to her chest and neck before lowering his makeshift weapon and giving her a nod.

Bailey lifted her arms to an offensive position and sunlight glinted hard off the blade of a dagger she held in her right hand.

"What the hell?" Cole ground out, trying hard to control his sudden anger. He watched as she flicked her wrist in awkward motions, attempting to recreate what Miles had just showed her, but all Cole could see was disaster in the making.

"Your little warrior doesn't seem to have a natural ability with sharp objects," Cisco observed.

"Who the hell gave her the damn blade, did you see? I'll have the man keelhauled for his lack of wits."

"They don't mean any harm; no one knows she cut you. They are only showing her what they know best—and for Miles, that is how to fight with a knife. What harm is there? She won't have a blade of her own, so there's nothing to fear."

"Fear? Christ, I do not fear her coming after me, you old ox, though I give you my deepest gratitude for your complete lack of confidence in my ability to defend myself. I'm thinking of what would happen to her if someone got that dagger away from her. It wouldn't be difficult—even the drunkest of fools could wrest the damn thing from her. Her grip is all wrong. Her stance is completely unguarded," he finished, not caring that he was scowling like a demon. He looked to his silent companion, who stared back at him with a mixture of confusion and expectation.

Cole ground out an oath, shoved the mug at his first mate and headed with purpose across the deck. He reached the group in no time, coming up unnoticed from an angle behind them. He could see Bailey's expression as she swung and stabbed the air, a look of pure concentration on her bruised face. He slipped up and spun her around to face him, grabbing her wrists and pulling them in a firm grasp down by her sides. A little more pressure to her right wrist caused her to cry out in pain and release the dagger. The weapon barely had time to clatter to the deck before Cole readjusted, holding both wrists in one hand while scooping up the dagger in the other.

"Let go! Let go! What are you doing? You're hurting me!" she cried, her light eyes sparking with anger.

"Oh, I beg your pardon, miss. I didn't mean to hurt you. I'm just a lust-filled, drunken, lawless pirate who's been thieving at sea and hasn't seen a women in three months. By all means, I'll just do as you say and let you go now," he mocked, dropping her wrists and bowing low.

Miles stared at his captain, eyes wide, mouth slack as a breathless moment of silence hung on the gentle sea breeze.

"You unchivalrous scoundrel!" Bailey scolded, sending a number of the onlooking sailors into riotous laughter.

Cole inclined his head to Miles and shrugged. It was the young man's undoing. He doubled over, laughing in earnest before gaining some control and moving to join the others at the railing.

"Why must you try to ruin everything for me?"

"Me? What exactly have I ruined for you? Oh, yes. I ruined your attempt to slice my throat open. And did I toss you overboard for attacking me? Hmmm, no, I didn't. Should have. But I didn't. I know that was your wish—to swim back to shore, so I suppose I ruined that as well." He moved closer, his body nearly touching hers. To his surprise, she didn't back up. Instead, she tilted her head back to glare up at him, her fists in balls on her hips.

"I would have been better off, to be sure. You refused to take me home, saying we were too far out to sea. And now you are trying to keep me from doing what I must to get home."

"And what is it you think you must do to get home? Fight? Fight who? Me?"

"No . . . of course not. But I must learn to protect myself. We will be parting company soon. And despite you, I *will* learn to face the world on my own."

Cole felt the warm breath of her defiant vow on his face, the fresh scent of herbs wafting about his head, making it hard to keep his anger burning. He hated to admit it, even to himself, but the girl had courage. And determination. But then, so did he.

"I have no intention of getting in irons about this."

"Then you concede." She backed up a step and smiled, her white teeth sparkling against the greenish-blue hue of the bruises that lingered.

"No, I do not. I simply refuse to argue the point."

"Good. Then I will continue. Excuse me."

He caught her by the elbow as she started to turn away. "You have yet to tell me who you wish to protect yourself from. No one onboard this ship is a threat to you."

"But I'm not going to be aboard the *Barracuda* for much longer. We will reach land soon, isn't that so?"

Her plan suddenly became as clear as rainwater. The girl was either unbelievably naive or she was daft. Either way, he would have to prove to her that she would stand no chance against the inhabitants of New Providence.

"That is so." He turned and ordered the group of sailors to disperse, saying that he would find plenty for them to do, if they couldn't entertain themselves elsewhere. One by one, the men shuffled away, some glancing back with sullen expressions. They looked as if they were leaving one of heaven's angels alone with the devil, Cole mused to himself. "Pitiful lot of pups running about my ship," he muttered, before turning back to face Bailey's frown.

"Now, do you want to continue or not?" He shook off his sleeveless waistcoat and tossed it aside.

"You? You wish to teach me?"

"Not to fight. Only to defend yourself."

"Please do not humor me. I know you don't think I can take care of myself," she said, turning her back to him.

Cole sighed, having caught the hurt look she tried to hide. It was true, though. In fact, that was exactly what he was trying to point out to her. She was only bringing this pain on herself. Why did she have to be so stubborn?

"I don't humor anyone. But you should know that we will reach the island tomorrow, and you are not going ashore, so you won't have need to defend yourself, anyway."

She turned around to face him, her blue eyes shining like the sun-tipped waves. "I said nothing of going ashore."

Cole gave her a knowing look and had to repress a smile as she pouted at being so easily read.

"But what if one of the pirates boards the *Barracuda* while you're gone? I know I'm not your responsibility, but you can't be heartless enough to leave me here with no way to protect myself."

He decided it was fruitless to continue this way. Like any other female, she would have to be humored. He would show her a few defensive tactics in order to gain her compliance about staying onboard for their brief stay in New Providence.

"Would you like to stop arguing with me long enough to learn something, or do you plan to use that tongue to cleave your imaginary assailants in two?" He hadn't meant to tease her, but something in her lively spirit brought out the mischief in him.

Her eyes widened and she clamped her mouth shut, but he didn't miss the slight shadow of a smile that touched her lips as she nodded and relaxed her stiff shoulders.

"Good. Now, the most important thing to remember is you must never let your enemy see your fear. Don't give him any reason to believe you are weak. Men will think they have a natural advantage over a woman. But a man's size or strength doesn't necessarily mean he can best you."

"You mean like David and Goliath?"

Cole couldn't help but smile. "That's an interesting example. However, I don't have a slingshot handy at the moment. Besides, I agreed to teach you to protect yourself, not to blind giants. Anyway, I don't think there are any giants residing in the Colonies these days. They fled when the English began arriving."

She giggled, the melodic sound catching on the wind and disappearing all too quickly under the whipping of sails and rigging. It took Cole a moment to recover, his tongue tied as if he had fallen under a siren's spell. She licked her lips and he felt his body respond. It had been an innocent mannerism, but it had him wondering what she would taste like. He pushed the thought aside as her voice broke through his hazy lust.

"Cole? What shall I do instead?"

"You begin by throwing your opponent off guard. That can be a very effective way to gain an early advantage."

"Throw him off guard. How?"

"Do whatever he would least expect you to do. Here, I'll show you." He stepped in close and gazed down at her up-turned face, expectant, trusting, as if she thought he might reveal some ancient secret power that would send her demons back to Hell. What he wouldn't give to possess such a power over his own demons. "Turn around."

She obeyed and turned as she swept a mass of wind-tumbled curls from her eyes. He groaned inwardly. Settling his hands on her hips, he could feel the warmth of her skin through the fabric that clung to her curves. He swallowed hard against the pleasurable feeling of those curves fitting into his palms so naturally.

He shouldn't have started this nonsense. But now he couldn't seem to tear himself away.

"When I get hold of you, I want you to try to get away. Do whatever you can and don't be concerned about hurting me. Understand?"

At her nod of acknowledgment, he wrapped his arms around her, one across her stomach, the other across her breasts, her back pressed tight against him, her arms trapped at her sides. She struggled fiercely, arched her back and tried to wiggle out of his hold. Cole felt his body react in a purely primitive way, triggering a strong and deep-seated impulse to release her.

But he couldn't let go. An even stronger feeling of protectiveness surged over him at the thought of another man—someone meaning to do her harm—holding her like this, feeling the same male hunger stirred to life.

And what such a predator would do to her to sate that hunger.

Suddenly it became serious to him. Suddenly it became imperative to him that she learn to handle herself in the dangerous world she had been thrown into. She tried to loosen her arms, while kicking her feet harmlessly in the air. Finally, he set her down and she turned to him, breathless.

"I couldn't move at all! I am not strong enough to fight a man—surely you see now that I need a weapon. You must give the dagger back to me!"

Cole shook his head, but before he could explain his reasons, she blurted, "It was a gift from Miles. You cannot mean to keep me from receiving a gift. No one would even know I have it—it will be harmless."

"No, it's not harmless and you well know it. You said it yourself: you are not strong enough, and that is the problem. It takes months, at the least, to learn to use weapons properly. You must face your weaknesses and learn to work with them. You can outwit your attacker, distract him—and then run to safety."

She huffed in exasperation, setting her fists on her hips and tilting her head to glare up at him, though the sun made it impossible for her not to squint. She was quite a sight, tussled curls whipping about in the wind, green and blue bruises like paint splotches on her fair skin, bare ankles and toes poking out from her borrowed breeches.

She had been through so much, yet her eyes still shone with light. With life. With hope for the future. He didn't understand how she could cling to it, how she could put her faith in such a useless emotion. Hope had done nothing for him. Still, he was fascinated by her spirit. And by the way she looked up at him, her luminous eyes threatening to swallow him whole. His traitorous body was reminding him of the long weeks since he'd been with a woman. It would be easy enough to satiate that primal yearning.

What plagued him worse than the physical discomfort was that Bailey stimulated his mind like no other woman he'd ever known. He wasn't used to it—and damn sure didn't like it.

"Did you hear me? Cole? How shall I outwit my opponent?"

"Enough, Bailey. This is a waste of time. There is no reason for you to defend yourself. But since it appears you are feeling better, I suggest you work, like everyone else onboard this ship." Bending, he scooped his vest off the deck and carelessly shrugged into it.

Bailey's mouth dropped open as she took a step back.

Confusion and anger mingled in her expression. She started to speak, but he stopped her, holding up his hand before she could utter a word.

"Report to the galley. Marcel will find something for you to do."

A distant rumble of thunder took his attention from the cold aqua shimmer in her eyes, to the deep purplish-gray of the sky. A wind gust blew sea spray into her face, upsetting her balance. Cole caught her by her elbows, steadying her as the ship rose on a wave, then dipped sharply.

He felt her stiffen under his grasp, though she didn't struggle for release. When the ship settled, she remained still except for the slight confrontational tilt of her head. Her full pink lips protruded in an angry pout. Desire pulled at him and he was swept into its powerful current.

He slipped one arm around her tiny waist and the other anchored at the back of her neck, drawing her close. He took her mouth in a kiss meant to conquer, effectively silencing her protest. She moaned and pushed feebly against him before surrendering, leaving her palms splayed against his chest. He coaxed her lips apart, delving his tongue into the sweet warmth of her mouth. He deepened the kiss, slanting his mouth hard across hers. Startled by his aggression, she leaned back and renewed her struggles. But as she arched her back, her breasts pressed intimately against him, firing his blood all the more. He slid his hand to cup her buttocks, pulling her hips flush to his aching body.

She gasped and twisted her head away, covering her mouth with a shaky hand. The distress in her expression wrenched him painfully back to the present. What did he expect? She was a blasted virgin, for Christ's sake.

But she didn't run from him. And she didn't slap him or rail at him. In fact, the unease he saw on her face wasn't nearly as evident as another emotion.

Passion.

He knew it when he saw it.

She lowered her hand and simply stared at him, her seafoam eyes heavy-lidded, her bruised lips parted slightly. She lifted her chin a notch.

As if she wanted him to kiss her.

As if that had been her plan all along.

It seemed even virgins knew how to destroy a man.

"You are dismissed."

He turned and walked away, determined to order her out of his thoughts as well.

Chapter Nine

Marcel did not seem surprised to see Bailey when she showed up in the galley a little while later. She suspected Cole had something to do with that, though Marcel didn't mention the captain at all. Bailey was grateful for that, as her thoughts had been consumed by him since the kiss. She didn't know how it had happened, but even before he lowered his head to hers, she had wanted him to kiss her. God help her, his embrace had felt so intoxicating. He could have had anything he wanted from her in that moment and the realization astonished her.

The old cook introduced her to Karl, a young sailor who nodded at her before turning back to the chicken he was plucking.

Marcel patted his wrinkled hand on a stool meant for Bailey. She sat on it at a tall counter and began chopping potatoes while Marcel helped Karl finish preparing the chickens for the boiling pot. It was stuffy in the small space, but Bailey preferred the heat to sitting alone in Cole's cabin with nothing but her thoughts to occupy her. She had lost so much in such a short time and now her entire future seemed to be in the hands of a man who hated her.

A man who had awoken the most confusing and earth-shaking emotions inside her. *Sweet Mary, why had he kissed her?*

Later, as she peeled and sliced the last potato, she still had not been able to answer her troubling questions.

"I have some onions, too. Are you almost done with those, *mademoiselle?*"

"All done," she replied. She dropped the potatoes in the pot and wiped her hands on her apron. "How many onions would you like?"

"How many are left?"

She dug in the sack and pulled out four small, slightly bruised yellow onions. Marcel nodded as she held them up. "That will have to do. We'll have to restock our supplies soon."

"In New Providence?"

Marcel poked at the soup with a large spoon, then turned to her, rubbing his hands across his low back. "Eh, probably not. But don't worry, we won't be there long."

Karl paused where he was unstacking pewter bowls, long enough to exchange glances with the cook, but then resumed his task without a word.

"Is it really so bad?"

"It's bad enough, *mademoiselle,*" Marcel replied.

"But Lew said there are women and even children who live there."

"Not all pirates are bloodthirsty, but they are still pirates. New Providence is their home. They follow their own laws and customs, and if you aren't familiar with their ways, you can get into trouble. As for the women Lew told you about, they are as brutal as the men in many ways. It's a difficult and violent life. The *capitaine* can't forget that for a minute when he's here with them. Certainly, you don't wish to go ashore, *mademoiselle? Non,* not after what you've been through."

"I need to go home." She turned to a disapproving sound behind her and saw Cole filling the doorway.

He shook his head, his brows angled down in displeasure. "The only way a pirate is going to aid you in getting home is if you are taken hostage and your precious James comes up with your ransom. You can't be that desperate to get your way."

Oh, why did he have to show up now? And looking so . . . well formed. She tried to ignore him. Thank goodness he didn't know what Lew had told her. If there was any chance that English officers were on the island, then she was going to find them. They would see that she got home. And when they heard what she'd been through, Cole was likely to find himself in chains, rotting in a damp, cold cell in Newgate. No, if he knew what she was thinking of doing, she didn't even want to consider what he might do to keep himself out of prison.

She rinsed her hands in the washbowl and dried them on her apron as she turned to face Cole. He leaned against the door frame, his thick arms crossed. She supposed he was trying to intimidate her and she was determined to ignore that, too.

"How are you different than the pirates, then? You are keeping me against my wishes, and you refuse to commit to when you will see me home. I am no better than a captive with you. I can do better on my own, and I demand that you release me when we reach the island. I'll take my chances there."

One dark brow rose, signaling the end of his patience. She refused to look away.

"You're done here. I'll escort you to my quarters. Marcel, would you be so kind as to bring Bailey her dinner?"

"*Oui, Capitaine.* Of course."

"I am not done here, Captain. There is still—"

"Shall I toss you over my shoulder and carry you?"

He had pulled her to him in order to whisper the question huskily against her ear. She prayed he could not detect the delicious tingle his breath sent through her. She stiffened her body as his arm tightened more intimately around her waist. To an observer it would appear that their relationship was less than innocent.

He was trying to embarrass her into submission!

Marcel stirred the soup and Karl looked around for something to do, both clearly uncomfortable with the scene. As much as she hated him right now, she refused to give Cole any more satisfaction.

She pushed away from him to remove her apron and then brushed past him down the corridor.

Once inside his cabin, she spun around, fully prepared to give the brute a piece of her mind. She would not allow him to treat her this way.

"I'll thank you to keep your hands off me, Captain," she said with as much rancor as she could muster.

"You didn't seem to mind my hands on you this afternoon, Miss Spencer," he reminded her, advancing a step. "Shall I remind you?"

She backed up, her body reacting to the seductive invitation. If this was a game he was playing, he was determined to win. And he would, she thought miserably, for she had no idea of the rules.

"That was innocent! That was nothing more than what you men do when you are learning the ways of fighting." She was going to completely ignore the fact that he was talking about the kiss.

He laughed and took another step. Her backside came in contact with the table in the center of the cabin.

"Well, since it's all so innocent, why don't we continue what we started up on deck?"

"You are just trying to distract me from what I was saying before," she accused. He was so close, his spicy, masculine scent entangled her like a net.

"And what was that, Bailey?" he asked, leaning down to trap her with his arms braced on the table on both sides of her.

Good Lord, she *was* distracted. What had she just said?

"Why must you try to humiliate me in front of your men?" she managed.

"Why must you continue to challenge me?" he asked. He

shifted his weight to lift his hand, tucking a stray lock of hair gently behind her ear.

"I . . . I just . . . I don't want to be here." She could barely get the breath out of her lungs. His angelic face lowered to mere inches above hers. If she lifted her chin, her lips would touch his. Did she dare?

"I don't want you to be here, either. But you are. We could try to enjoy it, Bailey."

His voice was seductive, low. Like a caress, it sent gooseflesh up her arms and neck. Part of her waited, breathless for whatever he might do next. Another part of her fought for control, to wake up and come to her senses. But if he was trying to intimidate her, she would show him she was not so easily subdued.

She took his face in her hands and pressed her lips to his, trying to mimic what he had done to her. She fully expected him to push her away, angry that she had taken control.

Instead, he lifted her to sit on the edge of the table, then stepped between her legs and wrapped his arms around her body. He kissed her back, his mouth insistent, demanding. She didn't know what he wanted from her, but God, she wanted to give it. She followed his lead, touching his tongue, his lips, his teeth as a liquid heat surged through her limbs. When she felt she couldn't stand the pleasure another second, she pulled away, dropping her head back. A moan escaped her lips, but she couldn't bring herself to care.

Cole pressed kisses down her throat, careful to avoid her injury. When his lips and tongue assaulted the sensitive skin along her collarbone, she nearly came off the table. She wasn't showing him anything—other than how easily he could steal her will. She needed him to stop.

But in truth, she prayed he wouldn't.

A loud knock at the door broke her from the spell and she gasped, pushing him away.

Cole cursed and straightened.

"Come in," he growled.

Bailey slipped past him to the opposite side of the table. Marcel entered with Bailey's dinner. She tried to act serene, but the old cook seemed to sense something amiss and left the cabin quickly without his usual friendly chatter.

"Cole, we have some things to settle," she managed.

"I don't have time for that right now. There's a storm coming."

"But you have time to torment me with your unwanted attentions?" she asked, irritated.

"Torment?" He grinned and shook his head. "You didn't appear tormented to me, Bailey. In fact, all you had to do was move away."

"I shouldn't have to move away. You should know to leave me alone."

"Oh, that's right. I forgot about James. His attentions aren't *unwanted,* are they, Bailey?"

"That is none of your business."

"You certainly don't like to talk about your true love, do you? Don't worry. I won't tell him that you kissed me."

"I did no such thing!" she gasped. "You are insufferable. And completely wrong! I would never kiss the likes of you. You kissed me."

"I'm glad we got that worked out. I must have been mistaken," he added with a smirk.

He was enjoying himself far too much. She wanted to strangle him.

"Bailey, this storm looks serious. You have to stay in here. Marcel will need to get the galley secured, so don't take too long to eat. If it gets bad enough to slide the chairs across the floor, blow the lamp out right away. That is important, do you understand?" He pulled his overcoat from a peg behind the door.

"Yes, of course I do."

He nodded and disappeared into the dark passageway without another word.

She closed the door, feeling as if she had just been thoroughly seduced. Not that she would know much about the act of seduction, but she suspected it must make one feel like she felt right now.

Confused. Exhilarated. Tingly and shaky all at the same time. Mercy, what would she be feeling right now if they hadn't been interrupted?

Despite what he had said, it took her a while before her stomach was settled enough for food. Marcel was still in the galley when she took her tray back, but the ship was beginning to roll, so she didn't linger. She wasn't much in the mood for company, anyway. She had to figure out what she was going to do.

Cole was unwilling to tell her anything about where they were going or when he would be ready to let her go. In fact, he seemed determined to keep her. But why, she couldn't fathom. She only knew that the more determined he was to keep her, the more determined she was to get away from him.

With all haste.

As she moved around restlessly, she began to think of a way to leave the *Barracuda* once they reached the island. She would sneak off the ship as soon as the men were gone. She prayed that Lew was right—that the King's Navy would be in place on the island. If not, she would have to get back onboard the *Barracuda* unnoticed and wait for their next stop. Or for Cole to make good on his word. But the more she came to know him, the more she knew that Cole was not a man who could be pushed. He would act only when he saw fit, and for the moment he didn't see fit to do her bidding.

She lit only the glass lamp that hung on the wall above Cole's desk. She removed the candles and brass holders from the table and tucked them into his sea chest, along with the porcelain pitcher and a few other loose objects that lay around the cabin. The last remnants of dusk were lost as the first bolt of lightning ripped through the dark clouds, followed by a loud clap of thunder. Bailey curled up in the window seat to watch the spectacular display.

Only hours before, the sky had looked so different.

Crystal blue, calm, with puffs of white clouds floating peacefully above. She had found herself laughing. It was hard to believe anything could make her laugh, or forget for just a moment the utter despair that clutched her heart. And even more surprising was the fact that Cole had been the one to lighten her mood and briefly ease her pain.

After a while, she stripped out of the breeches and crossed to the captain's desk, holding on to the table for support as the ship rocked on the rough waves. She blew out the lamp and made her way back to the bunk, listening to the protesting groans of the ship and the steady patter of rain.

She lay on her back, staring into the darkness, wondering about the man whose bed she occupied. Today, she had seen more in Cole than the gruff, serious loner with nothing in his heart but revenge. He insisted that revenge was all that mattered to him. If that was true, then he might never see fit to help her get home. He was on a path leading to disaster and she refused to let him take her with him. She had to make her own way, the sooner, the better. And once she had left him behind, she prayed she wouldn't be haunted by memories of disturbing silver eyes that focused on her with an intensity that made her tremble.

An hour later, Bailey still lay awake, her thoughts a jumbled mess of broken dreams and a dismal future. She wished she was back in Beaufort, living a safe, predictable life with her brother and father, but that was not to be. She sighed and thought of her dependable friend—the man she would finally consent to marry. So, James had turned out to be right—they were meant to be together. She would become his wife. She didn't feel capable of facing the hardships of a future alone, and she didn't want to live in fear and uncertainty. James had declared his love to her and promised to keep her safe. She was more than ready to feel safe. Love would come with time. Wouldn't it?

Oh, tomorrow could not come soon enough.

* * *

"Tomorrow cannot come soon enough," Cole grumbled as he downed the last swallow of rum from his cup.

A clap of thunder punctuated his complaint. The ship rode another swollen wave as Cole steadied the teetering bottle of spirits.

"You think he will be there?" Cisco asked. He reached out a beefy hand to catch their pile of plates as they slid across the table toward him.

"I don't know. But at least I can get off this blasted ship for a few hours."

"Ah. I was wondering why you were so interested in my company tonight. What has she done now?" The big man chuckled as he lit a fat cigar.

"Nothing. I hadn't given her a thought."

Cisco nodded, puffed hard on his cigar, then blew out a thick line of smoke, the sweet odor hanging in the air above them. "Then I'm sure you haven't thought of what you will do if the navy is there when we arrive. You can be rid of her easily enough. They would consider it their duty to see her safely home. I could personally see to it once we dock."

"No. I think it's still too soon for their ships to be arriving."

"But, if they are—"

"I won't be turning her over to them."

"I see. Do you plan to turn her over to *him,* then? Would you really go that far to get what you want?"

"No. That is something *he* would do. I haven't fallen that far into hell, yet, old man."

"I know. But you are thinking of how to turn this in your favor, aren't you?"

"Why shouldn't I use the situation to my favor? What's the harm as long as she isn't hurt—and she wouldn't be. She doesn't even have to know what's happening. I wouldn't let the bastard see her, just the threat of her would be enough to spark his interest. But I would have to have her—and I would have to prove that I have her."

"Are you willing to keep her with you until the end, then? Until your revenge is complete? Because if you do this, if you bring her into this in any way, you won't be able to send her back to Beaufort until the Dragon is dead."

Cole knew. He had known from the moment he considered the idea. If he went through with this, no one in Beaufort could keep Bailey safe as long as the Dragon lived. He would have to protect her until it was over. For some reason, the thought of keeping her, even by force, didn't bother him as much as he thought it would. A few days ago, the thought of him taking responsibility for the safety of any woman would have made him laugh. But he had the opportunity to use a woman to get what he wanted and he felt justified.

"I'm aware of the consequences." He reached for a cigar and bit off the tip before continuing. "But how can I not use this situation to my benefit? It's just too perfect. It's as though she was brought to me just for this purpose. What are the chances of something like this? Admit it, even your grandmother would say it was meant to be."

"*Mi abuela* would whip you raw for even thinking of using the girl for your own ends," Cisco replied.

"What about you, old friend? Do you think I've crossed the line into hell? Have I become as depraved as the pirate? Christ, I don't know anymore."

"I'm not about to tell you your mind. I'm here no matter what you decide to do. But whether you use her or not, I know you won't take the girl to Beaufort. It's the last place she would be safe, and you will not send her to her death."

"You are so sure of my honor, aren't you, old man?" Cole lost his interest in smoking the cigar and tossed it, unlit, onto his plate.

Cisco shrugged, squinting at the smoke that weaved about his face.

"Don't be. The girl means nothing to me. But her life likely depends on my protection, so she shouldn't be opposed to do something for me in return. That's not so honorable, but there it is, that's what I want."

Cisco shrugged again. "It sounds like you have it all figured out, *amigo*." The *Barracuda* dipped sharply at the bow as she came off another large wave. Cisco deftly caught his cigar and the ashtray before they slid to the floor.

"Damn!" Cole's empty glass just missed his grasp as it flew off the end of the table and shattered against a beam. "Not yet, but I will. I will." Cole heard the faint sound of a bell over the pouring rain. "Ten o'clock."

"*Sí.* Have you figured out where you'll sleep tonight?" Cisco asked with a grin.

"You seem to be enjoying all my recent misfortunes, my friend. That is why I will be staying right here. I plan to annoy you in return for the duration of the night."

"Fine by me. But you'll have to squeeze in with the four others that will be coming in any time now."

Cole understood. "Hell and fire. Everything's full up?"

"Everything but the hold. But you said you didn't want any of them down there, catching God knows what. With the storm, they can't sleep on deck, but they could . . ."

"They could what?"

"Well, just because you want to avoid her, doesn't mean all the men do. I'm sure you won't have a problem getting a couple of volunteers to share your cabin with Miss Spencer."

Cole stood up, grabbed his coat from the back of the chair and stabbed his finger in the air at his first mate. "You know, you won't be grinning like that when we get to Lochinvar and I tell Analee how you've tortured me. She'll turn you out to sleep in the sugar fields, no matter how long it's been since you warmed her bed."

He left with the sound of Cisco's robust laughter taunting him down the passageway.

Chapter Ten

Bailey rolled to her back, bracing herself with her right hand splayed against the wall, her left gripping the edge of the mattress. The *Barracuda* tipped deeply starboard, and then as she righted herself, Bailey released her grip and waited for the next wave to come. She'd never experienced anything like this feeling of being lifted and dropped, tossed and turned, like a leaf in the wind. It was exactly how she felt ever since the attack—like a leaf, torn from its tree, spinning out of control and toward the complete unknown.

And to make matters worse, her usual levelheaded temperament seemed to have abandoned her ever since she had met Cole Leighton. One minute he infuriated her with his arrogance and the next she found herself amused at his wry humor. And heaven help her, but she couldn't begin to explain the chaotic emotions she felt today on deck when he had his hands on her. With the sun on his face, his dark hair blowing loose from the leather tie, he had looked recklessly handsome. Her skin tingled, her entire body came alive from the inside when he had hold of her. She felt the sculpted muscles of his arms, his back, awed by the sheer power and masculinity of him as she watched him move.

For the tenth time this past hour, she relived the moment

that Cole had taunted her in his cabin before he left tonight. Each time she thought of it, the details seemed more dreadful than before. It had been past midday, the sun's heat intense, despite the sweet, salty breeze. Cole's keen silver-gray gaze had paralyzed her, as they stood with barely an inch between their bodies, her wrists captured securely in his hands behind her back. She was supposed to demonstrate how she'd learned to get away, but for the life of her, she couldn't remember what he had just shown her. All her traitorous mind would focus on was the dark stubble on his face, the perfect firm line of his lips . . . and how those lips might feel against hers. It seemed as though she stood there unmoving, for an eternity. She was certain he had read the sway of her thoughts, the unabashed desire in her eyes. She squeezed her eyes shut against the embarrassment that continued to grip her even now, as she recalled how he had abruptly released her, as if she was poison.

But then, why had he tried to seduce her into kissing him only a few hours ago? Thank God Marcel had knocked, for she was almost sure she would have given in in another breath.

All of a sudden, a wooden crash thundered above the din of the storm, startling Bailey, and she gasped loudly, rolling over to face the room.

"Ouch!" A male voice growled into the darkness.

"Who's there!" Bailey demanded.

"It's only me, Bailey. I didn't mean to scare you. I just ran over a blasted chair. I may have broken my knee," he grumbled.

"Oh." She let out a breath of relief. "I'm sorry. They have been sliding about all evening. I didn't know what to do with them."

"You're not to blame. I forgot to secure them before I left," he answered, his tone calmer now.

Bailey heard the scratch of flint and soon the dim glow of lamplight illuminated the space. "What are you doing? Are you going to sleep in here?" she asked. She watched as Cole dug around in a desk drawer, coming away with several large, curved hooks that he then secured in iron rings hanging on the far wall.

"This *is* my cabin, if I remember correctly." One by one, he retrieved the chairs and placed them on the hooks, tugging each to make sure they were hung securely.

"I just thought—well, I thought you were being a gentleman, giving up your cabin for my privacy. Oh, I was wondering what those rings were used for," she finished, trying to change the subject. Why should she show so much interest in where he was sleeping, anyway?

Cole turned to face her, the glow from the flame bathing his face with warm, orange light. "There's no such thing as privacy aboard a ship," he replied without further explanation. He pulled the leather cord from his nape, tossed it on the desk and ran his hands roughly through his hair. "As for the hooks, I also revel in hanging people on them from time to time. Especially troublesome women who keep me from my own bed." His tone was halfheartedly accusing.

"Hmph. Perhaps you should remember that the next time you plan to hold a woman against her wishes. You'll have to find another location in which to keep her—one with more proper accommodations," she retorted.

"There will never be a next time. I only regret that I wasn't aware of your presence before we sailed. If I had been, neither of us would be in this unfortunate situation," he replied, his tone icy.

His words wouldn't have stung so much if she wasn't still haunted by how she had made such a fool of herself on deck earlier. "You may rest assured, Captain, we shall not be in this unfortunate situation for much longer. I will see to that. Good night." Bailey was proud of herself for keeping the emotion she was feeling out of her voice. Nonetheless, she rolled to face the wall and pulled the blanket up tight under her chin, hoping to dismiss Cole from her thoughts as easily as from her sight.

But it was not to be.

She lay still, her bruised muscles aching from tension as she listened to Cole moving around the cabin. She gritted her teeth against the memory of his body pressed against her back, his arms wrapped tightly around her. The point of the exercise had been lost on her. Rather than feel the threat of a would-be attacker, she had breathed in the fresh and spicy scent that was Cole and she had felt safe. Safer than she could ever remember feeling.

Cole saw the flicker of hurt in Bailey's expression before she turned away from him, but he refused to feel repentant. He had only spoken the truth. Why should he lie? Lies were more damaging than the truth, he thought bitterly.

Her veiled threat to leave him once they reached land was not lost on him. She was getting desperate, and Cole was beginning to think she would do just about anything, no matter how foolish, to get away from him. Or was she desperate to get back to her lover, James?

He couldn't let that happen. Not just yet. Not when the temptation to use her was beginning to win out over the shadow of conscience that lingered somewhere deep within him.

That conscience had reared up from its dark hiding place in his core more than once during the afternoon with Bailey. He hadn't counted on becoming so relaxed in her presence. He hadn't bargained on the passion that surfaced, intensifying every time he touched her. And once, as he held her body captive against his, she had looked up at him with seductive aqua eyes that invited him, nay, begged him to kiss her. It was no wonder he hadn't been able to fight his desire. It was just his physical body, reacting in its most natural, male way.

Bloody hell, it hadn't even gotten her out of his system.

He'd practically ravished her the second time. Though the wench would have deserved it. She probably thought that he would let her go ashore if he was too numb with passion to think clearly. But she'd failed miserably. She was too innocent to realize how her game would turn against her. He'd seen the desire in her eyes. Felt it in her body—and, damn him, he'd felt it in his, too.

Hell, it had been too long since he had indulged in the pleasures of a woman's flesh. That was why his body was so reactive to Bailey. Aye, as soon as he slaked his thirst for simple physical release, his mind would release him from thoughts of Bailey Spencer.

Cole spent a mere few minutes recording in his ledger as the storm continued to buffet the *Barracuda* to and fro with increasing intensity. Once he was satisfied the ink was dry, he closed the leather book and tucked it into the top drawer of the built-in desk. He drew the quilt from his sea chest, took a small pillow from the window seat and went again to his desk to extinguish the single lamp that burned there. He hesitated, then turned to peruse the girl in his bed. She lay with her back to him, bundled to her neck with covers, a few curls spilling across the pillow, glowing red-gold in the candlelight. Whether it was curiosity or something else that made him stand there and watch her for the next full minute, he refused to examine. She looked so small in the large bunk, built specifically to fit his tall frame. He started to imagine himself lying there with her and instantly his loins tightened. He muttered a curse against his traitorous body, swearing to himself that he would conquer his lust before leaving New Providence. He would cease to be plagued by this girl once one of the eager young pirate women took care of him, and then he could get his mind back on Bailey's true purpose. Luring his enemy. Those thoughts eased his immediate physical discomfort, but still agitated, he doused the candle and roughly settled himself on the oak floor.

It didn't take long for the damp cold from the bare wood to seep into Cole's body, chilling him to the bone. Worse yet, each new wave that buffeted the *Barracuda,* took her bow from a steep upward angle to a sudden drop, where she would then rock from port to starboard in the rough water like a child's toy. Late-summer storms in the southern Atlantic could be quite severe, and just as unpredictable. Cole was used to riding out bad weather, however, he'd never had to attempt it lying on the floor.

As the ship lurched suddenly to port, Cole half-rolled and half-slid painfully into one of the thick, carved legs of the table, eliciting a whispered curse as he rubbed a bump on his head.

"Are you hurt?"

"I am fine," Cole answered, noting the slight tone of guilt along with concern in her voice. "I thought you were asleep."

"How can anyone possibly sleep this way? Do you ever get used to being tossed about so?"

He could tell she had turned to face the room, and with a flash of lightning, he could see her gripping the carved post of the bunk with a delicate, white hand. He repositioned himself, dragging the pillow and quilt back to his narrow place between the table and the window seat before answering. "Aye, somewhat. This isn't a particularly bad storm, but the direction of the wind is making it feel worse than it is. I doubt it will last much longer."

At that, the ship keeled violently, sending Cole smacking into the solid base of the window seat, then scrambling to get a hold on something solid as he slid headfirst toward the bunk.

"I do not believe you'll get much sleep down there. Is there nowhere else onboard you could go?"

"If there was, Bailey, believe me, I would be there. The men who usually sleep on deck are doubled in the berths or bunked on the floor with the officers. Our accommodations are limited, you will just have to make due with my presence."

Bailey gritted her teeth at his pompous tone. To think she had actually been concerned about his welfare for the briefest of moments. "Very well. But could you please keep yourself from rolling about? The raucous noise of your bones cracking against the furniture is keeping me awake."

She had made the request in the most mean-spirited tone she could, and yet, she could hear his dry chuckle mingle with the steady rainfall.

"That might not be possible, but I will do my best," he replied mockingly.

"Do you have a rope, sir? I will gladly tie your sorry carcass to the table legs, and be quite happy to leave you there when we reach the island. I'm sure at some point after I'm quite gone, one of your crewmen will find you and release you." Oh, how the man could goad her patience!

"I believe I will decline. You'll have to save those types of games for your betrothed. Is good old James aware of your colorful tastes?"

Bailey refused the bait, though she was glad for the darkness to hide her heated blush.

Light spilled into the room as another brief flash came and went. Bailey could see Cole sitting against the window seat, his knees raised up, the quilt wrapped around him, his head resting on his knees. A pang of guilt assailed her, the sight of him branded in her mind and then reinforced by another quick flash of light. He appeared so innocent, so vulnerable, and she lost her inner struggle to suppress the words she had been determined not to utter.

"Cole? This is ridiculous. Why don't you—" She was interrupted as the *Barracuda* was assaulted by another wave, the *whack* as loud as a cannon explosion. The ship lurched up and dropped down at a frightening angle, Bailey's breath caught in her throat. She lost her hold on the thick bedpost and tumbled out of the bunk, with a thud. Pain exploded through her as her injured body was aggrieved further by the fall. In a futile effort, she tried to stop herself from sliding across the floor, her arms reaching blindly for something to grab on to in the dark.

Suddenly she felt Cole's hands on her, firm and sure, yet gentle as he steadied them both while the *Barracuda* balanced herself again.

"Are you all right?" All signs of mockery were gone from his voice.

"No. Well, yes, it's just that I fell on one of my bruises. It's noth—oh!"

Bailey was surprised into silence as Cole lifted her and placed her gently on the bunk just as another wave hit the ship. She braced herself, and watched Cole's dark outline as he steadied himself against the post as the hull settled into a cushion of the ocean once again.

"Cole, you cannot sleep on the floor. It's not safe . . ." She hesitated too long.

"Bailey, I told you, there is nowhere else for me to go." He spoke as if explaining the situation to a child. Her ire at his tone unfortunately was not enough to entirely subdue her nerves at what she was about to offer.

"You can sleep with me—I mean to say, we can share the bunk." She cringed at the deafening silence that was his reply. The blood pounding in her ears nearly drowned out the noise of the storm. "But—you must remain above the covers!" She rolled to face the wall, humiliation warming her from cheeks to toes. She lay perfectly still, despite the rocking motion of the ship, grasping the edge of the mattress with her fingers to keep herself firmly in place.

"How sensible of you, Miss Spencer."

The way her proper name slipped off his tongue, like a caress in the dark, sounded so improper, it released a tingle down her spine. She heard his boots hit the floor and then she felt the mattress sink with his weight. Bailey tightened her grip as though she would drop into the pit of Hell if she dared let go.

"Stay above the sheet!" she ordered as she felt him settle next to her. Oh, Sweet Mary, maybe this was not such a good idea. Her body rolled into his as his body bore into the mattress and, try as she might, she couldn't press any closer to the wall than she was. Did he have to be so . . . big? And warm? She curled in a ball, but then her buttocks pressed firmly against some part of him and she heard him stifle a groan, so she assumed he was as displeased with the contact as she was.

After what felt like an eternity, Cole spoke, startling Bailey into an even more rigid posture. His deep voice rose above the sharp rain patter, though a distinct chill filled each word. "You needn't worry. I gave up ravishing unwilling women long ago. And even the willing ones aren't worth more than a few hours of a man's time. Mostly harlots, clinging to a man's breeches while reaching for his coin as he tries to make his escape," he snorted. "I can do without the lot of you."

"Really? And which lot do you place me in, Captain? Come, come, please continue. I find your ideas fascinating. You obviously have an extensive knowledge of women. Enlighten me." Bailey hoped the sarcasm in her tone would make up for the fact that it was too dark for him to see her scathing glare, even if she could bring herself to roll over and face him.

"I do not claim to have extensive knowledge. I have my own experiences and that is all I need to make my observations. As for you, Bailey, I do not know where you fit. I haven't given you that much thought."

She was surprised at how deeply that comment cut her. "Good. Then you won't give much thought to my absence once we reach New Providence and I bid you and the *Barracuda* my most eager farewell."

"You won't be bidding anyone farewell until we are far

away from New Providence. You might as well banish that idea right now."

"But you just said—"

"We have been over this. I am responsible for you."

"No, you are not. I am not your ward—or your property. When I choose to go, there is nothing you can do to stop me." How dare he pretend to be noble, protecting her, after insulting her so. The man was so flawed in character, he couldn't rise to redeem himself the slightest little bit.

"Bailey, I've told you. New Providence is not safe. You cannot go ashore there."

"Then where? Do you plan to take me back to Beaufort once we leave the island?"

"I don't know. Where I go will depend on what I find out in New Providence."

"About the Dragon?"

"Yes. I have come close to him twice now, and if I find out that he has been seen in these waters, I must stay and search for him. I have no time to waste sailing back to the Colonies while the Dragon is secreting himself away. There are hundreds of cays and islands and inlets in the area. He could hide for months and I will not take that chance."

"Oh! And how do you suppose I will be safe with you chasing after the Dragon? I thought you said he would hunt me until he is sure I am dead."

"I also told you I will protect you."

"Why should I believe you? You have shown me the extent of your chivalry. And your lovely description of women . . . Well, I understood your meaning fully. I am nothing to you." *Less than nothing, if his disdain for women extended beyond the range of the one who had hurt him so deeply,* she thought, but dared not say aloud.

"Because I gave you my word."

"And you honor your word." She made sure he would hear the skepticism in her voice.

"Always." He sighed, a long, drawn-out breath that said more than his words possibly could. He sounded weary. Not just tired, but soul-tired. What had damaged him so? What was it that he was longing for? Was he suffering inside as she was, from something the Dragon had done to him—or perhaps to someone he loved? She couldn't contain her curious desire to know more about him.

"Are you married?" The question slipped past her lips before she could stop the silent thought from resounding between them like a clash of cymbals. Reacting instinctively, she bit her lip, groaning at the sharp sting of her teeth against the cut there. She waited for a breathless moment, praying that perhaps he had not heard her above the creaking wood and pounding rain.

"Hmm, as much as I appreciate the offer, I believe you are spoken for," he replied.

As arrogant as ever.

"I am not—" she stopped herself. She didn't see fit to elaborate on her relationship with James. Perhaps if he thought she was going to marry James, he'd release her sooner, lest he have to face an angry fiancé and his family. "Silly me. What could you know about marriage? I cannot imagine any woman with a grain of good sense agreeing to marry you. Why, I can scarcely stand to be in the same room with you. I was only wondering why you are searching for the Dragon. I thought perhaps he had killed someone . . . important to you."

"Someone like a wife. Nay, nothing like that. I'm sure you're quite right in your keen observation of my disposition. I doubt there's a woman to be found who would want to be married to the likes of me. And I am all the more happy because of the fact. Marriage is for fools and tenderhearted dupes. And before you ask, I haven't decided which of those you are, either."

She was so caught up in their conversation, Bailey all but forgot her timidity and rolled onto her back in order to hear him better. "Do you jest about everything? Or just topics with which you are uncomfortable?"

"I am not uncomfortable. You are the one bound inside the blankets like an insect within a cocoon. Ask me whatever you wish to know. If I see fit to answer, then you may be assured I will answer you honestly."

"How did you become so intolerably arrogant?" Bailey asked the boards above her, shaking her head in the dark. She felt Cole's head turn on the pillow to face her, felt his breath tickle her cheek when he answered.

"Survival is all about arrogance, Bailey. Understanding that the only person you can believe in is yourself. You are on your own now. It wouldn't surprise me if you became arrogant someday, too."

"Never. I do believe in myself, but I could never forsake having people around me. I cannot even imagine such a desolate life. No one deserves such loneliness."

"I desire it."

"Cole, do you really hate all women so?"

There was a long pause before he answered. "Perhaps some more than others. But there isn't one of you I trust."

"Who hurt you so deeply? Did you love her?"

His low growl indicated his loss of patience with her questions on the topic.

"I don't care to discuss this. And you are too inquisitive."

"I just find it very sad, that's all. What about your mother? Surely you trust her."

A long silence followed. First she thought he was ignoring her, then she thought he might have fallen asleep. But finally, he responded in a low voice, tight and filled with venom. "She is the very last woman I would ever trust. But she's dead now."

"Oh. I'm sorry."

"I'm not."

"You cannot mean that. What could she possibly have done to make her own child say such a thing?"

"The heartless whore murdered my father," he stated flatly.

Bailey was stunned into silence. Her instinct was to refuse to believe it. Cole's mother had killed his father? She had never heard of anything so aberrant. She couldn't have helped her reaction if she tried—her heart broke for him.

"I am sorry I made you think of it."

"You didn't. There isn't a moment when I am not thinking about what that bitch did to our family."

Bailey turned her head on the pillow, wishing she could see his face, but he was shielded by the darkness. There were so many more questions burning on her tongue, but she dared not push Cole further. His voice had begun to sound so strained, so tortured. She couldn't bring herself to pry any more than she had. Perhaps it was because she had recently experienced the same type of soul-wrenching pain that she suddenly felt a sense of kinship with Cole. Her instinct was to reach out to him. She believed that some part of him longed for comfort as much as she longed to offer it. A part that was likely buried so deep he didn't even realize it himself. There was much more to this man than the harsh, thorny shell of his exterior and she found herself wanting to get beneath that hard skin to see more of the man he was concealing.

Minutes passed without a word between them. The combination of the binding covers, and the heat from Cole's body so close to her, made her fidgety.

"Would you please find a position and just stay still?" His voice sounded strained.

"I'm sorry," she replied, finally coming to rest on her back.

Thunder rolled, rain pounded and the ship continued to rock and sway. For the life of her, she couldn't seem to think about anything but the feel of the terribly complicated man next to her as the ship jostled them closer, tighter. No sleep came to bring her peace. Their bodies seemed to move together with the rhythm of the waves. It was a most unsettling feeling, and soon began brewing the most wicked thoughts her innocent mind could conjure. She imagined how this man's warm bare skin would feel against hers, how his muscles might feel beneath her fingers.

"Are you asleep?"

"N—No," she choked out. Oh, Sweet Mary, she prayed he couldn't read her mind.

"I was thinking you might be more comfortable wearing something other than Tom's shirt and breeches. It won't be difficult to find something for you on New Providence. I doubt it will be the latest fashion, but at least it won't be a man's breeches."

"Breeches do feel a little strange, but I must admit, they are quite comfortable. Perhaps if I wear Tom's clothes and tie my hair up under a cap, I could go ashore in New Providence. No one would know I am anything other than your hired cabin boy."

She could tell by his chuckle what he thought of her idea. "The island's habitants do spend a great deal of time intoxicated. But, Bailey, there isn't enough rum in the Caribbean to make any man mistake you for a boy."

Innocent though she was, there was no mistaking the distinct edge of lust in his gravely reply. She clamped her mouth shut, grateful for the blackness that concealed the color she knew would be bright from the heat on her cheeks. And the warmth didn't stop there. It flooded her limbs, making her breasts tingle and a strange ache settle deep between her thighs.

"Now there will be no more discussion about you going ashore. You will have to trust me on this and come tomorrow you must do exactly as I say."

"How can you ask me to trust you when you cannot trust in return? You said yourself that I have only myself to rely on, and so I shall."

"You will not win in this, Bailey. If you attempt to defy me tomorrow, I will tie you to one of these oak posts and gag you myself. The long day would prove to be very hot and uncomfortable for you, so, just put it out of your head once and for all."

What tomorrow was going to prove was that Bailey was not a meek and obedient little mouse to be ordered about by the likes of Cole Leighton. She had a gold ring that would easily pay her passage to the Colonies and she made a silent vow that she would be well on her way home before Cole returned to his empty cabin.

Chapter Eleven

Cole woke and studied Bailey's sleeping form as the first stirrings of morning tinted the cabin with a pale light. She lay on her side curled up, her knees against Cole's thighs, her right forearm flat against his chest. Her hand was small and light against his tanned skin, her fingers splayed over his heart. Thick brown lashes nearly disappeared against the backdrop of the dark bruise that rimmed her eye and cheek. The strip of cloth wrapped around her throat had a thin brown stain of blood marring its stark whiteness.

She would bear a scar from the vicious cut—a mark to remind her for the rest of her life what the Dragon had done to her. Such a flaw might be seen as destructive to the fragile beauty of most women of the day, but that would not be true of Bailey. There was a vibrancy about her, a grace and natural sensuality that was as much a part of her as her stubborn determination. He lay with his face close to hers and noticed how she lacked the milky-white complexion of upper-class women. Ladies who appeared gaunt and drawn, especially when they powdered and twisted their hair up into the impossible styles of the day.

If his mother hadn't forever quelled his capacity to love, then he imagined Bailey might be the kind of woman he would be drawn to. Even as the errant thought occurred to him, he cursed himself for his weakness. There was a time when he had entertained the possibility of a future with a wife and family. But he was much younger then. And untarnished by the truth. Once enlightened, he had banished such fanciful myths and had never since been bothered by false promises of things that were not to be. His path had been firmly set, his heart was cold and he would be a fool to trust another woman.

He recited that silently to himself again and again, as one might a well-loved poem. All too soon, Bailey's eyelids fluttered and she sighed, her full lips parting as she started to come awake. Cole stayed still, waiting for her to blush with hot anger or bolt from the bed, but she did neither. Her eyes were wide and he could see dark flecks that were more green than blue, giving their depths all the hues within the shallows of the Caribbean Sea. The scent of lavender clung to her, filling his nose. Her delicate palm seemed to brand his chest. The impulse overtook him before he could reconcile his body with his brain, his lips touched hers. Softly, barely a taste, but enough to spark a desire for more. He steeled himself against a persuasive and growing need and reluctantly drew back.

To his wonder, she leaned into him, her moist lips meeting his again, but remaining still, unsure, as her warm exhale caressed his mouth. Desire like he had never known blindsided him and he took over then, deepening the kiss, coaxing her mouth open gently, as if the fragile moment could be shattered by anything more forceful. The slightest moan escaped from her throat and as he felt her body soften, his own hardened and throbbed with need. His tongue swept inside her mouth, flicking, teasing and he felt her tremble against him. Her sleepy, unguarded acceptance rendered him defenseless and he gave in to it fully, slanting his mouth hard across hers in total possession of her lips.

Suddenly, she cried out and jerked away, pressing her fingers to the swollen cut on her lip. Cole cursed out loud for his unintentional roughness, but more for the complete loss of control that had led him to such a regretful act in the first place. Damn it, he had sworn he wouldn't let it happen again.

Sworn he felt nothing for her.

He rolled from the bunk, grabbed his shirt from the back of the chair scooped up his boots and withdrew from the cabin before either of them could utter a word.

A brisk wind filled the sails as Cole inhaled the tangy morning air. He stood with his legs braced apart as the *Barracuda* skimmed along, slicing the calm surface, peeling layers of white-tipped waves away from her hull. The leagues fell away behind them with ease, unlike the unease that bore down on Cole with a relentless hold.

He couldn't shake the kiss from his mind. Nearly an hour had passed since he'd left her, but it was as if he could still feel the soft tremble of her lips on his own. Could still smell the lavender of her skin and the spicy scent of her tangled hair clinging to him. His body still felt tight, every muscle alert, every nerve aroused. He couldn't remember ever feeling so physically lured by a woman. He had been out of control, not like last night when he'd had her backed against the table. He'd been in complete control then, teasing her desire to the surface. Daring her to kiss him. He had done it only to prove to himself she was like every other woman—innocent or not. But his thoughtless flirtation had backfired and he was paying for it with a good deal of physical discomfort this morning.

Not to mention the inkling of guilt that would not ease up.

"Bloody hell," he muttered, rubbing his fingers and thumb hard against his tired eyes. He wished he could rub the memory of last night away, too. He had revealed so much of himself to her—more than he had confided to anyone, except Cisco, in many long years.

Emotional ammunition. That's what he'd given her. Damn

his eyes for his carelessness. It was only a matter of time before she tried to hurt him with what he'd told her. They always did.

"That's no way to greet a man who's only come to inquire on the health of his captain," Cisco quipped as he approached Cole on the raised platform. "I expected you to be abed late this morn. *La señorita,* she didn't warm up to you, eh?"

Cole slid his first mate a black look but made no effort to reply.

"I can see she did not claw out your eyes, or slip a blade in your back. Maybe that is as friendly as she gets. Who would have believed it? A living, breathing woman who's not reduced to a quivering mass in the presence of Colby Leighton. Could it be she doesn't find you so *guapo?* No, can't be. Maybe she feels simple next to you. Most women aren't used to men as pretty as you," he said and laughed.

"There's nothing simple about her," Cole replied before he could help himself.

"What exactly happened between you and your warrior?"

Cisco's grin broadened but Cole put up a hand to stop him before he could start an inquisition. He didn't want to talk about the strange way Bailey was affecting him—the attraction that was growing stronger each time he was near her. He seemed to be losing a grip on the cool reserve that had become so much a part of him. But one thing was for certain: he had better get control of his simpering tongue when in the company of his opinionated friend, or he would never hear the end of it. He needed to change the subject. "I'm merely trying to figure out the best way to handle her."

"Handle her?"

Cole thumped the compass with his forefinger. "Nothing. Never mind."

"Oh, no, *mi amigo.* You spend one night with *the señorita,* and now I find you with a frown that would wither the devil himself. You have never had to figure out how to handle a woman before, they are usually more than happy to be handled. You are losing your touch, I think."

Cole had never cared for the fact that women seemed to find him beguiling. He certainly didn't prevail upon them to share his company, so if he was losing his touch, then he was pleased to hear it. "She is still angling to go ashore in New Providence and trade that ring for passage. I told her she cannot make a deal with pirates, but she is threatening to do just that if I don't take her home immediately. She is too stubborn for her own good."

"You of all people ought to recognize that fine trait. So, why not just accept the ring as payment and take her back? You will have your connection to the Dragon and she will be out from under your thin skin."

Cole ignored the barb. "It's true enough. I don't want to let that ring get away. But it might not be enough. I need something more. And I have it in her. I just have to figure out how best to use her."

"Cole, you are not thinking right. You are talking about the girl's life."

Cole shook his head but didn't reply. He knew Cisco was right. He was on the verge of going too far. But he could practically taste the sweet nectar of revenge easing away the bitterness that had burned on his tongue for so long. It would be so easy. Why the hell shouldn't he use her? She was nothing to him.

He continued the silent argument in his head as the *Barracuda* began to come to life and men began to emerge from below. One young bleary-eyed sailor ascended the ladder singing a bawdy tune in a low, rich voice, causing a trail of laughter to follow him as he made his way across the deck. Seeing his carefree expression, Cole realized he hadn't felt that way since he was a boy, fishing in the river or riding bareback across the lush fields of Rosegate with his brother. He had been forced to see the ugliness of the world—of people and of love—before he could even form his own opinions on such matters and he could never get his innocence back. The only thing that would satisfy him now was revenge.

"I could make it work, old man. You know I could. I wouldn't let her anywhere near that black-hearted bastard. All I have to do is prove that she is alive and that I have her."

He turned to Cisco and lowered his voice as much as the wind in the sails would allow. "Admit it. It's not a bad plan. I would wager my ship that it would lure him out," he said as casually as he could manage.

Cisco cocked his head, squinting his dark eyes in dubious contemplation. "Knowing that he left a victim alive has probably boiled his blood. I suspect he would do just about anything to remedy that damning blow to his reputation. Blackbeard is always complaining that he's going to have to do more than just light his whiskers on fire to be as feared as that bastard. The Dragon's ego would probably goad him to take your bait. Cole, I know you want this man, and I know you have no care for women. But I also know you would never let an innocent lay on the slaughtering block just to get what you want."

Cole huffed a sigh. "She's no lamb, and her tongue is too sharp for an innocent, but none of that is the point. She won't be in danger. In fact she is in more danger out there on her own, and if I can convince her of that, then she might even willingly cooperate. The sooner the Dragon is dead, the sooner she can go home. And I will finally be able to lay my father's soul to rest with honor."

"Honor!" Cisco slapped his huge palm against his lined forehead, then dragged his brown fingers down his face and through his beard. "Where is the honor in what you will do to the girl? This is not like you. No matter how bad things have gotten, you have never given up your honor, and I see no honor in this."

Cole inclined his head, feeling somewhat defeated and more than a little weary. "I know that. Don't you think I bloody know there's no honor in it? I don't care, old man. Do you understand? I devoted my life to killing that bastard and I've tried every honorable way to do it for the last five god-forsaken years. Now, fate has finally deemed to grant me an advantage. You think I'm going to let honor get in my way now? Honor has done nothing for me."

A long moment passed before Cisco blew out a sigh and turned to face Cole. "Then do what you must. And be assured that I will always be there to guard your back."

Cole nodded and swallowed hard against the strength of the emotion that kept him from responding to his unyieldingly loyal friend. But Cisco did not wait for an answer and was already off to see to the day's duties, leaving Cole alone to consider abandoning the only noble emotion he had left. All for the sake of retribution.

Chapter Twelve

Bailey bit her lip in a nervous gesture, then winced and pressed her fingers tenderly against the healing cut. She wanted to stay below and as far away from Cole as possible, but the tropical climate was turning the cabin into an oven. The sweltering heat had become stronger than the humiliation that filled her since he'd left so abruptly just after dawn.

Why had he seemed so angry? He had kissed her! In fact, if anyone should be angry, it should be she. The fact that she wasn't was a puzzle she didn't wish to solve, and she was running out of things to distract her mind in the stuffy cabin.

She climbed up the last step and with a steadying breath, emerged from the shadowed passageway into the bright sunshine. A light wind caressed her cheek and blew tendrils of hair free from the loose braid she had made and tied with a leather cord. She glanced around, trying not to be obvious as she searched the deck for Cole. She spotted him almost immediately, standing at the base of the mainmast, pulling on a heavy lanyard attached to the foresail. She recognized the sailor from the galley, Karl, and watched as he shimmied up the notched wood to work on the heavy mainsail.

Below the young man, Cole stepped back and called out orders to him and several bare-chested sailors working the

rigging and sails. Cole was devoid of a shirt as well, though
he looked nothing like the slim, wiry young men around him.
Standing a good head above the tallest of them, he was a for-
midable sight, indeed. Thick tanned cords of muscle rippled
with each contraction, glistening with a thin layer of sweat.
His straight dark hair blew across his shoulders, in sweat-
damp strands, somehow making him appear less than decent.
She felt the familiar butterflies stirring inside her and wasted
no time in making her way as far from the men as possible.
That point turned out to be at the stern, where she was, bless-
edly, quite alone. She sat on a large crate and breathed in the
salty air, careful to keep her eyes averted from the object of
her disconcertment.

In the distance ahead, she could see the dark outline of land.

It must be New Providence, she thought as a shiver crawled
up her spine.

The pirate island. Fear bubbled up inside her at the possible dangers that awaited her. Perhaps her decision to go out
on her own was rash. Perhaps she should stay safely hidden
away on the *Barracuda*. But then she would have to face Cole
and she wasn't sure she had the courage.

He had left the cabin this morning as if he couldn't get
away from her fast enough. Lord, her behavior had been in-
excusably wanton. Inviting him to share the bunk had been a
serious error in judgment. She had convinced herself that the
storm had provided a sound reason and that she was only
acting out of concern for the captain. But this morning she
had known his attentions and did nothing to stop him. Instead, she found herself returning his kiss with a passion she
was not aware she possessed.

James had kissed her once—an entirely unsolicited kiss
that had caught her quite by surprise. It had been quick and
chaste. His kiss had not make her tingle from the inside out
and most certainly didn't make her want to kiss him back
the way she had kissed Cole.

When she awoke to find Cole watching her, it had unnerved her. But more than that, she felt a strange kind of excitement, a delicious stirring that welled up inside her. She felt paralyzed, and when he leaned in and his lips caressed hers like the wings of a butterfly, God's mercy, she could not move away. She didn't want to move away, and when he started to draw back, she found that she didn't want him to go. She wanted more of him, so she brazenly pressed against his body and gave her lips over to him. When he eagerly responded, taking possession of her mouth, she thought she would drown in the sheer pleasure of what she was feeling. Heaven help her, what was wrong with her? She had behaved no better than a cheap tavern hussy, and she regretted it with every bit of her being. That kiss had tortured her thoughts for the entire morning as she had performed her toilette and then righted the storm-tossed cabin. That kiss—and the brooding, rogue of a captain who was responsible for these alarming sensations.

Was he attempting to manipulate her feelings so she would follow his orders? She was certain he was capable of it. But did his disdain for women run so deep that kissing her had been too much for him? Was that why he had left angry? Or was it her? She was undeniably innocent. Had she done something wrong? Oh, she could go mad trying to figure him out! Cole was a complicated man, full of secrets, and a darkness that lurked in his shadowed mind that she was beginning to believe would make him do anything to get what he wanted. And what he wanted was the Dragon. Yes, she was beginning to realize with startling clarity that Cole would do whatever it took to find his enemy. And she was his only link to the pirate. So if he thought kissing her would help him, then he would lower himself to the task. That stark realization stung.

Oh, why couldn't she break free from thoughts of him, even for a moment? He was invading her mind with as much quiet force as he ran his ship. She was beginning to fear that

Cole Leighton was more dangerous to her than anything she had yet endured.

She sighed. "Oh, stop being such a nit. He is just a man. He has no magic power over me," she chided herself. Still, she knew the only way to truly put him out of her mind was to get away from him.

Today.

She pulled the ring out of her shirt and examined the gold *L* as it caught the sunlight and tried to imagine Cole's mother. Did she have the same silver eyes? Had she been a raven-haired beauty in her youth? Did she have the same menace brewing deep within her—and was that what had led her to kill Cole's father? Bailey wondered if Cole had that same uncontrolled fury inside him. How far could she push him before she saw the worst of it?

She shivered, though the morning air already held an oppressive heat. Nerves fluttered to life in her stomach as she began to think about leaving the *Barracuda* and making her own way on New Providence. Her only hope would be one of the English ships Lew had told her about. She said a quick prayer that luck would be on her side. The emerald outline of land was rapidly expanding in size. She had to think of a way to slip away from the dark captain.

"You look so serious, Bailey. What are you thinking about?"

She startled at the gruffness in his deep voice, barely hearing the question. How had he managed to sneak up on her?

"I . . . What?" She dropped the ring back inside the open neck of her shirt. She couldn't risk him demanding it back, it was her only hope.

"I asked what has you in such a deeply thoughtful state. You seem . . . unsettled." He leaned back, his tanned elbows resting on the rail, and stared out across the ship.

Her cheeks flamed. It probably appeared to him that she was upset about the way he had callously left her this morning. The arrogant cad. "Oh," she smiled weakly and tried to sound nonchalant, though her heart was thrumming heavily and she felt oddly short of breath. "I was thinking about home."

He nodded, though his expression looked less than convinced. "Beaufort."

"Yes, Beaufort. And my family." She was having trouble concentrating. He had put on a white shirt, worn open to the waist, the sleeves rolled carelessly up to his elbows. His morning toilet must have consisted of dumping a bucket of water over his head, she noted in vexation. Several droplets of water covered his chest and the ripples of his stomach. His wet dark hair was slicked back in a queue, the sun reflecting it like liquid. Tan breeches clung to his legs, his thigh muscles seeming to strain against the fabric. No gentleman would ever dare to be seen in such a state of . . . of . . . indecency. But despite her limited knowledge of propriety, she couldn't convince herself that he truly looked indecent. In fact, the hard silver gleam in his eyes and the dangerous set of his jaw only made him seem that much more handsome. And he didn't seem the least aware of his appeal. Suddenly she realized she was holding her breath and she turned away, gulping in a draft of air.

"Mmm-hmm. Right. And James."

Looking back at his profile, she could fathom nothing from the strange tone in his voice. He was such a guarded man, with brooding, dark traits he seemed to wear as well as his own skin. Was one of those dark traits the ability to see into her soul? She prayed not.

"Bailey, we have to talk."

She swung her head back to find his eyes fixed on her, silver flecks lit by sunlight, holding her gaze hostage. He was going to apologize for the kiss.

He dipped his head toward her. "I'll be going ashore tonight."

She worked to hide her surprise. He seemed to have forgotten it had even happened. Well, then, so could she. "We reach the island tonight?"

"Yes, we do. And you must stay onboard while I make inquiries. It's not safe for you to be seen. People would want to know who you are."

She had expected him to order her, command her obedience, but he was speaking to her most reasonably.

She nodded weakly. A wave of guilt rushed over her, knowing that from here on out, everything she said to him would likely be some form of a lie. But she had no choice—she had only herself to rely on. He had said as much himself.

His intense gaze held her for what seemed an eternity, sending a delicious shiver through her, as if he had physically touched her. She could not break the contact, though she needed desperately to draw a breath. Finally, he released her, looking over her shoulder across the water.

"Good. So I have your promise that you will do exactly as I say—"

She cast her eyes downward, unable to form the words that would convince him she would obey.

"Bailey," he drawled out in a warning tone. "You *will* stay on the *Barracuda,* out of sight, until I return. Understood?"

She nodded again, but her thoughts were marred by doubt and mistrust. Doubts about her own abilities to get herself out of this mess and mistrust toward this man at her side who could very well be using her to meet his own goals.

"I have your word, then? You'll stay put—you won't give me any reason to lock you in my quarters?"

An unwelcome heat rushed to her cheeks. "You wouldn't dare!"

"Oh, but I would. I would tie you to the bunk, lock you in and post a guard at the door, if I felt it was warranted."

She wanted to scream at him, shove him overboard and watch that arrogant expression get washed off his face while he sputtered in the crystal-blue water below. That thought gave her a small amount of satisfaction. At least enough to keep her from choking on the distasteful lie she was about to tell.

"Of course you have my word, for mercy's sake," she said, feeling only the slightest twinge of guilt.

"Good enough. It's for the best, Bailey, that you see the wisdom in not defying me. You are too naive by far, and would only end up in dire circumstances if you had thought to go ashore on your own."

Until now. Now she didn't even feel the twinge. And when he raised that dark brow and that cocky grin slipped onto his lips, she felt positive she had made the right decision: to leave the arrogant Captain Leighton as soon as they reached New Providence.

Yes, she would leave him far, far behind and she would never look back.

The afternoon hours dragged with little to do other than watch the speck of land in the distance. The wind had died and the *Barracuda* was making slow progress. Sailors gathered about, playing loo or other card games, smoking or trying to nap in the hot sun. She strolled absently, trailing her hand along the rail, deep in thought. She came across Lew, who seemed pleased enough to talk to her, until he suddenly made an excuse and hurried away. She turned and saw Cole on the quarterdeck, watching her, his arms draped casually over the railing. She had felt trapped by his gaze all morning and decided she'd had enough. She refused to let him claim her, even if his possessiveness was all in her mind.

She sent him a charming smile, hoping to shame him into looking away.

He winked at her.

Her heart skipped and she gasped. She should have known—the man had no shame. Suddenly, she felt exhausted. She would need to be rested when they reached the island, so she went below for a nap.

Rhythmic creaking and metallic clinking of hooks and

pulleys lulled her and she drifted off feeling a little more confident. But once sleep claimed her, she had no control over the dreams. Dreams of her silver-eyed captain, his strong arms wrapped around her waist, his breath in her ear as he whispered her name. The feeling of pleasure that spread up from somewhere deep in her belly when he turned her face-up for a kiss that swept the breath from her lungs. The kiss ended too soon, but an intoxicating feeling lingered and she let her dark captain pull her along by the hand into a dense gray fog. He didn't offer any words of reassurance, but she didn't need them. She felt safe with him, safer than she could ever remember. They neared the edge of the concealing fog and walked into a clear, starlit night, the sky a strange but lovely shade of purple. Her captain turned and gently kissed her, then took her hands in his.

"Trust me. I'll keep you safe."

He whispered the words over and over as he slipped his mother's ring from around her neck, then nudged her forward. She took a few steps and could just make out a beautiful colored light glowing far in the distance. Glancing back, she found the captain had disappeared, but she could still hear his voice echoing low from the fog.

"Trust me. Trust me."

The golden-red light beckoned and she ran toward it, eager to discover the origin of such beauty. She was upon it in no time, the glow becoming so bright she had to shield her eyes. When she lowered her arm she was nearly engulfed in blood-red flames. At the center of the fire was her home and she could hear the agonizing screams coming from within. She tried to run to the house, but her legs wouldn't budge from the thick sand that sucked at her ankles. Harsh laughter rang in her ears and she watched in horror as the Dragon walked out of the fire, flames falling off his body like droplets of water as he stalked toward her, closer . . . closer . . .

Bailey woke with a scream strangling in her throat. Her

eyes darted about the cabin as she reoriented herself with her surroundings, letting the nightmare fade and her racing heart return to a normal rhythm. The last light of dusk filtered through the salt-spattered porthole, its rosy hue helping ease the cold fear of her dream. Nervous excitement rose up to fuel her tired limbs. She sprang from the bunk and splashed her face, but then had to stop herself from rushing out of the cabin and up on deck. For once she heeded the warning her father had so often offered about her tendency to rush into fires without so much as a pail of water in hand. She had to admit, though with fondness, that she had inherited her mother's impetuous nature. As she paced the cabin, she promised herself that from this moment forward, she would think carefully before acting. She had no idea of what she might face on the island, but she was fully aware that things would be very different from what she had ever experienced. Hopefully, that knowledge would be enough to keep her cautious and out of harm's way.

Marcel knocked and called out a warm greeting as he entered the cabin, leaving her with a meal of biscuits, honeyed ham and wine. She ate as much as she could stand and then folded the leftover biscuits in a square of linen to take with her. She tucked her napkin under the single pillow on the bunk, smoothed the wrinkles from her breeches and left the cabin in what she hoped appeared to be a dispassionate pace.

Lew and Miles greeted Bailey, then rushed off in different directions. In fact, the deck of the *Barracuda* was buzzing with activity. All hands prepared for their slow entry into the more shallow water, with its many dangerous reefs and shoals.

Shielding her eyes from the brilliant orange sun on the horizon, she could just make out two sailors in the rigging, pulling on lines and wrapping sails, while another shouted orders from the deck. The giant bearded man she had seen on deck that first day tipped his head, then winked as he strode past her. There was nothing insulting about the gesture, in fact, it seemed almost friendly, which both surprised and confused her. She didn't have time to ponder the matter further when she spotted Cole coming her way.

Her breath caught at the sight of him, stalking toward her with long strides, the muscles in his thighs flexing against white breeches that contrasted nicely with his tall black boots. He wore a black shirt, open to the waist, the sleeves billowing carelessly in the breeze. A large gold cross encrusted with rubies hung on a thick chain to the center of his chest. A deep-purple sash was tied loosely at his waist and a leather scabbard slung across his hips sheathed a long sword with an intricately carved hilt. Another carved hilt, this one silver, was visible just at the side of his knee, hiding some kind of knife blade on the inside of the boot. His shiny black hair was partially hidden underneath a black scarf that was tied about his head, emphasizing the fine angles of his jaw and the bright silver light in his eyes. Eyes that were locked on her in a mesmerizing grip that she was unable or unwilling to break. He looked just like . . . a pirate, she thought with unease.

Despite her distaste at that thought, she knew she would never look upon a man so striking as him if she lived to be a hundred years old. As he approached, one side of his mouth lifted in a crooked, yet thoroughly arrogant grin, as if he had caught her with her fingers in the honeypot.

"What I would give to know your thoughts right now, Bailey." One crescent-shaped dimple poked into the side of his mouth and she felt her face ignite. Heaven help her, why couldn't she control her reaction to him? So he was handsome. So what? No, not handsome.

Magnificent. And he knew it, the beast.

"I am horrified. You look just like one of those bloodthirsty outlaws. I hope you are pleased with yourself."

"Thank you. I am."

"But, you're not a . . . Are you one of them?" she asked, her voice rising a pitch.

"I told you I'm not. But it helps to look a bit more like the locals when I'm here. Puts them at ease. The only gentlemen planters they ever see are bound and gagged and usually being held for ransom."

"Oh. So, is that what you are? A planter?"

"You left out 'gentleman.'"

"No, I didn't. That is a matter of opinion."

He laughed. A rich, full, deep laugh that accentuated his intrepid good looks. It was a pleasant sound that sent gooseflesh across her skin.

"So, am I to understand my appearance does not meet with your approval?"

She bristled at the humor in his tone, embarrassed at her unabashed ogling of him. "I didn't realize my approval was so important to you, Captain Leighton."

"Ah, but that is my problem, you see. Certain things about you are beginning to become important to me."

Her heart skipped. Had his kisses meant something, after all? "Is that an attempt to charm me? Because if it is, Captain, then I will save you the trouble straight away." Ignoring his droll chuckle, she turned to him, tilting her face up to look directly in his mocking eyes. Oh, how she wished those haunting gray eyes didn't affect her so. She needed to think of nothing but how she was going to get away from him. "I know exactly where your interest lies." She was bluffing, of course, but perhaps he would say something to give away his intentions.

One ebony brow arched as he crossed his arms over his chest and a warning seemed to issue forth from the tight line of his mouth.

"Do you, now?" he drawled. "Go on."

"You don't want me to go ashore because no matter what, you would lose. If I find the Royal Navy, I go home. But even if I was killed, you would lose your means of luring the Dragon to you. That is what you care about. That is why you want me to stay hidden. Isn't it? What is it you have planned, Cole? If you find the Dragon, do you plan to tell him you have me? Will you turn me over to him? Or perhaps you will merely dangle me from the mainmast, like a mouse before a starving hawk."

"Don't push me, Bailey."

"If I could be taken so easily, what about you?"

"Worried for me, Bailey? Or just hoping to be free of me?"

She actually hadn't considered it until this very moment. What would become of her if something happened to him?

"Believe me," he said, "I'll fare better than you would. I've done this before, Bailey, the pirates are used to me."

"Why do they let you come here? Why would they ever tell you where the Dragon is? Isn't it a huge risk?"

"I suppose it is." He shrugged. "But I pay well for good information. Pirates lose their strength when they are separated. Loyalty is a fleeting trait among thieves."

"But if he is there, won't he hear that you have arrived?"

"Yes, most likely."

"He would kill you!"

"He would try."

"How can you smile like that? Are you not afraid to die?"

"Afraid? Not in the least." His laugh was caustic. "He has already done his worst. Death is just death. No, I am not afraid of the Dragon. But do you see now why it would be pure foolishness for me to take you ashore?"

"Yes," she answered honestly. Going ashore with him would be a terrible mistake. He was living on the very edge of reason—what type of person didn't care whether they lived or died? No, she must go ashore alone, but only if she saw English ships in port. Let the pirates' attention be on him, she would surely be safer that way.

"Good. Then I won't have to tie you to my bunk?"

"N—No!" she gasped.

"Fine. Don't make me regret trusting you, Bailey. I promise you will like me even less if you betray me."

She gave a half-nod. She had no idea what that meant, but from his dire expression, she prayed she would never know. But he was asking for too much. He said he was trusting her, but he had admitted he was incapable of it. He expected her to blindly trust him. But even if she did, she had no assurances of her safety if Cole got himself killed. God, she couldn't let herself think of that. No one would expect her to depend on Cole under these circumstances, and no one would blame her for breaking her word to him. She could not think of a soul who would agree to such a thing.

"It looks beautiful," she said, anxious to change the subject.

"Aye. That is Nassau. The town of New Providence will be coming into view soon."

"It looks so peaceful from here."

"It's deceptive. When we get closer, you'll see that the nature here is no match for the pirates and their way of life."

"You mean they don't take care of the island?"

"They do as little as they possibly can to get by. They don't worry about next year or even tomorrow—for a lot of them there are very few tomorrows left."

"Where do they live?"

"Mostly in tents, but there are some crudely built shanties as well. The town is dirty, unkempt, just like the pirates and their families."

"Families? You mean there are children here, too?"

"Yes. Some."

"And marriage?"

"There are a few. There are some marriages, so to speak, but for the most part there's a lot of fighting over who belongs to whom and very little fidelity from either men or women. Some of the women were hostages taken during attacks and for whatever reason were never ransomed. They are just trying to make the best of their situations."

"How can anyone live that way?"

"For many of them, it's all they know. Or it's at least a better life than they've had before." He gently pulled the wide collar of her borrowed shirt out from where it had gotten blown inside her neckline by the wind. His fingers were warm against her skin and she felt her pulse quicken at his touch.

Bailey sighed, reflecting on how simple her life had been in comparison. Her daily chores that went on from dawn until dusk didn't seem nearly as tiresome when she thought about the constant perils and conflicts that seemed commonplace on that small bit of land ahead. Cole made it sound like a strange world all unto itself. She gazed at the brilliant green fringe lined by a sparkling white sand border and wondered if he was right. She had never been far outside of Beaufort, so she didn't know much about strange lands other than what she'd read in books.

"We'll be docking in a couple of hours. It won't be quite dark, so it will be best if you go below as soon as we approach the mooring."

She nodded, at a loss for what to say. Cole had no way of knowing this might be their last conversation. But even if he had, she knew he wouldn't feel the same sense of loss—that tiny nit of regret that she was feeling. She looked at his face, trying to memorize every fleck of silver in his eyes, the thick, straight line of his eyebrows, the unyielding set of his stubbled jaw. Those lips. She knew she would never forget those lips. And how they felt against hers.

Despite the puzzlement on his face, he said nothing. She dropped her gaze and turned to stroll along the starboard side of the ship. She tried to turn her thoughts to Beaufort. To rebuilding her life. A rebuilding that would happen with James. Once they were together, James would be the one to kiss her. The only one. And he would make her forget her brief, turbulent encounter with the dark Colby Leighton.

Chapter Thirteen

Bailey strained to see through the salt clinging to the porthole, but all she could make out from her vantage point was the tiniest strip of beach and forest that appeared to be completely deserted. She needed to be on deck, to get a better idea of what to expect. She also wanted to watch Cole depart the ship, so she'd know which direction not to go in, lest she run smack into him. Oh, she could just imagine if he caught her. His arms would bulge, folded tight across his wide chest, his dark head would be cocked, his brows lowered over narrowed eyes the color of a thundercloud, shooting blades in her direction. But really, what could he do? Drag her back to the ship by her hair? Not likely. She knew he wanted to avoid any undue attention and dragging a screaming woman through the streets would definitely garner many unwanted stares.

She smiled at the thought. For all of the confidence and commanding authority that rose about him like morning mist, he really had no control over her. Not as long as she refused to allow it. And she wouldn't.

With that bit of bravado driving her, she tiptoed to the door and turned the knob. The smooth brass moved slightly to the right and then stopped dead.

No! He didn't! she thought in dismay.

She jiggled the knob back and forth with all her might, but it held fast. That was the faint click she thought she heard when he'd left. He had locked her in!

Fuming, she raised her fists to pound the polished oak to the ground, but stopped herself before she landed the first blow. If there was anyone onboard, she didn't want them to think she was being held against her will. Even if one of the crew was aware that she was locked in, she must pretend that she was going along with it for her own safety. But she must find a way to get out of here.

She only had to call out twice before she heard footsteps hurrying down the ladder.

"Miss? You all right in there?"

"I beg your pardon. I know you must have more important matters to attend to, but it is terribly stuffy in here."

"Sorry 'bout that, but I don't think I can do nothin' about it. I'm not supposed to let you out."

"No, no, I understand. Oh, I do apologize, I'm sure you'd much rather be off on the island, rather than stuck here with me. It's just that . . ." She let the volume of her voice deliberately trail off.

"What's that, miss? I can't hear you so good. Hold on a minute."

She heard the key turn in the lock and rushed to sit on the window seat, affecting a composed posture while fanning herself with a folded piece of parchment.

"Crikey! It's hot as hellfire in here."

"Aye, it is, Karl." She recognized the young blond sailor she'd met in the galley and smiled inwardly at her good luck. He seemed shy and eager to please when he was around her. "I understand it's for my safety that I stay hidden. It's just that I'm feeling a little queasy."

He nodded, momentarily distracted by the open neck of her shirt. She swallowed her embarrassment, and decided that just this once, it would be all right to use her wiles to her favor.

"It might help to have a cool drink. I think Marcel has some lemons left. I know how to make a wonderful drink with lemons and sugar. I'd be happy to make us both one, if you think we can spare a small amount of water. Does that sound all right?"

He looked interested, so she pushed on. "We haven't had much of a chance to talk." She smiled encouragingly.

"Nay, miss," he answered with a returning grin.

"Why don't I go to the galley and get everything ready? Then I'll bring the drinks back here. You could go finish up whatever task you were doing and I'll call for you when I'm ready."

She got up and walked out into the corridor, as if she had all the confidence that he wouldn't think of stopping her. As she entered the open doorway of the galley, her heart was pounding fast, but she looked back at him, following, and smiled. "Just go about your duties and don't let me be a bother. I'll be ready soon."

"I'd rather stay with you. I can help," he said.

She dismissed the odd glint in his eye as harmless flirtation.

"Uh, that would be nice." She hadn't counted on that, but she couldn't refuse or do anything else to make him suspicious.

Bailey busied herself with the motions of slicing the lemons and mixing them with a pitcher of fresh, tepid water. She thought for an instant of the knife she held. Could she use it on Karl? Could she injure him just enough for her to make her escape? Never, she realized, the mere idea unthinkable.

"You sure are pretty, miss. I thought so right away that first day I saw you on deck with the captain . . ."

His voice faded, as if he realized he was about to embarrass her.

"You are very kind to say so, Karl." She was starting to feel uncomfortable. The tiny space in the galley felt barely large enough for the two of them, and the heat was beginning to truly make her nauseous.

"If you don't mind me sayin' so, miss . . ."

She stopped slicing and turned to listen to him, the knife poised unintentionally in front of her. Karl reached forward and gently pressed on her wrist to angle the blade away from him.

"Oh! I'm terribly sorry." She put down the knife.

"You don't wanna be here, do you?"

"No, not really. I'm aboard the *Barracuda* quite by accident, I'm afraid."

"Well, I don't think what the cap'n is doin' to you is right. An' I think he's puttin' you in danger. He's selfish. It ain't right to keep you from yer family."

"But what can I do, Karl? I would like nothing better than to disembark, but Captain Leighton has ordered me to stay on the ship." A flutter of excitement ran through her. Could she get Karl to let her go?

"Well," he drawled, as if considering what to do. "I know the island pretty good. And I seen a couple of the Royal Navy's ships docked on the other side of the island when we sailed in. I bet one o' them would take you back to North Carolina in a hurry."

Bailey gasped, unable to hide her excitement. "You did? Truly? Oh, Karl, would you take me to one of them? Please?"

"I don't know. If the cap'n ever found out, he'd skin my hide but good. He'd put me off the ship an' I'd have nowhere to go."

"I would never say a word, Karl. You could say that I escaped without your knowledge. You can't possibly watch every inch of the ship at every moment. How could he hold you responsible?"

"I guess we could make it look like you got away by yerself."

"Oh, Karl, thank you! Thank you!" she said, clapping her hands together.

Everything is going to be all right, she thought, handing a mug to Karl. Nothing could go wrong now.

* * *

Up on deck, Bailey realized that getting off the *Barracuda* wouldn't be as difficult as she thought, even if she didn't have Karl to assist her. There were many people buzzing about the docks, just like any other busy port would have. Though she had to admit the odd and exceedingly bright clothing the people wore was out of the ordinary. In the dusky light, she could see the majority of people engrossed in something down the dock to her right. A crowd had formed there, where a large merchant vessel was just easing into a berth. Some of the ship's square sails were tattered and hanging limp from broken yards that swayed like snapped tree limbs.

Men and women alike shouted to the ragged sailors on the damaged vessel, who returned the greetings with whoops and yells of their own. Some of the men onboard were bandaged, and most were filthy, covered with black soot from head to toe, but all were celebrating as if they'd returned victorious from a great battle. Then her eye caught sight of the white skull and crossed swords on the red flag dangling from the cracked mainmast, and the situation became frighteningly clear and very real. They were pirates, and that was what a ship full of the wild brigands looked like. A shiver crossed over her, raising bumps on her skin, despite the evening heat. She rubbed her arms and inhaled deeply to calm the knot of fear that had dropped like a stone to the pit of her stomach. She prayed it wouldn't take long to locate the English sailors.

In all her imaginings she could not have prepared herself for this. The night she was attacked there had been three pirates' voices at most, and the only one she actually saw was the Dragon himself. He had not looked like any of these men, and had not screamed and hollered as if the Devil was lighting his feet on fire. He had been dressed in black, masked down to his full lips and had moved quietly, with purpose and almost with grace. His voice had been rough but controlled and filled with deadly calm.

"Ready, miss?"

Karl's quiet approach startled her out of her trance. "Oh. Uh, yes, I am." She took a deep, steadying breath, shoving aside her doubts.

"Let's be off, then. If we get movin' while they're un-loadin', then we ain't likely to be seen."

"All right, let's go," she answered, bolstering her courage once again. She could hardly believe it. She'd soon be on her way home.

The knowledge that she would never see Cole again hurt more than she wanted to admit. The pangs of regret would fade, but the vision of him . . .

She would never be able to forget.

A short half hour later, Karl dragged the skiff out of the water and helped Bailey step from the small vessel. She stumbled the first few steps, as her legs adjusted to being on land for the first time in days. Karl glanced about, seeming nervous, then impatiently took her elbow and led her up the beach to a narrow path that disappeared into a dense forest. They walked along for what seemed a long time, stopping only once at a freshwater hole that Karl found with little difficulty. She brushed aside an odd feeling of trepidation at Karl's easy knowledge of the island. Of course he would know the island. Cole had said they were here often. *There's nothing to be concerned about,* she reminded herself. Loud calls of night birds echoed above them, and the heady scent of flowers drifted to her on the tropical breeze. Her excitement grew the farther they walked, because that meant she was getting closer and closer to the Royal Navy's officers. And home.

But then, why couldn't she shake the dread that remained in the back of her mind? It made no sense, but something didn't feel quite right. She decided she was just feeling guilty about lying. It was not commonplace for her to tell so many lies, and it seemed that in the last few days, she had told one after the other. She was certain God would forgive her, since she wasn't hurting anyone with her lies. She was only trying to protect herself.

The path began to widen, and up ahead Bailey could see several tents set up and a few small fires burning near them. Even from here she could also see that many of the tents were torn and filthy. But the welcoming smell of roasting meat drifted to her nose, giving the scene a more cozy appeal.

As they left the path and walked into the open field, four women hailed Karl and rose from their place by one of the fires, heading toward them. Bailey turned to ask Karl who they were, and why they looked so ragged and worn, but she never got the words out. Karl grabbed her and roughly shoved a small vile of liquid between her parted lips. She started to choke on a scream until he silenced her by forcing her mouth closed. Despite her intuition not to, she was forced to swallow the liquid or choke further. One hand held her in a punishing grip, his face having lost all signs of the boyish charm she had seen earlier. His other hand left her mouth and moved to her breast, brutally squeezing until she screamed. Her head was beginning to spin wildy, the earth and sky swirling together as if they were one. She tried to focus on his narrow brown eyes, and as he spoke, she felt as though she might become sick.

"Yer gonna bring me riches way beyond what I'm gonna need to quit breakin' my bloody ass on that damn ship of his. High and mighty, he thinks he is, but he ain't shit. What kinda stupid fool would leave a well-to-do plantation to go pirate huntin'? He can have 'em, but I ain't gonna take his orders no more. I got plans to sign up with Captain Edward Low. We're gonna be the richest pirates of all. I been waitin' a long time for my chance, Miss Spencer, and I got you to thank. So, thanks," he finished, then dipped his head to lick her from her chin to her nose.

Nausea overwhelmed Bailey, her confused, fuzzy mind trying to grasp what was happening. Sweet Mary, how could she have been so gullible? She wanted to get home so desperately, she willingly traipsed off with a boy—no, a man—she knew less about than the man she had been trying to escape. Her limbs felt heavy, numb, and as she started to slump to her knees, she heard loud cackling laughter and ribald feminine voices behind her. It must be the women she had seen approaching them a moment before. All hope of their helping her dissolved as she felt herself being grabbed by one or more of them as Karl pushed her away from him. Somewhere in the haze of her mind, she heard him ask for his payment and heard one of the voices respond. He reached over her to retrieve some kind of pouch and then she heard him laugh as he thanked the women.

"Don't worry, miss. These good ladies'll find you a fine new home," he whispered in her ear, then laughed a frightening, promise-filled laugh. She watched the traitorous fiend walk into the forest, back toward the *Barracuda*. Her last thought before she lost her fight to stay conscious was of Cole. Would he care that she was gone? Of course. She was his only link to the Dragon. He would come, if only to use her for his own purposes. *God,* she prayed, *please let him come.*

"Get up, ye lazy chit!"

"Lizzy, you know it ain't the lazy bug, is the laudanum bug that's bit her."

Bailey started to come around and through a sluggish haze, she heard one of the women saying something about a bug. She tried to make sense of it in her fog-thickened mind, but their grating laughter increased her confusion, making it hard to think at all. She opened her eyes, then groaned and squeezed them shut against the blinding morning sun. She wanted to rub the cold clamminess from her skin, but for some reason her arms wouldn't budge. They seemed to be stuck behind her back. She struggled to sit up and found herself being wrenched painfully to her feet by her shoulders. A strange taste had settled in the back of her mouth and though her sight was blurry, she was able to make out two women standing in front of her smiling like tomcats. She tried to move her arms again when one of them stepped forward and leaned in close to her ear.

"You ain't gonna be able to get loose, chit. I tied them knots meself. Might as well get cozy."

Bailey tried to speak, to ask what was happening, but before she could finish the question, the one called Lizzy came around in front of her and slapped her hard across the mouth.

"Shut up, whore. We ain't got the time or the care to tell you what yer in for. If yer thinkin' to beg us to keep you, yer plain crazy. We ain't gonna let you steal away our men with yer soft skin and them fine tits. No sir, we ain't gonna share with the likes o' you."

"Aye, we don't want you here, bitch," another spit out.

"An' we know just how to get rid o' you fer good, don't we, Jane?" Lizzy finished as Jane and the others began to laugh, causing a ringing in Bailey's ears.

The four women surrounded her, shoving from all sides, forcing her to walk. They followed a different path from the one she and Karl had come in on, leading away from the small camp into the palm-shaded woods. The smell of hibiscus and frangipani lay heavy in the still air. Bailey couldn't understand why she felt so dizzy. All she wanted to do was lie down and sleep. A brief flash of Karl's face swam before her, and she remembered the liquid he had forced down her throat. A wave of shame passed over her at her own stupidity. She had done this to herself. God help her, these women were going to get rid of her so she wouldn't steal their men? It was almost too ludicrous to imagine! If only she could explain to them what had happened to her, but her confused mind wouldn't cooperate. All she could do was wonder where they were taking her and what they planned to do to her. Perhaps she could bargain her way out . . . She tried to blink away the haze and looked down for the leather cord around her neck. Her heart dropped.

The ring was gone!

Mercifully, her mind refused to focus and she absently listened to the shrieks of the strange birds from above. Suddenly, she realized the rushing noise she'd been hearing was the sound of the ocean to her right. She tried to sharpen her thoughts, trying to plan out a way to escape. The path beneath her bare feet began to soften, the hard branches and forest debris giving way to pearly sand. They left the woods and came out onto a narrow, cluttered street that was all but deserted. Several more turns and shortcuts through alleyways behind ramshackle buildings finally brought them out on what appeared to be the main street.

The smell of too many unclean bodies mixed with the tang of animals and their droppings, the dust hanging over everything like an ivory cloud.

Lizzy grabbed Bailey's elbow and dragged her through a throng of men and women, dressed in the gaudiest array of dirty, torn finery she could imagine. As they neared the front, Bailey realized with horror the reason for the crowd. Before her stood a platform with several crude posts anchored into roughly cut holes. On each of the poles were two sets of chains, one about midway up, the other at the bottom of each pole. Bailey gasped at the sight of people shackled in the chains, some by the wrist, others by the ankle. There was one set of chains not yet occupied and Bailey felt the bile rise in her throat as she was dragged toward the platform.

Lizzy shoved her at a barrel-chested pirate with a huge scar pulling down one sightless eye. Bailey let out a terror-filled scream and began to fight in earnest. She twisted and pulled, trying to gain release, and when that didn't work she tried kicking her captor. Whoops and raucous laughter rose from the rowdy crowd as they encouraged her attack. The pirate's fingers dug cruelly into Bailey's arm. He held her and as he motioned to two young thugs behind him, she bent her head and bit his hand as hard as she could. The pirate hollered in pain and backhanded her to the ground with a curse.

"Take the bitch," he growled as the two others approached.

They yanked her to her feet and wrestled her up the rickety steps of the platform. Out of breath and reeling from the vicious hit, Bailey fought with all her remaining strength to break free before they could chain her. She cried out as one wrist was locked in the iron, thrashing and kicking to keep them from getting to her other wrist. The two pirates laughed along with the growing crowd, seeming to enjoy her resistance. They had been playing with her! And now, as if they were tired of their game, they bowed to the crowd. Then, one pirate jumped off the platform while the larger of the two wrenched her arm from behind her back and locked her other wrist in the heavy band of iron.

"All right, mates. Got a fresh one for ye. Young an' pretty she is."

Bailey fought the urge to throw up. She focused on the crowd, praying to see one of the sailors from the *Barracuda*.

"Show us more!" came a yell from the crowd.

"Aye, more! More!" echoed more voices.

"As you like, me fine brothers," the filthy pirate answered, stepping forward and ripping the front of Bailey's shirt with his grubby thick fingers.

She screamed and kicked at him hard, but did little damage in her bare feet. He laughed at the feeble effort. Thank goodness he had only been able to tear the material enough to fall off her shoulder. Though from the disgusting comments and rude stares, she may as well be naked.

"Aye, fine and feisty, mates. She be a live one, good for many a night's pleasure before ye tire of the wench. Come on, now, well worth a hefty sum, if I do say so. Who's got a bid?"

"I got a gold doubloon here that says the chit is mine."

"Two gold pieces an' a ruby earring," another voice rang out.

And so it went on for agonizing minutes that seemed more like hours. Bailey shut her eyes, trying to block it all out, willing herself to be anywhere but here—being sold as a slave. She knew of slavery, of course, but her family had been far from wealthy and had never owned any type of servant. The only place she had ever seen slaves had been at Lady Hawthorne's home, but somehow the reality of their situation had never really sunk in. But standing here, being shown like horseflesh, she had an inkling of the humiliation that went along with the unbelievably barbaric practice of buying and selling human beings. God help her, she had to get out of this. But how? Her head was still reeling from the mixture of whatever Karl had given her and the searing late-morning sun. She blinked hard to clear her eyes and spotted one man at the back of the crowd whose tall form stood well above the other men.

Her heart soared at the sight of him. He had found her, thank God!

Standing with his arms crossed over his chest, a sheen of sweat sparkling in the sun, Cole looked like a pirate god risen from the sea. He had never looked so powerful, so raw.

Or so angry.

His molten eyes were nearly slits with no sign of the usual silver sparkle and she shuddered at the fury she saw there. She had lied to him about staying on the *Barracuda* and now she was caught. She knew she owed him the grandest apology of all time, and she would gladly offer it as soon as she was liberated from this hellish nightmare.

She caught his eye and attempted to smile bravely through her trembling lips but he only glared at her in return. She supposed she deserved his anger and she would accept whatever harsh criticism he wished to offer, but couldn't he just hurry up and get her out of there?

The crowd was growing more rowdy as the bidding

increased and some of the men were shouting to see more of the "goods."

She held his eyes, her expression imploring him to help her, but she got no reaction. In fact the line of his mouth seemed to harden more. He turned to a wiry, raggedly dressed pirate and said something that made the old man laugh and then nod. Then, without as much as one last glance at her, he turned and walked away.

Chapter Fourteen

He left her! Good Lord, he actually turned and strolled away as if she was nothing to him. She couldn't believe his heart was so cold.

But it was.

She had seen it in his eyes just before he had turned and walked calmly away from her.

Yes, she had lied to him about staying put, but was he really so driven by his own pride? Even if he hated her for betraying him, didn't he still want to keep her to get the Dragon? It appeared not, because he had left her here to fend for herself. Yes, now she was truly all alone, her future uncertain at best, but despite how much she didn't want to, all she could think about was how Cole had just abandoned her. She wondered miserably if he was aware of who had taken her or where she was headed. She wondered if he cared a whit about what was going to happen to her.

A tear slipped down her cheek. She would give anything just to see his arrogant face again. Oh, she must be daft to have such thoughts!

Damn him. I hate him. I'm glad I will never have to lay eyes on that dreadful lout again.

He clearly had no goodness in his tarnished soul if he could leave her to the mercy of pirates and she would waste no more tears on him. She choked back her fear and despair, refusing to let her ravished dignity fall away completely as the rowdy crowd began to whoop and cheer at the generous sum that had just been offered for her. Heaven help her! Someone in the crowd had just succeeded in buying her. She would not let this happen! She would find a way to escape whoever it was, and she would do it without any help from Cole Leighton. The Devil could take him for all she cared! And if her prayers were answered, the Devil would gladly have him, and not only for the fact that he'd left her to the whims of these lawless thieves and cutthroats. She was sure the captain had committed more than enough sins to gain an uproarious entry into the fiery realm before she had ever crossed his path.

Simmering anger kept her strong through the next miserable minutes during which her wrists were unchained and retied with a length of hemp that was used to tug her forward and off the platform. She could do little to keep her torn shirt together, but at least with her arms pulled in front of her, she had a small allowance of modesty. Once on the ground, she caught a glimpse of the old wiry pirate the captain had spoken to. He was leering at her with a gap-toothed grin on his grizzled face.

Sensing someone coming up behind her, she turned her head, but too late to see the old pirate's accomplice. She was grabbed and blindfolded with a thick scarf and led a few steps away before being shoved to the ground and told to sit.

Oh, dear Lord, was the old man the one who had bought her? Really, what difference did it make which of these filthy riffraff took her? They were likely one as bad as the other. At least she might stand a chance to escape the old pirate, she thought. He was small and bony and looked as frail as old driftwood.

Hope began to rekindle in her. And as it did, so did the hurt she had felt when Cole had turned his back on her and walked away. She understood his anger at her disobedience, but could he really be that surprised? Wouldn't he have done the same thing in her situation? Of course he would have. In the short amount of time she had been with him, he had made it quite clear that his goal was the only thing that mattered. He'd also made it clear she was nothing more than a hindrance to him, so it was her own gullible nature that had her starting to believe that a small part of him actually liked her. Was he just pretending to be attracted to her when he kissed her? Deep down, she didn't think so.

Maybe he never intended to use her as bait. She suddenly felt very unsure of herself. Maybe he really had been prepared to take her home. How could she have been so wrong? It wasn't like her to judge so harshly, though she had had no problem thinking the worst of Cole. Then again, what kind of man would consider *this* a just punishment for telling a lie? Cole Leighton, that was who. At least one part of him. The one part who despised women—the one part who was leaving her here, to become the property of a pirate. And all she could think about was that she was never going to see him again.

That realization hit her like a blow to the stomach. Why, she couldn't fathom; after all, she had left the ship this morning knowing she would never lay eyes on the man again. But now that was a certainty, and it hurt. More than she cared to think about. How was it possible that such a ruthless, uncaring man could have her wishing that she was with him again?

No, she told herself firmly. It wasn't that she wished to be with him, it was just that she was scared. Scared about her current predicament. A predicament that needed her full attention if she was going to figure a way out of it.

She forced the dark captain from her mind as she blinked back tears that were forming behind her eyes. She was given no more time to ponder her fate, though, as she was roughly hauled to her feet by huge hands. She could feel the heat from the massive body in front of her, could smell the stale rum and old tobacco rising off him. It wasn't the wiry old pirate, these hands felt too meaty, too strong. Her head continued to spin and her stomach threatened to heave from the fear that engulfed her.

"Come on, wench. The master wants ye dressed like the rest of our fine ladies. Least til he wants ye dressed in nothin' at all." The smelly pirate laughed as he scooped her up and tossed her over his thick shoulder. She heard a thin voice in front of them call out the order to follow. The old pirate, she thought, hoping beyond hope that the giant who had her wouldn't be staying with them for long. She would have a hard time getting past him if he was as big as she thought he was. The giant started walking—long, heavy steps that jarred her teeth and bounced her about, causing great pain to her injured ribs. She bit her lip to keep from crying out and tried her best not to pass out.

Bailey woke on a scratchy, hard pallet feeling disoriented and suffering from a terrible pounding in her head. Where was she? What had that awful smelly pirate done, dropped her on her head? No, she remembered now. She'd been drugged by Karl, and dragged to the slave block by those wicked pirate women.

She groaned and eased herself to a sitting position, holding her ribs protectively, and surveyed her surroundings. She was in a small tent, held up by one crooked, rotted-looking wood stake in the center. The front was flipped open, allowing the small amount of the dusk light inside, though Bailey was sure she'd prefer to not be able to see about her. A small three-legged table nestled in the sand floor next to the pallet, covered with a strip of green-tassled velvet cloth. There was a silver lamp on the table that would have looked perfectly at home in the finest of drawing rooms, if not for the dents and chipped globe. A small mirror dangled by a length of hemp looped through a small hook affixed in the tent pole, catching the deep orange glow of sunlight among its cracks.

As she started to rise, the rustle of silk caught her attention. How had she not noticed her attire straight away? Someone had dressed her in the most gaudy gown she could ever have imagined. She stumbled over miles of red fabric as she hurried to stand up, and rushed to the mirror. Unable to hold back a gasp, she assessed herself in shock. The square neckline of the dress was indecently low, nearly exposing her breasts. The bodice was so tight that it only accentuated her cleavage more, pressing her skin into firm mounds above the black lace that lined the edge of the bodice. The stomacher was tied with black ribbon, the ends hanging all the way down the front of the red silk skirt. The fitted sleeves were elbow length, ending with layers of black silk and tied through with red ribbons that hung to her wrists. She reached down and fingered the multitiered petticoat made of black lace that matched the bodice, hardly able to believe her eyes. She had certainly never seen a gown like this on anyone in Beaufort, and she'd never been to London, where fashion was all the buzz, but she doubted this was an example of how fine English ladies dressed. No, this was the dress of a common doxie. Exactly what the pirate who'd paid for her would expect, Bailey thought miserably.

How was she going to fight or run with all this fabric enveloping her? Her own dresses were simple compared with this. Besides, she had become accustomed to the breeches and the freedom of movement they allowed. It would have been much easier to escape in Tom's clothing. But she wouldn't give up. She hadn't survived the Dragon's attack only to end up the property of one of his devil brethren.

Voices outside the tent drew her attention and she went to peer out of the opening.

She recognized two of the women who had taken her to the

slave block. They wore dresses that surpassed hers in brightness and ornament, to her complete amazement.

"We're here ta get the girl."

She started to duck back into the solitude of the tent, when a beefy, tattooed arm snuck out and grabbed her arm, pulling her out into the fading daylight. Was this the giant pirate who had carried her here from the platform? He smelled the same. She looked up into his deeply tanned face, heavily bearded and marked with scars. He grinned, revealing two gold teeth in the front of his mouth. His grip was like iron, though it seemed like no exertion in the least to him. Her heart sank. She would find it impossible to get away with this brute hovering about her. She would have to think of a way to outsmart him, as she would be no match for his strength or speed.

"Come on, chit. 'Tis a fine night fer a party, 'an you don't wanna miss it, now do ya?"

"Hope ye like the dress, missy. Lizzy don't like ta part with 'er finery. But yer new owner paid a pretty penny ta getcha outta them breeches, he did. Yer one lucky chit ta have a man like that ta take care a ya."

Lizzy snorted out a laugh. "Aw, Jane, you know she'll be takin' care o' him to pay it off, if ya know what I mean."

"I'm startin' to forget what ya mean," the woman called Jane whined. "I ain't had any pleasures since that bastard Doc gave me them bugs. The rest o' them cowards all scared they'll catch it. Don't be lookin' at me like that, wench. You'll be catchin' something, too, I promise ya that. With that fine face and them high tits, you'll get used up quicker than I was."

Both women laughed, as if they shared some kind of jest at Bailey's expense. But she understood perfectly well their crude insinuations. That decrepit, wrinkled pirate was not going to lay one bony finger on her! And just to show her lowlife companions what she thought about their assessment of her future, she picked up her skirts and stalked away from

them. Their cackling laughter followed her as all three made
their way toward the bright bonfire a ways down the beach.

The moon was still high in the sky, but already Bailey's
nerves felt stretched to the limit. The pirates had been drinking for hours, getting louder and bawdier with each new keg
and bottle of rum. The remnants of a roasted boar lay about
the ground, as if dogs had been tearing the carcass directly off
the spit. She had eaten little, her stomach upset by the crude
comments about her new position in life. She had been
handed a large cup of rum and despite the temptation to use
the drink to ease her nerves, Bailey was determined to keep
her wits about her. Bit by bit, she secretly poured the rum into
the sand, so her companions wouldn't get suspicious.

The pirates taunted her with rumors about the man they all
acknowledged as her owner. She consoled herself with the
belief that the pirates were greatly exaggerating their tales of
the man's deeds, and did her best to ignore everyone around
her. She had yet to see the old man, though she had hoped to
be able to observe him in order to determine a weakness that
would enable her to escape him. The huge tattooed pirate remained nearby, though, ever watchful and vigilant in keeping
away the many curious and zealous pirate admirers who
thought to steal a grope, or even more. If she could be grateful for anything about her current situation, then she was
grateful for her tattooed guard.

Wild howls, a shot from a flintlock pistol and the crackling
fire all mixed with the strange brand of music the pirates were
making. Some attempted to play broken instruments. Several
blew odd melodies on homemade flutes. One drunken reveler
kept rhythm beating a dented drum while others tapped dag-
gers against copper and pewter pots and mugs.

Several women got up and began dancing around the fire,
stripping off pieces of clothing and swinging them gaily

above their heads. Some ended up bare-breasted, long color-ful beads and gold chains swinging seductively against their firelit skin. Others stripped completely, gyrating their full naked hips in provocative thrusts, teasing and thrilling their cheering male counterparts. Their eyes held the merriment of the power they had over the pirates who watched them, en-tranced. A young pirate with long blond hair and a snake tattoo on his chest stepped into the circle and swooped up a naked dancing redhead. Her squeal of delight echoed back to the revellers as they disappeared from the circle of firelight into the darkness. Lizzy pulled herself out of the arms of a portly pirate who was reluctant to let her go, laughed and then staggered over to Bailey. She plopped herself down as if they were the best of friends and tossed her arm about Bailey's shoulder. She tipped up a half-drunk bottle and swallowed deeply, then offered some to Bailey.

"No," Bailey replied. She tipped her cup to show it was still half full.

Lizzy broke into raucous laugher. "That's the way, sweet-heart! Yer gettin' the 'ang of it. It helps ta be smashed the first few times—these bastards don't know nothin' about being gentle when they have their way. But ye'll get used to it. Ye even start ta like it rough after a while. Yep, ye'll make a mighty fine whore for that man, that beautiful man. Ye lucky chit."

Bailey couldn't imagine why Lizzy thought she was lucky, but she figured there were many things about these people she didn't understand. She sat quietly next to her odd com-panion for a few minutes, listening to the broken drum rhythm that was beginning to make her head pound.

"Whooboy, here he comes! Ya better git yerself ready, chit, cause yer man has come ta claim what's his."

Lizzy's cackle of laughter grated against Bailey's frayed nerves. She hadn't noticed the man approaching from the shadows outside the bonfire. She felt the sudden urge to throw up, but refused to show the old twig of a man her fear.

Lizzy's drunken giggle continued and she poked Bailey in her side one too many times. Bailey dragged her eyes from the approaching man to glare at Lizzy, shoving the woman's elbow aside. Then she noticed with dismay that many of the partying crowd had turned their attention to her and the pirate who had paid such an enormous amount to own her. Oh, God, what were they expecting to happen? She wanted more than anything to fight her way out of here right now. But she couldn't allow her impetuous nature to surface just yet.

There was no more time to think. He entered the circle of firelight and stalked toward her like a hungry lion. Lizzy squirmed excitedly beside her and Bailey straightened her spine, lifting her chin a notch. She couldn't take her eyes from the dark figure looming closer. He was much too big to be Old Twig, but one quick glance behind her told her the burly tattooed pirate was still at her back. Was this another of the old man's thugs, come to drag her off to him? The pirates began to chant, and Bailey's heart thumped hard inside her chest. The man leaned down, his features in silhouette with the blazing fire behind him. He reached out his hand to her, palm up.

"I will not go willingly," she hissed, her hands squeezing the cup.

The pirates laughed at her resistance, then cheered her possessor on, shouting out explicit and filthy suggestions of what he should spend the next few hours doing to her.

"All the more pleasurable for me, wench."

Bailey gasped at the low, barely controlled rage in the deep voice she knew so well. "Co—!" He swept her up, his name cut short as her stomach connected hard with his shoulder and with each bouncing, angry step as he took them away from the raucous pirates.

Chapter Fifteen

Cole strode away from the bawdy crowd, their encouragement echoing in the clear night air. He bent slightly, carrying his sputtering burden through the flaps of a large tent that had been set up for him and his *purchase*. He dropped Bailey unceremoniously on the mattress. She tumbled over in a swirl of red and black fabric, mixing with the deep blues of the silk bedding. He raked his hand through his hair and turned from her to close and tie the tent flaps, the distant sound of whistles and howls marking the pirates' hearty approval.

He poured himself a drink and sat in a ridiculously ornate chair across from Bailey, stretching out his legs in front of him.

"I can't believe it's you," she said, her voice shaking with emotion. Her sea-blue eyes held great relief.

"You were expecting someone else? Stede Bonnet? Perhaps Blackbeard himself? Sorry to disappoint you." He could barely control his rage—and the overwhelming urge to toss up her skirt and spank her shapely backside until her buttocks were as red as her dress.

"No. Oh, Cole, I am so glad to see you!"

"Are you, now?"

"Of course I am. But I don't understand. What about that

disgusting old pirate who . . . bought me?" she spit out. "What will happen when he finds out I am gone?"

"Be careful how you speak about Bones."

"His name is Bones?" she asked, her face wrinkled in distaste.

Cole wasn't sure how long he could maintain this pretense of casual disinterest. He was so angry at her but relieved at the same time. He tried to drown his anger with a mouthful of rum, then nodded. "He is a friend of mine."

"Do you think you can convince him to let me go?" She nearly swayed off the mattress in her anticipation of his answer.

He shrugged. "You're definitely more trouble than you're worth."

"I deserve that."

"Consorting with Lizzy and Jane has made you agreeable, I see."

"Cole, I never should have left the *Barracuda*," she said, sniffling. "I know you won't believe me, but I am sorry I lied to you."

She sounded so forlorn—and sincere. To keep himself from giving in and comforting her, he remained silent, sipped his rum, then folded his arms across his chest.

"I saw you in the crowd. You looked so angry. And then you left—you left me there. But here you are. I don't understand. I thought you sailed away."

"Because of your deceptive act of rebellion, we are unable to leave the island until tomorrow."

"We?" Her small voice sounded so hopeful.

"For some reason beyond my own comprehension, I found I couldn't leave you here, as much as you thought you wished it. But I told you there would be questions. These people know me as a man who would never give two shillings for a woman, much less the amount of gold it took to free you from old Bones."

"Free me?" She was leaning so far forward now, he was surprised she hadn't tumbled head over heels at his feet.

"It took quite a bit of convincing for him to sell your papers to me. And it raised a lot of eyebrows in the process. One old hag even suggested that you must be a princess from some foreign land. She accused me of trying to cheat the brotherhood out of a royal fortune in ransom. I had to convince them you were not a princess."

"You said Bones sold my papers? What exactly does that mean?" she asked hesitantly.

"Just what you might think it means. I own you. You owe me. And they are expecting me to collect—tonight," he said, not bothering to soften the truth. In the last few hours he had done things he swore he would never do for a woman and the last thing he felt at the moment was sympathetic.

She gasped. "You don't have to be so indelicate. I didn't mean for any of this to happen. Karl said that English ships were here. But he lied. He made me drink some drug, I think, and then he gave me to those women. And then, well, you know the rest."

"I know all of it. I had my doubts about that boy when I agreed to take him on, and I should have trusted my instincts. But I have taken care of the situation."

Bailey was afraid to ask what he'd done to the boy, but Cole's angry countenance made her desperate to say something that would appease him. "I will pay you back, every bit. I promise."

"Splendid! I'll tell you what. Give me my mother's ring and I will forgive the entire amount it took me to get you away from Bones. I will hand these papers over to you and you can burn them to ashes." He knew full well the ring had been stolen, but he wasn't in the mood to ease her guilt.

She hesitated, lowering her head, then let out a defeated sigh. "I would. I really would give you the ring . . . if I could. But I cannot."

"Why not?"

"I don't have it," she admitted brokenly.

"What do you mean, you don't have it?"

"The women must have found it. When I woke from the drug, it was gone. I suppose they wouldn't consider giving it back?"

"Unlikely."

She frowned, her brow furrowing beneath the tangles of her hair.

"Well, then. Where do you suppose that leaves us, Bailey?"

"I don't know. Where?"

"The way I see it, you are indebted to me for quite a large sum of money. And it appears you don't have a way to pay."

"I will find a way. Somehow."

"Do you know what these are?" he asked, taking a ribbon-tied parchment from the table and waving it in the air. "These are the papers that say that I own you. You belong to me. You are my property. Like this chair, these clothes, my ship. Like any one of the horses that fill my stables at home. For the next seven years, the length of time written in here, you are beholden to me. You have no say in your life anymore. Not until you have worked off your debt. Is this all clear to you?"

Tears gathered in her eyes, but he pressed on. He had to make her see how much danger she'd been in. He had almost lost her. If he hadn't come up Bay Street when he had, she could easily be the plaything of a pirate right now, completely at his mercy. He had to make her see how close she'd come to hell.

"Do you at last understand the seriousness of what happened to you on that block today? You were sold to a pirate who could have done anything he pleased with you. And he would have, I promise you that. Then after he was tired of you, he would have shared you with whoever wanted a turn with you. But see here, Bailey. It matters naught that it was me who secured your papers. In the end, the fact remains the same. You have been purchased. You are mine to do with as I see fit."

"But you don't even want me. So, why can't you—?"

"Oh, but there is something that I want. I want the Dragon. And since there's no chance of you giving me the ring to bait him, I am now prepared to use the next best thing."

Her eyes narrowed, a worried frown creasing her lovely brow. He nodded as his intention sunk in.

"Yes, you. I don't see any other way, do you?"

She lowered her head and clasped her hands in the folds of red and black. "No. I don't. You are right. I owe you my life. I will do whatever I can to help you get the Dragon. I'm afraid that is the only way I can repay you and though it isn't money, I know you value revenge more than any amount of money— probably more than your own life. I'm truly sorry for all the trouble I have caused you."

He hadn't expected her contrition. He had expected her to fight, to refuse him, to deny being owned like so much property, especially by him. The fact that she was so relieved— even glad—to see him meant only one thing. She had been so terrified by her ordeal on the block that being with him was better than the alternatives presented by the pirates.

He felt a prickle of guilt at his harsh words and treatment of her and the look of sheer exhaustion that drooped her shoulders. He blew out a sigh and ran his fingers across his forehead to release the tension there. He was a little surprised to find that he didn't want to break her. He admired her courage, her spirit, reckless though she was at times. Damn, he didn't know what to think anymore. The woman had him at a loss.

"We can discuss it later. It's late." He got up, set his glass on the table and bent to peer out of the tent.

"Are you leaving?"

He nodded.

"I don't understand. Whose tent is this?"

"Yours. I don't share my quarters with women who betray me. You had no intention of staying on the *Barracuda* and you could have gotten us all killed for getting your pretty hide out of this mess. You are the most selfish, deceitful woman I have ever come across and you are right. I don't trust you at all. You proved that I can't."

"But you never did in the first place. You refused to even try!" She jumped to her feet, swaying slightly. "You gave me no choice."

He stormed over to her stand above her so she had to tilt her face up to him.

"I didn't have to try—I was right about you from the beginning. You are like all other wo—"

"I am not like all other women. At least not the ones you have known. But you are too pigheaded to see me for who I am. You are afraid of finding out you are wrong."

The fire was back in her eyes and a pink flush in her cheeks. She threw her shoulders back as she poked him in the chest with her finger. God, to think she had nearly been lost to him. The little fool. She still had no idea what he had saved her from. The thought of what she would have gone through at the hands of Bones and any number of the other pirates tore through his gut like a grappling hook. He felt a desperation tugging at a part of his heart that he had thought was long dead.

He reached out and cupped the back of her head in his hand, crushing her to him and claiming her lips in a punishing kiss. He held back none of the volatile emotions that were churning his insides. He felt her melt into him almost immediately as she responded to his kiss with all the emotion inside her. A soft moan released from her throat, but then suddenly she shoved against him with both of her palms.

Breathless, she lifted the back of her hand to her rosy mouth and gazed at him with a look he couldn't fathom. Was it anger? Hatred? Damn his eyes. He shouldn't have let himself kiss her, but she seemed to melt his iron will to liquid fire.

Her eyes held him captive, as if she was trying to see inside his soul and he couldn't look away if he'd wanted to. He didn't.

Amazingly, she stepped into him and grasped his shirt in her fists, pulling him down to her as she tilted her face up and touched his lips with hers. He felt her hunger, though she was slightly hesitant. Her obvious inexperience did nothing to cool his hunger, indeed, her innocent boldness brought his entire body to life. He encouraged her lips apart with his own and flicked his tongue against hers. She moaned and opened her mouth to receive more of him. This time she met his tongue with her own. He felt his groin swell as his need for her burned deep within him. He let his hand slip down to her décolletage, his fingers sweeping across the velvety smoothness of her breasts. She inhaled and arched more fully into him.

He should stop.

Leave her alone.

God help him, he couldn't. She was breathtaking. He broke his lips away from hers to trail kisses down the slim line of her throat, feeling the wild beat of her pulse against his lips. She dropped her head back, her sigh of pleasure nearly undoing him. He let his tongue explore the delicious hollow of her collarbone, careful to avoid the angry cut that was healing at the base of her neck. She moaned, a throaty, soft, purely seductive sound that he took as an invitation to intensify his pleasurable assault. He tugged on the bodice of her dress, the material just releasing her glorious breasts from their silk prison. He squeezed his fingers into their fullness, then teased the hardened nipples, one by one with his ravenous tongue. She mumbled softly, dropping her arms by her sides, her head back, eyes closed. With her back slightly arched, the pink tips of her breasts seemed to beckon him for more. He pulled the fabric lower, until the square neckline rested under the full swells, pressing them upward to his waiting mouth. He suckled first one, then the other, lavishing them with attention, his cock aching painfully with each pleasurable whimper that escaped her lips.

As if she could stand no more, she straightened up and opened her eyes. They glistened with passion. She tried to lift her arms around his neck, but the lowered bodice held her arms captive at her sides. She settled her hands on his hips instead, and lifted her face for another kiss. Cole lowered them both to the mattress, covering her body with his, her lips with his own. Bailey wriggled to free her arms from her sleeves, then tore open the front of Cole's shirt, pulling it off of his shoulders. Her hands came to rest lightly against his biceps, allowing him better access to her satin flesh once again. He didn't hesitate to accommodate her with his mouth, his tongue, his hands.

He began to push her skirt up, feeling the soft skin of her thigh against his palm.

Suddenly, a voice broke through Cole's passion-hazed mind, and he tore his lips from Bailey's breasts. Bailey gasped at the intrusion, and struggled to cover herself.

"Hell and fire, what is it?" Cole ground out as he swung around to find two grizzled faces watching them with interest through a slit in the tent flap.

"We hate to throw cold water on ye, Cap'n Leighton, but Bones wanted us to check an' see if the lady is farin' well," one said.

"Yeah, maybe she's had herself a change o' mind an' wants ta stay here, with 'im," said the other.

"Holy Christ!" Cole muttered in disgust. "Bailey, Bones would like to know if you are well, or if you might like to stay here with him. Would you please indulge these men with a reply before I run a sword through their hearts?"

"I am fine," she said thickly, from behind Cole's broad back.

"No bother, then. We'll just give ol' Bones the message, Cap'n."

"Brilliant," Cole grumbled.

He heard a rustle of fabric behind him and knew Bailey was redressing herself in the concealing shadows. He couldn't bear facing her just now. He couldn't believe how completely he had lost his tightly reigned control. She was like the mythical sirens who lured sailors to their deaths on the treacherous ocean rocks. He had forgotten that for a moment. She had made him forget. But he would not be led onto the rocks. Not again.

By all rights, she was now his property and she needed to accept that fact. He could use her to his own ends and she had no say in the matter. By damn, he would use her to find the Dragon, so help him, God. She owed it to him.

"I should not have touched you. I assure you it won't happen again. Good night."

He steeled himself against the hurt look on her flushed face, ignored her trembling lips, still swollen from his kisses. "Hear me well, Bailey. I *will* make you sorry if you even attempt to leave this tent."

As he stalked into the darkness, somewhere in the deepest, most closed-off part of him, a thought kindled and sputtered to life with a will of its own.

What would he have done if she had uttered just one word to show that she wanted him to stay?

He smothered the dangerous thought immediately, reminding himself of the damage such musings would inevitably render upon his life.

Chapter Sixteen

Bailey woke from the pressure of a hand over her mouth and tried to scream.

"Shh, it's me. We have to go. Now."

She heard the urgency in his whisper and moved quickly. "Cole, what's wrong?"

"We don't have time for this," he responded and grabbed her hand, leading her out of the tent into the darkness of predawn.

Bailey tried her best to keep up, as Cole half-ran down the beach, towing her along. She held her skirts up with her left hand, but still tripped up now and then on pieces of the hem. Her feet sank deep into the cool, wet sand, making the going even more difficult, but she could tell from his serious manner that something was amiss, so she dared not ask him to slow down. Soon they reached a bend in the beach, where two shadowed figures waited knee-high in the lapping water next to a longboat. As they reached them, Bailey barely had time to recognize Miles and Lew before she was helped into the longboat and the two men began rowing out of the surf. The *Barracuda* waited a short distance out, dark and silent in the black water and as they reached her, Bailey could see several men on deck, quietly preparing the ship to sail.

Once on deck, Cole spoke briefly to Miles, who then silently escorted Bailey to the captain's cabin, tipped his hat and mumbled, "Sorry" before closing the door. She heard the lock click in place, but there was little she could do to protest at the moment. She made her way in the darkness to the window seat and stared out the porthole at the beach. The pirates' bonfire had dwindled, but still a small orange glow radiated out, illuminating the white-tipped waves that peeled up on the beach.

Late on the third day, Bailey stood at the railing near the bow, enduring the hot afternoon sun to watch as they approached Cole's home. Lush, tall palm trees followed the line of blush-colored sand as it arced out into the teal water and back in, forming several gentle curves that made up the island. The *Barracuda* slid into a protected cove, and the sailors began working to secure the few heavy sails that had remained unfurled as they eased into the shallow water.

An hour later, Bailey strolled along the soft sand, cooling her feet in the crystal water as boxes, trunks, barrels, and crates of various sizes were unloaded and brought up the beach. Miles and another sailor had disappeared down a shaded path in the trees soon after escorting her to the beach, but now they returned with two large horse-drawn carts leading two additional tethered horses behind them. Bailey saw Cole once or twice as he moved back and forth among the men, but not once did he look her way. Except for the sash, headband and weapons, he wore his black pirate attire, despite the intense heat of the day. Even from a distance, he seemed to move slowly, as if he had gotten little rest since leaving New Providence. She hoped she was the cause of his lack of sleep, as he had been the cause of hers these last two nights. When the carts were nearly loaded, Miles approached her with the smaller of the horses that had been tied to the carts and helped her mount.

"We'll be goin' up to the house now, miss. It won't be much longer and you'll have a comfortable place to rest an' a bite to eat."

She thanked him and he took the horse's reins and led the animal off the beach and up the slight incline of the shady path he had come down earlier.

"Isn't anyone else coming, Miles?"

"To be sure, miss. The captain wanted me to get you outta the sun and up to the house. He figured you must be about to boil in all them layers. I don't know how you women wear all that mess of stuff, I sure don't."

After her time spent in breeches, Bailey understood that sentiment well, though she kept that finding to herself.

After climbing the winding path, Miles led the horse into a large clearing of deep green dotted with wildflowers. Cole's house nestled at the top of the hill, amidst tall palms and other trees Bailey did not recognize. She could hear the rush and splash of the ocean breaking below them off to the right. They approached the side of the house, the horse's hooves clicking up the brick drive to the circular courtyard. In the center of the courtyard was a fountain, surrounded by a multitude of plants, blooming with flowers in all sizes and colors. Bailey admired the beautiful mermaid statue at the center of the fountain and breathed in the sweet fragrances that filled the afternoon air.

Miles helped Bailey down from the horse as several young men and women emerged from the house, followed by a curvaceous woman with dark curly hair spilling down to her hips. The woman was obviously in charge, calling out instructions in an authoritative, yet kind voice that was heavily accented. Miles smiled broadly and stepped forward to greet her.

"Mistress Analee. How d'ya fare, ma'am?"

"Very well, Miles, thank you. Is my fine-looking husband on his way up to see his lovely wife, or does he plan to make me wait another three months?" She laughed, tilting her head and planting her hands on her ample hips in mock anger.

"He's comin' right along, Mistress. Cap'n Leighton wanted me to get Miss Bailey up here quick like."

"*Eh, me llamo Analee.* And you must be the one who Miles is speaking of," the woman said, coming around the sailor to give Bailey a once-over. "Well, aren't you just as lovely as a summer morning! Bailey, *sí?* I'm so pleased to meet you."

"The pleasure is mine," Bailey replied with a smile. The bubbling joy coming from the beautiful dark-skinned woman flowed through her, improving Bailey's mood considerably.

"How wonderful to have another woman to talk to. We'll just be the best of friends, I know it. Now, you come inside and let's get you something to eat. Maetta, hurry, dear, and get a room ready for Miss Bailey. The blue room will suit nicely. And Maetta, have Pansy prepare her a healing salve," she finished, tipping Bailey's chin up to gently examine her neck.

"Yes'm." A young girl with coffee-colored skin and beautiful almond eyes nodded briefly and skipped off to do Analee's bidding.

"I know you must be exhausted, Bailey, but it will take a little while for the girls to get your room ready, and I'm just bursting with curiosity about you. Come with me into the drawing room and we'll get acquainted. You must tell me everything!" she exclaimed, looping her arm through Bailey's and patting her hand.

"Thank you, Analee." Bailey smiled at the beautiful woman, feeling completely at ease with her candid manner. "It will be a great relief to tell someone all that has happened to me these last few days. I am glad that someone will be you," she said sincerely.

Analee smiled, her brown eyes twinkling. "I am, too, *chica dulce.*"

* * *

The island was breathtaking. Bailey had spent the past two days leisurely exploring the wonders of Cole's home. Analee had taught her the names of many of the exotic plants and flowers during their friendly walks. Bailey felt as if they had known each other for years. Analee had accepted Bailey's story of how she'd come to be with Cole without an ounce of judgment, cursing the demon pirates who had brought so much pain to her family.

Bailey listened with rapt attention when Analee spoke of Cole, which was often. It was evident she cared a great deal for him and even seemed a bit protective, which made Bailey's curiosity rise. She hadn't seen Cole since that morning they had left New Providence in such a hurry, and try as she might, she couldn't help but feel hurt. Twice now, he had abruptly left her during what she considered to be rather intimate moments. At least more intimate than she had ever experienced. Lord, she should have learned after that first time. In fact, she had sworn to herself she wouldn't let him kiss her again, but she had proven to be more than weak where he was concerned.

And now, listening to Analee go on about how wonderful he was, how kind, honorable—and misunderstood—well, she thought she might go mad. Honorable, indeed! The man out-right told her she was his property and he would do with her as he pleased! There was nothing to misunderstand about that. And for all she knew, he was concocting a plan to snare the Dragon with her at the heart of it. She had to find a way to buy back her freedom.

She raised her gaze to stare out at the ocean, and sipped her warm herb tea. This was her favorite spot, she decided, and she would miss her quiet mornings here when she left. The two-story limestone terrace ran the length of the back of the house, supported by six artfully carved columns. Here, on the main floor, the terrace was only two stairs from the ground, blending easily with the beautifully manicured lawn that swept down a gentle hill, allowing an exceptional view of the ocean below.

Bailey skimmed the missive once again, before carefully folding it and tucking it in the pocket of Analee's borrowed blue cotton dress. The only thing she had left to include was how to find the island. She would have to ask Analee to help her with that bit of information and then she could finish the letter and send it to James.

She knew she would be laying a heavy burden on him, and not only because of the money she owed to Cole. But she didn't know what else to do. James was her only hope of getting her life back to a semblance of normalcy. He had declared his love to her not long before that fateful night though he had yet to ask her to marry him. Bailey saw him only as a friend but he believed that with some time, she would come to have deeper feelings for him. She had been hoping for a great love, love she thought she might find out in the world beyond Beaufort. But now she wondered if she had just been restless and immature. Everything she needed for a safe, stable life was with James. He was a good man and not the least bit domineering. He would be good to her and treat her with respect, unlike . . . She stopped herself before she could even think of Cole.

Besides, she would have a lifetime to fall in love with James. It would come with time. Wouldn't it?

Later that morning, Bailey found Analee in the cookhouse, settling a squabble between two young servant girls.

"But coconut pie is Master Cole's favorite!" exclaimed one, as she stomped a bare foot on the tile floor.

"We's havin' coconut fish for dinner, I keep tellin' you, girl! That's just too dang much coconut!" the other debated. "Make that pineapple cake 'nstead."

"Girls, girls!" Analee clapped her hands, then spotted

Bailey at the door and winked at her. "I know you both want to please Master Cole, but all this shouting does not please me. Now, let's talk this over and make some sense of it. Mary, you already have the fish marinating, so we will have the coconut fish after the soup. Beatrice, you make the finest pineapple cake on the island, and you should be quite proud. Now, Master Cole will be taking his dinner in his room this evening, so neither of you need to preen about so."

"Again?" both girls whined at once.

"We ain't even seen him since he got back," added Mary.

"And you won't be seeing him this evening, either. The two of you! You're behaving like lovesick ninnies. Now, remember that you are friends and stop bickering with each other."

Despite the reprimand, Analee smiled at the girls, who grinned back at her and then at each other before falling into an easy banter as they bustled about the kitchen as if nothing had happened.

Analee met Bailey at the door and they walked together toward the house.

"What has been keeping Cole so busy?" Bailey asked, trying to sound uninterested.

"I'm not really able to say. But you don't need to worry yourself."

Worry? Why would she say that?

"I almost forgot. Didn't you want to discuss something with me?"

"Oh, yes. My letter."

"That's right. You have written a letter to your young man in North Carolina, did I remember that right?"

Bailey nodded. "I just need to be able to tell him how to find me. Where exactly is this island?"

Analee's expression became thoughtful and she lowered her thick black lashes to shield her cocoa-colored eyes for a moment as if trying to decide what to say.

"That will be a problem, *chica,*" she said with an apologetic shake of her head.

"Why?"

"Lochinvar is Cole's home, but also his hideaway, so to speak. The island's location is not charted, and few people know how to find it. That is the way he intended it to be. Even if I knew how to direct a ship here, I would not."

"But what am I to do? I can't stay here with him."

"Have you forgotten, *chica dulce?*"

"What?"

"You are no longer a free woman. Please forgive me for being indelicate, I don't mean to hurt you. But the papers Cole purchased are binding. You belong to him now. The sooner you accept that fact, the sooner you will be able to find peace."

Peace? How could anyone find peace knowing another human being believes they own them . . . like a piece of property. Or an animal.

"But, Analee, I owe him more than I can pay. And if I cannot pay him, then Cole plans to use me to get revenge against the Dragon."

"I'm sure he spoke in haste. Cole would never do such a thing."

"No, I agreed to it. I told him I would help him. But I can't go through with it. If I help him he might be killed. I cannot be a part of a plan that might lead to his death."

"Please, don't be upset. As soon as Cole—has a moment, we will go and speak with him about sending your letter. I'm sure he will be reasonable. If you truly wish to go and be with James, then I know Cole will not keep you from him."

"Then I must speak with him immediately."

"No!" Analee responded hastily.

She fluttered her hands nervously as she moved to stand in front of Bailey, who was growing more confused by the moment.

"What in the world is going on around here? The sooner I

speak with Cole, the sooner I can be on my way. Whatever is the matter? Analee?" she asked, growing concerned for the woman whose usual smile was replaced by a worried frown.

"Nothing, *chica*. Cole is occupied with very important business and he has ordered that he not be disturbed."

"For how long?"

"I don't know. For as long as it takes, I suppose. Now, why don't we take a stroll to the west gardens. I want to check on the mango trees. It's a little early, but we may be able to find one or two that are ripe enough to pick."

Bailey mumbled a response, falling into step next to Analee, who chattered on as they walked along in the hot sunshine. But her mind wasn't on mangos. Her mind was on Cole, and what business he was taking care of that would keep him locked in his quarters for the fourth day in a row. Maybe if she hadn't thrown herself at him in the tent that night, she wouldn't be feeling so sensitive right now—like he was specifically avoiding her. She blamed her lack of self-control that night on her overwhelming relief that she was not the property of a pirate, and vowed she would never be in such a dire situation again.

And then she made another vow. She would see Cole and discuss her letter with him before this day was out.

Chapter Seventeen

Bailey sat at her dressing table watching in the mirror as the young maid braided her hair. Maetta was full of harmless gossip about the diverse group of people who lived on the island. Bailey learned that Cole had recently offered land to any of his crewmen who wished to make the island their home as well. Several had accepted, and the girl seemed especially pleased that Daniel Lewis had decided to stay. She positively beamed when she talked about him and Bailey couldn't contain her smile the third time his name was mentioned.

"Daniel's gonna build his place on the other side of the island. There's a cove where we saw dolphins play. I told him it's my favorite place of all the island."

"It sounds as if Lew is thinking of settling down, Maetta. What do you think about that?"

"I guess so," she said, golden light sparkling in her brown eyes. She twisted the braid into a knot and secured it at Bailey's neck. "He wouldn't say anything about that to me, though," she finished, suddenly shy.

"Hmm, well, you seem to have very good instincts, Maetta. I wouldn't be surprised if he doesn't talk to you soon." She would never have given the girl this kind of hope, but Lew had told her about a beautiful golden-eyed girl who worked in Cole's

island home. He said he had grown to care for her on their last
stay there and he was hoping she had not forgotten him.

Maetta laughed sweetly as she bounced on her toes in excitement. She caught herself and made a quick curtsy. "Sorry,
Miss Bailey."

"Don't be. There's nothing at all wrong with being happy."
In the mirror, she studied the girl whose expression held so
much promise for the future. She fought a feeling of sadness
for the girlish dreams she herself had once held on to. That
seemed like a lifetime ago.

"That's the last one. You're all done, Miss Bailey."

Maetta put the extra pins on the table and stepped back to
admire her work.

"Thank you, Maetta. I couldn't possibly have done such a
good job. You are gifted."

"You're welcome, Miss Bailey. Will you be coming down
for the afternoon meal?"

"Yes, I'll be there shortly," she answered as the maid left
the room.

Bailey stood and smoothed her skirt. She would have felt
at a disadvantage facing Cole in the red and black disaster she
had been wearing on New Providence. But thanks to Analee's
generosity, she had a wardrobe full of dresses to wear. The
white linen she wore now had delicate yellow flowers and
vines of light green, and fit nicely, though the hem was
slightly short. The elbow-length sleeves were sheer and the
modest neckline dipped in the front as well as the back. The
simple design and light material would allow for some comfort in the tropical heat.

She took a deep breath and left the room, tucking an escaped wisp of hair behind her ear. The sudden flutter in her
stomach must be due to the confrontation she was planning
to have with Cole, not because she was going to see him for
the first time since their encounter in the tent. The places
where he had touched and kissed her still tingled when she

thought about it. She tried not to but her resolve seemed to weaken, especially when she lay awake in the dark.

How did he feel about what had passed between them? Was that why she hadn't seen him since? He must know as well as she did, they had gone too far. She was as much to blame as he. She had allowed—nay, welcomed—his attentions. Her reaction to him frightened her and made it more clear than ever that she must convince him to let her go. She nurtured her determination and steeled herself for the storm ahead, as she peered into the dining room.

She was early. The table was just being set with patterned china, lovely crystal and fragrant flowers. Bailey was somewhat relieved that she wouldn't have to try to put food in her stomach just now. She slipped away to conduct a casual search of the ground floor. Cole was nowhere to be found. None of the servants would give her any information, brushing aside her inquiries with noncommittal answers or shrugging as if they didn't understand her English at all. She had discovered a room that was obviously Cole's study, but the room was dark, the shutters drawn. There were no papers littering the desk, no quill and ink bottle, and a brand new wick in the lamp showed it had yet to be used. A slight musty smell filled the room; the smell of a room unused for some time. Bailey could not hold back her suspicion. He had not been working these last days. In fact, it appeared that Cole had not come to his study at all since they had arrived on the island.

So, where was he and what was he doing? And why wouldn't anyone tell her anything?

Bailey heard footsteps and a low female voice as someone descended the stairs. Then she heard Analee's voice respond in a strangely tight tone. Bailey ducked into the drawing room and pressed herself against the wall, waiting breathlessly for the two women to leave. She listened as the rustle of skirts faded and heard their footsteps echo off the polished wood floor at the back of the house before she peered out of the drawing room into the empty hall. She crossed the floor and tiptoed up the stairs, determined to put an end to the mystery of where Cole was and what everyone was keeping from her.

He must be up here somewhere, she thought as she stalked like a thief down the wide hallway in the opposite direction of her room. Finding nothing, she turned and searched the other way down the hall, pausing at each door to listen for sounds inside. She moved past each slowly, hearing nothing until she reached the room to the door next to hers; the last room on the floor. She heard a low male voice coming from inside, then heavy footsteps, then the voice again.

"No, Cole! You're not ready."

This was it! He was in there. She screwed up her courage, put on her best stern look and barged into the room.

The giant bearded man from the *Barracuda* stood in the center of the room. She knew that this was Cisco, Analee's beloved husband. He still looked frightening to Bailey, especially now as he stared back at her with a mix of surprise and disapproval on his grizzled face.

Suddenly, he broke into a wide grin. He must be mad, Bailey thought. In fact, she was wondering if the entire household was a bit daft.

"Día bueno," the giant greeted her with good cheer.

"Cisco, get her out of here," Cole growled from a large wing chair by the double set of open French doors.

"Maybe you can talk some sense into him, *señorita.*"

"What do you mean?" Bailey asked the big man, never taking her eyes from Cole's angry face.

"I have to see about something. *Dispénseme,*" Cisco said, excusing himself.

"Damn it, man! Take her with you," Cole ground out.

Cisco ignored him, tipped his head to Bailey and left them alone.

Bailey took a few steps into the large bedchamber, barely noticing the carved white marble fireplace or most of the elegant furnishings that made up the room. One piece stood out above all the others, and she was determined to ignore it. But nevertheless, her eyes strayed to the huge four-poster bed, with vibrant shades of green and cream bedding strewn about as if that part of the room, alone, had suffered a hurricane. Cole didn't look much better, she realized, when she came to stand a few feet away from him. A light breeze came through the doors, stirring the sheer curtains, and despite the comfortable temperature, Cole's forehead carried a sheen of sweat.

"I want you to leave, Bailey." He stood up and held out his hand as if that gesture would make her obey him.

"That is precisely what I am here to discuss with you. I wish to go home."

"I meant I want you to leave this room."

"I know what you meant. I don't care a whit what you want. Is this why you have been avoiding me? Is it your intention to keep me until you find the Dragon? I know what I said, but I have changed my mind. I will not let you use me, Cole."

"You seem to be forgetting a very important fact. I own you. If I so choose, you could be scrubbing this floor on your hands and knees until the sun sets tonight."

She gasped in anger, despite her best effort to remain unmoved. His voice sounded strained as he continued.

"If you think that sounds bad, you should consider yourself extremely lucky that I got you instead of Bones. Ah, but, in truth, I'm not surprised that you are completely ungrateful."

"You know good and well that I am grateful for what you did for me on New Providence. But it was because of you that I ended up in that terrible position. You have done nothing but play havoc with my emotions and force me to put myself in danger to be free of you. And then you have the audacity to hold that sham of a proceeding in New Providence against me? It stops right now, Cole. I am no longer going to even pretend to do what you tell me to. I will not be owned by you—or anyone. No, what I will do before the sun sets tonight is have this letter on its way," she said, pulling the stationery out of her pocket and waving it at him.

"All of this because you want a letter mailed?" he asked, referring to her agitation with a mocking flick of his hand.

She ignored him, feeling more confident after successfully giving him a piece of her mind. "No. All of this because I am going home. This letter is to James. He will pay you whatever it takes to free me," she sneered. "Once he receives this, James will come for me and I will owe him, not you."

"You have yet to send the letter? Why, I'm surprised you haven't climbed a tree and snared a parrot to fly your plea to good old James the first day we arrived. What ever is holding you up?"

"I . . . I don't know how to direct him here. You must tell me where we are." Her confidence faltered slightly as his face took on a strange pallor.

Cole laughed, then. A harsh, cold sound that turned into a fit of coughing. He grimaced and leaned into his left side, and she could see he was trying to hide some type of discomfort. Before she could ask if he was all right, he answered her with a chilled edge to his words.

"No way in hell."

"No, you won't tell me where we are?"

"No to all of it. You have no say in what happens to you now. And your lover has even less say. You answer to me. You belong to me, and you'd better get yourself accustomed to it. I bought you, Bailey. Like a horse. And you had best be careful not to continue to vex me, or you will find yourself harnessed and pulling a cart through the cane fields."

She settled her fists on her hips, ready for battle. "I will *not* let you use me for your revenge. Ever! You will have to kill me first, do you hear me!"

"I believe the entire island heard you. Not only did you not find the English Navy, but you lost the only thing that could have aided me in finding the Dragon. You *owe* me. And now that you are my property, I will collect on that debt any damn way I see fit. If that means I dangle you out a window with your hair on fire, then so be it. Do you hear me?"

"You are barbaric!" She advanced on him in her anger. "You are worse than the slimiest of those pirates on New Providence. I have just as much reason to hate the Dragon as you, but I am not willing to destroy myself in the name of revenge. But you . . . ! Revenge is all that is important to you, and you will die because of it. The only other person on the earth who will be with you in the end will be your most hated enemy. Well, I wish you the utmost luck. I hope you find him. I hope you both come to a miserable end at the hand of the other! Then maybe I will finally find some peace!" She started to spin away but Cole grabbed her wrists.

"Yes, I'm barbaric, I'm no better than a pirate. I heard every venom-filled word. I will try my best to fulfill at least half of that wish, though your wish for my death may also be granted in the process. But until that happens, you go nowhere but where I say you go; you do nothing unless I grant you permission. And I did not grant you permission to write any letters," he said, reaching out his hand, palm up.

She didn't want to give him the letter, her only hope of escaping him and his dangerous life. Why hadn't she realized he would be so unreasonable?

"Do you want me to come after it?"

Bailey scowled at him and reluctantly handed him the wrinkled parchment. "I will find another way, I promise you that."

"Thank you for the warning. I will be sure not to give you enough freedom to fulfill that promise. Now, are you finished throwing your tantrum? Because if not, it will have to wait because I have pressing business to attend to."

"Pressing business? Your study looks as if you are still away. Actually, it doesn't appear that you've left this room since we arrived. What type of business are you conducting from your bedchamber, Cole?"

"Would you really like to know what happens in here?" he asked, drawing her forcefully closer to him.

She struggled to free her fists from his grasp, when suddenly Cole let go. The ashy color drained from his face and he seemed to sway as his dull gray eyes blinked down at her.

"Cole?"

She had no more time to wonder about his strange behavior before he crumpled to the floor at her feet.

"Cole!" Oh, God's Mercy! What was wrong with him?

She dropped to her knees at his side and turned him to lie on his back. He groaned and she drew her hands away, noticing with horror the blood on her hand and on the floor where he had fallen.

"Help, someone! Analee! Maetta! Please, come quickly! Cole needs help!"

She opened Cole's shirt and discovered the source of the blood. A bandage had been wrapped about his abdomen and the fresh blood was soaking through the white linen. When had this happened? she wondered. Had he found the Dragon on New Providence? Had they fought? Oh, God, what she had said to him . . . She hadn't meant it. She didn't want him to die.

"Cole? Can you hear me?"

He moaned. She wiped the sweat from his face with her trembling fingers, wishing desperately that she knew what to do.

Within moments, Analee rushed in, followed by Pansy,

Maetta, and Cisco, who rushed to Cole's side. The big man gently lifted Cole off the floor and carried him to the bed.

"Where is Marcel? Someone needs to get him. Quickly!" Bailey cried, looking at Analee and Cisco.

"He's out in the bay, fishing with some of the men," Cisco replied. "They won't be back for hours."

"Maetta, go down to the cove and tell whoever is there to get a boat out to the bay. Tell them to hurry," Analee said, patting the frightened maid's back as she turned the girl toward the door.

"Damn! It's bleeding again," Cisco said to his worried wife.

"*Sí*. He must be stitched again. And he must be made to lay still."

"What is going on? What is wrong with him?" Bailey asked in a rush of emotion.

"He was stabbed just before we left New Providence."

"Why? Oh, God, was it the Dragon?"

"No. But I'm afraid I can't tell you anything more about it. There's no time. He's been bleeding for most of a week now, we must get it to stop." Cisco turned to Analee and added gravely, "I don't think he has much time left."

"We cannot wait for the infection to heal. We must try to stitch him up again and hope that it holds this time."

"Let me see," Bailey said, and moved between Cisco and Analee. She pulled back the edge of the bandage and saw the jagged edge of the wound. The infected skin was swollen and red, but the inside of the cut appeared clean. "I have seen this type of wound before—on one of the fishermen. The cut is not straight enough to stitch, and the infected skin will not hold stitches for long. The bad skin must be cut away first. Then, we can draw the wound tighter together and cover it to stop the bleeding."

"Can you do this?" Analee asked with hope.

"I have only seen it done, but I believe I can do it."

"Tell Pansy what you will need."

Within half an hour, the maid was back with the requested sharp knife, plaster mixture and bandages. Cole had regained consciousness, too weak to protest verbally, though his wary gaze never left Bailey's as she picked up the knife with an unsteady hand. She looked into his pain-dulled eyes, and seeing the mistrust there she leaned down and whispered close to his ear, "This is not your day to die."

Then, she bent over his body and concentrated solely on the difficult task ahead, though she was aware of his eyes on her the entire time. As gently as possible, she cut away as much of the infection as she could, leaving almost enough skin to fully cover the wound. Then, Bailey instructed Analee on how to apply the sticky plaster to the edges of the wound, and though Analee gave Bailey a dubious look, she did as she was told. She stepped back and Bailey pressed the bandage into the sticky poultice on one side, then the other, pulling the wound closed as much as possible. Then, with Cisco's help in lifting Cole, she wrapped a clean linen bandage around his abdomen and tied it tightly on his uninjured side.

"It is done," Bailey said quietly. Her eyes locked with Cole's, the expression in those gray depths holding her captive with the intensity of unspoken emotion. Gratitude and relief, yes, that was all it was. Surely she was mistaken to think she had seen a glimmer of trust shining back at her before he closed his eyes.

Cole's chest contracted as he let out a heavy breath in sleep. Bailey took a piece of linen and wiped the sweat from his skin. Cisco grinned and Analee fell into the big man's outstretched arms for a well-deserved hug.

"Cole has been sent *un ángel* this day," Analee said as she went to embrace Bailey. "We are so blessed that you were here today. *¡Gracias eres un ángel!*" Analee gushed her thanks as she squeezed Bailey tight.

Bailey felt guilty for the praise she knew she didn't deserve. Not an hour before she had stood in this very room vocalizing her earnest desire to see Cole dead, and now he lay seriously injured with a wound and infection that might likely make those cruel and hastily spoken words come true.

"Why don't you sit with him for a while. Pansy, bring Miss Bailey some cool water," Analee said over her shoulder, and then to Bailey, ". . . so you can keep the fever away. I'll have a tray sent up for you." She cupped Bailey's cheek and patted her face affectionately, then whispered in a conspiratorial tone for Bailey's ears alone. "You are good for him, *chica*. I can see it as plain as a cloudless sky. Cisco, come with me, *querido*. It is time you and I shared a meal and some rest."

Bailey stood in awkward silence as Analee and Cisco closed the door behind them, leaving her alone with Cole. She felt a blush warm her face, remembering all the places his warm lips had caressed her that night in the tent. She had spent enough tears on the three-day voyage to Cole's home, fretting over her part in the near seduction; chastising herself for how easily she had let it happen for a second time. She absolutely could not lose her heart to Cole. Not to a man whose sole purpose for living was for revenge. His life meant nothing to him and he was not afraid to die to get that revenge. He was a man who, by his own words, could never—would never—love or trust another woman. It was a hopeless situation, and Bailey had suffered enough hopelessness to last the rest of her life. If she was honest with herself, she could no longer deny that she felt a strong attraction to Cole. He was undeniably the most ruggedly handsome, commanding man she had ever known, but she had allowed her infatuation to go further than she should have. She would not let it happen again. She had a much safer life waiting for her in Beaufort, with James—if he would still have her. A quiet, safe life. That's what she needed. That's what she wanted. And as soon as she got away from Cole, the attraction she felt now would be forgotten.

Moving quietly so as not to wake him, Bailey went to retrieve the chair that he had been sitting in earlier. She moved behind the chair, thinking to push it over by the bed, when a breeze caught the sheer white curtain, blowing it around to ensnare her legs. She stepped out of the cocoon of material and swept the curtain aside, when something twinkled up at her from a blood spot on the floor. She bent down for a closer look and recognized the gold sparkle immediately. Her heart dropped to her stomach.

The ring!

Bailey picked up the gold band, smeared with Cole's blood, her brows knit in confusion. It couldn't be. She examined it closely, but there was no question it was the ring that had been taken from her on New Providence. Cole must have had it on him when he collapsed—after he had just finished telling her in rude detail how she owed him for losing it.

She glanced at the bed to ensure that Cole had not awakened to witness her discovery. She picked up a torn scrap of linen and wiped the blood from the ring before slipping it in her pocket. Then she slid the chair across the floor next to the bed and sat down. Her mind raced with questions. Cole had gotten the ring back somehow before they had left New Providence. Was that why they had left before dawn in such a hurry? Of course! And that's why he hadn't come back to the tent all night. He had been tracking down the ring. He must have gotten stabbed fighting to recover it. Whatever the truth was, one thing was certain: Cole was deceiving her, making her believe the ring was lost for good. But why? What did he have to gain from such a deception? Suddenly, a sickening thought came to her. What if Cole intended to keep her, despite having his mother's ring back? He must believe that she herself was the only foolproof way to entice the Dragon. But how far would he go? How close would he let the Dragon get to her? A shiver passed over her skin, raising gooseflesh on her arms. She was starting to believe that Cole was so lost to his obsession for revenge that he was capable of viewing her as property and sacrificing her as he saw fit. She had thought he was starting to care for her, just a little bit. What a fool she was!

She cursed herself for the pain that tore at her heart and reminded herself once again that only a fool would lose her heart to such a beast.

"You will not have my heart, Cole Leighton," she whispered to his sleeping form as she leaned forward and touched the back of her hand to his forehead. Just then, Bailey heard a light knock and Pansy entered the room with a pitcher of fresh water. The shy servant retrieved a bowl from the washstand and poured the fresh water, then placed the bowl next to Bailey on a table by the bed.

"Is he in fever?" she asked in her heavily accented voice.

"No. He is cool."

"You need else, miss?"

"No, thank you. I'll just be leaving now that you are here."

"Oh, no, miss. Mistress Analee says Miss Bailey have to stay with him. She told me bring water and go."

"But I—"

"I must to go. Ship with supplies comes tomorrow and Maetta and me still got to clean the dry goods barrels for the kitchen. I go," the girl said in a rush.

Bailey nodded, and waved the girl out of the room, distracted by the servant's news. A supply ship—coming here. Tomorrow.

Merciful heaven! Bailey bit her lip to stifle her outcry. Her chance had finally come! No matter what it took, she was going to be on that ship when it left the island.

Chapter Eighteen

Unable to sleep, Bailey sat in a chair next to the fireplace, her gaze fixed on the gilt-framed painting over the bed. Firelight from several candles leapt in patterns against the shadowed walls, as chaotic as her thoughts.

During supper, she had been surprised to learn that every detail of the elegant home had been overseen by Cole. The serene elegance and beauty that surrounded her was not something she would have imagined him capable of appreciating. It certainly seemed to contradict the indifference he preferred her to see. He had commissioned this painting, which showed an exquisite view of the island and ocean below. He would have had to bring the artist to Lochinvar, for the painting had been done from the balcony of this very room. She tucked her knees up in the chair, wondering about the gentile side of Cole that would be capable of creating such elegant surroundings. It was a quite hidden side, to be sure. Bailey had a hard time imagining Cole taking pleasure in anything other than his quest for revenge.

She looked around at the lovely shades of blue and gold, from the tiny floral pattern on the thick, quilted bedding to the hand-painted paper that covered the walls. White sheer curtains just like the ones in Cole's room next door, hung from the single set of French doors, open to the sweetly scented night air. She stood and began to pace, noticing for the first time a door next to the fireplace. There was a door in Cole's room in the same location. The rooms were connected. Had this room been intended for a wife? Perhaps a lover he kept on the island? She felt the sharp tongue of jealousy lick at her insides. How ridiculous! She cared not a whit who this chamber was meant for. He could fill it with a hundred women, for after this night it would be empty. She stared down at the pattern on the rug as her bare feet padded along the border of intricate shapes. It was now past midnight, but she was still too agitated to sleep. She knew she had been too quiet at supper. She had noticed the concerned glances exchanged between Cisco and Analee. She couldn't very well tell them of her plan to escape on the supply ship, so she pled exhaustion and escaped to the solitude of her room. Her desire to leave Cole made perfect sense. What made no sense at all was the pang of guilt that had gnawed at her since the moment she made the decision to go.

She disrobed, hanging the borrowed dress in the wardrobe with loving care. In the morning, for her voyage home, she would don the red and black lace dress she had worn in New Providence. As much as she hated the gaudy attire, she could not bear to take anything from Analee. She had been so kind and Bailey didn't want to disrespect that kindness in even the smallest way. She had nothing to leave in payment for taking any of the dresses, and she needed the gold ring to barter for passage home, so that was that. She hoped James and the other folk in Beaufort would be too relieved to see her to care that she looked like a ragged pirate castoff. She donned a white silk nightdress, also belonging to Analee, and began to extinguish the candles.

An insistent knocking at the door startled her. She picked up the candle she was about to blow out and opened the door. Analee stood there, her bronze face a mask of emotion.

"What is it?" Bailey asked, taking the woman's hand.

"He is bad."

"Fever?"

"*Sí.* I don't think he will live through the night," Analee cried.

"What can I do?" Bailey asked, fear drawing her throat tight.

"He is in a fitful state. He calls for you. You must come," she pleaded, pulling Bailey along as she hurried next door.

Cole lay on the bed, his skin pasty and covered in sweat, despite the violent shaking that racked his body. Bailey rushed over and sat on the mattress next to him, taking his hand as he called out her name, among other unintelligible moans. The vulnerability and sheer need she heard in his broken words upset her greatly. She had never seen him show any type of weakness, which made this sight of him so much more frightening. As she watched his face, contorted by demons that chased him in his delirium, she became consumed with heartwrenching fear. No matter what it meant for her—for her future—she did not want him to die.

The night wore on, hour after hour, seemingly without end. Marcel had been summoned, bringing with him a hot tea made with elder flowers, peppermint, white yarrow, and feverfew, which Bailey patiently coaxed Cole to drink. She wiped the resulting perspiration from his body with damp cloths, soothing his torment with soft words spoken close to his ear. Once, he had opened his fever-glazed eyes, his gaze, even then powerful enough to steal her breath, until she had lulled him back to sleep, breaking the spell.

Analee had come and gone through the long night, bringing water and fresh towels as they were needed. The sun had yet to break the darkness, though now the very first morning birds could be heard chirping and twittering in anticipation of the new day. Analee shooed the assisting servants to their beds for a few hours' rest and kissed Cisco soundly on the mouth before sending him off as well.

"I'm sorry to leave you, *mi amor,*" he told her. "But I have to prepare to meet the *Sea Spirit* and see that everything is unloaded and documented. Cole would not want the captain's schedule to be impaired because of him."

"Cole will be grateful to you for handling the shipment," Analee said.

"God willing, I pray he is up and about soon to complain about how I paid too much for the flour, or some such nonsense. You need to get some sleep, *esposa,*" he said tenderly, cupping his wife's cheek gently in his big hand.

"Go on, now. I am hale as the day we met. There will be plenty of time to sleep—when he's out of danger. Besides, there is nothing you can do. All that is left is to wait for the infection to subside."

Bailey tried not to be obvious as she watched the tender exchange between husband and wife. She had become quite fond of Analee and it didn't take long for her to begin to admire her big, gruff husband, too. Their love was plain for everyone to see. They shared a closeness that reminded her of how her parents were when she was young. Sadly, Analee had never conceived a child, but she shared the endless love in her heart with all the inhabitants of Lochinvar, making the island a warm, well-run home as well as a successful sugar farm.

Bailey longed for a love such as theirs. And a family to share her life with. But how was she going to have all those things when the only man who occupied her thoughts was reckless with his life, ill-mannered, incapable of love . . . and now on the edge of death.

Maetta came into the room just as Cisco left, balancing a tray filled with fruit and bread and a pot of tea. With a wide yawn she set it on the round table next to the gray marble fireplace. Analee thanked the girl and sent her off to bed before pouring the aromatic tea and coming to sit next to Bailey.

"Thank you," Bailey said as she blew on the steamy tea, then took a shallow sip. "Cisco is very good to you. You are blessed to have each other."

"*Sí*. He is a good man. To think I almost refused to marry him." She laughed.

"Truly?"

Analee nodded, pushing her thick brown hair back from her face. "He was just so . . . intimidating. And loud. I thought he was more a bear than a man. How could he know anything about love?"

Bailey smiled. "How did he convince you?"

"He courted me as patiently as a saint. He brought me flowers, read me poems, took me for long walks through my family's vineyards." She smiled. "It must have driven him nearly mad when I refused him after months of that. I was so young, and he was so full of experience. But still, he did not give up. And one day, as we came to sit beneath my favorite Willow tree, I saw a tiny bird laying on the ground. It was moving about, trying to get up and fly, but the poor thing had broken a wing in the fall. Cisco picked up the little bird so gently and cradled it in his big, rough palm all the way back to the villa. We cared for that little bird together and Cisco took him home with him that day. I never saw him without little Afortunato again. He was unable to fly, but the silly bird would sit right on his shoulder, and every time Cisco came to call, Afortunato was right there with him. The next time Cisco asked me to marry him, I said yes right away."

"My mother used to say that you can only make a fair assessment of a person when you look at his heart," Bailey said, wistfully.

"It's hard to tell that to a fanciful, young girl. My eyes were searching for a handsome knight, not a bellowing bear," she said, laughing. "As it turns out, I got both."

Bailey nodded thoughtfully, her eyes straying to the bed, where Cole rolled his head fitfully back and forth. She stood and removed the damp pillow, replacing it with a fresh one and wiping Cole's neck and brow with a cool cloth. Then she sat back down next to Analee, who sliced small round slices of a green fruit with dark seeds unlike any fruit Bailey had ever seen. Analee handed her several pieces of the fruit, telling her it was called kiwi fruit.

"Your mother sounds like she was a wise woman. Remind me, *ángel,* how old were you when she died?"

"Twelve. I remember a lot about her, but sometimes it feels like I have forgotten much more than I have been able to hold on to."

"You were blessed to have a mother who loved you, even if you were so young when she died. Some people are not so fortunate."

Bailey placed her teacup on the saucer and looked into her friend's eyes, hoping she would elaborate. Analee reached out and covered Bailey's hand with her own. "I have come to understand there are many things that have made Cole the way he is."

"Cold? Unreachable? Infuriating?"

Analee grinned. "Cisco and I didn't know Cole until later— when he was looking for a crew for the *Barracuda*. But I feel it, in here," she said, tapping her fingers over her heart. "And I see it in his eyes sometimes. He longs for things he feels he no longer can trust. So he fights to deny the longings."

"And he does so exceptionally well. He should remain quite safe."

Analee gave her a wise, too all-knowing look. "I have always believed that someday he would meet his match in that fight. *Un ángel* who could make him believe again."

"If she exists, then I wish the fair-sainted lady luck. She will need it," Bailey replied, then took notice as Cole began to roll his head and mumble again. She stood and hurried to wet a cloth, wrung it out and wiped his forehead with care.

"*Sí*, but I believe you will be up to the task."

Bailey concentrated on making Cole as comfortable as possible, and thought she must have misunderstood Analee's accented English. She glanced back at her new friend and caught the mischievous sparkle in her coffee-colored eyes. It was apparent she had not misunderstood at all. Bailey started to protest with much force, but Analee planted a peck on her cheek and headed for the door.

"I'd best go see that the household is up and running this morning. You should go and get a few hours of sleep. I'll have Maetta come sit with him."

"Oh . . . I'd rather stay myself, uh, if it's all right." She suddenly felt very sheepish.

Again, the sparkle lit in Analee's eyes, reaching all the way to her flash of white teeth as she smiled broadly. "Of course, *chica*. I'll send up some strong coffee."

This means nothing, I just don't wish for the man to die, that is not so strange, Bailey told herself as Analee closed the door.

An hour later, Bailey stood and stretched, rubbing her hands across the arch of her lower back. She straightened up the room and opened the doors wide to let the morning breeze drift inside. Moments later, she heard Cole's voice and went back to sit next to him, watching him. He seemed awake, though his eyes still had a faraway look to them.

"You cut me open."

"Yes. I did. Would you rather have died?"

He grunted in response.

"No, you won't allow yourself to die until you get your revenge. I know you at least that well."

"If you only knew . . ."

"Shh, don't talk. You need to rest."

He shook his head. ". . . what happened . . . Then you would understand."

"You can tell me later. I want you to rest now."

He shook his head again. "Now."

Bailey knew his look all too well. She gave up and leaned close so he wouldn't have to strain too hard to speak. "I'm listening."

"She—my mother," he said with bitterness, "had an affair. Her lover convinced her to poison my father. Said he wanted to marry her." He coughed and then took a moment to catch his breath.

Bailey dabbed his forehead with a cool cloth, softly coaxing him to continue. "Didn't your mother love your father?"

"He told her my father didn't love her. But he did love her."

"Of course he did," Bailey said soothingly.

Cole nodded. "I was away at school. But Griff was still young. He was there when . . ."

"He was there when what, Cole? What happened next?"

"The man told her she must get rid of Griff—and me. He wanted his own sons."

"He wanted her to kill you and your brother?" Bailey gasped.

"She refused. Said she would ruin him. Reveal the truth about him."

"What truth?"

"His true identity. He is . . . the Dragon," Cole spit out the name, then coughed.

Bailey jerked upright in her chair, smothering a gasp with her palm. She remembered Cole telling her that the Dragon was somehow able to move about the Colonies as if he was one of them. And his mother had been knowingly sleeping with the beast! Bailey's heart broke for Cole. No wonder he held on to so much anger.

"But your mother did not betray him, did she?"

"She couldn't, even if she would have. He stabbed her . . . in the heart. Left her to die. I had been called back from school when my father got ill. I got home too late for him. A day after this had happened. She had been asking for me—would only talk to me. She told me everything. Almost everything. Mother wanted my forgiveness first," he said bitterly.

Bailey squeezed her eyes shut, understanding at once. Cole had not given his forgiveness and it had cost him the name of the Dragon. "Your mother died before she could tell you who he was." Her voice was barely a whisper.

He nodded, looking at her, his expression empty. He appeared as if his emotions were spent and he had nothing left inside. Bailey couldn't bear to see him defeated. She longed for the anger, the arrogance, something. Anything of the unbreakable man she had come to know.

"Your mother loved you, Cole. You see that, don't you? She made mistakes, terrible mistakes. But she couldn't go through with killing you and your brother. It seems that your mother was going to do the right thing, after all."

"It's my fault. I didn't forgive her. And now I chase a ghost."

Bailey leaned close and turned his face to her. "None of it is your fault. None of it, you hear me? No one could blame you for being too angry to forgive her. It was a shock—you had no time to sort through it all before she died. You can still forgive her."

He reached out and stroked his fingers down the side of her face. Then he dropped his hand and closed his eyes. "No," he breathed, falling back into a deep sleep.

She studied his sleeping form, seeing him with new eyes. He was as damaged as she was, perhaps more. He didn't seem able or willing to let go of any of the pain of his past. It had been difficult and she prayed every night for the strength to be happy again. Her father had always told her that her mother wouldn't want them to be sad forever. So Bailey had learned to be happy after her mother's death. And she was trying her best to follow her father's words again.

Cole was not going to find happiness again. He fought it.

She wished he wouldn't. A part of her wished she could heal him and stay with him forever. But she knew he had chosen his path and would not stray from it for anything. Even ravaged with fever, his face held the strain of the truth he had revealed to her.

She sighed and walked through the open French doors to stand on the balcony. She breathed in the fresh morning breeze and surveyed the beauty of the morning. Out in the ocean to her left, she spotted the large square sails against the pale blue-gray sky.

The supply ship had arrived.

Bailey hugged her arms to her body watching the progress of the ship as it docked. She should be bursting with excitement. This was the ship that would take her home.

Away from here.

Away from Cole.

So, why did a part of her wish that the ship out there was just a figment of her imagination?

She rubbed her arms vigorously, as if to rub away her conflicted emotions, and returned to Cole's bedside. She was simply feeling empathy for him, for the terrible tragedy that had befallen his family at the hands of the Dragon. It was something they shared, the destruction of their loved ones by the very same vile pirate, so it was only natural that she would feel compassion for Cole. But it was nothing more than that. She couldn't allow it to be more.

The sun had yet to reach its peak in the sky, yet the heat was settling like a thick blanket on the upper floor of the house, when Bailey woke from a light doze. Thankfully, the island winds were fairly constant, allowing a nice breeze to drift into the room. Her head had been resting on her forearm on the mattress next to Cole and she groaned, feeling the stiffness in her muscles. Bailey touched the back of her hand to Cole's dry forehead and let out an audible sigh of relief. She watched his sleeping form as she rubbed her sore neck and stood to stretch.

Analee came into the room, followed by a servant carrying a pitcher of fresh water.

"How is he?" she asked, worry evident in the wrinkles on her forehead.

"The fever is gone," Bailey managed, her voice filled with emotion.

"—*¡Gracias a Dios!*" Analee said, giving her thanks to God, and the two women hugged each other, laughing, as much from fatigue as from relief.

Together, they cleaned Cole's wound and rebandaged him before sharing a few minutes of quiet conversation on the sun-drenched balcony. After being interrupted by two young maids, Analee excused herself to go and see to their problem. Not long after she left, the embracing warmth of the sunshine wrapped around Bailey and she felt exhaustion taking over her mind and body. Feeling confident that Cole was out of danger, she decided to go to her room and lie down. It would be hours until the supply ship was ready to leave and it would benefit her to be rested for the voyage home. She prayed she could convince the captain of the vessel to take her to the Colonies, despite her inability to pay for her passage.

She went to Cole's bedside one last time, grateful that his eyes were not open to see deep into her soul. She reached into her pocket and removed the ring, taking one last look at the bold *L* engraved in the gold before sliding it onto the fifth finger of Cole's left hand. She hoped having his mother's ring would somehow bring him the peace he sorely needed. Then, impulsively, she bent over him and placed a soft kiss of good-bye upon his warm, full lips.

Chapter Nineteen

The next day, Cole refused to stay in bed. There was nothing Analee could do to keep him quiet or subdued as he paced the length of his room. Enough time had been wasted on his injury and he had urgent business to attend to. In typical fashion, he refused to tell her what was so important that he couldn't rest for a few days. Analee's pleas went ignored. He had ordered the *Barracuda* to be ready to sail in two days' time. Cisco was as confused as the rest of the crew, for he had been told nothing of their destination.

The truth was, Cole didn't know what to say to them. He was filled with a mixture of fury and disbelief. Bailey had left the island on the *Sea Spirit* and he was going to get her back.

His foggy memory cleared just enough to remember telling her everything in his fever-induced state. She had been so appalled, she took the first opportunity to run from him. Forget that he had saved her from the grim fate of slavery, his confession had been too much for her. He supposed he shouldn't blame her, but the wench owed him and he wasn't about to let her just sail away without giving him his due. Any pangs of conscience he had had about how he had treated her on New Providence burned away with every minute that crept by, dragging the morning into endless hell. Damn his conscience, anyway. He had thought it had been killed the day his mother had made her own sinful confessions, but it seemed a small part had survived. Survived to betray him once again.

But it would be the last time, he vowed to himself, groaning with pain as he shrugged into a clean shirt. When he found her, he would show no mercy. Whatever it took, in whatever way he found necessary, he would use her to draw out the Dragon. He stared into the cold fireplace and took a long swig of wine from a crystal glass on a tray filled with uneaten food. He calculated how many hours had passed since the *Sea Spirit* had departed the island, his anger swelling as he absently squeezed the delicate crystal until the pop of glass shattered his thoughts.

"Damn!" he cursed, shaking the broken pieces of glass onto the floor.

"What happened? Are you all right?"

Cole swung around abruptly at the voice that was so foreign, yet so familiar to him.

"What are you doing here?" he barked as Bailey crossed his bedroom in a swish of light green silk skirts.

"Let me see," she said, ignoring his question as she set down a basket on the table next to the fireplace.

She took out a strip of clean cloth and motioned for him to come and sit in the adjacent chair. Still stunned by her presence, he did as he was told without thinking to refuse. She knelt on the thick carpet, between his casually spread knees and took his hand in hers, gently brushing away the tiny shards of glass that glittered in his palm.

"Hold still. There are a few pieces quite stuck in there. What in heaven's name were you thinking about to break a glass in your hand?" she asked as she carefully plucked out one, two, then three good-sized slivers of glass, dropping them on the silver tray where his cold food sat.

"I don't know. It was an accident." He stared down at the top of her head, several golden-red waves of hair draping forward in her face. She paused to tuck the strands behind her ear and continued, her forehead wrinkled and lips puckered in concentration. He glanced down, to the low neckline of the dress that seemed to barely hold the full curves of her bosom.

To his chagrin, he found his anger slipping away, as another fiery emotion started to take hold of his body. Kneeling between his legs as she was, with her head tilted just so, he began to imagine a completely different kind of attention she could be paying to his body and he felt that part of him react instantly. He groaned, wishing he had the strength to tell her to go.

"Oh. I'm sorry. Did I hurt you?"

"No," he growled.

"There! I think I got it all," she said, releasing his hand and standing up.

"What are you doing here?" he asked again, sucking a drop of blood from his middle finger.

"I came to see if your bandage needs to be changed. I'm afraid it's been too long since you've been checked. I was just told that Analee has been occupied and I'm embarrassed to admit that I slept quite late this morning. I only woke an hour ago."

"What happened yesterday." He had meant it as a question, but it sounded to his own ears like an accusation. "I mean to say, who tended me yesterday?" He had been told that Bailey had not left his side, but he thought Analee was trying to keep the truth from him so he would lie still.

"Analee and I have been taking care of you. And Maetta has been a wonderful help to us. You had a terrible infection in the wound in your side. And a fever. You almost died."

"When did the fever break?"

"Yesterday morning. A little after daybreak."

Cole made the connections in his mind but still couldn't fathom the truth of it. He had to know.

"Why didn't you leave?" At her look of astonishment, he continued in a cool tone. "Yesterday, on the *Sea Spirit*."

"How . . . How did you know?" she asked, her clear eyes wide and bright with color against her pale face.

"I was awake when you put this on my finger," he said, briefly flashing the ring on his finger. He watched the pink flood her face. "The kiss was unnecessary, though," he added, knowing the comment was hurtful, but telling himself he didn't care. He didn't want there to be a chance that she could sense the relief he was feeling that she was still here.

"Awake? What were you doing, playing the spy?" she asked, flustered.

Cole laughed, then cringed at the pain it caused him.

"Are you all right?" she asked immediately, stepping toward him again.

Cole sobered at the genuine concern in her voice, on her face. He held up a hand. "I am fine. It's no more than I deserve for being such a churl. I appreciate what you did for me, Bailey. Really, I do. Now, answer my question. Why didn't you leave when you had the chance? That is why you gave me the ring, isn't it? As a sort of payment?"

She shook her head. "Not really. I just thought you might want it someday. Besides, it wouldn't have been nearly enough. But I promise I was going to find a way to pay you back."

He shook his head. "That's not what I'm interested in. Tell me. Why?"

"You had a fever," she offered quietly.

"But the fever was gone by daybreak, you said so yourself. The *Sea Spirit* didn't leave until the evening tide." Her look of exasperation amused him and he couldn't help but smile at the show of emotion that she was too innocent to conceal.

She hesitated a long moment before replying, tipping her head shyly, her hands folded in front of her as she squeezed her fingers to white. "You needed me."

"And now?"

"Now, what?" she asked, looking as if she was about to melt with embarrassment.

"Now that you are staying, do you want this back?" he asked, holding up his hand to display the gold ring.

She shook her head. "It doesn't belong with me. It isn't going to help me get home, and that is all I want. You should have it—for whatever purpose you see fit."

Cole felt a sudden tug of conscience at her gesture. In a way, it seemed she was telling him she hoped that he was successful in his quest for the pirate. But the best way for his success to be assured was for him to continue with his plan to use her. So he swallowed his conscience and told her the lie he knew would keep her satisfied for at least a little while longer.

"As soon as I am fit, I will see you home."

He expected a look of joy on her face. But there was no joy there. Surprise, perhaps, but then something else as well. Did she suspect that he was lying?

"You don't believe me?"

"No, of course I do. I . . . uh . . . Thank you," she said quietly. Then she hastily excused herself and rushed from the room.

Chapter Twenty

Life on the island returned to its normal easy pace once Cole began roaming about, showing everyone that the master of Lochinvar was well on the mend. He had spent one full day in his study going over Lochinvar's accounts, the room's tall white shutters flung wide to let in the cool ocean breezes and dispell the musty scent of disuse.

Cole had spent another day catching up with the different crews that worked the various crops on the farm. Yesterday had been taken up overseeing the light repairs and maintenance of the *Barracuda,* for he didn't expect to stay long at his island paradise. While in New Providence, Cole had made arrangements for the word to spread that there was a survivor in the Beaufort raid; a survivor who could identify the infamous Dragon. Once the rumor reached its target, Cole was certain the pirate would come out of hiding to hunt down that survivor. The other thing Cole was certain of was that the Dragon would never rest until that person was dead. Though the rumor would not be specific about who the survivor was, Cole knew that he was making it impossible to let Bailey leave him. He knew it three days ago when he promised to take her home.

Something had come over him while he lay half-conscious

and felt her slip the Dragon's ring on his finger. He was certain he would wake to find her gone. But that next day when she had walked into the room, her aqua eyes rimmed with red and worry, the lie had slipped too easily off his tongue. No matter how much he regretted the events he'd put into motion, there was no turning back. If she got angry that she wouldn't be going home, then so be it. He was now her only protection.

Damn! How she set his guilt aflame. She was wreaking havoc on his mind despite the fact that he hadn't seen her these past three days. He had no idea what she was occupying her time with, and no matter how busy he tried to keep himself, she was never far from his thoughts. He still couldn't fully understand why she hadn't sailed with the supply ship when she had the chance. It was no secret the ship was bound for the Colonies and knowing Captain Winthrop as well as he did, Cole had no doubt the soft-hearted seaman would have seen her safely to Beaufort.

You needed me.

Her words still rang in his head. She had given up her chance to get away from him, simply because she felt he had needed her? It was too selfless for him to comprehend. She knew what her future held if she stayed with him, he had been brutally clear about his intentions. She put her own wishes—nay, her very freedom—aside, to see him through his fever. He had done nothing to gain her concern, in fact, everything he had done since they were thrown together had warranted the complete opposite. He would never understand the twisted makings of a woman's mind.

Irritably, he tightened the cinch on his horse's saddle, wincing at the pain that shot through the healing wound at his side. The animal snickered and danced, as if sensing his owner's mood.

"Sorry, Maximilian, old boy. I shouldn't take out my surly temper on you."

"Would you rather take it out on me?"

Cole spun around to find Bailey standing in the doorway

of the stable, the bright sun lighting her from behind, making her expression unreadable.

"I am losing precious days with this nonsense," he said, gesturing with a nod to his bandaged midsection.

"That 'nonsense' nearly took your life. I would think a few days are a small price to pay."

"I have already paid more than my share; it is past time for me to make up for my losses."

"Or die trying?" she asked. As she walked into the stable, he noticed that she appeared much improved since the last time he saw her. Dressed in lavender, her burnished gold curls tamed with matching ribbons, she looked as fresh as any of the flowers that bloomed across the island. "I would think you would have learned the lesson of patience. I have had to learn it in the past days, yet soon I will be rewarded by going home."

Her voice held excitement and more than a note of hope. He should just tell her the way of it right now; get it over with once and for all. Her anger he could take. Her happiness made him squirm. Cole finished with the buckles on the saddle and moved to fit the bridle over the horse's head, ready to change the topic before his guilt undid him. He felt the sudden need to distract her from the topic at hand.

"Would you like me to show you around the island?"

"I've seen quite a bit of it already. Analee and I walk almost every day."

"You don't want to come?"

"No. I mean, yes. I was just saying that . . . oh, never mind. I'd love to see more of your lovely island."

"Give me a moment to saddle another horse."

"I don't know how to ride."

Cole heaved out a sigh. "Of course you don't," he muttered under his breath.

"Pardon?" she asked, stepping close enough that he could smell the light floral scent of the soap on her skin.

"You will ride with me. Come, turn around," he said, waiting patiently for her to comply. When she finally moved close enough, he placed his hands on her small waist, ready to lift her up.

"Your wound! You cannot lift me. I will stay here," she protested trying to move out of his hold.

"The only thing irritating my wound is your wiggling. Now, be still," he commanded her before lifting her up and settling her on the horse.

She smiled down at him, her face filled with the excitement of a new experience, and then giggled when he rolled his eyes before climbing up behind her and leading the horse out of the stable.

The island was paradise, and although Cole never took for granted the beauty of his island retreat, seeing it through Bailey's eyes proved to reignite his enthusiasm for all the color, sounds, and fragrances surrounding them.

They rode up a wide, sun-drenched path lined with vibrant pink hibiscus and the scent of frangipani hanging in the humid air. Cole pointed out some of the brightly colored birds perched above their heads, squawking loudly in the branches of Caribbean Pine and Calabash trees.

The path opened up to large fields stretching out in both directions, lined with neat rows of sugarcane plants drinking in the sun. As they rode along the rows, Cole checked the condition of the plants, explaining to Bailey the arduous process of harvesting and processing the plants into sugar. Many of the surrounding islands grew sugarcane and exported huge amounts of the profitable crop to Europe and the Colonies. But sugarcane was a brutal crop to harvest, requiring many workers; slaves who saw none of the profits of their blood and sweat. Cole had lived his entire life being taught that slavery was a necessary part of running the vast, self-contained plantations in the New World. From his great-grandfather, who had built Rosegate, to his father and all of their peers, slavery had become an accepted way of life in the colonies, just as it had been for hundreds of years in many parts of the world. But Cole had traveled the world and had seen the evils that men committed on the ones they dominated, and he had grown to hate the institution. None of the people who lived and worked at Lochinvar were slaves—at least not since they had found their way here. He couldn't change the world. He couldn't even free his own people at Rosegate without dire consequences to his and Griffin's livelihood, but he could do whatever he damn well pleased here.

He was thankful that Bailey wasn't aware of this particular belief, or his *purchase* of her in New Providence would mean nothing and she would undoubtedly try to leave him again when she found out how long she might have to wait. Besides, now that he had involved her in his plot for revenge, leaving was not an option. She would have to stay with him until the end.

Cole knew he couldn't stall forever. He needed to tell her what he'd done to put her at risk, if only to convince her that she was safer with him than in Beaufort. But each time he thought to tell her, she interrupted with a smile, or a laugh, or a question about some plant or strange-looking animal that went scurrying as they rode past. He hated to admit it, but he was enjoying Bailey's company and the pleasure she was experiencing at his home.

They left the cane fields and rode through orchards of citrus trees, then mango and banana trees, past a field of low strawberry plants, and finally the many rows of vegetable gardens, closer to the main house. They were almost back, he realized, acknowledging the slightest disappointment. It had been hours that seemed like minutes. They had talked easily, Bailey laughing often, even as she recounted memories of a life that was all but shattered fragments of what it had once been. She had been sheltered and protected by her father as well as by the simple life the Spencers had led, and as the day wore on, he found himself warming to the notion of being her protector, rather than her persecutor. But before he could be seduced by any more such reckless thoughts, he pulled on the reins and turned Max toward the stables, anxious to put some distance between Bailey and his dangerous imaginings.

Bailey strolled along the beach, dragging her toes in the delicious warmth of the powdery, soft sand. The time she had spent with Cole yesterday had felt like the rarest of gifts. Cole had revealed even more of himself to her, a side of him that Bailey found incredibly attractive. His mother may have damaged his caring spirit, but Bailey realized that the lady had not killed it.

She hoped to catch sight of Cole this morning, so she had collected herbs from the side garden, where she could keep an eye on the stables. But the morning faded and he didn't come. After depositing the herbs in the kitchen and sharing tea with Analee, Bailey excused herself for a solitary walk. She needed to sort out her feelings for Cole, feelings that were growing, despite her better judgment. Not leaving on the *Sea Spirit* had been a surprise that she couldn't explain to herself. Seeing him lying in bed so weak and helpless, he was a far cry from the indomitable, arrogant man who claimed to live only for the sake of vengeance. And after he had shared his painful secrets with her, she felt a bond with him that she couldn't explain. His trust in her had touched her deeply, though she doubted he even remembered what he'd told her. Lately she found herself wishing he would share more with her.

It was senseless, she knew. There was no future to be had with Cole, not as long as he sought revenge against the Dragon. He would never be safe, and neither would she. Nothing she longed for—family, security, love—would ever be possible with Cole.

Regret tugged at her heart, but she took a deep breath and tried to think of what her future would hold. She walked down to the shoreline to cool her feet in the crystalline water, hiking her blush-pink petticoat up to her calves. The rhythmic roll and crash of breaking waves helped to ease her mind away from the painful truths about Cole. Mingled with the roar of the ocean and cries of seagulls came a high-pitched whinny and Bailey turned around to find Cole riding Max down the beach toward her. Her heart skipped and her breath caught at the sight of him straddling the horse, barefoot, in fitted brown breeches and a white shirt, open to the waist. He reached her before she could recover herself and swung down from the horse, dropping the reins and letting the animal wander a short distance to the shady palms lining the beach.

"I see you've found my favorite stretch of beach on the island," he said casually, pushing his dark hair back from his sparkling eyes.

"Is it? I can certainly see why you love it here. The water is the most exquisite color I've ever seen," she said, hoping he didn't realize the effect he was having on her.

"The exact color of your eyes. At this moment, anyway. When you're angry, they are quite a different shade altogether. Much deeper, more blue than green."

Her knees felt weak. Since when had he noticed her eyes? "I came upon this place by accident. I was following the most beautiful trail of the berries you showed me yesterday." She suddenly realized she still held her skirt up and dropped it immediately, the hemline instantly soaking up water. "I can leave if you want to be alone."

"No need. In fact, if you wish, I could show you how to dig for clams. I find some of the best ones right along this stretch," he said with a wave of his muscular forearm. He whistled and Max reared his head and trotted casually toward them. Cole retrieved two metal tools resembling tiny shovels and handed her one, before leading the horse behind him.

Against every ounce of good sense that said nay, she found herself following as easily as Max. "I make the best clam stew in two counties," she boasted playfully as she caught up to him to walk side by side with him down the beach.

"You may just have to prove that tonight, Bailey."

The way he said her name, like a caress, sent gooseflesh skimming across her arms.

Soon, they were ankle-deep in the clear ocean, bent over, thrusting their hands into the gooey mixture of sand and salty water to recover the clams that weren't fortunate enough to be buried deep enough to escape capture. It was difficult to move the sand and the continuous waves aided the clams more than their captors and before long they were laughing like children caught playing in a mud puddle.

"You are a mess, Colby Leighton. Here, allow me to rinse you off," she teased, scooping up as much water as she could and drenching his face completely.

He sputtered and blinked his eyes in an exaggerated fashion, as if he had just recovered from a near drowning. "Mmm. Salty," he said, licking the edges of his lips. "You must try some." He advanced on her, moving with comical awkwardness in the shallow waves toward her as she backed away, giggling.

Her wet skirt was weighing her down considerably and she tried to lift it in order to move faster, when suddenly a wave caught her in the backs of her knees, knocking her off her feet. She landed on her backside in the water and when she recovered, wiping the salty water from her eyes, Cole stood directly above her, hands on his hips, a huge grin covering his face. It was a breathtaking sight, despite the fact that it was due to her clumsiness and resulting embarrassment.

"You!"

"Me? I didn't touch you. You managed this act of grace all by yourself," he teased. "Would you like some assistance now?"

He reached out and she placed her hands in his palms, allowing him to lift her heavy, wet weight out of the water. He groaned and panted as if he was lifting Max, and once she was firmly on her feet, she shoved against his bare chest with the flat of her palms.

"You are a despicable oaf, and you must be punished," she said in her most wicked voice.

He stepped back, one gleaming dark brow raised in curiosity and interest as she bent and scooped up a handful of wet sand. His other brow raised and he tilted his head to the other side, as he comprehended the mischief she was about. She slowly circled him as he followed with his gaze, then let out a growl and spun on her, trapping her wrists in his wet grip before she could dump the sand down his waistband.

"Oh, my, my. So, you are a devilish little wench today, aren't you, Bailey?"

"I . . . It was an accident?"

"I think not." He turned her palms, forcing her to drop the clumps of sand.

"No?"

His eyes shone like liquid silver fire. He shook his head. "And allow me to repeat your own words of just a moment ago." As he spoke, he pulled her wrists around and held them behind her back. "You must be punished."

Before she could utter a denial, his lips crushed hers in a damp, salty kiss. Against every reaction she knew to be sane, she responded by pressing her body more closely to his, her breasts crushing against his bare skin, her nipples hardening beneath the wet, thin fabric of her bodice. She moaned deep in her throat and felt Cole deepen the kiss in response, slanting his mouth over hers possessively, completely.

He dropped her wrists and she felt him lift her and carry her just out of the water before he set her down once again, her feet touching the damp, packed sand.

"Tell me to stop," he said, desperation edging his husky voice. He kissed the hollow of her neck, then moved to her shoulder.

Did he truly want a response? His lips moved back to her neck, his tongue making a hot trail up to the sensitive tip of her ear, where it lingered, making a shiver travel up her spine.

"Tell me," he breathed into her ear.

"Don't. Stop." She dropped her head to give him better access and moaned as he readily accommodated her.

As his lips and tongue continued their torturous assault, she explored his bare chest with her hands, feeling the hard muscles underneath the tiny grains of sand. He lifted his head and looked into her eyes, as if he was searching for some sign that she wanted him to put an end to the madness that was overtaking them. In response, she pushed his wet linen shirt off his shoulders and down his arms, until the heavy weight of it pulled the material out of the loose breeches and it fell to the sand. Then, wordlessly, she pulled at the laces holding her bodice together and pulled the pale silk garment aside, leaving her breasts all but exposed in the transparent chemise that left nothing to the imagination.

"You are trying to kill me, wench," he murmured as he drank in the sight of her without touching.

"If that is so, then isn't this a preferable way to go than at the end of a blade, or with your neck in a noose?"

"It is all the same when said and done."

"I admit I don't know much about it, but I don't believe this is supposed to kill a man."

"With that siren's body and those sea-blue eyes that make such promises, I almost believe you," he moaned, sliding his thumbs down the curves of her face.

She was throwing herself at him, fully accepting of what they were about to do, yet he still held back, unable to fully trust her. Wanting so badly to reach him and release him from the pain that held chains around his heart, Bailey pushed aside her remaining inhibitions and called to the woman in her. The woman that Cole had been coaxing out of her these past weeks. Not quite sure of what to do, but knowing generally where the core of his passion existed, she slid her hand slowly down the front of him. Down the hard plane of his chest, past the ripples of his stomach, past the ties on his breeches and lower still until she heard his sharp intake of breath.

She felt that hard part of him press against her palm, straining against the fabric that separated skin from skin and she felt a surge of power she had never felt before. She looked up into his eyes, his gaze filled with restrained passion—passion that she longed for him to give in to.

"You don't understand the consequences of—"

"I don't understand you, either, but I don't care. I don't care about anything, except how you make me feel. I want this as much as you do."

"I don't . . . Ah, God, Bailey." He couldn't finish his denial.

With that, she knew he wanted her.

For now, she could forget about whatever might come tomorrow.

As if to seal her fate, she innocently stroked the hard shaft beneath her hand, feeling it come alive again with her unpracticed caress.

Cole could stand no more. He wanted her. Badly. More than he had ever wanted any woman before. Trust be damned. Betrayal be damned. He would sell his soul this very second just for this one chance to feel himself buried deep inside her sweetness. Somehow, he knew that if he took her, he would never be the same, but he didn't care. He felt as reckless as she did and they would likely both pay dearly for it, but like she had just breathlessly confessed, he didn't give a damn, either.

He pulled her hand from his throbbing member, kissing her fingers and then her open palm.

"Am I doing something wrong?" she asked shyly.

"No, dove. On the contrary. I'm afraid you will have this ended before it's begun if you're not careful." He laughed gently at her confused look. "Don't frown. We'll get there. I'll show you everything, all in good time. Now, why don't we start with you?" he asked and grinned wickedly. He lowered them to the packed sand and rolled playfully, pulling her beneath him.

Cole settled his weight on top of her and took her eager lips in a long, sensual kiss. His tongue licked at her salty lips, teasing them apart, then stroking her tongue with his, he coaxed her to respond and reveled in the moan that came from deep in her throat. She became restless, her body moving beneath him, unknowingly begging him for a release he knew she wasn't even aware she desired. She arched up, clutching her fingers into his back, her uninhibited response to him making his ache almost unbearable. He tore his lips from hers and ripped open the flimsy chemise, burying his face in the cool, wet skin of her breasts. He suckled them, one by one, fondling each cool, wet mound with his fingers, then licked one hard nipple with the tip of his tongue while teasing the other to tighten beneath his fingers. She arched again, pressing her body more fully into his mouth, moaning and breathing in rasping gulps of air.

"Cole . . . Cole."

"What is it, dove?" *Christ, please don't ask me to stop*.

"Please . . ."

"Do you want me to stop?"

"No! I just . . . I feel so strange. It aches."

"I know, sweet, I know. But it won't for much longer, I promise," he said, knowing he told her the truth about that, at least.

He rose to his knees and slid her heavy skirts up to her thighs, revealing her long, slender legs. She was trembling, so he rubbed his hands up and down her legs, then placed kisses along the length of the inside of one shapely limb, stopping only when he ran into the folds of pink silk fabric.

"I fear I am at the verge of my own ruin, yet I am powerless to resist you."

In response, she raked her luminous gaze over his half-naked form, unconsciously touching her tongue to her parted lips in a most sensual gesture.

"You are a vixen, after all, I see. I am yours, vixen, have

mercy," he breathed as he began unfastening the tangled ties on his wet breeches.

Before he could finish the task, Cole was rudely wrenched from the moment as the sounds of laughing and loud voices carried to him on the wind. Instantly, he was on the move, pulling Bailey's skirt down and moving off of her to retrieve his discarded shirt. She recovered almost as quickly, scrambling to sit up and cover herself, for her ripped chemise was beyond hope and would offer no cover for her bare breasts. Cole tossed her his shirt and helped her stand up just as the group of intruders burst through the scrubby bushes and rushed the beach. A dozen children, laughing and shouting gaily, darted past them, without so much as a second look and ran straight into the ocean, frolicking and splashing without a care in the world.

Cole felt as if his balls had been caught in a vise, the pain streaking a direct path to his erection and up his body to a deafening roar and pounding in his head. He could see that Bailey wasn't doing much better, though he couldn't imagine that she could be suffering as much as he was at the moment.

"I'm sorry, Bailey. This is not how it's supposed to end. I promise you there is great pleasure involved in what we were about to do." *And I will prove it to you the very next chance I get,* he swore to himself.

"This was wrong," she said, her voice sounding strained. "I cannot be alone with you again," she cried and tried to wrench away from him.

Her words didn't register in his passion-dulled mind, as he hurried them along to where Max stood patiently munching on a bright green leaf. And even if her words had hit home, his body was demanding every bit of his attention, just to ease his considerable discomfort. And so he remained, the entire ride back to the house, with Bailey's soft backside pressed between his legs and the vision of her willing body writhing on the sand burning a hole into his passion-sotted brain.

Chapter Twenty-One

When they arrived at the house, Bailey rushed through the garden entrance on the side of the house, fleeing like a half-drowned wraith past two startled housemaids as she made her way to her room. Thankfully, she had seen no one else on her way upstairs and now she burst into her room and slammed and locked the door behind her.

Cole had told her he would have a bath sent up, but at the moment, she didn't care about a bath or anything else. All she could think about was how she had let her body nearly betray every moral fiber of her being. She had been a breath away from giving herself—completely willingly—to a man she was not married to. A man who by his own words would never marry. Or even love, for that matter! Sweet Mary, what had come over her? Had she lost complete control over her own senses since the night of the attack? By all that was holy, it seemed so.

"What am I to do?" she cried softly to herself as she paced the carpet in her bare feet.

For one thing, she could not be alone with Colby Leighton again. Ever! She forgot everything that mattered when she was near him. Her desire for a family and to live a safe, quiet life; even the basic duty of protecting her already-fragile reputation fled her brain when she was around Cole.

At a knock on the door, she spun around, releasing drying salt and sand from her skirt to litter the thick carpet.

"Go away!" she cried, wringing her hands in front of her.

"I have water for your bath, miss," came a timid reply from the hallway.

Bailey sighed, collecting herself. There was no call to be rude to Maetta, who had been so good to her. She opened the door, apologized for her curtness and allowed the girl to enter the room, followed by three young men carrying buckets of steaming water. Bailey went to stand on the balcony, her back to the room while her bath was prepared, and soon the servant came to tell her all was ready. Bailey dismissed Maetta, and once she was alone again the lure of the luxurious bath soon had her standing next to the tub, examining all the different oils and soaps that had been placed on a low table there. She chose a combination of rosemary and lavender oils, dripping them both and watching them swirl as she dragged her fingers through the warm water. In no time she had shed Cole's shirt and her heavy, briny clothes and was soaking away all of the tension and guilt amassed from her downfall on the beach.

A mere half hour later, Bailey was feeling much better. The bath had refreshed her, body and spirit. The deep physical discomfort she had felt had eased as well, though she felt the strangest sense of emptiness. As if a part of her was missing something. She shook off the odd feeling and poured a glass of the deep red wine that Maetta had brought along. Bless her heart, Bailey thought. The lively dark-eyed girl always seemed to know what she needed and when.

The afternoon air was hot and the breeze that tussled the sheer curtains tempted Bailey outside to the balcony. She wore only a dressing robe, filmy white silk that felt cool and sinful against her skin. She ran her fingers through her damp hair, tossing her head to catch the breeze, allowing the fragrant air to dry her wavy locks. She closed her eyes and tilted her head back, feeling a drift of wind sneak under the robe and caress her legs. She imagined that it was Cole caressing her, his large, rough hands gently stroking her the way they had on the beach. Heaven help her, no matter how hard she tried, she could not put him out of her mind. She had wanted his touch then. And she wanted it still.

Suddenly, as if she had drawn him by sheer will, she felt him behind her, wrapping his arms around her waist, burying his lips against her neck.

"No," she murmured, thinking she must be dreaming. But then, if it was a dream, what was the harm? "Mmm, yes."

"No or yes? Pray, make up your mind quickly, wench, before I go too far."

This was no dream. She tried to turn, but he held her in place, nuzzling his face in the damp hair against her neck.

"You smell like heaven."

He breathed in and then exhaled a long, warm breath next to her ear, making her shiver with delight. "But this is not heaven, and I fear you are the devil here to tempt me," she responded. It was the best she could think of to dissuade him.

He nestled his body closer to her backside, sliding his hands down the silky fabric along the curves of her hips and thighs, then again encircling her waist.

"You have yet to answer me. Is it 'yes,' or do I throw myself over the balcony and end this unbearable torture for good?"

She giggled, despite herself. But still, she was unable to answer him. She hadn't the strength to tell him no or the courage to say yes. She tilted her head to give him better access to her neck and half-prayed that he would not require her answer after all.

She felt his lips and tongue burn a path down her neck to the hollow at her shoulder. He shoved the fabric down, baring her skin to his delicious onslaught and she moaned in response. As his lips caressed and his teeth raked her shoulder, his hand slid around and found its way inside the robe, capturing the full weight of her breast. He fondled and caressed and she arched into his hand more fully, laying her head back on his shoulder with a soft mewl of pleasure. He smelled of salt and seaweed and ocean. He gently squeezed her nipple, rolling it between his thumb and forefinger, sending a searing heat shooting down into her core. He reached his other hand around, capturing the other breast and lavishing it with the same slow, deliberate attention.

She thought she would go mad with pleasure, her body felt weightless, as if she floated above the earth. She ached to touch him in return, and struggled to turn and face him. He held her still, tightening his arms like steel bands around her body.

"Not yet, sweet. I have more territory to conquer," he whispered huskily in her ear before nipping the lobe with his teeth.

"But I wish to conquer, too," she replied in a husky voice.

"Ah, but you already have. God, how you have conquered me," he breathed heavily, as if fully defeated.

She took in his words, her heart leaping at the possibilities she heard in them. Could it be possible? Did they have a chance to be together? Was it possible she could not fight these strong feelings for him because she was meant to feel them? In this moment of sheer madness, she pretended it was so.

She released her grip on the balcony railing, dropping her arms to her sides in complete surrender to his well-practiced caresses. He reached down and untied the robe, pulling the garment off her body with one swift motion. She gasped as the silk fell down her limbs and pooled at her feet in a puddle of white, leaving her completely naked and vulnerable to his touch.

"Cole! This is indecent!" She struggled to cover herself but he held her arms down by her sides.

"There is nothing indecent about this—or you. Nothing."

"But . . . We are outside!"

"We were outside on the beach, too," he agreed devilishly, as his hands roamed her body.

He stroked her breasts, the gentle slope of her stomach and lower until his hands brushed lightly against the most secret, private part of her. She inhaled sharply as she felt his fingers brush the curls between her legs, then move lower to tease the skin of her inner thighs.

"Cole, no." Her protest sounded weak, even to her own ears. She prayed he would ignore it.

"Does it feel good, sweet?" he coaxed.

"Mmm. Yes," she moaned, unable to lie, yet still embarrassed by her inexperience.

"Let me show you more. There is so much more," he whispered, sweeping her hair aside and kissing the back of her neck.

His hands swept down her back, cupping her buttocks, squeezing them before sliding around her hips to the front of her once again. He pressed his palm into the mound of curls, rubbing gently, until his fingers naturally felt their way inside her woman's lips. Bailey felt a searing heat flood her cheeks as well as a different kind of heat that swirled deep within her core, just out of reach of Cole's fingers. She was startled and a bit afraid of these new and strange sensations, yet she was not afraid of Cole. She wanted him to be the one to bring out these sensual feelings, to teach her what it felt like to be a woman, completely and totally.

She moaned as his fingers toyed with the sensitive nub, arching instinctively into his hand as he whispered words in her ear that deepened the hot flush on her cheeks. He slipped a finger deep inside her, then out, and repeated the motion again. And again.

"You are so wet," he groaned. "So hot, my little virgin dove."

She sighed in response to the pet name he had given her

in their moments of physical pleasure, trying to ignore the warnings in her head reminding her that if she let him continue, she would no longer be a virgin. But in truth, she didn't care. This was all she cared about. Cole's hands on her. His kisses on her neck. His body pressed hotly against hers. She wanted more of him. All of him. And she wanted to give all of herself to him in return.

"Please, Cole. I want . . ."

"What is it, dove? What do you want?" he asked, his hands cupping her breasts and squeezing.

"I want . . . I am not sure. I want . . . I want you, Cole. All of you."

"And I want you, Bailey. God, how I want you."

Roughly, Cole swept her up in his arms and carried her across the adjoining balcony and through the open sets of French doors to his room, the curtains grazing their skin as they walked through them. He set her on the floor, her body sliding down his chest, catching the rough bits of dried salt and sand that still clung to him.

She had no idea what she should do, or what would come next. Her pulse beat a frantic rhythm as she stood before Cole, naked, her lips and body still tingling from his caresses. He took her hands in his and guided them to the fastenings on his breeches, helping her release them and slide them down his thighs. He stepped out of the damp garment, kicking it aside and then smiled wickedly when he caught her gaping at his nakedness.

Her self-consciousness threatened to overwhelm her but as if he sensed her uncertainty, he lowered his head and captured her lips in a consuming kiss. His hands roamed her body; he had the power to make her crave his touch as if she needed it to breathe. He lowered her to the bed and covered her body with his, smothering her face and neck with kisses before moving lower. He trapped her bent arms to the bed while his mouth found her breasts, teasing one sensitive nipple and then the other with his tongue and teeth. He released her arms as his lips traveled lower, kissing and licking her belly button playfully. She giggled, losing a bit of her self-consciousness and he raised his dark head to gift her with a seductive smile and a promise in the depths of his deep gray eyes.

She saw more there, too. Passion. Feeling. The man that lay deep within the hard shell he had created on the outside. More than anything, she wanted to reach that man, to bring him back to the surface of life. She reached down and entwined her fingers in his silky hair. He nipped at the slight curve of her belly, then slid farther down her body, his warm breath stirring the golden triangle of hair between her thighs.

Before she knew what he intended, he spread her thighs apart and nestled his face into the patch of curls, his tongue entering the folds of her flesh in the most intimate of caresses. She gasped, and tried to push him away, but he laughed deep in his throat and captured her wrists before continuing to pleasure her.

She felt her loins melt and tingle with sensations she had never experienced before. She moaned and tossed her head as the tingling grew and spiraled up and up, throughout her entire body. She began to move her hips instinctively, her pleasure increasing with each flick of his tongue on her sensitive sex. He moaned and moved up, covering her body with his, pressing her thighs farther apart with his weight.

"I have to be inside you. Now," he nearly growled.

"Yes," she agreed, not fully understanding but knowing there must be more and she needed it as much as he did.

He slid between her thighs, filling her completely with his thick, hard shaft. She inhaled sharply at the unexpected, searing pain, digging her nails into his back and holding her breath.

"It will be better soon. I promise," he whispered raggedly. She didn't know why, but she believed him and nodded as he stared down into her eyes.

He began to move then, slowly at first and then faster and harder. She hesitantly moved her hips, matching his rhythm until his movements became too fast and too powerful for her to follow. He cupped her buttocks and guided her legs to wrap about his hips. He pounded into her, a hard rhythm that carried her heavenward. She moaned his name over and over, some unknown hunger building in her until she thought she might die from the intensity of it. She cried out his name and felt her body quiver, as wave after wave of rapture exploded from deep within her body. It was frightening and exquisite all at the same time but soon she felt the pulsing ease as her body floated back down to Earth. She opened her eyes to find him watching her, an expression of pure male pride lighting his features. She held his eyes with hers, his thrusts becoming deeper, harder, as he found his own release, his body shuddering before he relaxed completely, a sheen of sweat covering his face and body.

He kissed her lips and adjusted his weight to rest on his stomach along the entire length of her, his face nuzzled comfortably in the curve of her neck. He wrapped his arm around her waist, as if to keep her from moving away. It was an arrogant gesture of total possession that was purely Cole.

Bailey sighed, a feeling of contentment and sanctuary washing over her.

Chapter Twenty-Two

The next few weeks were like a dream. Bailey was amazed and delighted at the change in Cole. She never would have believed it possible, if she hadn't spent almost every moment with him. He laughed often and winked when he smiled at her, or when he mischievously slapped her backside. Sun-drenched days went by, riding Maximilian across the island or swimming naked in the freshwater pool that Cole claimed no one could find but him. They made love there, in the soft grass or on a secluded stretch of pink beach, the sun's warmth mingling with the heat and sweat of their bodies. At night they made love in his big bed among the layers of soft white covers and pillows. Cole had brought about some changes within her as well, as night after night he coaxed out the vixen within her.

Even on the days when Cole was occupied with work, she saw the difference in him. His attitude was relaxed as he went about the island estate overseeing tasks with an easy author-ity. Gone was the air of tightly subdued rage she had become familiar with on the *Barracuda*. Everyone from field hands to the housemaids noticed the improved mood of the master of Lochinvar, though the only one who dared make a point of it was Cisco. And no amount of ribbing from the old Spaniard could break the wonderful spell.

Now she watched from the grassy bank as Cole walked out of the water, droplets sparkling against his tanned skin like brilliant yellow crystals in the afternoon light. He raked his hands through his hair, smoothing the glossy black back from his face. He smiled at her now, a single dimple poking into his cheek, visible despite the dark stubble that shadowed his unshaven jaw. His teeth flashed white with the smile, though it was more of a wicked leer, she decided as a delicious shiver of pleasure ran up her spine.

"What are you thinking?" he asked, coming to recline on the grass next to her.

"I am wondering if there is a single inch of you that has not been tanned by all of this time you spend without clothing," she teased.

"Hmm. In case you haven't noticed, you have been naked just as much as I. I daresay my innocent little dove is no longer snow-white," he said, raking his eyes down the length of her bare body.

She glanced down her frame, noticing the golden color of her limbs and the light sprinkling of freckles that covered her skin. "Oh, dear! How could I have not noticed this before? I tend to get freckles on my face if I don't wear my hat, but I have always been so careful. Heavens, I have made a mess of myself." She laughed, trying to keep the distress from her voice. James's aunt Charlotte always said that only ladies of low moral character allowed their skin to freckle in the sun. And here she was, her body bared not only to the sun, but to a man who was not her husband. A gloriously handsome rake of a man who, with a mere touch, could make her practically beg him to make love to her.

Just as he was doing now, as he kissed the soft curve of her shoulder while his hand cupped her breast.

"The color suits you. You were looking entirely too priggish with all that pale skin."

She gasped, her brain working to come up with a suitable retort, when she heard his chuckle and realized he had been teasing her.

"I believe you must have some freckles marking that fine, dark body I know you admire so much," she teased back, narrowing her eyes to search his face for the offending spots.

Would you like to examine me more closely?" he offered suggestively, moving to straddle her narrow hips.

She ran her hands up the firm ripples of his stomach, over his ribs and across his wide chest. Cool water dripped from his hair, wetting her skin as he lowered himself over her and took her mouth in a hungry kiss, making her forget what they were bantering about. She opened to him completely, meeting his tongue with hers as his mouth slanted across hers, his skillful assault igniting her desire all over again. His hands roamed her body, skimming the curves of his hips, her breasts, the delicate skin on the inside of her thighs. His lips moved from hers to explore her body, the hard evidence of his arousal brushing against her as he moved lower. And lower.

"Cole . . ."

"What is it, dove?" he asked, his voice husky with want.

"We cannot—that is—we just did *that,*" she finished in near whisper, feeling her cheeks fill with heat.

He chuckled and pressed a kiss on her inner thigh. "Yes, we did, but I have had ample time to recover and I believe we should do 'that' again."

She lifted up on her elbows, eyeing him with astonished embarrassment, making him laugh deeply, bright silver light sparking from his hungry gaze.

"You, sir, are insatiable," she lightly reprimanded him.

"Very well. I will leave you alone, if that is your wish." He made a theatrical display of rolling off of her, landing on his back and sighing heavily.

"Oh, no. That is not my wish at all, rogue," she replied. She climbed on top of his muscular body, kneeling astride his hips.

He angled his head, his gaze saturated with lust. "And what is your wish, then? I shall do my best to fulfill it."

"Ohh!" Bailey covered her face with her hands. She would have thought that the last few weeks had drained all inhibition from her being, but she supposed there was a little bit left, and it was now attempting to appeal to what tiny bit of virtue that remained inside her. Every time Cole introduced her to something new, she thought she would never be able to comply, yet each time she did.

Willingly.

And eagerly.

It seemed she had become as wanton as a gill-flirt and, to her shocked surprise, it was becoming more and more difficult to care about the state of her reputation.

"It pleases me to hear you say that you want me," he said gently, his teasing manner gone. He peeled her hand from her face and kissed the tips of her fingers, letting his tongue and teeth scrape the sensitive pads.

Her eyes locked with his as he continued the seduction, a look of immense pleasure settling on his face, weighting his eyelids heavily. She sucked in a long breath, amazed at the effect he had on her mind and body. She tingled all the way from the fingertips he held to the innermost part of her—the intimate part that he had become quite familiar with of late. Even if she had the will to refuse him, she would not.

"I do want you. I want to please you . . . the way you please me." She felt shy saying the words, as if she was more exposed than simply lying next to him, out of doors and naked. But she felt exhilarated, too. More alive than she had ever felt.

"You do, sweet. You do. Now, why don't you please me

once more before I come undone?" he growled, pulling her down for a thorough kiss.

She wasn't sure what to do next, but before she could worry over it, he lifted her and eased her onto his hard cock. Holding her hips, he guided her movements until she caught on and began to move at her own pace. She was controlling their lovemaking in a way she had never done and she felt powerful and sensual at the same time. His eyes held her own gaze captive, the possessiveness in those silver depths beckoning her closer, closer. She felt almost as if their souls were melting together, creating one body. Cole moaned underneath her and began to move, faster and harder, until all she could do was hold on to him. He sat up, cupping her buttocks and she wrapped her arms around his neck, her head dropping back as he brought them both to a shattering climax.

The rest of the afternoon was spent much the same way, relaxing on the soft grass, eating bread, fruit and wine from a basket Bailey had packed and swimming in the clear blue water of the fresh spring. They had even made love again, this time in the water, as he stood holding her to him while she wrapped her legs around his strong, lean hips. She was learning not to be shocked by the bold and inventive ways that Cole took her, in fact, she reveled in how free and natural it felt whenever her body was joined with his.

The first twinges of evening began to tint the sky as the sun made its gradual change from yellow to deep gold. The few puffy clouds that floated above were becoming saturated with color and the busy calls of birds high on their branches had started to wane. Bailey sighed, nestling more deeply into the crook of Cole's arms as he stroked her hair.

"Could we stay here forever? Just like this?" she whispered, more to herself than to Cole, though she felt him tense and his fingers fell away from her hair. She turned to look up at him and thought she saw a faraway look in his gray eyes. She pulled away and sat up. "Is something wrong?"

He shook his head. "It's getting late. We should be getting back to the house. I have a few matters to attend to before we sail." He smiled and kissed her, before rising and helping her up.

"We are sailing? When?"

"Tomorrow."

"Tomorrow!"

"Yes, tomorrow," he said, pulling on his breeches. "Now, unless you care to sail like that, which is quite fine by me," he teased, "I suggest you get dressed. We have much to do."

He went to get Max, while Bailey dressed and collected the glasses and food and repacked the basket in silent contemplation. It seemed he was finally going to take her back to Beaufort. It was what she had wanted for so long. Only, now . . . how could he take her back after everything they had shared these last weeks? Did he want to be rid of her? Did he feel nothing for her?

No, she refused to believe that. It wasn't possible that he could be so tender and passionate with her and not feel for her the way she felt for him.

It was true.

She had finally admitted to herself what he meant to her. Despite her best intentions and efforts to smother her feelings for him, they refused to die. He was flawed and impossible at times, yet she was seeing evidence of the kindhearted, generous man that lived beneath the scars. And when she gave herself to him that first time, she knew she could no longer deny that he had gotten into her heart.

Weeks ago! She could scarcely believe it had been mere weeks since their relationship had changed so. She felt as if she had known him forever. She had dared not share her feelings with him, though. A small part of her had felt unsure, as if any tiny crack in their blissful world would split it into a thousand, unreachable pieces.

And now that was just what was happening. He was finally

ready to take her home and she did not want to leave him. She couldn't blame him, either. It was all she had asked of him from the very beginning. No, not asked. Demanded.

Oh, why? she thought as sadness crept into her heart. *Why now?*

Cole returned, leading Maximilian, rubbing his nose and speaking in a low tone to him. She watched him as he loaded and secured the blanket and basket on the horse's back and then came over and bent to retrieve his shirt from the grass. He straightened and looked at her in question, one dark brow raised above eyes the color of polished silver. She knew that color meant he was happy. Happy to get rid of her? She had to know.

"Where are we going?" she asked as casually as she could manage, despite her fear of his answer.

He went and looped his shirt through a strap on Max's blanket saddle and answered just as casually. "We are going to Virginia. To Rosegate."

"Rosegate? Your plantation?"

"Yes." He walked back to her and took her hands in his. "I know it's not what you want, but I was hoping you might come with me willingly. The plantation is—"

"Oh, Cole! Of course I will go with you. I am quite excited to see where you grew up. And your brother. I will meet Griffin, won't I? Do you think he will like me? Oh, but I have nothing proper to wear. Your brother is going to think you are dragging home a woman of the lowest virtue when he sees me in that gaudy red dress."

Cole laughed, and kissed her palms, one by one. "Aye, you will meet Griffin, and I'm sure he will like you, even if you are wearing a sugar sack. But I have a feeling that Analee will be more than happy to let you keep the frocks you've been wearing. You have made a loyal friend in her and I have a feeling she will not be so happy to see you leave. Now, come along, let's get you up on Max."

As they rode, Bailey leaned back into Cole, enjoying the sweetly fragrant air and the feel of his chest against her back. She felt a thrilling sense of relief. If Cole was taking her home, it must mean that he had given up his quest for revenge. The weeks they had shared here had shown him what he was missing—joy and peace. She smiled and made a silent promise to bring him so much happiness he would never look back into his painful past again.

"How long will it take us to get to Rosegate?"

Bailey could barely contain her excitement as the *Barracuda* slid out of the thick shade of the sheltered mooring, moving with care out of the shallows toward the open sea. It had been difficult to say good-bye to Analee, and as they hugged and cried they promised to see each other again soon. Bailey was thrilled for Analee when she revealed that Cisco would be staying on the island to begin building their own home, close to Lochinvar.

"It's about a week's sail to Tidewater and then a few hours down the river to Harrison's Landing. Rosegate is on the river, just beyond Berkeley so we won't have to travel by wagon at all. The roads in Virginia are no better than in North Carolina, though at least there is little mud this time of year."

"I would walk to Rosegate in the mud if it was our only way of getting there. But I admit I'm thankful I won't have to." She giggled.

"I expected you to fight me over this. I am pleased that you have come around to trust me." He picked up her hand, turning it over to place a warm kiss in her palm.

"I do trust you."

"Good. And you must remember that if I tell you to do something, you must do it without question. But don't be afraid. I will do everything in my power to keep the Dragon from getting too close."

"I am not afraid anymore. Why would I be? The Dragon knows nothing about where I am, or even the fact that I am alive. And we are going to Rosegate. I am sure I will feel perfectly safe there, and with time we will forget him and every evil thing he has done to us both."

Cole tightened his grip on her hand and searched her eyes, his expression turning deadly serious.

"No, Bailey, that's not going to happen. I will never forget and I will not stop until I have my revenge."

"But you are taking me to your home! I thought you had given up chasing after the Dragon."

He shook his head. "No, Bailey. I will never give up. Not until I have killed the bastard with my own hands."

"Or until he kills you?"

He didn't answer, but she could see the resignation in his eyes. His own death was a distinct possibility and he still behaved as if he didn't care. With some effort, she pulled her hand from his grasp and backed away from him, until she felt her body make contact with the railing.

"You lied to me!" she cried. "You said we would go to your home!"

"We are."

"But you said you were going to forget your revenge." Even as the words left her mouth, she knew it wasn't true. She had wished to hear him say those words, but in truth, he had not, she thought miserably.

He closed the space between them, bracing his hands on the railing on either side of her, trapping her. She suddenly felt as though she couldn't catch her breath.

"You know I never said that."

"Then why are you taking me to Rosegate?"

"I have received information that the Dragon is back in the Colonies, using his titled identity. His greed is beginning to overwhelm his caution. I am getting close, Bailey. Very close, and the bastard is too wrapped up in himself to see me coming."

Bailey shivered at the faraway look in Cole's stormy eyes. The man she had grown to love at Lochinvar was lost to her. He was lost to everything, save his consuming desire for revenge. Despite what she had hoped—nay, prayed for—nothing had changed for him. Sadness filled her but soon diminished with her growing anger.

"You have yet to explain why you are bringing me with you. I have nothing to do with your revenge and there is nothing I will do to help you," she said, allowing the ice that was engulfing her heart to saturate her words as well.

He tilted his head, the telltale arch of his eyebrow hinting at a response she well knew would bring her pain.

"Why would I not bring my own property with me? I find that I am in need of a housemaid. One who can sufficiently warm my bed and satisfy my most personal needs. That, my dove, is you."

"Never!"

"Oh, but it is much too late to say never, Bailey. We have come much too far to undo the things we have done. And I find that I was indeed missing the considerable feminine pleasures that I have been denying myself of late."

"How dare you speak to me this way! I am not your whore and I refuse to let you treat me as one."

"Whore? No, I would not waste so much time on a whore. But since the seduction has yielded me nothing, why don't you just agree to be my lure? Then you may be rid of me all the sooner."

Bailey felt her palm make stinging contact with Cole's unyielding cheek, even before she realized she had slapped him. His only reaction was a heavy pulse in his hard jaw and the slight downward angle of his brows. Both gave his countenance an angry, cold mask that she feared as much as loathed at the moment. But she had lost too much to care, and now she was losing him—though apparently she had never had him to lose. She was ashamed at how wrong she had been about him. And even more ashamed about how freely she had given herself to him when all the while he was seducing her to gain her submission in the only thing he was capable of caring about. Revenge.

"No more! I should have sent that letter to James when I had the chance. I should have left on the *Sea Spirit*—stupid girl!" she reprimanded herself. "Well, mark my words, Colby Leighton, I am no longer an innocent cully and you cannot seduce me or force me to aid you in your ill-advised fixation with the Dragon. I will not be your pawn in this game you play."

"You will do exactly as you are told. You have no other choice." He bit out each word with menace. "I will do whatever it takes to meet my ends. And you will do well to remember that you are not free to leave me."

Refusing to let him see how his threats affected her, Bailey lifted her chin and shoved his arm away from the railing, freeing herself from the prison of his body. She held her composure all the way across the deck, until she was safely away from her dark captain, in the solitude of his large cabin.

She glared at the mahogany bunk they would have shared through the next long nights at sea and felt a cold emptiness wash over her. She would not stay in his quarters one more minute, she decided, and stood to gather her things when she heard heavy footsteps, the distinct metal clink of the cabin door being locked and then the footsteps again, as they retreated down the passageway.

She was once again his unwilling prisoner. Only now, her heart was imprisoned as well.

Several flatboats had been lowered from the *Barraduca* and loaded before they were ready to leave the busy dock. Bailey sat on the hard seat and watched with feigned indifference as Cole jumped in the lead boat, sparing her barely a glance. They rowed out of the bay and after an hour or so the men were able to simply guide the boats as they floated along with the brisk current.

The air along the river felt hot and sticky and lacked the cool breeziness that was so much a part of the Caribbean. Virginia resembled North Carolina in many ways, and Bailey felt the stirrings of homesickness, along with the pain that still surfaced whenever she thought of Adam and her father. As they floated past plantations, with acres and acres of land, she let her gaze roam over the trees and brush that lined the river's edge, to rolling fields filled with grazing cattle and sheep. She had not spoken to Cole in three days, and he had not come to his cabin once since they had argued.

Bailey sighed and tilted the fringed mint-green parasol back in order to see the vast white home that was just becoming visible on top of a gentle hill through the trees ahead. A long dock stretched out into the river just ahead and Miles guided the flatboats to come up behind the two that preceded them. Cole was already on the dock, motioning to the other small vessels and calling out orders to the crew. The dock and grounds were abuzz with activity as several black-skinned men rushed to help unload the crates and trunks from the flatboats.

A well-dressed young man with wavy hair the color of Cole's charged up to him and grabbed him in a fierce embrace. Cole returned the hug, slapping the man's back and then shoving him away and clapping his hands on the smaller man's shoulders. As Bailey's boat approached the dock, she feigned indifference as Cole spoke to the man, who appeared to listen with rapt interest. Miles assisted her from the small boat and she thanked him, retrieving her parasol from Dewey and fidgeting with the tassled handle as she stood, feeling awkward.

The man broke into laughter, startling a crow from a nearby tree and causing Cole to drop his head and run his hands through his dark hair. Bailey felt her cheeks flame as both men turned to look at her. What had he told the man? It seemed that insensitive dolt was not going to allow her the smallest bit of dignity, but he had sorely misjudged her if he thought she was going to let it bother her. She picked up her skirts, raised her chin and walked down the dock, intent on sweeping past without a second glance.

The younger dolt left Cole's side and rushed down the dock to meet her halfway, kissing her hand and bowing gallantly. If he was making fun of her, she would skin him like a rabbit.

"My brother tells me you are Bailey Spencer. Miss Spencer, it is a great pleasure to make your acquaintance. I am Griffin Leighton. Welcome to Rosegate."

"Thank you, sir. I am very pleased to be here." She didn't mean to lie, she was just caught so off guard by his perfect manners and genuine smile. Griffin had the same dark hair and similar features, but his eyes were a warm brandy color and his face lacked the mistrust and pain that was so evident in his older brother.

"Bosh, don't be formal with me. 'Griffin,'" he said, tapping his forefinger against his crisp white cravat. He grinned and offered her his arm. She looped her hand through the crook of his elbow and he led her to the end of the dock and right past Cole, engaging her in conversation the entire way, making it impossible for his brother to object. But Bailey couldn't miss the hard line of Cole's mouth and the deep, stormy color of his eyes that spoke volumes of his displeasure. She gifted Griffin with a bright smile and said a silent prayer of thanks for this lighthearted man who might just prove to be her beacon in the dark.

"Hell's bells, it's good to have you home, old boy," Griffin said, lifting his scotch in toast of his older brother.

Cole nodded in acknowledgment, but only grunted a reply

before swallowing the entire contents of his glass. He refilled the etched crystal and then walked to the cold fireplace where he leaned casually, his legs crossed at the ankle. He swirled the brassy liquid in lazy circles, regarding his younger brother with care. Griffin had changed since Cole last saw him two years past. Mischief was still evident in his eyes, yet the boyish uncertainty had been replaced by confidence. Cole felt a surge of relief that Griffin had been spared their mother's deathbed confession. Though Griffin knew what she had done, he had not had to look in her fading eyes as she pleaded for forgiveness. Forgiveness that she did not deserve. No, Griffin had been spared the damage that fine lady had brought upon Cole; damage that reached so far as to prevent him from ever trusting a woman again. Not so, Griffin. His younger brother actually enjoyed being swarmed with feminine company, and had from the time they were boys. He had an easy charm and a devilish wit that women could not seem to resist. Cole saw Bailey taken by that charm the minute they had arrived at Rosegate and he didn't like it. Not one bit.

"I wish you would have written, Cole. I would have made special arrangements for your homecoming."

"I shudder to think about it. The afternoon was unbearable enough, thank you."

"Unbearable? Hmmm. What about the afternoon was unbearable, brother? Seeing me for the first time in two years? Eating a meal consisting of more than moldy cheese and dried meat? Bringing a lovely, charming lady home with you?"

"I told you why she is here, and you insisted on misrepresenting her to everyone within earshot. She is already difficult and now you have made my situation with her even more so. She is my property, not a guest. Do not forget that again."

"*I* have made your situation more difficult? That is rich!" Griffin laughed heartily, then rose from one of a matching set of embroidered boroque chairs. He splashed another shot of scotch in his glass, then turned to face his older brother. "Cole,

I have the utmost confidence in your ability to complicate your own life. Give me no credit."

Cole glared at his brother's jovial grin. Griffin was forever goading and it appeared that his newfound maturity had done nothing to diminish that annoying trait.

"Griff, I am asking you to not introduce Bailey as your guest. For once, keep your meddlesome mouth closed and let me handle this."

"What is there to handle? If you're going to use her, then by all means, bait the line and throw her in, brother. What are you waiting for?"

"I told you," Cole growled, "I will only use her if I run out of other options. Speaking of which, have you heard anything from your informants?"

"There are a couple of suspicious fellows just arrived in the last few weeks. One is a Spaniard, who is looking to settle in Charles Towne, with his wife. The other is English, just arrived, but no one knows from where. He is traveling alone and is currently residing in Williamsburg."

"Interesting."

"Very. Oh, something else interesting."

Cole grimaced at the mischievous gleam in his brother's eyes. "Dare I ask?"

"Julie."

"Holy Hell," Cole groaned. "She cannot possibly know I have returned."

"Hmm, I wouldn't be so sure, brother. You know Julia."

"Unfortunately, I do." Cole couldn't help but grin at his little brother's deep, full laughter. "When is the hurricane expected to arrive?"

"Next week. But I think it's safe to say that if she finds out you have already returned, it will be much, much sooner. Better keep your newly acquired *property* hidden away, brother."

Cole sighed heavily and nodded, then downed the last of his scotch and bid his brother good night.

Chapter Twenty-Three

"My, my, what a pleasant way to greet the morning."

Bailey descended the last step and smiled shyly at the compliment, as Griffin extended his arm for her. "You are too kind. I fear these dark circles under my eyes will never fade."

"Well, I happen to be quite taken by that particular shade of blue. Or is that black?" Griffin teased with a smile.

Bailey laughed at his charming wit that made her feel so at ease. But she couldn't help fidget with the high lace collar, adjusting it to hide her healing scar.

"Don't," Griffin said, brushing her fingers away. "There is nothing there that can take away from your beauty."

She smiled again and let her hand fall back to her side as Griffin led her into the dining room for the morning meal. Just like yesterday, the table was set like nothing Bailey had ever seen. A lovely white linen tablecloth lay beneath delicate peach and gold china plates and gold-rimmed crystal glasses. A basket of fruit sat at one end of the table and warm scented bread at the other. Once seated, a dark-skinned girl no older than Bailey entered the room with coffee, cream and sugar. An older woman with the same deeply colored skin pushed a wheeled cart into the room and set it against one wall.

"It's all right, Tessa. You may begin serving." Griffin turned his attention to Bailey and said, "Cole will not be joining us this morning. He left early to attend to his ship and crew. I expect he will be back before dinner."

"I'm sure I will not miss him in the least," Bailey replied. She doubted her tone carried the frostiness she intended, as Griffin smiled in response.

"I have taken care of your letter, Bailey. It should make it to Beaufort in a couple of weeks. I hope you will make yourself at home here while you wait for a reply."

"That depends, I suppose."

"On what?" Griffin asked, smearing melted butter on a hot roll.

"On how long Cole is away," she replied, grinning when Griffin chortled in appreciation.

"Well said, Bailey. Well said, indeed. How would you like a tour of the grounds after breakfast?"

"I would love that. Is Rosegate very big?"

"About ten-thousand acres. Our grandparents were granted the land by The Virginia Company of London. They were among the first to settle in the Virginia Colony."

"They must have been very brave. My father brought my mother to the Colonies to live a free life. They had both served in the household of a duke, who was kind enough to help them secure passage to North Carolina when my mother became pregnant with my brother. I was too young to remember living in England, though I doubt the duke's estate was as grand as Rosegate. I cannot imagine how you keep track of ten thousand acres of land."

"Good point. I suppose we shouldn't try to see it all in one day, hmm?"

Bailey laughed, then turned serious. "How is it that you are so different from your brother? Why, I would not even believe the two of you are related, if it wasn't for the resemblance."

Griffin swallowed a bite of eggs, his expression turning thoughtful. "Cole has had a difficult time of it. Father counted on him to be the man of the house when he sailed, which was often when we were boys. Mother always seemed sad to me, but now that I'm older, I understand she suffered from melancholia. She leaned heavily on Cole for emotional support. Too much, I think. She finally relented to Father's requests and Cole was sent to study in England when he was twelve. He came home often to see after Mother, but . . ."

"There was nothing he could do to cure her illness."

"I know. But he blames himself for her . . . mistakes. He feels like he failed our father. And ever since, he has sworn to make it up to him, to the family name."

"That is a dreadful burden for a young man to carry."

Griffin nodded. "Cole has a good heart, Bailey. I have never known anyone who was so giving. But sometimes the events in our lives take us to dark places and show us the worst of the world. Some people make it back but others are lost to the darkness forever."

"You don't believe that Cole is lost forever, do you?"

"I had my doubts, Bailey. I had serious doubts these past several years, ever since he sailed off, hell-bent on finding the Dragon. But now—now that you are here, I am beginning to have hope again."

"Now that I am here? What on Earth have I done to give you hope?"

"You have brought him home for the first time since our mother died."

"No, that was not me. He has had news of the Dragon's return to the Colonies. He has only brought me along to use me as he sees fit."

Griffin shook his head and wiped the edge of his mouth with an embroidered napkin. "No, no. I don't think so. I see something in Cole's eyes when he speaks of you. Something I have not seen there since we were young. He may not recognize it, but you are bringing him back from the darkness,

Bailey. And I, for one, salute you," he finished, raising his china coffee cup and tilting his dark head at her, smiling.

Bailey remained silent, taking in Griffin's words carefully as memories of the past weeks softened her anger and melted her heart. Oh, if only Griffin was right. If only Cole would come out of the darkness of his bitterness, his hatred . . . They could be happy together, she knew it. But it was too much to ask. She knew him well enough by now to know he would never give up his vow to kill the Dragon. His deep sense of honor was something she had grown to admire, despite where it was leading him, and she knew that honor would not allow him to give up until he had avenged his father's death.

"I cannot bring him out of it, Griffin. The choice is his, and he has made it. He would rather die in this quest of his than give it up. For anything. And I cannot stay here and watch him die. I have lost everyone I care about. My heart cannot take any more."

Besides, she thought, it was too late, anyway. Griffin had sent her letter to James. She would return to Beaufort with him, and she would never see Cole again. There was no turning back.

"I apologize for making you think of such upsetting matters. Please forgive me. I'm afraid your charming beauty has turned my brain to oatmeal. Let's go for that ride, now, shall we?"

Bailey pushed back from the table and rose, accepting Griffin's arm. They walked out into the cheery sunshine, but despite the bright warmth of the day, her heart remained chilled, her thoughts never far from the troubled, dark captain of the *Barracuda*.

July came, dragging on heavy wings, the oppressive, humid air slowing down everything and everyone at Rosegate to a languid crawl. Bailey sat on the wide columned porch facing the river, cooling herself with a fan she had just completed embroidering the day before. Yellow bumblebees floated among pink and blue flowers on the stiff white silk.

Sophie sat next to her, chattering away, while snapping off the ends of a large basket of green beans. Griffin had sent Sophie to Bailey's room the day after she arrived, and the women had taken an instant liking to each other. Sophie was more than pleased to be elevated to the status of lady's maid. There had been no ladies to look after at Rosegate in much too long, she had declared.

"I don't believe I will ever get used to the summer heat, Sophie," Bailey said to the young black woman who had become her companion and friend.

"Well, Miss Bailey, we can go for a soak in the rivah later on, if ya like. Seems that's the only way to keep cool round here, lest ya walk about without a stitch on." She giggled.

"Sophie!" Bailey frowned at the girl with feigned admonishment before breaking into laughter. "That would be a sight, indeed."

"Something I wouldn't be opposed to seeing."

Bailey jumped at the deep, sultry sound of Cole's voice in the doorway behind them.

"Sophie, we will be receiving company soon. Would you please go and help Tessa prepare tea and refreshments?"

"Yessir, Master Cole," Sophie said, unable to contain her grin of embarrassment at being caught in an indecent conversation with her new mistress. Bailey grinned back at her and winked, setting the girl into a fit of giggling as she disappeared down the stairs of the porch and across the lawn toward the cookhouse.

"You have corrupted her, it seems," Cole reprimanded dryly. He sat in the cushioned chair next to Bailey, stretching his legs out long in front of him and crossing his booted feet.

She swallowed the sudden tightness in her throat. It was the first time she had been alone with Cole since arriving. She had missed him, despite the insults and hurtful words that had made up their last conversation. "Me? No, I think Sophie is much more worldly than I will ever be. Did you know that her parents escaped an actual slave ship that was heading for the Colonies? They were almost drowned in a storm. Sophie was almost never born!"

"I know."

"I'm sorry. Of course you know. Your father rescued them from the ocean and brought them to live at Rosegate. He told them they could leave, that he would help them to return to their homeland, but Sophie's mother was too weak to travel."

Cole nodded. "And when her mother died giving birth to her, her father could not bear the pain. He returned to his continent without his daughter. Sophie has been here her whole life. My parents always thought of her more like a daughter than a slave."

"Your parents were kindhearted people, despite the mistakes they may have made."

She saw a thick pulse had taken to throbbing in his jaw as he stared out over the river. Bailey wasn't sure if he remembered that he'd told her about his mother while he'd had the fever. If he would only open up his heart to her, perhaps he could start to heal. She sat quietly on the wide cushioned bench, fanning herself until he finally spoke.

"The only mistake my father made was trusting that his wife wouldn't betray him while he was working to secure his family's future."

"Was your mother always . . . unhappy?"

"Not at first. At least not that I could see. But on my visits home over the years, I could see that she was not the same. My father spent a lot of time away. He had invested in a ship-building business with an old friend from college. They were setting up the business in New York, so he had to sail there often."

"So your mother was lonely?"

"Apparently she had been having the affair for about a year.

The Dragon convinced her that my father didn't love her anymore and told her that he wanted to marry her. She began poisoning my father shortly after that, when he came home for the winter. By the time I received the missive and got home, it was spring. He had died two weeks before."

"But your mother was still alive then, wasn't she?"

"Yes, she had been stabbed in the heart . . . But I told you that already, didn't I?"

"Yes," Bailey replied. She smiled gently, urging him on with her expression. "She wanted to talk to you, didn't she?"

He nodded. "The stubborn woman refused to die. She held on for two days until I arrived home. After she told me what she'd done she told me she'd suffered terrible guilt. She couldn't save Father, but she refused to kill Griff and me. The Dragon threatened her and she told him she'd rather die than murder her sons. So, he stabbed her. Then, he thrilled in telling her that he was the notorious Dragon. And that his true purpose in charming her was to steal the Leighton inheritance. He said he had done the same many times before with many other wealthy ladies in the Colonies. He told me how he hated the upper class and how he was going to destroy them all."

"Dear Lord," Bailey whispered, dropping the fan in her lap. "I'm so sorry, Cole."

"It doesn't matter."

"Of course it does. It matters a great deal. Griffin told me how you took care of him. And everyone else at Rosegate. I know how hard it was for you to overcome the scandal. There weren't many who stood by you, though there were others who had been through the same thing. You were alone."

He looked at her as if she had revealed a secret he'd been keeping from the world. She longed to tell him he wasn't alone anymore. But something in his expression stopped her.

"How is it possible that he has not been captured? Surely one of those other families has spoken up after all this time?"

"No one else knows that the lord and the pirate are one and the same. The man only admitted he was the Dragon because he knew my mother would carry the information to her grave. If I had just told her what she wanted to hear—"

"No, Cole. Even if you had forgiven her, she may have died before she could tell you who he was. You didn't do anything wrong."

"How many innocent people would be alive today if I had gotten his name that day? Your family—"

"Please don't. I won't let you hold yourself responsible. None of it is your fault. I don't blame you. I could never blame you." Bailey wiped at the tears that fell freely down her cheeks. She was beginning to understand how Cole's heart had grown cold. He carried pain and guilt and let no one comfort him. He believed nothing but revenge could comfort him.

"Now do you understand why I continue to search for the Dragon?"

She did. She pushed aside the strange feeling of foreboding that suddenly came over her.

She nodded, her head dipped in study of a pink butterfly on her fan. She felt Cole's thumb on her cheek, gently wiping away a tear. She sniffled and lifted her head, gracing him with a smile. He was starting to trust her. He had finally shared the dark secrets that tormented him. In turn, she would try to bring more lightness into his life.

"Tell me, who is this company and when are they going to be here?" she asked, flicking her fan back and forth.

"The lady's name is Julia Hayward," Cole replied. "Her family has been our closest neighbor since my father was a young boy. She should be here within the hour, I suppose."

Bailey looked up at him with interest as Cole stood and stretched. "Are you quite anxious to see her?" she asked, trying to sound bored.

"Jealous, dove?" Cole teased, offering his hand to help her up.

"No, I am not jealous!" she snapped, brushing aside his hand and standing on her own.

"Even though she and I were once betrothed?" he goaded.

She glared at the wicked smile that showcased white teeth against the tan of his face. He was enjoying this, she knew, as she struggled to keep quiet. She would swallow her tongue before she asked him about it.

"All right, I will indulge you, as I see you about to bust wide-open with curiosity."

"I really do not care who you were, or are, engaged to, Colby Leighton."

He wrapped his arms around her middle as she started to walk away from him into the house, his whispered answer tickling her ear. "We were five. She asked me to marry her and I said I would if she would let me ride her horse."

Bailey tilted her head to look at him in amused interest. "Truly?"

"Of course. He was much faster than the old mare I learned to ride on. It only lasted a week before she changed her mind and asked our other neighbor, Robert Warren."

Bailey laughed, tipping her neck to allow Cole's lips better access as he nuzzled her. She had missed him too much to let their last angry encounter keep her from the pleasure of his teasing and the warmth of his lips.

"Mm, well, I hope she is not here to change her mind back. I might just have to reject her for you—on behalf of Maximilian, of course."

"Oh, of course," he agreed dramatically.

She felt a familiar delicious tingle as he wrapped his arm possessively around her waist to guide her through the wide back door. She was beginning to feel very much at home. The feeling unnerved her almost as much as the feeling of foreboding that refused to be ignored.

* * *

An hour later, Bailey descended the curved staircase in one of the simple cotton dresses she had brought from Lochinvar. The striped blue skirt and white petticoat had been lengthened, so her ankles no longer peeked out indecently. She had also had the waist nipped in and the bust of the pale blue bodice adjusted to fit her form perfectly. It wasn't a fancy dress, but then Bailey had never owned a fancy dress. Nor did she feel the need for one now, despite the butterflies that danced about in her stomach in anticipation of Julia Hayward's arrival. She fussed with the ribbon at the elbow-length sleeve and wondered what a wealthy planter's daughter would be like.

She didn't have long to wait. Bailey barely had time to situate herself in the parlor when Griffin entered and announced that Lady Hayward's carriage was coming up the oak-lined drive.

"Where is Cole?" Bailey asked, unable to explain her intense nervousness.

"Hiding, I would imagine," Griffin said, smiling with mischief.

"If I thought it was possible she wouldn't find me, I just might consider it," Cole answered as he entered the parlor.

He hadn't bothered to change clothes for the arrival of company, though to Bailey, he couldn't have looked more handsome, anyway. Dressed in perfectly fitted breeches fastened below the knee and a single-breasted midnight blue coat, he was the picture of a gentleman. The green and blue satin waistcoat he wore was tasteful and contrasted nicely with the pure-white cravat tied in a careless knot around his neck. As usual, he was wigless, his dark, shiny hair pulled back neatly in a queue.

"Come, now, big brother. Don't tell me you haven't missed our little Julie even a tiny bit? She's probably not even still angry at you for—"

"Enough, Griff. Do you ever stop prattling away?"

"Well, I don't know, it just seems that when there's a good story to tell, one should tell it."

Cole gave his brother a threatening glare, but Griffin merely slapped him on the back and then winked at Bailey on his way to the lowboy. "We might as well start with a stiff one, it could be a long afternoon."

"I hate to say this, but the two of you are making me quite nervous. You make Miss Hayward sound a bit frightening."

"My apologies, Bailey. I just can't refrain from making my brother's life miserable. He's been away so long and I have missed so many opportunities to torture him. You see, Julie has always been somewhat . . . smitten with my big brother. And though he has never encouraged her, she has yet to give up on becoming Mrs. Colby Leighton. Even her brief marriage to the ancient, rich-as-clotted-cream Lord Hayward did not sway her from her ultimate goal of becoming the mistress of Rosegate." He poured two glasses of bourbon and handed one to Cole. He offered Bailey a small, delicate glass with a splash of sherry, which she took merely to keep her hands busy.

"If Julia wants to become Mistress of Rosegate, then she will have to marry you, then. And we both know how little affection she holds for you," Cole said.

Griffin laughed and went to look out the window. "Ah, then I suppose Rosegate, as well as the two of us, are safe from our little Julie."

"Pay no heed to him, Bailey. I am sure Julia has more than gotten over her childhood infatuation with me. I have not even seen her for, what, a good six or seven years. Not since the funeral that made her a very rich widow."

"Good point, brother. I wonder what this visit will bring," Griffin said, swirling the golden liquor in his glass.

Minutes later, a servant announced Lady Julia Hayward. Bailey's breath caught in her throat at the first sight of Lady Hayward. She didn't even notice Griffin move forward to kiss her hand and welcome her into the parlor. She did, however, notice Cole's complete lack of manners as he held his position by the fireplace, merely nodding to the woman in greeting.

"Well, Colby Matthew Leighton, I believe all that time alone on your ship with those filthy sailors has robbed you of your fine manners. Darling, come over here and greet me properly," she cooed, opening her arms with nothing less than complete expectation of his compliance.

"Hello, Julia," Cole responded cooly, making no movement toward her.

The woman didn't flinch at the blatant slight but covered quickly by turning her attention to Bailey. Bailey felt her heart skip and suddenly felt incredibly plain. Julia was stunningly blonde, stunningly beautiful, and impeccably dressed in the palest mint-colored silk that brought out the color of her cool green eyes. She removed her plumed hat to reveal unpowdered yellow-white hair, piled intricately on her head in swirls of glorious curls. She glided over to the settee, where Bailey sat, dumbfounded, watching the graceful swish of the woman's skirts as she moved closer.

"My dear, I believe these boys are too uncivilized to introduce us. I don't believe we've ever met and I pride myself on knowing everyone in Williamsburg's gentry."

Her emerald gaze was filled with suspicion as she examined Bailey's simple attire. "I am Lady Hayward, of Hayward Hall. But you must call me Julia." She held out her gloved hand limply, angled in such a way it seemed as if she expected Bailey to kiss it.

Just as Bailey was about to blather some inane comment, forgetting her name entirely, Cole stepped forward and spoke up.

"Julia, I would like to introduce you to Miss Bailey Spencer. She was the unfortunate victim of a shipwreck off the coast. Luckily, I came upon the vessel just before she sank completely below the waves." Bailey recognized the annoyance in the deep hue of his eyes, narrowed slightly at the blond woman as he continued. "Miss Spencer was the only survivor. She has agreed to be our guest until other arrangements can be made."

"Oh, my darling girl," Julia breathed, her hand fluttering against her chest. "I just knew there had to be a reasonable explanation for that horrid dress! You poor, darling creature. You will have to let me lend you something decent to wear."

If Bailey had felt the smallest bit of guilt over the lie Cole had told, it was gone the second Julia uttered her first "darling." Bailey had never felt so embarrassed in her life. If it hadn't been for his lie, she would have burst into flames from her acute shame.

"That won't be necessary, Julie. I am taking care of all of Miss Spencer's needs while she is here," Cole said.

"Colby Leighton, you know you cannot let her stay here . . . with the two of you," Julia gasped. "No, it's completely inappropriate! The darling girl has lost her maid and she simply cannot be expected to stay at Rosegate without a proper chaperone. Her reputation would be ruined if anyone found out."

Cole didn't appear to be the least bit affected by the woman's sugarcoated threat. He stood, unmoving, behind a chair, casually leaning on the window sill. But a closer look at him revealed the sign that helped Bailey relax: that telltale throb in his hard-angled jaw showed her that he was affected by Julia's words. And he didn't like what she had to say.

Cole's quiet reaction gave her all the courage she needed. "Why, thank you, Julia. You are quite generous to offer, but I am sure I will make do just fine. I will be leaving for North Carolina soon, anyway."

"Pooh, that is too bad," Julia replied with a heavy-lipped pout. "Well, you cannot go very soon, darling. That is precisely why I am here. I have come to invite you . . . all," she said, nodding at Bailey with a forced smile, "to a ball at Hayward Hall, Saturday after next."

"I don't think—" Cole began.

"No, no! You cannot say no, Colby." She rushed to his side. "Now, if I had had any idea that you were home, well, I would have held the ball in your honor. But since you are here, you will just have to consider yourself the second most important reason I am throwing this party. Since I am sure you all are just beside yourselves, wanting to know what the first reason is, I will have to give in and tell you. No one else will know until the ball, but I do consider you . . . more than just a friend," she purred, running her gloved fingers down the sleeve of Cole's coat.

Griffin was the first to break the uncomfortable silence. Bailey saw the gleam in his eye and braced herself for more of his impishness. "But won't all the other gents from here to Williamsburg be jealous, Julie? After all, I hear a few of them believe they are more than just your friend, too."

Bailey nearly choked on a sip of her sherry.

"Do stop calling me that! You know I hate that ridiculous nickname. And as for jealous, I am sure you are right. There will be more than one jealous man at Hayward Manor when I make my announcement. And I believe one of them is in this very room." She lowered her voice for the last comment, though only for effect. Her words still carried across the quiet parlor. "Perhaps you will finally come to your senses and stop me before it is too late," she said, casting a seductive glance up at Cole.

"By all means, don't tempt us further. What is this big news?" Griffin asked.

"No." She pouted, fixing her hat back up on the top of her curls. "I have changed my mind. You will just have to wait. Griffin, you always have a way of spoiling things for everyone else. You should learn to tame that insidious humor of yours. Now, I must go. I have one more stop before dark.

Come, darling, walk me out," she insisted, pulling on Cole's arm as she turned her back to Bailey and Griffin.

Griffin walked over to the brocade settee, gave Bailey a re-assuring wink and offered her his hand. They followed Cole and Julia out of the parlor, stopping at the top of the wide front porch. Julia dragged Cole down the steps, then reached up and held his face, kissing him on his unyielding mouth. She lingered near him to whisper something in his ear. As far as Bailey could tell, he didn't respond in any way before he backed up onto the bottom step and watched Julia flounce to her carriage.

She turned to wave at Bailey and Griffin, and in a voice loud enough for passing servants, she said, "Bailey, darling, you mustn't feel the least bit ashamed about losing all your fine clothes. I will find you the perfect gown for the ball, so you needn't worry about fitting in. And I will send you my maid—I am certain she can do something with your hair. Ta!"

Just as Bailey was about to lose her composure completely, Cole spoke up.

"Julia!"

"Yes, darling?" She spun around, the tall green plume on her hat brushing against one of the horses' hindquarters. The animal stomped, swishing his tail furiously at the ticklish in-truder, knocking Julia's hat off her perfectly coifed head. The green feathered silk and felt landed in a warm pile of fresh manure directly below the horse's rear end, invoking a horri-fied shriek from Lady Hayward.

Griffin and Cole fell into unchivalrous laughter, while Julia stood fuming, her gloved hands planted firmly on her shapely hips. Bailey covered her mouth discreetly, suddenly overcome by a fit of coughing, while a few gathered servants rushed away in search of any task other than retrieving the lady's hat.

"Never mind," Cole said with a grin.

"That hat was French!" Julia squealed, stomping her foot, as her driver jumped down to fish the hat out of the pile of manure. Another fit of laughter assailed Cole and Griffin. The driver looked as if he was at a loss to know what to do with the ruined hat, and finally held it out to her in question. "You oaf! Leave it! Get me out of here," she ordered, climbing up in an unladylike poof of green silk skirts.

Cole walked up the steps to join his brother and Bailey, a smile lingering on his face. He took Bailey's chin in his hand and kissed her mouth soundly, surprising her.

"What was that for?"

"Any woman who handles a first meeting with Julie as well as you just did deserves at least a kiss."

She laughed and let him guide her into the house, the comforting warmth of his hand at the small of her back sending a wave of pleasure up her spine. Griffin was still chuckling behind them as he closed the door.

Chapter Twenty-Four

"Looks like it will be a good year for corn," Cole observed, nudging his horse Maximilian out of a row of the tall stalks. Griffin waited on the worn path atop a sleek black stallion, who pawed the soft dirt impatiently.

"Yes, all of our crops have done well this year. We were lucky to have had plenty of rain this spring."

"I saw the books, Griff. You have managed to increase profits again this year—and without any additional labor. My hat is off to you, little brother. You are running this place as if it was merely a day at the races."

Griffin laughed. "It's nothing more than survival, brother, but I thank you for the praise. This is the first time you've taken an interest in years. Are you finally ready to take over?"

"Hell, no."

"You know it wouldn't bother me. It is your birthright, brother, not mine. I have only been managing the place while you have been . . . occupied."

"Still the same self-less, noble saphead you were when we were boys. You are too good for your own good, Griff. I still can't figure out how you have remained so untouched."

"I had someone there to protect me," he said with a

meaningful look at Cole. "You did not. I owe my attitude to you, brother."

"That sounds almost humorous, wouldn't you say?"

Griffin laughed and nodded. "Almost? Damned humorous, I would say. You know what else I could find humorous?"

"I cannot imagine," Cole drawled, scowling in his brother's direction.

"That it appears you are headed for the altar before me."

"Holy Christ! What is the matter with you?"

"There isn't a thing the matter with me, brother, but I am fairly certain that something is very wrong with you. You have broken your promise to yourself, and that is just not like you. Not like you a'tall," he said, grinning like a cat. "What is the world coming to, when a man can't keep a promise to himself." He shook his head in a dramatic gesture of disbelief.

"I am not beyond giving you a sound beating, whelp."

"Ah, but you are out of practice, brother. And I have learned to defend myself since way back then. Besides, it looks as if it's going to rain and I really would prefer to stay out of the mud today. What do you say?"

Cole shook his head at his troublesome sibling. "I say I cannot wait until you meet the woman who makes that witty tongue of yours drag the floor."

"Well, in your defense, I have to say that if it was anyone other than Bailey, you would have stood a chance."

"But it *is* her."

"Yes. Yes, I see your problem. Tricky business. My sympathies, old boy. My deepest sympathies." He laughed deeply at his own sarcasm.

Griffin's laughter hung in the air, annoying Cole as much as the heavy, warm drops of rain that had begun to fall. He had no time to reply before Griffin spurred his horse into a gallop in the direction of the stables. But Cole couldn't think of a convincing denial to his brother's observations, anyway. More and more of late, he was finding it difficult to hold on to his mistrust. With every new discovery he made about Bailey, he was coming to realize that she was not like any other woman. Those promises he made to himself seemed a lifetime away—and he wasn't sure he wanted to stick to them after all.

A half hour later, Cole and Griffin left the stables, and entered the cookhouse to deposit their wet hose and muddy boots. Tessa stood at the stone dry sink, peeling potatoes, while a young girl pulled a hot loaf of bread from the brick oven.

"Oh, Master Griffin, I'm so glad y'all are back. Miss Bailey is in the parlor and I'm thinkin' y'all need to get in there right away!"

"What is it, Tessa? What's the matter?" Cole asked, his voice low. Cole and Griffin had grown up with Tessa looking after them like a mother hen, and both men knew when her feathers were ruffled.

"Miss Bailey says everything is fine, but she looks mighty worried. This gentleman came callin' today, an' I heard him say he's come to take Miss Bailey away! He—"

Before he heard another word, Cole tore out of the door and ran toward the main house. He entered the back of the house, slipping around the corner as his bare feet connected with the polished wood floor. His heart thudded hard in his throat as a horrible vision assaulted him: Bailey's white throat being squeezed in the brutal hands of the Dragon, waiting for Cole to discover them before he snapped her fragile neck, killing her before Cole could reach her.

He grabbed the door frame, throwing his body down the long hallway, rainwater flying off of him to spatter the walls and furniture as he flew past. He grabbed the doorway of the parlor to stop himself, swinging his body into the room, breathing heavily and assuming a stance that bespoke of a warrior.

"What the hell is going on here!" he shouted, in immediate confusion. This man could not be the Dragon. He seemed to be barely out of his teens.

"Cole!" Bailey rose, a look of stunned disbelief on her otherwise beautiful face. She appeared unhurt, and mostly at ease, considering he had probably just frightened the life out of her. "What on earth happened to you?"

"Nothing," he said, sweeping back a hunk of wet hair from his face. "Rain. Who are you?" he rushed on to ask the stranger, unconcerned with the formality of manners. He moved to stand protectively in front of Bailey.

"Ah, Cole, could I speak with you in private for a moment?"

"I don't think that is necessary, Bailey."

So, the meek little fellow on the settee could speak after all, Cole thought, as fingers of jealousy scratched at him, making his skin crawl.

"What's going on here?" Griffin demanded, rushing into the room, lowering the pistol he gripped in both hands.

"Griffin, would you mind? I need a moment with Cole," Bailey pleaded.

"No!"

"No!"

Cole and the stranger shouted at once. "You know this man?" Cole demanded of Bailey as he narrowed his eyes at the younger man. The stranger eyed him right back and squared his shoulders, as if ready for battle.

"I think we had better do this first, Bailey," Griffin said, moving into the room with his hand extended. "I am Griffin Leighton. That scowling beast is my brother, Cole. Welcome to Rosegate."

"My name is James Fulton. I am here to take Bailey home," he said pointedly, glaring at Cole as if he was nothing more than a lowlife kidnapper.

"Really?" Cole drawled, crossing his arms over his wide chest. "And how do you plan to get past me to accomplish that?"

"Why would you force me to challenge you?"

"Because she is not going anywhere . . . friend."

"You cannot mean to keep her against her will. If you insist on making this unpleasant for her, then I have come prepared. I have brought money to begin to repay you for . . . coming to her aid on that vile pirate island. I will have the rest soon."

"She is not here against her will."

"Then why am I here, sir?" James asked, puffing out his chest.

Cole looked at Bailey, who came around to stand in front of him, her eyes filled with some emotion he could not read.

"May we please speak in private now?" she whispered up at him, her hands wringing together in front of her.

Cole started to escort her from the room when James piped up, his voice almost taunting. "She wrote to me and begged me to come and get her away from you. And that is exactly what I intend to do. Bailey, come along. We will stay in Williamsburg until we secure passage to Beaufort. I will not allow you to stay here another minute."

"You will not *allow?"* Cole thundered, the pain of James's words sinking in like a lead stone. "Let me straighten something out for you, James. Bailey is not free to go with you. I own her. Despite your belief that she is your betrothed, she became my legal property the day I bought her off a slave block in New Providence. And unless I decide that it is worth it to me to sell her back to you, then you have no claim on her. And I believe that concludes your business here."

Bailey wrenched her arm from his grasp. Cole hadn't even realized he had taken hold of her, he was so intent on getting this boy out of Rosegate and as far away from Bailey as possible. Anger and hurt felt like a brand on his heart. He couldn't believe she had actually written James. He thought she had given up that idea while they were at Lochinvar. He thought she was happy being with him. What a fool he was. The truth was so clear to him now as she stood before him, her hands fisted on her hips, her face a mask of uncontained rage. She hated him. She had been merely biding her time until *this boy* came for her.

Damn her for her betrayal. And damn himself for being so stupid. But he still had the upper hand. He owned her and she could do nothing about that fact. She wasn't going anywhere with James Fulton until he had damn well gotten his use out of her.

"I suggest you tame that temper of yours and retire to your room until dinner," he ordered Bailey. She gasped and fled, while James sputtered some comment from across the room, coaxing a grin of angry satisfaction to spread across Cole's face. Griffin stood quietly next to James, a look of pleading on his face, but Cole was too angry to back down. He felt duped and betrayed—emotions he was well equipped to deal with—and for the first time in weeks, he knew exactly how to react.

"Bailey was remiss in not conveying to you that I am reluctant to part with her. You have traveled a long way for nothing. But please, at least join us for dinner before you return to your lodgings," Cole offered coolly.

"I . . . I have not had time to secure lodgings yet. But I thank you for your hospitality. I will stay for dinner so that we may come to an agreement." The boy looked sufficiently ill at ease.

"Cole, why don't you inform Tessa that we will have a guest for dinner," Griffin insisted. He might as well have shoved Cole out the door. "I would like to get to know our guest . . . without all the snorting and hoof stomping," he added for Cole's ears alone.

Cole rolled his eyes at his brother, then cast a warning glance at James before stalking out of the room.

Dinner seemed to go on forever and Bailey had never felt so awkward in her life. Or so conflicted. When she had sent the letter to James, she was sure she wanted to go home, sure that Cole could never give her the safe, peaceful life she wanted. She had been angry at him for making her believe he had given up his plan for revenge, although she admitted to herself that he hadn't lied to her—she had made an incorrect assumption.

She had let Cole into her heart, had let him make love to her and then let her common sense fly away on the wind. She had fantasized about a life with him because she had wanted so badly for it to be possible, and when he crushed her hopes with the truth, she had hastily sent that letter.

As much as she might have had second thoughts when she first saw James today, leaving with him would be for the best, she knew. She didn't belong in Cole's world of hate, bitterness and destruction. And she could not bear to love him, only to suffer her worst heartache of all if he died as a result of his bloodlust.

She sipped her wine, letting the warm bite of the buttery gold fluid sear a path down her throat to her fluttery stomach. The conversation had been quite civil, thanks to Griffin's extraordinary ability to charm anyone he came in contact with, and James was no exception. Bailey could barely look at her childhood friend as he discussed plans for their wedding. She knew she could never marry him now, but that explanation would have to wait until they had more privacy. James talked as if there was nothing standing in his way of taking her home, but she had heard Cole's cruel words as clear as a church bell. He had refused to let her go. Hadn't he?

"James, I, uh, I am not sure when I will be able to return home. My debts to Cole are more than I can repay. It will take some time—"

"You are free to go, Bailey," Cole interrupted, his voice sharp, cold.

"Excuse me?"

"I have decided that you will be leaving with James tomorrow."

She could not have been more shocked if he had punched her. "Tomorrow?"

"Isn't it wonderful? Captain Leighton has agreed to absolve you of your debt. We can be married as soon as we get back. I know losing Adam and your father has been hard for you and I think the sooner we get married, the better."

Bailey looked at Cole, whose face was like stone, then at Griffin, who was examining the raspberries in his tart with the sharp points of his dessert fork. James seemed oblivious to the somber mood in the room and chattered on throughout dessert and coffee. Bailey had eaten little dinner and hadn't even bothered to attempt one of Tessa's berry tarts, even though the sumptuous fragrance of the warm sweets filled the room. She was trying to understand what had happened between Cole and James in the short time she was in her room. At the very least Cole had been adamant that he would not release her until he had used her to find the Dragon. Why would he change his mind about that now?

"Has there been news about the Dragon?" she asked Cole softly. He ignored her.

"All of Beaufort is on alert for the brigand," James said. "The governor has ships sailing up and down the coast—it is only a matter of time before the pirate is caught. You have nothing to fear, Bailey, I will keep you safe," he insisted. "I best be on my way. I will be back first thing in the morning to pick Bailey up."

"There's no need for you to go, James. Please be our guest for the night," Griffin offered. "Williamsburg is a fair distance, even by river."

Bailey felt a lump form in her throat, then looked to see Cole's reaction. He gave her a look that chilled her. It was the same way he had looked at her the first day she met him, when he had her pinned to the deck of his ship after she had attacked him.

"By all means, do stay the night. Then there will be no

need to prolong your departure in the morning," Cole added, keeping his gaze on James.

Griffin coughed in the heavy silence, drawing attention away from the oath that rode on Bailey's open lips. She slid her chair back from the table and rose abruptly, throwing her napkin down and excusing herself, but not before her anger bested her.

"If only we could travel in the dark, I would be most happy to leave this very minute! Unfortunately, I will have to wait. Good night, Griffin. I will never forget your kindness while I was your guest here. Thank you."

James rose to escort her to the door, lifting her hand to kiss her knuckles. "Rest well, Bailey. I look forward to the morning."

"As do I," she replied, cutting her eyes at Cole, who lifted his wineglass and tipped it toward her in a silent toast.

She spun around and hurried up the stairs before her anger could turn to despair, revealing her for a fool in front of them all.

Bailey slammed the door to her bedchamber and gave in to the tears that had threatened her all through dinner. What a fool she was! She had let herself care about him again! Had she learned nothing about Cole, nothing at all? Revenge mattered more to him than she ever could! Why had she not gotten that through her thick head? Why had she let herself hope that he might be able to let go of the hate he carried in his heart and replace it with love?

"Idiot!" she hissed at herself, pounding her fist into a downy pillow. She pushed herself off the bed, swiped the tears from her lashes and cheeks and began gathering her few belongings.

Why had he bothered to spend so much time with her since they had arrived at Rosegate? Why all the hand-holding? Why all the kisses? Why had he spent every evening with her on the back porch looking at stars and listening to the summer insects? Why had he knocked on her door every night for the past three, just to see if she required anything?

What had all of that attention meant?

And, most important of all, why would he suddenly give up his only tangible connection to the one thing he wanted more than life itself?

"He wouldn't!" she gasped.

She had made the mistake of assuming he could let it go once before. But now she knew he would keep her for as long as he had a purpose for her, bound by those ridiculous papers that declared her his property, and nothing, he had said, could refute that. Whether he could actually bring himself to use her was yet to be determined, but she knew he would never give up the option.

He was up to something, she could feel it as clearly as she felt the goose bumps tickling the hair on her arms. James was downstairs likely getting himself maneuvered to Cole's design and he had no way of knowing what he was up against.

After pacing the room until the clock downstairs struck the hour, Bailey finished folding her clothes and dressed for bed. She sat at the dressing table brushing her hair, her reflection staring back at her with red-rimmed eyes. It was no use. No matter how long she fretted over it, she would never be able to change Cole. And despite the common sense that screamed otherwise, she knew deep down she wouldn't want to change him. There was so much about his stubborn determination that she admired, so much about his moody personality that she had grown to care about. Faults aside, she had come to know a side of him that perhaps he didn't even realize he had shown her. That was the Colby Leighton she had grown to love.

There it was: the truth. As she looked into her own blue eyes, moistening with new tears, she faced herself and the truth she had been denying for weeks.

She loved Cole. More than she ever thought possible. But she had suffered so much loss, she knew her heart could not stand to lose him, too. Hunting the Dragon to the death was what Cole wanted more than anything, and she could not ask him to give that up for her.

So she had no choice but to leave.

She wouldn't think about her future just now. She would think about that in the days and weeks to come, after the warmth in her heart had grown cold, after her memories of Cole had faded. And, Heaven-help-her, she prayed they would.

Bailey dabbed at her eyes and took a few calming breaths, running the brush through her hair a few last strokes before climbing into bed. As exhausted as she was, she didn't want to fall asleep. It was her last night under the same roof with the man she loved and though she knew it was wrong, she wished the night could last forever.

Cole's head ached as if he'd gone a few rounds with a bear. But he still hadn't managed to get her out of his mind. He had drunk way too much last night, but at least he had retained enough sense to wait until that Fulton boy had retired before he sank all the way into the bottle. Griffin had stayed up with him but had remained too clearheaded to be of any use. His attempts to fix Cole's life had become so annoying that Cole had nearly tossed his little brother out on his meddling ass. Luckily, his black mood was enough to send Griff stalking out before it had come to that. Soon after, Cole had closed himself in the study with a full bottle of whiskey and now, as he shifted in the leather chair where he'd passed the night, the half-empty bottle fell with a slosh and thud on the thick Persian rug.

Cole groaned as he rose, trying to stretch out his stiff muscles while he made his way across the room. He shielded his eyes with his hand as he pulled the dark green curtains closed to shut out the blinding morning light. Once all the windows were sufficiently covered, he returned to the chair and sank down, rubbing his temples in an attempt to banish his headache.

The clock in the hallway sprang to life. Seven chimes. They would have left at dawn.

She was gone.

He retrieved the bottle from the floor and lifted the glass to his lips. His stomach nearly recoiled as the pungent whiskey filled his nostrils, but he took a swig, anyway. He swished the liquor around in his mouth and swallowed, grimacing at the burn that slid a path down his throat. The pounding in his head began to diminish, though his memory was still intact.

How much would he have to drink before he could forget her? Would he die first? Doubtful, but he couldn't let that happen, he reminded himself. He had too much to live for. Revenge. He couldn't die until he had gotten his revenge. It was all that had mattered to him for what felt like a lifetime.

But now for some reason it didn't seem to matter at all.

Bailey was gone and he'd had no idea what that would feel like. He never thought he would have a reason to know. He had been able to keep her with a perfectly logical excuse and there had been no need for any emotion behind it at all. She was his property and he had a purpose for keeping that property.

That is, until yesterday, when he'd agreed to let her go home with James. He couldn't fathom his reasoning, but something in her wide blue-green eyes had touched him and he knew it was wrong for him to keep her. She had been through a hell of a lot—and not all of it at the hands of the Dragon. He had to accept responsibility for his part in her recent unhappiness, too. But he thought she'd come to be happy for some of that time. Was he wrong to think that she had felt some of the lightness that he had felt since they had made love?

Of course he was wrong. He was wrong to have taken her at all. She was innocent . . . and saving herself for her childhood love. He had taken advantage of her kindness, her gentle tending of him while he recovered from his stab wound. He had shown her the first physical tenderness she had seen since her family had been murdered and of course she had clung to that. She had allowed him to make love to her, but if he hadn't been keeping her against her will, she would never have allowed him to touch her. She would have been back in Beaufort, planning a proper wedding to a proper young man, who would never have treated her as indelicately as Cole had these past few months.

Cole got up and stumbled over his boots as he began to pace the room. He felt like a caged animal, who longed to be released into the wild. But it wasn't freedom Cole longed for and while he tried to walk off the alcohol haze that muddled his head, he finally began to understand exactly what it was he had been longing for. Yes, he wanted revenge. Yes, he had promised to regain his family's honor. He wanted those things desperately. However, there was something he longed for even more.

Bailey.

But knowing she was miserable with him, he had let her go and he knew he would never see her again. It was eating a hole in his gut that no amount of whiskey could ever fill, but there was no changing it now. He would accept that she was better off with James and that he was better off fulfilling the promise he had made to his murdered father.

"Damn her!" he growled, throwing the near-empty bottle at the solid oak door. It crashed into pieces, the clatter sending a piercing ache through Cole's head. He squeezed his eyes shut, pressing his palms against his ears, waiting for the pain to subside.

He opened his eyes to an impossible vision and blinked hard. He blinked again and shook his head, groaning at the persistent throb. He was going mad, the vision was still there.

"You are drunk!" Despite the accusatory tone, her voice was a balm to his pain.

Bailey walked into the room, carefully stepping over the whiskey puddle and chunks of glass, and closed the door. She was as beautiful as a spring morning. Her red-gold hair was pulled back in a simple style that allowed the short wisps to fall about her lovely face. She was dressed in rich blue, making her eyes sparkle like the depths of the ocean.

"You are here," he said, not meaning for his voice to sound so gruff.

"Yes, I am here," she replied. Either her voice was unsteady, or his hearing was, he wasn't sure which.

"I thought you would have been gone by now. It's getting late. When are you leaving?"

"I am not leaving," she said, crossing her arms in a defensive gesture.

Now his ears were playing tricks on him. Cole couldn't take much more of this. He went to the leather chair behind the desk and flopped down, fully expecting the vision of her to have disappeared by the time he looked up.

She was still there.

"Obviously, this is not a good time to talk to you, you have apparently besotted yourself to the point of complete idiocy. I will come back later."

"No! No, stay. I just . . . I have a slight headache, but I am perfectly capable of having a conversation. You were saying something about not leaving . . ."

She nodded, biting her bottom lip. "What do you think about that?"

"What do I think?" His heart had been begun to race the moment he realized she was flesh and blood and not some trick of his whiskey-soaked brain. What he was thinking was that this was too good to be true, that he didn't deserve for her to be standing here in front of him. What he was thinking was, *What is she thinking?* "I think you are making a mistake."

She lowered her face, but not before he saw the hurt look that came into her eyes. He hated that he was the cause of it. And he hated that he was too much of a coward to say to her what he really wanted to say. But he could tell her one thing. "I let you go, Bailey, because I am not going to use you to get to the Dragon. You don't owe me anything. Your debt to me is more than paid."

"I am not here because of any debt I owe you. I am here because I find that it's impossible for me to leave you. I am here because of what I feel for you." She uncrossed her arms and wiped a lone tear from her cheek.

Cole was still feeling very much the coward, but he also felt the first stirrings of hope he had allowed himself in years. Her words were beginning to light the darkness that had covered a part of his soul in apathy and distrust for a long time. He wasn't sure he could face this, wasn't sure he knew what to do. But he had been given a second chance and one thing was certain: he was not going to give her a reason to leave him again.

"And what is that?" he asked gently. He reached out and captured her wrist, drawing her forward to stand between his knees.

"I love you," she whispered, her luminous eyes filled with emotion. "You are not the cold, hard, empty man that I thought you were when I first met you. You are a good man, Cole. And despite how hard you've tried to hide that part of you . . . I have always seen it."

"Say it again." He knew there was pleading in his voice. He didn't care.

"I love you, Cole. I can't go back with James. I don't want to marry him, I never did. I know that you don't share my feelings, but it's all right. I don't care. Just please don't send me—"

"You are wrong, Bailey." He shushed her before she could reply and pulled her down to sit on his lap. She gave him a wobbly smile before he took her face in his hands and kissed her. When she opened her lips to him and moaned, he thought he would die from the need of her. He kissed her with a furious desire, his mouth conveying all the feeling behind the words he could not speak.

"You won't . . . send me . . . away?" she asked between breathless kisses.

"Never again."

The urgency of that promise seemed to inflame her and he felt his body harden in quick response. She pulled at the silk ties of her chemise and freed her breasts, allowing the full creamy flesh to brush against Cole's eager lips.

"I need to feel your touch, Cole, please . . ."

It was all the encouragement he needed. More than enough. He took his fill of her lips, her neck, her taut pink nipples. She reached down and tugged at his breeches impatiently. He obliged her immediately, working on the fastenings as she started to rise. He slipped the material down and grabbed her by the hips, turning her away from him and sliding her skirt up her thighs. She understood and as she lowered herself, he guided her down until he felt his hard shaft fill her completely. He reached around and cupped her breasts, pulling her gently back so his lips had access to the soft skin of her neck. She made soft, pleading noises as she writhed on his lap and he began to move in answer to her demands. As her mewls of pleasure increased, he moved faster, guiding her hips up and down with his hands. She moved with him, arching her back, her moans growing and mingling with his own until she cried out, her release coming just moments before his own. She collapsed against his chest, her head resting on his shoulder and he wrapped his arms around her. He held her back against him for long moments, comforted by the feel of her breathing as it gradually returned to normal.

She was real. She was here.

And she was his.

Chapter Twenty-Five

"I've never been to a ball before," Bailey said, hooking her arm through Cole's as they entered the dining room for breakfast.

"I know, dove, you've mentioned it once or twice," Cole teased, squeezing her hand affectionately.

Bailey pouted sweetly at him and slipped out of his grasp to hug James. "Good morning, James. Thank you again for being so understanding. You know how important you are to me and I would never want to hurt you," she said, for his ears alone. Then, more cheerily, "I'm so happy you decided to stay until after the ball. Did you find something suitable to wear?"

James returned her hug and nodded, while casting a furtive glance at Cole, who seemed unaffected by the couple's show of affection.

"Morning, all," Griffin chimed in as he entered the room, plucking a fat piece of sausage off a silver tray on the buffet. Tessa squinted hard at him, shooing him away so she could serve the food. "James is going to catch every woman's eye in the room tonight, Bailey. Of course, how can you miss with my fancy green frock coat on, my man?" Griffin slapped James's shoulder good-naturedly and took the chair at the head of the table.

James nodded and smiled. "I thank you for the loan, Griffin. And, again, for your hospitality in having me here and including me in your plans for tonight. I must apologize in advance, I don't mean any disrespect, but I feel I must say this." He looked at Bailey. "If you change your mind, you mustn't hesitate to tell me that you wish to go home with me. I haven't forgotten what you said about us getting married, and I promise I wouldn't push you to change your mind. It's just that Beaufort is your home and I want you to feel comfortable returning there—as my future wife, or not." He looked at Cole then. "I mean you no disrespect, sir. Bailey and I have known each other nearly our entire lives and I only want what is best for her."

Cole swallowed a bite of ham and shook his head casually. "No need to apologize, James. I would only be displeased if I found that you were not looking out for her best interests. But since you are, there is no harm done. Bailey knows she is free to go if she chooses."

"All right, gentlemen, there's no need to talk about me like I'm a sack of wheat. I can speak for myself and, believe it or not, I can think for myself as well. I appreciate that you both care for me and want the best for me and I also appreciate that you both are going to respect my decision without any hard feelings." She glanced at James and gave him a heartfelt smile.

He hesitated, looking a bit uncomfortable, but at her gentle prodding, returned her smile and proceeded to fill his plate with eggs and ham. The atmosphere in the room became relaxed and the easy conversation went from crops and profits, to embarrassing childhood stories to the upcoming evening at Hayward Hall.

Eager anticipation kept Bailey as fidgety as a kitten all morning. She had collected eggs, weeded and cut fresh herbs from the kitchen garden, and learned to churn butter in a large wooden barrel, though her arms gave out before the cream had completely turned. She took the leftover buttermilk to the kitchen for Tessa to use in her delicious biscuits. One of the young girls who worked spinning wool had recently given birth, and Bailey went to visit the mother and her new son.

By the time she left the small hut and headed back to the main house, it was after noon. She would soak in a cool bath and try to nap, though she wasn't sure she would be able to sleep. Happiness seemed to be making her giddy and she couldn't wait to spend the evening dancing in Cole's arms. And she couldn't wait to wear the breathtaking gown he had bought her, either. Just last night, he had presented her with a large box, a gift he had purchased in Williamsburg soon after Julia had come with her invitation. He told her how beautiful she was, with or without a stitch of clothing, but that she deserved a gown to make Julia's face turn green with envy. Hers had turned as red as a tomato at the compliment, though his words had warmed her heart and made her feel as beautiful as she was in Cole's eyes. Sophie was working to raise the hemline, but other than that, the ready-made London gown fit nearly to perfection. The cheery servant gushed over the lavish gift all afternoon, telling Bailey how uncommon ready-made gowns were in the colonies and therefore how expensive it must have been.

Bailey entered the house and floated up the stairs, with lovely imaginings of her first ball dancing about in her head.

Cole stood frozen, unable to move forward or retreat out of the room his parents had shared for as long as he could remember. He had come in here for a purpose, but at the moment that purpose was forgotten as he gazed about the large bedroom where memories seemed to fly at him from every corner. The décor was different, but he could still picture it the way it was the day he raced in to find his mother dying, her last words a breathless whisper for his forgiveness. Cole felt his heart twist with pain and turned abruptly to leave, only to come face-to-face with his younger brother, who stood quietly in the doorway.

"Should I come back later?" Griffin asked, one arm braced on the door frame.

"No, of course not. I . . . I just came in here for—"

"Are you all right? Do you mind that I changed it? I just thought it would help me move on to happier times here, if I started anew."

Cole nodded thoughtfully. "I didn't realize you had been so affected by it all."

"You and father weren't the only ones she betrayed, you know."

"I know," Cole acknowledged quietly.

"I just had to find a way to accept things—I had nowhere to go. I couldn't bear to see Rosegate fall, Father would have hated that."

"I understand, Griff. You did nothing wrong. I did. I didn't see what it had done to you, and I left you. I'm sorry."

Griffin shrugged and walked into the room, his characteristic grin back in place. "Hell, I did all right without you around to give me your big-brother lectures, and tweak my ears when you got tired of me following you around."

"Christ, I haven't done that since you were twelve. Will you ever let go of that, Frog?"

Griffin laughed and sat on the edge of the bed. "Only if you forget that you ever used to call me that. Deal?"

Cole laughed in return. "Deal. I like what you've done in here. It was much too dark before."

"Thanks. I thought it needed a bit of brightening up, myself. If I ever get the chance to share this room, I'd prefer to be able to see the lovely lady in all possible light."

"Oh, really? So, do you have anyone in particular in mind?"

Griffin shook his head, laughing. "No, no. Seeing you

these last couple of weeks has just started to put thoughts in my head, that's all."

"Those thoughts better not have anything to do with Bailey, or I'll be doing more damage than tweaking your big ears."

"I'll do my best to work up a fear, old boy. In the meantime, why don't you do something about keeping her, and you won't have to worry about me or James or anyone else," Griffin ribbed his big brother.

"As a matter of fact, that's part of why I came in here."

At Griffin's questioning look, Cole reached into his pocket and pulled out a small leather pouch and dropped the contents into Griffin's palm. Griffin stared at the large, pear-shaped faceted stone, the same crystal shade of the ocean surrounding Lochinvar.

"I purchased this from one of my pirate friends in New Providence. Don't look at me like that, I had no idea what I was going to do with it when I bought it. Hell, at that point, she was lucky I bought her out of the mess she was in; giving her a gift was the last thing on my mind."

"I suppose the color just reminded you of something," Griffin suggested wryly.

"That will be enough from you, I haven't forgotten how to hurt you," Cole threatened halfheartedly.

"I still don't understand, what are you looking for in here?"

"I had the stone mounted in Williamsburg and I was thinking of putting the pendant on Mother's pearls. I am hoping Bailey will like it. I thought maybe it would aid me in my cause, so to speak."

"Hmmm. You going to ask her tonight, then?"

Cole swung his head to look at his grinning brother. "No one likes a wise-acre, you know."

Griffin laughed and pounded his brother on the back. He rose from the bed and went to a tall bureau in the corner. He opened two small doors and retrieved a carved wooden box from the hutch in the dresser and brought the box to a table by the bed. Upon opening the box, he and Cole stared at the adornments inside, momentarily caught up in memories their mother's jewelry stirred in each.

"Here it is," Griffin said, pulling out the short strand of glowing pinkish pearls. He picked up the sea-blue pendant and attached it to the pearls, then handed the necklace to Cole. "It will be good to see it on her."

Cole nodded thoughtfully.

"Bailey is nothing like her, you know."

"I know. I used to think all women were like our mother— to some degree or another. I've known so many who lie to get what they want, or work toward a secret purpose they will stop at nothing to fulfill . . . I was beginning to think it was inherently female." He chuckled, slightly embarrassed. Bailey was nothing like he had thought, and never had been. But he had been blinded by mistrust and bitterness for too long to see the truth until he had almost lost her. He felt a strong welling of emotion inside him at the realization of just how close he had come to losing Bailey. That would never happen again, he would see to it. He would make things right for her—for them both. Tonight.

"Looks like it's going to be a night to remember, brother. I, for one, am looking forward to Julia's reaction when she hears the happy news."

Griffin's prediction jarred Cole back to the moment. "No, I want this to be between us for now. Understand? I mean it, Griff," Cole warned his mischievous sibling. "I have my reasons."

"You won't hear a word out of me. I swear it," Griffin promised. "Now, why don't you get out of here and get cleaned up? As much as Bailey loves Maximilian, I don't think you want to smell like him when you ask her the big question. Go take a bath."

Cole rolled his eyes and slipped the necklace into the leather pouch as he preceded his brother out the door. He hesitated in the hallway and tilted his head to speak over his shoulder. "By the way, Frog, I'll be expecting you to keep Julie well occupied on the dance floor tonight."

He strode away, chuckling at the string of exaggerated oaths that followed him.

Bailey stood in front of the long oval mirror, trying to press an errant curl back into its proper place. It refused to stay put, even with Sophie's careful attention, so Bailey gently brushed the girl's fingers aside and tucked the curl behind her ear.

"There, see? No one will even notice that one little curl. You've done a splendid job, Sophie, I had no idea you were so artistic. Thank you so much."

Sophie smiled and beamed with pride. "It was nothin', Miss Bailey. I haven't gotten to fix up a lady's hair in a long time. Miss Catherine used to let me fix her hair when she was goin' to town. That's how I learned. Oh, Miss Bailey, you look prettier than any lady I've ever seen. You're gonna have so much fun at that ball."

"I hope so, Sophie. I must admit, I am a little nervous, though. None of the ladies I used to know in Beaufort looked anything like Julia Hayward. She is quite a beautiful woman." She sighed.

Sophie clucked her tongue, her opinion obviously different. Bailey smiled at the girl's unabashed honesty. "I know, she does seem to be a little difficult, but I am not going to let her worry me tonight. I am going to dance until my feet ache and there is only one person who will have my attention tonight."

Both women giggled at that and Bailey twirled about in the mirror, watching the ivory and peach silk of her skirt catch the candlelight.

"Am I interrupting?"

Bailey gasped, and spun toward the door. She had forgotten

that they had left it open when Sophie had gone to search for hairpins. Cole filled the doorway, dressed in a dark blue coat and breeches. His vest was deep gold, embroidered with vines of green and burgundy. A snowy white cravat was tied at his neck, making his tanned features look incredibly masculine. His hair was unpowdered, the dark strands tied neatly at the nape of his neck. Fine dark hose and highly polished shoes with silver buckles completed his outfit. She would never get used to how handsome he was, whether he was dressed like the wealthy gentleman or like the rugged sea captain pirate hunter.

"No, of course not. Am I late? Is it time to go?"

Cole walked inside, grinning. "Anxious, dove? Don't worry, we'll be leaving soon. We have a few minutes. I was hoping to speak to you."

Bailey nodded and thanked Sophie again, before excusing her for the night. "Should we go down to the parlor?"

"No, here is fine. Come, sit," he took her hand and led her to one of a matching set of embroidered chairs by the fireplace. He sat on the edge of the other, leaning forward with his elbows on his knees, his hands clasped together. "You look more lovely in the gown than I even imagined."

"Thank you," Bailey said, feeling a blush creep into her cheeks. She was suddenly feeling nervous, but she thought it must be because Cole seemed to be nervous and that was something she was not used to. She prayed nothing was wrong.

"I have something to ask you, but I don't want you to answer until later tonight—midnight. I want you to think long and hard about your answer, and I want you to know that whatever you decide, I will see to it that you never have to worry about your welfare."

"Cole, what is it? You are starting to frighten me."

He smiled. "I don't mean to. I have never done this before— actually, I thought I never would do this, so it's not surprising that I'm making a mess of it."

"Cole?" Bailey's heart started pounding a wild beat in her chest. This could not be happening. He wasn't actually—

"I want you to marry me. I want us to be married."

He was, actually! Bailey felt like all the air had been sucked from her lungs. She couldn't believe what she was hearing. Colby Leighton had just asked her to marry him. She couldn't respond even if he had wanted her to.

"Oh, and I have something for you." He took the pouch from his vest pocket and handed it to her.

She took it and reached inside, pulling the necklace out with a gasp. The huge crystal-blue stone was the most incredible shade of blue she had ever seen. "Oh, Cole! It's beautiful! It looks like the ocean surrounding Lochinvar."

"It looks like your eyes."

She felt the sudden sting of tears threatening. She hadn't thought she could be any happier, then he did something surprising that made her love him even more.

Cole stood up and took the glistening pearls from her limp fingers, clasping the necklace around her throat and placing a soft kiss against the skin there. She shivered from the delicious contact of his warm lips.

"Why must I wait to answer you?"

"Because I am still the same man I was when you met me. You have changed me in some ways, that is true, but there is a part of me that will never be able to let go of the past until I have righted it. And that isn't going to happen until I have found the Dragon. I am going after him until I find him, whether it takes me another year or another twenty years. And when I find him, there is going to be a fight to the death— mine or his." He knelt in front of her and took her trembling hands in his before continuing. "If you agree to marry me, you will have to accept that about me . . . And you will have to allow me to do what I must to avenge my father's death. I swore to him that I would, I cannot go back on my word. Not even for you."

She leaned forward and kissed him, feeling a tear slide down her cheek. How could she go from such a height of happiness to such a low of emptiness so quickly? Her mind whirled. Perhaps it was for the best that James was still there. He would be leaving after tonight and had made it clear that she could go with him, with no promises about the future. She lowered her head, unable to meet Cole's hopeful gaze.

Cole stood up and she reluctantly let her fingers slip from his grasp. She felt her heart breaking, all the hopeful joy she had felt, shadowed by the bleak circumstances that mapped their future. Cole leaned down and lifted the stone that lay just below her throat, rubbing it gently between his fingers. His eyes were dark, stormy gray, but his voice was light when he spoke.

"I didn't mean to upset you. I was hoping my gift would make you smile."

He was going to ignore all the rest of what he had said—very well, then. She didn't want to think about it, either. She just wanted to enjoy every minute with him, especially if this was to be their last night.

"I love your gift—it is the most lovely thing I have ever seen. Thank you for it," she said, and touched his fingers where they lingered on the pendant and the skin at her throat. "Now, are you going to take me to a ball tonight, or not? I am expecting to be whirled about until my feet fall off," she said, as lightly as she could manage. She sniffled back her emotions and offered her hand to Cole, who helped her up and escorted her out of her room.

Griffin and James were waiting for them in the library, discussing politics over brandy. Bailey put on a brave smile as she and Cole joined them for a drink before they piled into a carriage and made the short trip to Hayward Hall.

By the time they arrived at Hayward Hall, Bailey was feeling a little better. On the short drive, Griffin kept the group in stitches doing impressions of Cole and Julia and some of the more eccentric people who would be attending the party. The driver pulled the carriage to a stop behind two others in the circular drive and Bailey pulled aside the curtain and peered out the window. Candles twinkled from ornate crystal chandeliers, casting rays of light out the open windows and double front doors to spill across the grounds.

The group made their way into the large brick house and were quickly met by joyful partygoers who were eager to see Colby Leighton after so many years away. There was also many a curious stare at Bailey, whose story had been spread as quickly as Julia's tongue could manage. After many introductions were made and acquaintances renewed, Griffin took James off in the direction of the refreshments and Cole led Bailey toward the ballroom. They had taken only a few steps down the hallway when Julia rushed out to greet them. Dressed in a deep blue gown with silver threads running through the bodice and sleeves, she was more beautiful—and more intimidating—than Bailey had remembered. She held her head so high, the angle appeared awkward, not to mention seemingly impossible when Bailey thought about how heavy her tall powdered wig must have been. Her face was powdered as well, which Bailey found quite odd, though the taller woman was undeniably beautiful, despite her strange appearance.

"Darling! I was almost ready to be angry with you for being so late," she admonished, taking Cole's arm and dragging him down the hallway. "You look absolutely delicious, darling, but then you always do."

Cole glanced back at Bailey, looking as if he had eaten a sour apple. She smiled at him and he winked, the affectionate gesture catching Julia's attention.

"Oh, yes, Bailey, it's lovely to see you again. I'm so sorry, I just wasn't able to part with my maid after all, but I see you were able to scrounge up a dress. You look quite fetching, dear. Come this way, there is someone you simply must meet! I have been dying to introduce you, darling, and to tell you my news."

Julia hurried her pace, entering the ballroom and weaving in and out of the crowd, making it difficult for Bailey to keep up. Suddenly, a jovial young man approached Bailey and blocked her path. He introduced himself and insisted on hearing absolutely everything about her before launching into a long story detailing his entire life up until that very moment. Bailey lost sight of Cole and couldn't seem to locate Griffin or James among all the powdered heads, so she accepted the young man's arm and was soon settled on a padded bench listening to her talkative companion.

Cole grit his teeth and tried to loosen the death grip Julia had on his arm. He could see Bailey across the room, engaged in a conversation with some dandy-looking youngster, whom he would rescue her from as soon as he could disengage from Julia. Until then, he supposed, he had to be polite. They approached a man, not quite as tall as Cole, dressed in black with a silver brocade vest. The man wore a heavily powdered long wig and his face was also lightly powdered, though Cole could tell from the stubble on his chin that the man's hair was dark. There was something about the aristocratic way he held himself and looked at Cole as if he believed he was the better man that made Cole instantly dislike him. So, this was Julia's guest? He appeared to be her perfect match.

"Cole, darling, I want you to meet my fiancé, Edwin Munroe, of London. Edwin, this is the man I was telling you about: Colby Leighton. Our families have been neighbors since before we were born. I used to believe that we were destined to marry"—she laughed, a cold, brittle humorless sound—"but, of course, that was before I met you, my love."

She stroked Edwin's arm until he gave an almost imperceptible shake of his shoulder to dodge her and extended his hand to Cole.

"Why, yes, Julia, I do remember you speaking of Mr. Leighton. Pleasure to meet you, sir."

"Actually, it's Captain."

"Ah, that's right. I remember now. You are the one who has dedicated his life to sailing all about the Colonies and Caribbean, searching for some nasty pirate, isn't that right?"

Cole ignored the scorn in the man's tone. "That's right."

"The Snake, Serpent, what was it, love?"

"The Dragon," Julia supplied, eager to be involved in any type of gossip. "I told you, didn't I, that he seduced Cole's mother into—"

"Enough, Julie," Cole growled, his use of her hated nickname having the desired effect of her snapping her lips shut in irritation.

"I remember. A downright tragedy, old fellow. Quite sorry to hear about it. I'm sure you'll be successful in bringing the brigand to justice. How long have you been searching for the man?" he asked, wiping a nonexistent piece of lint from his sleeve.

Cole didn't answer, but narrowed his eyes on the man, wondering at his interest.

"Five years, but I know I told you that, my love. Don't you remember?" Julia asked.

"When did you arrive in the Colonies, Mr. Munroe?" Cole asked, accepting a glass of champagne from a passing servant.

"Only recently, as it happens. I was fortunate enough to meet this lovely lady while she was visiting friends in London and we fell in love almost immediately. I would have married her straight away, but Julia wanted more than anything to be married at her beloved Hayward Hall. We'll be returning to England next spring."

"Julia wanted to be married here?" Cole asked, his voice edged with confusion.

"Yes, why? Do you find that so strange?"

"I suppose not. I just would have thought that she would want to be married somewhere different this time."

Julia sputtered as she sipped her champagne, then dabbed at her lips with a lace handkerchief. "Cole, must you be so indelicate, darling? Edwin and I fell in love so suddenly, there wasn't much time to plan a wedding in London and settle all my affairs here. Besides, I'm sure my late husband would wish for me to be happy, and I wouldn't think of getting married without all of my friends around me. Surely you understand that," she snapped, then regained her composure in the blink of an eye. "Besides, it would have worried you terribly if I had run off to England without so much as a by-your-leave. We're practically family, after all," she purred.

"Indeed," Cole replied smoothly. Something about the situation didn't sit well with him, but he couldn't quite figure out what. He wasn't going to waste any more time on the matter, though, because Julia's affairs held no interest for him. She was a grown woman with one rich, old husband behind her and apparently another rich, young one ahead. What he was interested in was finding Bailey. "My sincere congratulations to you both. I'm sure we'll speak again, but at the moment, I need to find—"

"Cole!"

"Leighton, I'll be damned!"

Two men approached the group and after a few more minutes of pleasantries, they ushered Cole away to smoke cigars in the library. Cole went grudgingly, eager to find Bailey, but happy to have an excuse to withdraw from Julia and her simpering Englishman. He caught a glimpse of Bailey as his two old friends preceded him out of the ballroom. She was standing in a small circle, chatting and laughing with several women near her age. She was radiant and lovely, her smile lighting the room as well as her face, and he felt his heart swell. He wanted nothing more than to go to her, but after the mess he'd made of his proposal, he felt she deserved some time to just enjoy herself. He would leave her be for a little while longer, just long enough to smoke one cigar and reacquaint himself with Phillip Baldwin and Randolph Turner.

Chapter Twenty-Six

Bailey's head swam pleasantly from the effects of the champagne she'd been sipping, but the room had become too stuffy to bear, so she excused herself from the group to get some air.

"Oh, what a good idea, honey. I'll come along with you."

Bailey gladly accepted the company of the young Mrs. Cameron, who clucked her tongue in mock rebuke as they left the ballroom and walked past the library. "Those men of ours! Honestly, we wait all year long for a glorious party such as this, and our men congregate in one tiny room and stink the place to high heaven with those awful cigars. *Humph!* I suppose we are just supposed to dance with each other," she said and laughed gaily.

"I may just have to take you up on that, Martha. I have yet to dance once and I made a promise to myself to dance until my feet ache," Bailey responded.

Martha laughed and hooked her arm around Bailey's as the two women made their way out to the terrace. The air was no cooler out here, but at least they had a reprieve from the crush of bodies and heat from all the candles. Torches were lit at the edges of the terrace and a short distance away stood a lovely garden trellis, surrounded by dozens of richly hued rosebushes. A few couples stood about or sat on benches, sipping punch or champagne and chatting in quiet tones. Bailey enjoyed Martha's friendly wit as they talked of nothing in particular. A short time later, a lively tune sprang up from inside the house as the musicians began to play, and the few remaining couples went back inside to enjoy more dancing.

"Oh, I simply must get Stuart. My feet just won't stay still a moment longer. Do you want to come and drag Cole away from the men, honey?"

"I'll be along shortly. I need to clear the champagne from my head a bit. Go on, I'll be quite all right."

"I'll see you on the dance floor, then!" Martha replied and swished into the house in a flurry of yellow taffeta.

Out of the corner of her eye, Bailey saw movement and turned to see a man coming out to join her on the terrace.

"Good evening," he greeted her.

"Good evening, sir," Bailey replied. The man was very well dressed, all in black, except for his silver-threaded vest and stark white wig.

"Allow me to introduce myself. I am Edwin Munroe," he said and dipped his head as he bowed slightly.

Bailey had never experienced such stiff manners, but supposed this was how a proper gentleman behaved. She immediately decided she preferred Cole's rough edges. Before she could respond he spoke again, his eyes resting well below her face.

"What a lovely pendant, madame. I don't believe I've seen anything that unusual before. What is it?" he asked, enthralled by Cole's lavish gift. "Here, let's move into the light, so I can see it better," he said and guided them closer to a bright torch.

"I . . . I'm afraid I don't know the proper name for it. I have never seen anything like it, either. It was a gift." She fingered the necklace, painfully aware that her scar was visible just beneath the lower strand of pearls. She wished she could just get over her self-consciousness at the ugly physical reminder of the Dragon's attack.

"Good Lord, sweetness, whatever in the world happened to you? It looks as if you have suffered a terrible accident."

Something inside Bailey recoiled at the man's words. His voice was deep and raspy, not unpleasant, yet somehow disturbing. His face was overly powdered, not quite masking the deep bronze of his skin. She looked into his eyes, cold and maleficent, despite their rich golden color. For some unexplained reason, she felt her skin crawl, felt her throat tighten as she continued to stare into his eyes, unable to tear her gaze away. There was something familiar about Edwin Munroe, though she was sure she had never met him before.

"N—No. It was not an accident, but I would rather not talk about it. I'm afraid it brings back unpleasant memories."

"Oh, of course. Forgive me. There are plenty of things we can talk about. You are not from Virginia, are you?"

His tone had become suspicious. He was practically sneering at her. Bailey decided that impolite or not, she was not going to converse with Edwin Munroe a minute longer. She started to back away and make her excuses to go inside when he stopped her with a firm grip on her forearm.

"I think we have more to talk about, sweetness. Please, do stay a while," he insisted, his white teeth flashing as he attempted a smile.

Fight me, sweetness, come on.

Fight me, sweetness . . . The memory of the words breathed in her ear by the masked pirate the night of the attack nearly made her faint.

"Oh, God. No." Bailey barely got the whispered denial out before he wrenched her arm behind her back and crushed his other hand across her mouth. She felt her teeth cut into the inside of her lips, though she tried to scream, anyway.

"Shut up, bitch, or I will slice you open right here. Yes, sweetness, you are right. It's me, your long, lost Dragon.

Finally, we're reunited. And what a pleasant surprise this is, Bailey Spencer," he rasped in her ear.

Bailey felt sick to her stomach, barely able to control her shaking legs as the Dragon half dragged her across the lawn toward the relative privacy of the dimly lit garden trellis. Nearly halfway there, a voice stopped them in their tracks.

"Edwin? Darling? Where are you going? Who is that?" Julia asked, her voice heavy with jealous concern.

"Julia, love, we were just going to look at your lovely roses. Why don't you open a bottle of champagne and come out and join us?"

Bailey struggled and tried to scream or turn around—anything to get Julia's attention, to warn her away. The Dragon twisted her arm without mercy, nearly bringing her to her knees from the pain. She sagged against him for a second, gaining a slight release of his hold.

"Stand up, wench, or I'll kill you both, do you understand?" he hissed in her ear. "Hurry up, love, we want to hear all about your garden."

"I'll just be a moment," Julia replied, her voice fading as she scurried into the house.

Once inside the garden trellis, the Dragon shoved her down on a bench next to him, farthest from the opening of the structure. With one hand covering her mouth, he pulled her face close to his and pressed the sharp tip of a dagger against her chest. "Your future welfare is entirely dependent on how you behave in the next few minutes. Now, if you're thinking that you don't care about your own life, hear this well. Julia's life depends on you, too. I will slice you both open and leave you here while I go inside and enjoy the bloody roast beef. Nod if you understand."

She nodded, feeling the bile rise in her throat. Sweet Mary, this could not be happening. Where was Cole? *Please, God, don't let him come looking for me now.*

Satisfied with her weak nod, the Dragon released her, but held the dagger out between them.

"Now, tell me—and don't dare mince the truth—what are you doing here? Who are you here with?"

Bailey thought for a moment to tempt fate and lie. She didn't want Cole to find the Dragon this way. He would be completely at a disadvantage and she was afraid he might act rashly. He might not come out of it alive. But she didn't know what else to say, without the pirate knowing she lied.

"I . . . I am staying at Rosegate."

The pirate laughed harshly. "So, the good Captain Leighton found you, eh? I suppose I have to give the man his due. I had heard a rumor that he had an offer for me—I guess the rumor was true." He laughed again, his next words filled with derision. "How does it feel to be offered up to me for the sake of vengeance?"

She swallowed her pride, thinking only to protect Cole in any way she could. "Not very good, to tell you the truth. Now that you have me, where are you going to take me?"

"Oh, no! No, not so fast. The fun is only beginning, sweetness. We aren't going anywhere."

Just then Julia started across the lawn, a bottle of champagne swinging from one hand, her other wrapped tightly through James's arm.

No, not James, too. Bailey felt overwhelmed with fear, grief and concern. The only people left in the world that she cared about were in imminent danger. It was a near duplicate of the night her father and brother were killed. She was being held by the same pirate, and she was unable to do anything to save her loved ones. She would gladly give her own life this very minute if it would save James and Cole. And even Julia. The woman might be a bit overbearing, but she did not deserve to be involved in this.

"Please, just send them away. I'll do whatever you want, I swear, just please let them go."

"Reliving the past? Not much you could do then and, sorry, love, but not much you can do now. My future depends on my past staying buried, and none of you will be allowed to plague me any further. Julia, please, my dear, join us," he finished loud enough for her to hear.

Julia and James stepped up inside the whitewashed garden structure and though Bailey tried to catch James's eye, he seemed reluctant to look at her. Julia, however, had no such problem, glaring openly at Bailey's proximity to her fiancé before sitting close on his other side.

"James, how the hell are you, boy? How's the family? Been a good year so far? Plenty of food on the table? I hear you might be buying a bit of land for yourself soon. Heard you might be getting married. Oh, wait. I believe your wife-to-be is sitting right here, isn't that right?"

James looked beseechingly at the Dragon, then cast a guilty look at Bailey before lowering his head and shaking it, as if in disbelief about what was occurring.

"James?" Bailey pleaded, dying inside at what seemed to be unfolding. "Do you know him?" she asked, on the verge of tears. When he didn't answer in the negative right away, she swallowed hard and found much more strength in her voice. "Do you?" she demanded.

"Hmmm, I don't think James is going to answer you, Bailey. Why don't I fill you in? After that unfortunate pirate attack on your little town, James here, decided to go after the brigands responsible. And, of course, after you, my sweetness. But in his search for the Dragon—uh, me—he stopped at an establishment where he ran into a rough couple of bastards who didn't care much for his line of questioning. These blokes were friends of mine, you see, and they were just trying to protect me. So, they made a deal with young James. He would visit that very tavern each and every month and reveal any news of merchant ships scheduled to sail in the vicinity of Beaufort or Ocracoke, and in return, he would be paid a sum of money that he could use in any way he may choose. A damn generous sum, if I do say so myself. After all, I was the one who came up with the idea—bloody good one, too, wouldn't you say?"

Bailey closed her eyes against the pain and disgust she felt, unable to look at James and barely able to believe the story. If James hadn't looked so guilty during the telling of it, she never would have given credence to the pirate's claim. Julia didn't look much better, her face a sickly shade of green. Her mouth gaped open, a look of horror frozen on her face, though she finally found her wits and tried to rise. The Dragon cursed and grabbed her wrist, yanking her down with the order for her to remain still.

"Who are you?" she asked, breathlessly.

"He is the pirate that Cole has been searching for. He is the Dragon," Bailey uttered miserably.

"Thank you for the introduction," he replied and kissed Bailey hard on the lips. "Oh, Julia, you are too far behind. I can't possibly catch you up. I'm afraid my time here is becoming limited. Unfortunate, since I was beginning to really enjoy this little soiree—and you, my dear. You definitely do provide some entertainment . . . at least in the bedroom. The rest of the time you can be a bit tedious."

Julia gasped and slapped the Dragon, who laughed in delighted pleasure.

"You are the one? You are the man who has been stealing the fortunes of all those women? Oh, dear God, you meant for me to be your next victim, didn't you?"

"You still will be, Julia, dear. I have no intention of giving up your considerable inheritance. You were crafty indeed to marry that old coot, but I am even craftier. We will be married, my love, but soon after our wedding, you will fall victim to an unfortunate accident. I will, of course, be so devastated at the loss of my beautiful bride, that I will return to England and leave the Colonies behind forever. After this, I will have enough money and power to destroy that unreasonable blood father of mine. The bastard dared to deny me my birthright."

"I will never agree to marry you! You are mad!" Julia spat, struggling to rise. The Dragon stood and backhanded her hard, sending her sprawling in a pile of blue silk on the floor.

"Leave her alone," James begged. "I will help you get your money some other way. And let Bailey go. She has no fortune. I swear I will see to it that she keeps quiet. We will all keep quiet—right, Julia? Bailey?"

Bailey felt nauseous at the simpering in James's voice. How could this be the same boy she had grown up with? How could he have agreed to work for the Dragon after what the villain had done to her and her family? God help her, but she couldn't find the heart to forgive him just now.

"You are after Cole, aren't you? You won't let me go, because you know that Cole will come after me. Well, you might as well kill me now, because I will not help you hurt him. I will *not* lead him to you. Never!"

"Aren't you the smart one. You *will* lead Cole to me, whether you want to or not. As a matter of fact, I could go ahead and kill you and my plan would still work. As long as Cole believes I have you, he will come. He doesn't have to know whether you are dead or alive, now does he?"

"You are despicable," she spat. "But it will never work, no matter what you do. Cole will never be beaten by you!"

The Dragon clapped, laughing at what he considered a jest. "Enough! I am getting bored with all of this whining. James, come over here, let's discuss your situation, boy."

James stood hesitantly, a hopeful look settling on his pale face. He approached the taller man, who blocked any chance of Julia slipping past him to escape the garden trellis. The Dragon reached out and clapped his arm around James's shoulder, shaking him and laughing. James let out a heavy breath and lifted his lips in an uneasy grin.

"You and Bailey are going to take a ride with me."

Julia screamed, her voice a hysterical squeal. "No, please don't hurt me! Please!"

"Shut your mouth, whore!" He shook her hard, causing the tall wig on her head to slip backward. "Shut up, do you hear me?"

Julia quieted to a whimper. Bailey sat quietly, praying that she could hold her emotions intact. She had to stay calm if she had any chance of living through this and helping Cole in the process.

"Julia, please. Just do as he says," she pleaded to the frightened woman.

"Good girl, Bailey. Listen to her, Julia, and you might just live long enough to enjoy being married to me for a while. If you do exactly what I tell you to do, I'll let you live—if not, I will kill you. Believe me, there is nowhere you would be able to hide—I will eventually find you. Isn't that so, sweetness?" he asked over his shoulder.

Bailey didn't respond. She prayed Julia would cooperate, at least for the time being.

The Dragon's voice was low as he instructed each of them on what he expected in the next few hours. Bailey died inside when he told her what she and James must do. Cole had finally learned to trust her and this was going to destroy him.

"Is . . . Is that all?" Julia sniffed, visibly shaking.

"Not quite. I want you to go inside and enjoy the ball. In exactly two hours I want you to go to Captain Leighton and tell him that you saw Bailey and James leave in a carriage together."

"What if he wishes to leave early? What if he comes searching for Bailey?"

"Obviously, you must keep him occupied as well. He mustn't be allowed to leave Hayward Hall until the two hours have passed. Do you understand?" he asked as if speaking to a small child.

Julia nodded, wiping her nose with the back of her hand and attempting to pull herself together.

"All right. Yes. Yes. I can do that."

The Dragon turned to dismiss her, but she tugged on his coat and he spun around, his temper flaring. "What?"

"Is that all? I mean, if I do this, you won't . . . hurt me?"

"Do what I tell you and don't say a word to anyone, and you will be safe, love. I promise." The Dragon smiled and pulled her to him, crushing her against his body and kissing her in a grossly intimate manner. He then shoved her away from him and ordered her to go. "Have my carriage brought around to the side," he added, as she fled the rose-covered platform.

Chapter Twenty-Seven

"Sorry, gents, but if I don't go and spend some time dancing with my wife, I'll be sleeping in the stables for a week," Phillip Baldwin said, snuffing out his cigar and rising from his chair.

"Thank goodness I don't have to worry about the whims of a wife," Griffin said with a grin. "All I have to worry about is which lovely young miss I'll dance with next." He winked at Cole, who followed him, Phillip and Randolph out of the library.

"Ho, but at least Phillip and I have the pleasure of climbing into bed every night with a warm, soft body and willing companion. You're likely to get challenged by an angry father or jealous rival if you try the same, Griff. Why don't you join the rest of us and settle down—it's not nearly as bad as ol' Phillip makes it out to be," Randolph jested. "And what about you, Cole? Didn't I see you arrive tonight with a woman too beautiful to give you the time of day?"

"Aye, who is she, Cole? Lovely girl," Phillip added. "There you are, Griff—there's your future wife. How nice of your brother to find her for you."

Cole remained silent while his friends laughed at his expense. Nothing would change with these two, they had been the instigators of their tight-knit gang since all four were boys, and Cole had become used to being ribbed about his aversion to marriage.

"I don't know, gentlemen," Griffin answered. "The lady is definitely not interested in me. And, furthermore, my brother might just surprise us all—very soon, if I am not mistaken."

Cole gave Griffin a warning glare that effectively silenced the younger man. He hadn't told Griffin about Bailey's reaction to his proposal, or that he had insisted she take tonight to think it over. Her reaction to his admission that he would still go after the Dragon had obviously hurt her. But more than that, it had scared her, too. He saw such a deep fear cloud her blue-green eyes that he wasn't sure she would be able to accept his dangerous lifestyle. As much as he now longed for a life with her, he shared her intense pain of a past filled with loss and he wasn't sure she could overcome that any better than he had.

Both Phillip and Randolph chuckled, muttering colorful comments of disbelief as all four men entered the ballroom and split up to find their respective wives and dance partners.

Cole and Griffin walked around the candlelit border of the room, past tall gilt mirrors, reflecting colorful gowns and jackets as the double line of men and women moved through the steps of a lively reel. Cole didn't see Bailey among any of the small groups of single ladies, but one petite beauty caught Griffin's eye and he excused himself from his brother's company. Cole ventured across the room, toward the refreshment table, and saw Julia coming his way in a rush of blue and sparkle. She seemed flustered, out of breath, though her face was deathly pale. Gads, how he detested the current fashion of powdering everything in sight until it looked like the unfortunate soul had been dunked in a flour barrel.

"Cole! There you are! I . . . I was hoping you would have a dance with me."

"I promised Bailey would have all of my dances, tonight. Sorry, Julie."

"But . . . She doesn't seem to be available at the moment. Come, why don't we just go out there for a little while. As soon as you see her, I'll give you up," she promised.

Her voice seemed oddly tense, despite the enthusiastic sing-song lilt. It was almost as if she was trying hard to be at ease, though Cole had never known Julia to be uncomfortable. Confidence was one thing she had in spades, though he was a little thrown off that she hadn't reprimanded him for calling her by her hated nickname.

"Perhaps later, Julia. I've neglected Bailey for far too long as it is. Excuse me," he said, bowing politely.

"Cole! Grand to see you, young man. I hardly believed it was true when Baldwin told me you were here. So sorry I haven't had a chance to come out to Rosegate since your return. Oh, but could I have a few words with you? I promise I won't keep you from our lovely hostess for too long, but it's rather important."

Cole sighed. He really didn't wish to discuss business tonight, but Etheridge Hamilton was not a man to take no for an answer. Cole had been restocking the Williamsburg merchant's store for years now, trading the man's crops for spices, sugar, fabrics and other items for as long as he'd been sailing. Etheridge had been his father's closest friend and had been in Cole and Griffin's life for as long as he could remember. He was a good man, though a bit long-winded, and Cole didn't wish to be tied up with him just now. He glanced around the ballroom again, but seeing no sign of Bailey, he nodded to the man.

"Julia, would you take a look around for Bailey and ask her to come to the library when you see her?"

Julia nodded mutely, her green eyes wide. Cole held her gaze for a moment, waiting for her to say something else, as he fully expected, but she remained strangely silent.

"Don't be angry with me, Julie. I'm sure Griffin will dance with you, if you ask him nicely." He grinned at her and turned to walk away with Etheridge. He glanced over his shoulder, expecting to hear a loud insult at any moment, but Julia had turned her back to him, tipping her full glass of champagne nearly upside down to her lips. Cole had no more time to wonder at her strange behavior since Etheridge began chattering nonstop as they left the ballroom.

Cole glanced at the clock in the hallway as Etheridge said good-bye and wandered outside for some air.

Damn! Two hours? The man had grown even more long-winded than Cole remembered. And he couldn't for the life of him recall what all the man had said. None of it was terribly important, after all. But Cole knew that since the man had become a widower with no living children, he needed someone to talk to, and Cole and Griffin were the closest he had to family.

He had become a little concerned that Bailey hadn't come to find him, but assumed that she was having a good time with some new friends. And, besides, he figured that Julia had never intended to find her for him, so he doubted Bailey even knew he was looking for her.

A quick look about the ballroom told him she wasn't there, so he went out on the terrace, where a good number of people had gone in search of a breeze. Julia sat on a bench, surrounded by women, but Bailey was not among them. He caught Julia's eye and she popped up from the bench and hurried toward him.

"What is it?" he asked, concerned at the look of worry on her face.

"I saw Bailey and James leave. They took a carriage. Together."

"What?"

"You must return to Rosegate."

"Slow down, Julia," Cole said, keeping his voice low to calm her.

"Now!" Her voice cracked, though she tried to cover up her distress.

"What is wrong? Is Bailey sick? Did she go back to Rosegate?"

"I don't know. Just, please stop asking me questions and go!"

Cole hurried down the stone stairs and bolted across the lawn, circling around to the front of the house. "Bring my carriage around. Quick!" Cole shouted, startling a bored footman into action.

Cole tore up the front steps and into Rosegate, calling for Bailey as he went. The steward met him in the foyer, wringing his hands, his dark face shadowed with distress.

"What is it, George? Is she all right?" Cole grabbed the mahogany railing and took the stairs two at a time before George could utter a response.

By the time Cole discovered that Bailey's bedroom was empty, George had made it to the top of the stairs and stood in the hallway. Sophie huddled against the wall, biting her fingernails, her face red and tear-streaked.

"Where is she? What is this all about?" Cole thundered.

"I'm sorry, sir. She done gone. She an' that man, James."

"What do you mean, gone?" Cole shouted, then caught himself. He took a deep breath and apologized to the servant.

"Follow me, sir."

George and the maid led Cole into Griffin's room. Clothes were strung everywhere, pillows and bedding rumpled, candlesticks and vases in pieces on the floor. The drawers on the tall bureau had been pulled out, contents hanging in disarray. The doors on the bureau were open, the wooden jewelry box gone. Cole felt a sinking in his stomach and shook his head, unwilling to believe.

"All Miss Catherine's jewelry is gone, sir. They's some things missing from downstairs, too. Some silver. And some money from the desk in the study."

Cole sank down on the edge of the bed and rubbed at the dull thud that had begun behind his forehead as George continued.

"I tried to stop her, sir. I begged her not to do it, but Miss Bailey, she didn't even answer me. She didn't say nothin', she just followed that man around the house and let him tear everything apart. Then, they left right outta here—got in some fancy black carriage and took off."

Cole was barely listening now. The thread of pain he had initially felt had spun into a ball of white-hot fury. He deserved this! He deserved her betrayal, because he had allowed himself to believe in her. To care about her. He knew he shouldn't have. From the moment he had started to feel something for her, he knew he should fight it. He had promised himself—damn his own hide—promised himself! But she had him convinced that she was different, so he let himself hope. And look at what that hope had done for him.

Damn her! She would be sorry for betraying him. As sorry as he was for ever trusting her. He would find her and once he did, he would sacrifice her to the Dragon without a second thought. It's what he should have done from the very beginning. He could have had his revenge and been well on with his life by now, if he hadn't listened to his damn conscience. She was just like the rest of them and, damn it, he had allowed himself to forget that long enough for her to spin her web of deceit.

"Don't blame yourself, George. You didn't stand a chance against her. Get this mess cleaned up before Griffin comes home, I don't want him to be any more upset than he has to be."

"Yes, sir. Where you going, Mr. Cole?" George asked, concerned.

"I'm going to go take care of this," Cole said and stalked from the room.

"Griffin, I need to talk to you," Cole said, pulling on his brother's coat sleeve. He had to speak up over the din of music and laughter from a nearby group of partygoers.

"Not now, Brother, I am occupied," Griffin growled over his shoulder. He turned and bestowed a charming smile on the petite brunette he had been dancing with earlier.

"Now," Cole ground out, pulling his little brother away from the girl, leaving her with a disappointed pout on her full lips.

Cole dragged Griffin outside, across the terrace and down onto the lawn, away from prying eyes and curious ears.

"What is wrong with you? Have you lost your mind? Is everyone around here mad? I swear, you and Julie are acting very peculiar."

"Bailey is gone. She left with James."

"What?"

"There's more. I'm sorry, Griff, it's all my fault." He hesitated, finding it difficult to voice what he had been trying to deny the whole ride back to Hayward Hall. "She stole Mother's jewelry. And money. She took money from the study—I don't know how much."

"What the hell? No, I don't believe it, brother."

"Believe it. I just came from Rosegate. George and one of the maids saw her follow James around the house while he sacked the place."

"There has to be some mistake. Bailey wouldn't do that."

"I know. I wouldn't have believed it either, but you know George, Griff. He doesn't lie." He sighed.

"She loves you, Cole."

"The hell she does."

"Cole!" Julia hurried out of the house and joined them, her hands wringing in the folds of blue skirts. "Did you find Bailey and James?"

"I can't talk to you right now, Ju—what did you say? How did you know James was with her?"

"I . . . uh . . . I didn't. I just assumed. He is in Virginia because of her, isn't he?"

"Don't mind her, Cole. Julia is upset because her intended seems to have disappeared from the party."

"He didn't disappear, Griffin. He had too much to drink and went to lie down," she nervously amended.

"I thought you said he went to drive Miss Elizabeth and her sister home, since their parents had left earlier."

"That's right. Of course. Silly me." Julia wiped a bead of sweat from her face, the drip making a flesh-colored path in her powder.

"Julie, for heaven's sake, what is wrong with you tonight?" Griffin asked.

Cole watched her closely. He had known Julia far too long for her to hide her feelings from him. She was frightened. But of what—or who? She fidgeted, toying with a gold pendant that hung from a long chain around her neck. Something about the odd shape caught Cole's attention and he felt the fine hairs on his neck bristle in warning.

Cole reached out and grabbed the pendant, pulling Julia close with a tug.

Griffin looked at him as if he'd lost his mind, but Julia complied and took a step closer to Cole, looking down at the pendant that had come loose from inside her bodice.

"I've seen this before."

"It . . . It was a gift from Edwin. He had it made for me. It's a sun. He said it reminds him of the light I've brought to his life."

"Tell me again, Julia, where did you meet Edwin?" Cole

asked, his voice deceptively calm. He had to concentrate to ignore the heavy weight pressing on his heart.

"Cole," Griffin interrupted, exasperated. "Don't we have more impor—"

"Tell me, Julia."

"In Kent. He was attending a hunting party at the estate where I was a guest."

"Why are you lying about him?" Cole demanded, his patience near the breaking point.

She gasped. Griffin looked at Cole, then at Julia.

"I've seen that pendant before, Julia. It belonged to Lady Jackson."

"By golly, you're right, Cole," Griffin agreed. "I remember when old Jackson gave it to her. At Rosegate, after one of Mother and Father's dinner parties. Their daughter had just turned a year old and they always called her 'Sunny.' Jackson had the pendant made in France. She was quite pleased with the gift, if I remember."

Cole nodded. "That would be about seven years ago now. Jackson was killed about six months after that."

"Didn't he accidentally shoot himself while he was hunting?" Griffin asked.

Cole nodded at his brother. "I never understood why, but Father never believed that story." He turned to Julia, lifting her quivering chin. "How did Edwin get it, Julia?"

She didn't answer, but tears welled in her eyes.

"His name isn't Munroe, is it? It's Montrose, isn't it, Julia?" Cole felt shame wash over him for doubting Bailey even for a moment. He should have had faith in her. God, he could feel it—she was in danger. He couldn't lose her.

She whimpered, shaking her head. Cole grabbed her shoulders and shook her.

"Bailey is in danger, Julia. And I have no doubt that you are, too. Talk!"

"Yes! Yes! He said his name is Montrose, but that he had a

falling out with his family. They are very wealthy and he didn't want anyone here to know about their difficulties. He wanted to keep his true identity as a lord secret until he can reconcile with his father. He said they have been corresponding and he is certain they will be reunited soon."

"Damn right they will be reunited soon—and I will be the one to reunite them. In Hell. He lied to you, Julia. Lord Montrose is dead. Murdered in an alley in London four years ago—no doubt at the hands of his bastard son's henchmen. And that bastard son will be joining him as soon as I find him."

"Whoa, can we slow down here?" Griffin asked, bewildered by the conversation taking place.

"Cole, you can't. He's expecting you to follow him. He will be ready for you—he will kill you!" she cried.

"What the devil is she talking about? What the hell are you insinuating, Cole?"

"Griffin, Munroe is really the bastard son of William Montrose."

"That old lord you tracked down in London?" Griffin asked.

"Yes. Edwin grew up bitter. Montrose refused to acknowledge him, as he was the hated byblow of his wife's infidelity. So, Edwin turned to piracy, to become rich enough to destroy all the Montroses. He studied and learned how to pass for a titled nobleman—at least in the Colonies. He conned widows out of their inheritances and took a secret identity in order to pirate our waters as well."

"Oh, God. No," Griffin said, understanding lighting his eyes. "He is the Dragon, isn't he?"

Cole nodded and Julia broke down in earnest.

"I'm so sorry, Cole. I swear that I am. I didn't know Edwin was that dreadful pirate until tonight. He said he would kill me if I said a word to anyone."

Cole felt a part of himself dying. God, he had been so

wrong. And because he had wasted time being angry at her—not trusting in her—Bailey could die. Could she ever forgive him? No, he knew that wasn't possible. And he also knew he didn't deserve her forgiveness.

"Montrose took them to Rosegate, didn't he? He made them raid the house and take the money and jewelry."

Julia nodded, wiping her nose with a lace handkerchief.

"Damn me! This is my fault," Cole said, looking at his brother. All the sorrow and betrayal he had experienced was nothing compared with this feeling of utter anguish that filled him like no pain he had ever imagined. "I can't lose her," he whispered.

Griffin nodded grimly in understanding. "We'll find her. She'll be all right."

"Where has he gone, Julia?" Cole asked the frightened woman.

"I don't know. He wants you to come after him, but he needed time to get ahead of you. He said he would leave word of where you can find him."

"Where?" he demanded. "Damn it, when!"

"I don't know! I don't know," she sobbed. "He didn't tell me anything more."

They turned to go but Julia reached out and grabbed Cole's arm in desperation.

"Cole, please . . . I'm afraid. He plans to force me to marry him after he . . . He says I will have an accident and then afterward he will return to England."

"It will be all right, Julia. I won't let it get that far. The bastard won't be coming back here."

"Julia, go back and say good night to your guests," Griffin told her. "Then, pack up some things—you'll come and stay with me at Rosegate. I won't let anything happen to you, don't worry," he said, squeezing her hand.

"Thank you," she cried in relief. "Thank you, both. Cole!"

she called out as they turned to go. "I will pray that you find her in time."

Cole nodded stiffly, looking at Griffin, whose face showed all the concern and dread that he himself felt in his heart.

Please, God Almighty, don't let me be too late.

Cole finished loading one pistol, then picked up a second, as Tessa entered the study with a fresh pot of strong coffee. He thanked her and excused the worried woman, who backed out of the study just as Griffin rushed in.

"Did you find out anything?" Cole asked his brother.

"No one saw any type of boat leave our dock or the dock at Hayward Hall. At least not that anyone can remember," Griffin said and sighed. "It was after midnight, Cole. No one would have noticed anything at that hour. Have you heard anything about the carriage?"

"Yes. It was found about a mile down the road, off in the brush—empty. I think he let it go loose, to throw us off his trail. I still believe he left by water. It's faster, and it's what he knows."

"Do you have any idea where he might be heading?"

Cole cursed and rubbed his eyes, dropping his hands in surrender. "I have no bloody idea. I'm going to leave for Williamsburg and get under way as soon as the *Barracuda* is ready to sail. Hopefully by then, I'll have some idea of where to go. I just can't stay here anymore and do nothing."

"I understand. I still want to go with you."

"No. I appreciate it, Griffin, but you are needed here. Besides, if I'm wrong, they could still be in the area. If that turns out to be the case, I need you here. I don't trust anyone else to take care of it."

Griffin nodded. "I'll do whatever I have to do."

"I know you will. I took some powder for these and a patch box," he said as he lifted the pistols and folded them in a square of deerskin. "How about that cutlass I sent you from Jamaica—you mind if I borrow that?"

"I'll get it." Griffin retrieved a key from his top desk drawer, then dropped it suddenly at the sound of voices outside, raised in alarm.

Cole had already bolted from the room and was out the front door in a flash when Griffin caught up with him. Griffin's blacksmith and his apprentice were half-carrying, half-dragging a barely conscious man up toward the main house from the direction of the stables. The man's head was drooped low, dangling, and his feet dragged in the dirt, creating a trail of dusty air. Cole's heart dropped. Even from here, he could tell the man was not Edwin.

"It must be James," he said to Griffin, before leaping down the steps and meeting up with the three men.

"Ben! Where did you find him? Never mind, it doesn't matter right now. Get him upstairs—first door on the left."

"Wait . . . Wait," James said in a strained gurgle. He spit blood onto the ground before continuing. "I . . . have to . . . tell you . . ."

Griffin signaled for Ben and his apprentice to put James down. They lowered him gently to the ground and Cole kneeled beside him, steadying him with a hand on his shoulder.

"What is it, James? Do you know where he took her?"

James nodded and tried to reach into his jacket, but dropped his arm to the ground, too weak. He passed out before he could say anything else, so Cole pulled open his jacket and found a rolled parchment in the pocket. He took it out and unrolled it, his eyes widening at the discovery.

"It's a map of the northern section of an island in the Bahamas. Looks like it's about one hundred and fifty miles southeast of Nassau," he said to Griffin, his voice tight.

"All right. Take him in. Thank you, Ben," Griffin said and followed Cole into the study once again.

"I've been here before, but it was difficult to search. The island is well over fifty miles long and the east side is entirely made up of rocks and cliffs. Damn it! I should have been more thorough, I could have put an end to this long ago."

Griffin shook his head. "I don't know much about these things, but there must be hundreds of cays and inlets along this section of the map alone. No one could be that thorough, Cole."

"Blast it! It will take more than a week to travel that distance."

"God willing the currents and weather will be with you. Because that point is exactly where he wants you to go," Griffin said, stabbing the marked location with his finger.

"Well, he's going to get just what he wants," Cole said in a deadly calm voice. All of his anger, pain and years of searching were coming down to this little strip of land, where he would finally face the enemy who had done so much damage to his life. But now there was much more at stake than he could ever have imagined. He had always been resigned to the fact that he might die in this quest, but Bailey deserved none of this. He had to save her, no matter what it meant for himself.

"When will you leave?" Griffin asked, unlocking the glass case holding the cutlass.

"Tomorrow. A few of my crew are out this way. Can you send someone for them? I'll round up the others when I get to Williamsburg in the afternoon."

Griffin nodded. Cole picked up the pistols, accepted the cutlass and looked across the desk at his younger brother, whose expression had turned far too serious.

"Cole . . . Godspeed, Brother." He swallowed hard and bent his head to stare at the cherry desk.

"I *will* be back, Griff. And I'll have Bailey with me. I promise."

It wasn't like him to make promises to others. But he knew

it was time. In his search for revenge, he had been courting death. He had never cared about that—until now. His parents were dead and nothing would change the past. All he had was the present and, God willing, a future. He cared about his brother and he cared about Bailey. He hadn't trusted anyone but himself and now Bailey's life depended on her trusting him to find her.

And he had to trust her as well. Trust that she loved him enough to do everything in her power to stay alive.

Chapter Twenty-Eight

Eight long days had passed since the *Mortico* had moored at the northern tip of the island. Bailey had been chained to the floor of the crumbling ruins of an old fortress on a rocky bluff overlooking the ocean. The stone room had no windows, just an arrow slit that allowed scant light and air inside. She'd spent her days trying to squeeze her foot out of the iron that held her but only succeeded in making her ankle swollen. During the nights she dreamed of Cole. She was brought food and water twice, but otherwise it seemed as if she'd been forgotten.

Until today. The Dragon had come and released her and ordered her out of the tower. She was weak from hunger and filled with fear, but as long as her will remained strong, she would not let him see that fear. They reached the bottom of the hill and left the shelter of the trees to walk down the beach. The blistering summer sun beat down on Bailey, the sweltering layers of ivory silk and petticoats slowing her barefoot progress through the powdery sand. The Dragon grabbed a handful of hair at the nape of her neck and shoved her down, bending over her and squeezing her neck in a cruel grip.

"You are as weak as a baby sparrow. I struggle to understand how you survived that bloody beating I gave you. Well, fear not, wench. You will not survive this time. Ah, I must amend that. You will survive for as long as I want you to. You will repay me for the time I lost. You inconvenienced me, forcing me to stay on this bloody island while your persistent Captain Leighton tried to hunt me down. I would have been comfortably married to Lady Hayward by this time if I hadn't had to hide from that damn savior of yours. But that is all going to end very soon."

"He will not come. He will know you are trying to trap him."

"Oh, but he will come, sweetness. I have you."

"He doesn't care about me. He only kept me to use against you. And now that you have me, I am no longer useful to him."

The Dragon dropped to his knees over her and pulled her head back as he sneered his answer close to her face. "You had better pray you are wrong about that."

She squealed in pain and he released her with a laugh of pure evil.

"Now, why don't we get started on that payment you owe me?"

"I have no money, nor would I pay you anything if I did," she spat at him.

"I don't want your money, wench. Your flesh will satisfy me even more."

She shoved at him and tried to rise and was rewarded with a hard backhand across her face that rolled her over in the sand. She wiped the grit from her face and then gasped when the Dragon grabbed hold of her by the decolletage of her gown. He spread his fingers, brushing the backs of them against her breasts and watched eagerly for her reaction. She glared at him but remained still. He laughed and drew her attention to his ship that lay berthed just off the island, down the beach.

"I'm feeling very generous today. I'm going to tell you what I intend to do to you, and then, depending on how . . . nice you are to me . . . I may decide to keep you alive for a while after I kill Cole. I could allow you to stay alive as long as you please me, and since we both know you aren't the innocent virgin anymore, that shouldn't be an issue, should it? All right, you don't have to answer me just yet."

He rose and pulled her up, forcing her to walk next to him down the beach toward his ship. "You see, I cannot afford to be the Dragon any longer. You and Cole have made that impossible. But it doesn't matter. I have acquired enough in money and goods to return to England a very wealthy man. I will be able to bring ruin to every last Montrose, until I am all that is left. By then, I will have created documented proof that I am the legal and sole heir, as I should have been from the beginning. Along with my ill-gotten fortune, the Montrose fortune will make me untouchable by any of those titled fops on the continent."

"It is all ill-gotten. You were never entitled to the Montrose fortune. You are a bastard and nothing you do can change that," Bailey taunted him. She didn't care. She had nothing to lose. He was going to kill her anyway. But not until he killed Cole while making her watch. She couldn't take that. She wanted to die first. It wasn't purely selfish, though. If she forced the Dragon to kill her before Cole came, then he wouldn't have the distraction of her to keep him from concentrating on the Dragon—on his revenge. That was how Cole had begun this journey and she wanted him to be able to finish it the way he would have wanted. She loved him too much to see him fail in his quest now, only to lose her, too. She would try her best to make sure things ended the way they should.

The Dragon laughed, hauling her up against him and holding her to his side with an arm around her waist.

"Ah, sweetness, no, no. Nothing you say to me is going to make me rush. I intend to savor every moment of you—now and when the time comes to dispose of you. You see, I have learned to be a very patient man. For gaining my rightful inheritance, for finishing Cole . . . and now, you," he purred in her ear. "But, alas, I cannot keep my beloved ship, as much as I want to. The *Mortico* is the Dragon's ship, and both ship and pirate will burn into the sea and all that will remain will become legend."

"Legend? You are mad! No one will even remember your name this time next year. Cole will come and kill you and throw your carcass into the ocean to rot among the fish."

"I think I'd prefer your tongue to be occupied with something other than conversation," he growled and crushed his lips to hers in a punishing kiss.

Bailey felt her stomach recoil, but fought to keep from letting her emotions rise to the surface. She had to keep her wits about her. She knew he preferred a struggle, so she tried to remain still, even when she felt her teeth dig in to the inside of her lips. The Dragon pressed her down onto her back in the sand and crawled on top of her. He bound her wrists above her head with a short rope and then began to rip at the laces on her bodice. Bailey held her breath, praying for strength, but knowing she would not be able to take much more of his pawing before she fought him in earnest. He lowered his head to kiss her neck, letting his tongue trace the thick scar that he had created with his own blade. Bailey swallowed the bile that had risen in her throat and closed her eyes against the memories of the last time she had lain beneath the Dragon. She couldn't stand it any longer; the feel of his weight on her, the heat of his tongue, the rasp of his voice—she had to get away from him. She brought her bound hands down, hitting the Dragon hard on the top of his head. He fell aside and she stumbled to her feet and began to run. She could hear him cursing and then gaining his feet and coming after her. Suddenly, she stopped and turned to face him.

No, she would not run anymore! She had been running her entire life, it seemed, and she was tired of trying to elude her problems. Her feelings. She had run from a commitment with

James, she had run from her burning home. She had run from Cole more than once, and for the time she was with him she had run from the love that had stirred her heart.

She was ready to stop running.

She was ready to face her life. Even if all that was left of it was right here on this strip of beach, she would face it and fight for whatever time she had left. And for every precious minute that was, she would think of how much she loved Cole and how much she regretted that they would not have a life together.

The Dragon reached her and slapped her, sending her sprawling to the ground. She started to get up when three of his men rushed toward them, hollering and cursing, drawing the pirate's attention away from her. He dragged her with him to meet them and shoved her at one of them while ordering another to speak.

"What is it, Pitts?" he barked irritably.

"The ship's here, sir. Can't tell how many he's got with 'im, but we took care of one of 'em already. What do you want us to do?"

Pitts's gruesome face was distorted by two long criss-crossed scars that ran from his mangled eye to his twisted mouth. The pirate who held Bailey muttered unintelligibly, keeping wary eyes on their surroundings.

"Watch them. Find out how many there are. And get those fish chopped up and in the water. Now! I have business to finish here," the Dragon responded darkly.

The scarred pirate tilted his face in order to get a look at Bailey with his good eye.

"The lady don't seem to be impressed by yer charms, Dragon. She looks as unfriendly as a coral crab," Pitts cackled.

Bailey could smell the stale rum from her position a few feet away. A gold hoop earring that hooked through his bulbous nose swung wildly with the pirate's mirth.

The Dragon moved away from her slowly and approached Pitts, who sobered instantly and took a step back, appearing to recognize the warning look in his captain's eyes. He shifted uneasily.

"Get back there and take care of those men." The Dragon's tone was filled with scorn, and Pitts looked as if he knew that somehow he would pay for his reckless tongue.

"Aye, C . . . Captain," he stuttered, then bowed formally and turned to make a hasty retreat.

"Pitts." It was a calmly spoken order and Pitts turned slowly back. "One more thing," the Dragon said as he approached Pitts, stopping a mere arm's length away from the taller, bulkier pirate.

"Aye, Dragon?" He tried to keep his tone level, without much success.

The Dragon's response was to reach up and hook a forefinger through the gold hoop in Pitts's nose. Pitts dared not speak, but stood dead still and silent, his wide brown eyes locked with his captain's brittle whiskey-colored gaze. A slow, malevolent smile spread across the Dragon's closed lips as time seemed to grind to an agonizing halt for the three pirates who stood rigid and silent in the stifling afternoon air. The Dragon carefully removed his finger from the gold hoop and began to laugh from deep within his belly as he looked over all of the wary pirates. One at a time, their laughter joined the Dragon's. Bailey shook her head in disgust.

Pitts was the last to join in, his laughter holding more than a hint of relief as he turned to his comrades and motioned for them to follow. He turned back to the Dragon and started to speak, but the words that initiated from his mouth turned to a wail of pain as the Dragon reached up and tore the gold hoop from Pitts's nose in one quick, vicious motion. Pitts fell to his knees in the sand, both hands pressed firmly to his face as blood poured through his fingers to drizzle haphazardly into the sand. The other pirates jerked upright and

Bailey took advantage of the distraction, pulling the rope from the one who held her. Seeing that the Dragon's fury was still high, they turned and left to do his bidding, kicking sand up as they hurried away.

"Get up, you lousy dog, and go with them!" the Dragon ordered, throwing the earring to the ground. It landed in the blood-soaked sand where Pitts still kneeled, moaning in pain. He stumbled up and started away, blood dripping through his fingers, the earring left forgotten in the red grains.

Bailey stood her ground, raising her chin as the Dragon approached her, though her courage had taken a beating, watching the Dragon's brutality with his man.

"More's the pity, it appears we don't have time for this, after all. Your savior has arrived a bit earlier than I expected. Ah, well. Come, sweetness, time to die," he sneered, grabbing the rope and leading her down the beach toward his ship.

Just before dawn, Cole and three crewmen had rowed to the island under the cover of darkness, splitting up to search the island. Now, as the sun reached just shy of midday, Cole stooped next to a stream to drink and splash his face. Frustration was threatening to turn to desperation, but he had to fight the urge to do something careless. Bailey's life depended on him keeping a cool head. It was noon—time to meet up with the others. Cole got his bearings and headed through the dense brush, back toward where they had beached the longboat. He prayed that one of them had discovered something, because he sure as hell had come up empty-handed, so far. He had been searching the interior of the island all morning and there was no sign of the Dragon's hideaway.

Cole shielded his eyes and scanned the beach before leaving the cover of tall palms. He walked near the tree line toward the designated meeting spot, when a distant sound caught his ear. He stopped and turned his head away from the wind, trying to block out the surf, and listened intently. It came again, the distinct sound of someone calling out for help. Cole ran toward the sound, trying his best to get a good footing in the shifting sand.

"Miles! Hold on!" He cursed roundly at the sight that greeted him.

Buried to his neck in the sand, Miles struggled to breathe as the surf rushed in to cover his head, then spit and coughed as the water receded.

"Cap'n!" he choked as the foamy water again blanketed his head, then slid back down the gentle slope of sand.

Cole threw his pistols and powder where they wouldn't get wet and fell to his knees. He tore at the hard-packed wet sand holding Miles captive. He pulled the cutlass from the scabbard at his hip and slashed openings in the sand, pulling at the loosened clumps furiously. Hearing something, he spun around, brandishing the blade as Dewey and Tom ran toward them. Together, they made fast work of the sand and before long Miles was bared to the chest and struggling to free his arms.

"Captain, look!" Dewey had stopped digging, his attention drawn to something down the beach, over a rocky crag.

Cole saw a thin rope of smoke licking a trail upward in the cloudless sky. The smoke seemed to thicken and darken as they watched. Whatever was on fire was going up fast and Cole had a sickening feeling that Bailey was in imminent danger.

"Can you two get him out of there?" he asked Dewey and Tom.

"Yessir!"

"Aye, Captain!"

"When you get him out, conceal him in the brushline and come along. Stay inside the woods, even as you make your way over those rocks—it could be some kind of trap."

"Aye, Captain," responded Dewey. Tom nodded, scooping an armful of wet sand away from Miles.

"Stay the course, Miles. You're almost free," Cole reassured the young man, rubbing his wet, sandy hair.

He left the cutlass with Dewey, and went to retrieve his pistols. He loaded and primed them both, then raced along the tree line toward the black smoke.

Cole lay on his stomach, peering over jagged rocks on the lower slope of land that formed a horseshoe, open to a small cay. The *Mortico* lay just offshore, and would have been extremely difficult to find without the trail of smoke. The Dragon wanted it to be found—he knew Cole was there. The ship had been set on fire at the stern, the flames beginning to catch the wind as they ate at the wood and spread steadily toward midship. Cole squinted to make out something hanging from a yard off the mainmast. Hoping to make himself less visible, he peeled off his bright white shirt and maneuvered closer, careful to stay low to the ground. It was a gibbet cage—the kind they hung pirates' bodies in to be displayed as a warning to their criminal brethren.

A frightened cry rang out and Cole's heart froze in his chest as a gust of wind blew the smoke aside and he saw Bailey hanging in the cage. Her wild curls shone in the sun—he knew that red-gold color as well as he knew his own reflection—it could be no one else.

He scrambled down the jagged face of the hill, knowing the Dragon was somewhere nearby and likely hoping for this reaction. He didn't care. He had to get her off that ship. Once at the bottom, he discreetly tossed the guns into the sand, behind a small rock. He had just reached the edge of the water when he heard clapping coming from behind him. He turned slowly to face his mortal enemy: the man he had been hunting for five long years.

The Dragon.

Edwin Montrose.

Dressed entirely in black, a black mask covering the upper half of his face, the pirate posed arrogantly, his feet braced apart.

"Well done, well done!" he called out, continuing to clap in a condescending manner. "You have found my private sanctuary—and it only took you five years! Quite the explorer, Leighton, though I doubt the king would grant you any funds for future endeavors." He let out a fiendish laugh and moved forward toward Cole, brandishing a pistol.

"I don't have time for you, Montrose. Maybe later," Cole sneered, glancing askance of the pirate to see the sun glinting off the metal of the pistols behind the rocks. He had to hope the pirate wouldn't notice. Damn, he should have kept one of them on him, but he knew he would lose the shot if the pistol got wet.

"Really? No, I can't let you give up after all this time. You've been after me like a hound chasing his tail and, to tell you the truth, I've grown weary of it. And I'm tired of you, too, Leighton. So, let's get some things straightened out between us."

Cole's agitation rose as he noticed the fire spreading closer to the mainmast, closer to the single rail of wood holding Bailey precariously over the water.

"I can see your priorities have changed. Not that I blame you—she is a fine little beauty—but I hate to see your attentions wane. I'm a jealous man, you see." He moved closer to Cole, gesturing to the *Mortico* with a nod of his head. "It appears as if we're running out of time. So, I won't keep you much longer. You have a choice, Leighton." He spread his arms wide, lifting his head to the sun.

"Speak your mind, Montrose, and be quick about it. I'm about to lose all patience with you," Cole growled, glancing over his shoulder to check the *Mortico* once again.

The Dragon chuckled, clearly enjoying his game. "Very well. Let's do this, Leighton. Let's bring this nonsense to an end." He tossed his gun aside to land with a thud in the sand. "You can fight me—or you can save your little bedmate. I should warn you that you only have a short time left to save the wench. If the flames don't break the yard and drop her into the water . . . very soon, by the looks of it, then the rum bottle I have filled with gunpowder under the mainmast should provide a large enough explosion to kill anyone on-board. Ah, and if she does end up in the water, I've made arrangements for the sharks to find her. My men are littering the water with chopped fish as we speak."

"You infernal bastard," Cole ground out.

The Dragon laughed. "Bastard, yes. But the circumstances of my birth aren't going to matter for much longer. I will be returning to England as the sole heir to my blood-sire's considerable fortune. Much against his wishes, but he has little say in the matter since he is dead."

"You aren't going anywhere."

"So, is that it? Have you chosen to fight me? Good! I must admit I was looking forward to killing you—and if there's any time left, I may just release my little wench and keep her for my own pleasures."

Bailey screamed, the shrill sound of her terror piercing the acrid, blackened air. Cole looked just in time to see the fire lick its way across the deck. Bits of flame fell from the shrouds above, landing on the narrow arm of wood, midway between the mast and the cage where Bailey struggled.

Cole ran into the water and turned back to see the Dragon running in the opposite direction. He threw himself into the waves and swam the short distance to the *Mortico*. He climbed the rope hanging over the side and pulled himself onto the deck near the bow. Smoke filled his lungs, choking him. Thick, sooty air and bits of ash burned his eyes and nose as he made his way around smoldering coils of rope on the deck.

"Bailey! Stay still, the cage will fall! Don't move!"

"Cole! Oh, Cole, I'm sorry! I tried to stay quiet. I didn't want to distract you. I'm sorry I screamed," she apologized frantically.

"Quiet, now. I'm here."

He had to shout over the fire, trying to calm her while making his way around the growing flames and up the thick wood of the mainmast. He climbed up to the yard, ducking as sparks rained down from the rigging above him. He started to crawl out on the long pole, but his weight was too much and the wood cracked in protest. He immediately retreated a few feet, his mind racing for a way to get to her.

"Cole—I have the key. He put it in my bodice."

"All right, love. Stay very still for me, I'm going to get you down."

"Please hurry, Cole!" she cried, her voice hoarse from thick smoke.

He tried to block out the desperation in her voice, knowing he couldn't help her if he gave in to the panic he was feeling in his gut. He started to make his way farther up the mast, reaching ropes holding a spar that had yet to burn. He grabbed the attached sail and started to shimmy down the heavy canvas to hover above the iron cage. A deafening crack sounded above him and he looked up to see the the rigging collapsing as it crumbled in sparks and flame. Cole ducked his head, praying that the wood and rigging would somehow fall to the side of them. The burning mass tumbled over him, scraping his back and shoulders as it made its way past him. The large yardarm squarely hit the smaller one holding Bailey and she screamed and jerked about, trying to dislodge bits of burning ash from her hair and dress.

"No, be still!" Cole yelled, but it was too late.

The yard holding her snapped with a sickening crack and Cole watched helplessly as it dropped straight down, taking the cage and Bailey with it. He concentrated on the exact spot where the cage crashed into the water and took a deep breath, dropping from the rigging.

He dove into the water, feet first and pulled himself to the surface. He saw the tip of the cage as it went under, the air under Bailey's skirt giving him precious extra seconds.

"Hold your breath!" he commanded, but she was facing away from him so he couldn't tell if she'd heard.

Cole dug his way through the disturbed water and dove down, feeling the edge of the cage. He reached into the bars and felt for Bailey's bodice, but grabbed only fabric. He moved up slightly and tried again, this time finding her waist and sliding his hand up to hook inside the low neckline of her gown. His fingers found the hard metal of the key and he grabbed hold of it, drawing it carefully through the iron bars. Feeling for the lock, he guided the key into place with his other hand. The lock sprang open and he freed it from the metal, opening the cage and pulling Bailey out.

She grabbed on to his shoulders and pulled herself away from the cage just as it slipped off the piece of yard jutting from the water. The heavy cage dropped toward the bottom as they fought for the surface. Cole's lungs were burning as they broke the surface of the water. Bailey struggled to stay above the water and Cole realized the weight of her skirts was going to pull her under. He sank under the waves and removed a dagger from his boot, then began to cut away at her skirts.

Something bumped him hard in the back and he spun around just as a large gray shark swam away from him. He rose for air, and saw the look of fear in Bailey's eyes. She had seen the shark, too. He went under and finished cutting away her skirts, then surfaced, the knife blade securely in his teeth.

They began to swim to shore, dodging falling burnout from the ship. Fearing the keg of powder would explode at any moment, Cole wanted to swim at an angle, away from the *Mortico,* but it didn't appear as if Bailey had the strength. She needed to get out of the water.

A fin sliced through the crest of a wave in front of them and Bailey stopped dead, looking back at Cole with wide eyes. He tried to reassure her with his expression, then quickly turned his attention to the shark that circled them where they tread water. He watched the shark as it neared them with each circle, pulling the blade from his teeth with his right hand. The shark swam around them in an arc and Cole motioned for Bailey to swim. Then he turned back, just in time to see the shark moving straight toward him. The beast's mouth was wide open, rows of blade-sharp teeth catching the sunlight. The shark was so close, Cole could see bits of bloody fish caught in between the rows. He waited until the shark was nearly upon him, then drove the dagger upward into the beast's mouth, his forearm dragging painfully across razorlike teeth. The shark jerked away, thrashing its head and tail in agony as it swam in frantic circles, trying to dislodge the dagger.

Cole turned and swam, blocking out the pain and fatigue of his body. He caught up to Bailey just as she found her footing on the rocky bottom of shallow water. She stood and turned to him, holding out her arm. He reached her and wrapped his injured arm about her waist as they pulled themselves through the surf to the beach.

Bailey collapsed onto the sand but Cole dragged her up, urging her up the beach away from the water.

"It's going to blow," he rasped, hurrying them toward the rise of land where he had hidden his pistols. He grabbed the pistols and thrust one of them at her, then pushed her forward and up the horseshoe incline of land. They reached the top of the small rise and knelt behind a grouping of large rocks. Cole covered Bailey with his body, just as the sound of the exploding ship rent the air, smothering the roar and crackle of the fire that had caused the keg to blow.

Burning wood, metal hooks and pulleys and other debris fell all around them, littering the beach and hill with small fires and smoking ash. Bailey moved underneath him and Cole lifted his upper body, wrapping his arms protectively around her as they caught their breath.

"It's over, isn't it?" she asked, her voice hoarse.

"Yes, dove, it's over," he sighed against her ear.

She turned her head and kissed him hard. "Thank you for saving my life," she whispered.

He found he couldn't form words over the hard lump that had formed in the back of his throat. Though he was aware how close he had come to losing her, he had sorely underestimated how hard that would have hit him—until this very moment. He held her tighter, resting his chin on her shoulder as they watched the *Mortico* melt into the ocean.

Long minutes passed and though the charred remains of the *Mortico* had fallen to the bottom of the clear blue water, small fires still burned on the sand near the surf. Bailey leaned back into Cole's chest and sighed, exhausted and weak.

"Cole, how did you find me so fast?" she asked softly.

"It's a long story. I'll tell you about it later," he said and kissed her nape.

"Is . . . Is James—" she couldn't finish. She had witnessed the Dragon beating him mercilessly and feared the worst. James had made a dreadful mistake falling in league with the pirate, but he didn't deserve to die because of it.

"I believe he will be all right. He is badly injured, but no more so than you were when I found you and look at you now. Fighting pirates and sharks all in one day," he teased gently.

"I wasn't the one fighting, you were. Are you sure you aren't hurt any more than this?" she asked, lightly touching the deep scrapes on his arm. She turned to hear his response and gasped in fear.

"What—?" Cole turned and saw what had frightened Bailey.

"You didn't truly think I'd just let you go, did you? Get up. Death has arrived to claim you at last."

"Montrose," Cole growled as he stood, pulling Bailey up and pushing her behind him. "You shouldn't have come back."

"That's quite a threat, Leighton. However, I am not affected by your threats. You've been my shadow for so many years now, I feel nothing but pity for you. You are weak—and you've proved that by falling for your whore instead of tempting me with her. I wish I'd known you had her—I could have killed you much sooner."

"What are you waiting for? Try it," Cole said with contempt, holding his arms out in invitation.

The Dragon laughed. "Ah, killing you is beneath me. But since the explosion and the sharks didn't take care of you, I suppose I will have to deal with you myself. Over here." He motioned with his gun for Cole to move away from the edge of the hill. He inclined his head toward Bailey then. "And you—I am pleasantly surprised that you are so resilient, sweetness. I am going to enjoy every bit of you, in due time."

"You're not going to touch her, Montrose," Cole growled.

Bailey felt her stomach turn and sank down against the rock. All of the horror from that night in May came rushing back. Her head swam with horrific memories of the fire and knowing her family was dead. She remembered the pirate's rum-soaked breath on her bare skin. The same feeling of utter helplessness filled her now and the same desperate urge to run, as she watched the Dragon with Cole. What could she do? She couldn't help him. Sweet Mary, she couldn't bear to see Cole die at this beast's hands. Feeling ill, she sank down and felt something hard beneath her. She reached down and felt the hilt of a pistol. God, please let it be loaded, she thought as she felt for the handle. She watched as the pirate led Cole into the open space at the top of the sandy incline, brandishing his gun all the while.

Did she dare try to shoot at the Dragon from this distance, with him standing so close to Cole?

"Are you going to fight me like a man, Montrose, or like the cowardly masked bastard that you are?" Cole taunted.

The Dragon instantly tossed his gun aside. "I am going to send you to hell, Leighton. Be sure and give your mother my best."

Bailey smothered a cry as Cole lunged forward and the two men began to fight. Cole threw his fist hard into the pirate's mouth, throwing him backward. He regained his footing and charged into Cole's midsection, pounding his fist into Cole's ribs. Cole grabbed the Dragon's fist and twisted his arm, kicking the pirate's feet out from under him, then pinning him to the ground with his foot. The Dragon reached to his side and pulled a small dagger from a hidden sheath, plunging it into Cole's thigh. Cole stumbled backward and the Dragon regained his feet.

Bailey bit her lip, so as not to cry out, and pulled the gun from its position under her. She stared down the length of the pistol, her aim as unsure as her trembling hands. Cole limped forward, bracing himself on his uninjured leg and dipping out of reach as the Dragon slashed out with the red-stained blade. Cole swung his fist into the pirate's jaw, spinning him around. The force of the blow threw Cole off balance and he stumbled to his knee as his injured leg took all of his weight. The Dragon was on him in an instant, grabbing Cole by the neck and pressing the point of the dagger under his chin.

"I have waited a long time for this, Leighton. Now . . . I want you to die knowing that I took great pleasure in ruining your family more than any other. You think you are so much better than those unfortunate enough to be born beneath you. Ha! But you are beneath me now, aren't you?"

Bailey saw Cole clench his fist and knew the Dragon must have pressed the knife into his skin. If she was going to get the courage to shoot, she'd better muster it now. She tried to aim again, but her hands shook uncontrollably. The thought of missing and hitting Cole made her queasy. She took a deep breath and tried to steady herself. A vision of her father and Adam flashed in her mind. Instead of filling her with sorrow, she drew on the love she felt for them and let the vision fill her with strength.

"You are beneath me and very nearly in the same position your little wench is going to be in soon after you are gone." The pirate laughed. "But I daresay I will enjoy the sight of her on her knees before me much more than I do you. Think on that while you bleed to death at my feet, Leighton. Your whore is going to become my whore before you're drained of your last drop of blood. If you stay conscious long enough, you can watch," he sneered, bending to Cole's ear.

The Dragon rose and called out over his shoulder to her. "Are you ready for me, sweetness? If you want to run, better start now. I'll catch up." He laughed again.

Bailey called out to the pirate, but held the pistol steady, as ready as she would ever be. He turned to look at her and she pulled the trigger.

Her mind was playing tricks on her. She thought she heard two shots.

The Dragon stumbled backward, clenching his midsection where the ball had hit him. He spun around, trying to get his balance and as he did, Bailey saw the reason for hearing the second shot. A dark hole marred the side of the pirate's head, blood trickling down his cheek. Bailey looked at Cole, who still knelt in the sand, the second of the pistols smoking in his hand. She rushed to Cole's side, dropping down next to him, bracing his weight with her body.

The Dragon continued to try to get his balance while the blood started to run from his stomach through his fingers, dripping into the sand as he tripped backward. He reached the edge of the incline and his foot slipped in the loose rocks. He tumbled then, his legs flying into the air above his head as he disappeared down the hill.

Bailey helped Cole stand and they made their way slowly to the edge. The Dragon's lifeless body lay in a cloud of disturbed sand at the foot of the hill. Small fires continued to burn nearby, remaining signs of the battle that had recently taken place. Bailey looked up at Cole, tears blurring her vision, and smiled.

"Thank you for saving my life . . . again," she said, attempting to tease him, despite the crack in her voice.

He smiled down at her and kissed the top of her head. "And thank you for saving mine."

She glanced up at him and tilted her head in question.

"You didn't know I had a weapon, did you?"

She shook her head. "I was so afraid I would hit you, I almost didn't pull the trigger."

"But you did pull it." He grinned.

She nodded. "I couldn't bear to think of living without you, but he was going to kill you. So, if you had to die, it might as well be by my hand, instead of your enemy's."

"Interesting logic," he said, his brow lifted in amusement.

"Don't make fun of me, I am still shaking. You asked me to marry you, then make me wait to give you an answer and then almost get killed before I can say yes."

Cole chuckled and turned her to face him, resting his hands on her hips. "Is that so? Well, I am here now and I don't intend on going anywhere for the moment, so why don't you give me your answer?"

"What was the question again?" she teased.

Cole tilted his head down at her in mock consternation.

"Yes! The answer is yes, as if you didn't know, you stubborn, arrogant man. I love you, Cole. I have loved you nearly since I met you, despite you doing everything in your power to make it impossible."

"*Me*, impossible? Hmm, let me think about this for a

minute. When I first laid eyes on you, you tried to kill me. From that moment, you have fought me, run from me, defied me . . . Oh, yes, and sent for another man to get you away from me. How could I have not known that you loved me?" He bent to give her a tender kiss, easing the bold teasing.

"That all sounds pretty terrible, when you say it."

"Indeed. Well, you have the rest of your life to make it up to me. How's that?"

"I cannot wait," she replied earnestly, tilting her head up for another kiss.

Shouts sounded out from below and they parted to see Miles, Tom, and Dewey on the beach below, sand- and sweat-covered, yet hale enough. They were waving up at them and Cole acknowledged them with a lift of his hand.

"Everything all right, Captain?" Miles shouted.

"Aye! Signal for the *Barracuda*. We'll meet you at the longboat!"

Cole then hung his arm around Bailey's shoulder and they found a way down a more gentle angle of the incline, pausing every so often to let Cole rest from the stab wound in his thigh. He would be all right, Bailey knew. He had suffered far worse. So had she. And now, finally, she knew without a doubt, that she was going to be all right, too. With Cole by her side, she would be more than all right.

Chapter Twenty-Nine

Bailey stood on the balcony, awed by the display of colors streaking through the evening sky. She felt Cole's arms wrap around her waist from behind and she sighed contentedly, leaning back into his embrace.

"I don't believe there is a place on earth where the sky is any more beautiful. I can't imagine ever getting tired of seeing the sunsets here."

"Not even if you saw them every night for the rest of your life?" he breathed next to her ear.

The warm caress of his breath tickled her skin and sent delicious shivers across her body. She knew that Cole's touch was something she would never tire of, either. Learning to love had been such a difficult journey for him, she felt honored to her very soul that she was the one who would have that gift. And for the rest of their lives. After leaving the Dragon's hideout, they had sailed to Lochinvar, where Cole had asked her once again to be his wife. She had said yes so quickly, he had laughed, but she reminded him how poorly it had gone when he gave her time to think about her answer.

"As long as you are by my side, I believe I could manage it," she teased.

"Will you be serious for just a moment, woman? I'm trying to figure out if you would like Lochinvar to be your home."

She turned in his arms and searched his silver-flecked eyes. "Truly? But what about Rosegate? Don't you want to live there? It is your home, Cole, and now that you have let the bad memories rest, you are free to return, aren't you? Griffin is there, don't you want to be near your brother?" she asked, concerned that maybe he hadn't gotten over the pain his mother had caused.

"We could live there, of course. I'm sure Griffin would be happy to have us. But I have come to feel like I belong at Lochinvar. I have rather pleasant memories of a particular few weeks spent here quite recently," he said, his hands caressing her waist and hips.

Bailey felt her cheeks flush with color, pleased all the same at his reference to their time here together.

"Lochinvar is where our love really began to blossom, isn't it?" she responded shyly.

"I would say it definitely took a turn toward the more . . . pleasurable," he said with a wicked grin.

"I can think of nowhere I would rather live with you, Colby Leighton. Do you think our many children will like it here?"

He nodded. "Of course. All ten of them."

"Ten!"

"Don't panic, love. We don't have to have them all at once, you know," he teased.

"We aren't even married yet, you are going to scandalize me."

"Aye, but that is something I intend to rectify very soon. How does a fall wedding at Rosegate sound to you?"

"Oh, Cole, I would love that."

"We'd have to stay through the winter, but then we could return to Lochinvar in the spring. Griffin will be ready to be rid of me by then, it's safe to say. I can be tough to handle at times." He grinned.

"You don't say? I never noticed."

She playfully hit him in the chest, then tilted her head for a kiss. He raised a brow suggestively and Bailey smiled at the gesture she had come to know so well. The evening breeze carried the scent of gardenia and a lone gull cried out overhead. The colors that painted the sky deepened as the sun plunged into the ocean. Bailey took Cole's hand and, stepping out of his embrace, led him through the gauzy curtains into their bedroom. She moved slowly, so as not to rush him. His thigh was still healing and for the time had left him with a slight limp.

She faced him and unlaced his breeches. She then pushed him to sit on the edge of the bed and knelt down in front of him. First she removed his boots, then she pulled his breeches off his hips and slid them down his legs, tossing them aside. She checked the wound and placed a gentle kiss on his thigh.

"I suppose we both have our scars from the Dragon, now," he said, reaching out to caress her neck lovingly.

She kissed his hand and stood back up, untying her filmy white robe. She let the garment slip down her body to lay in a pool of silk at her feet. She moved to stand between Cole's legs and wrapped her arms about his neck.

"And we will likely never be able to forget the pain he brought to both of our lives. But he isn't able to touch us anymore. And I will be damned if I let him have any more power over me. He can't hurt me anymore. No one can. As long as I have your love, I am safe."

"Then, believe me, love, you are safe for the rest of your life," he said, pulling her down and rolling them over so the warm weight of his body covered hers.

"Show me," she whispered huskily.

"With pleasure," he responded.

Put a Little Romance in Your Life With
Georgina Gentry

Cheyenne Song
0-8217-5844-6 $5.99US/$7.99CAN

Apache Tears
0-8217-6435-7 $5.99US/$7.99CAN

Warrior's Heart
0-8217-7076-4 $5.99US/$7.99CAN

To Tame a Savage
0-8217-7077-2 $5.99US/$7.99CAN

To Tame a Texan
0-8217-7402-6 $5.99US/$7.99CAN

To Tame a Rebel
0-8217-7403-4 $5.99US/$7.99CAN

To Tempt a Texan
0-8217-7705-X $5.99US/$7.99CAN

Available Wherever Books Are Sold!

Visit our website at **www.kensingtonbooks.com.**

Discover the Romances of
Hannah Howell

My Valiant Knight	0-8217-5186-7	**$5.50**US/**$7.00**CAN
Only for You	0-8217-5943-4	**$5.99**US/**$7.50**CAN
A Taste of Fire	0-8217-7133-7	**$5.99**US/**$7.50**CAN
A Stockingful of Joy	0-8217-6754-2	**$5.99**US/**$7.50**CAN
Highland Destiny	0-8217-5921-3	**$5.99**US/**$7.50**CAN
Highland Honor	0-8217-6095-5	**$5.99**US/**$7.50**CAN
Highland Promise	0-8217-6254-0	**$5.99**US/**$7.50**CAN
Highland Vow	0-8217-6614-7	**$5.99**US/**$7.50**CAN
Highland Knight	0-8217-6817-4	**$5.99**US/**$7.50**CAN
Highland Hearts	0-8217-6925-1	**$5.99**US/**$7.50**CAN
Highland Bride	0-8217-7397-6	**$6.50**US/**$8.99**CAN
Highland Angel	0-8217-7426-3	**$6.50**US/**$8.99**CAN
Highland Groom	0-8217-7427-1	**$6.50**US/**$8.99**CAN
Highland Warrior	0-8217-7428-X	**$6.50**US/**$8.99**CAN
Reckless	0-8217-6917-0	**$6.50**US/**$8.99**CAN

Available Wherever Books Are Sold!

Visit our website at **www.kensingtonbooks.com**